NINE

UNFROZEN FOUR
SERIES

DAYS

Nine Days
Copyright © 2022 Joelina Falk

All rights reserved. No part of this publication may be reproduced, distribute or transmitted in any form without written permission of the publisher, except for brief passages by a reviewer for review purpose only.

This is a work of fiction. All names, characters, locations, and incidents are a product of the author's imagination and used fictitiously. Any resemblance to actual persons, events or things—living or dead—is entirely coincidental.

You can find me here:

https://www.instagram.com/authorjoelinafalk/
https://twitter.com/joelinafalk

To my mother because she will not only drown me in holy water after this, but she will also provide me with ten therapists.
I love you though, so that's okay.

NOTE TO READER:

This book discusses mental health, more specifically depression and suicidal thoughts.
If this specific topic is a trigger for you, I do not recommend reading this.

PLAYLIST

all the kids are depressed—Jeremy Zucker

In My Blood—Shawn Mendes

sex—EDEN

It's You—Henry

comethru—Jeremy Zucker

Roxanne—Chase Atlantic

Dandelions—Ruth B

Little Things—One Direction

Empty Space—James Arthur

this is how you fall in love—Jeremy Zucker

Memories—Shawn Mendes

Power Over Me—Dermot Kennedy

Chapter 1

"wouldn't it be nice to live inside a world that isn't black and white?"—Wonder by Shawn Mendes

Lily

Dear whoever reads this,

they say time heals all wounds…
they were wrong.
It's been exactly 5840 days and I'm still hurting.
Oh, maybe I should start this off with some more information than that, although I'm sure you are someone close to me, otherwise you wouldn't have found this book.
I'm Lily Heaven Reyes…and I live in fucking hell.
Not literally, but it feels like it. Which is quite ironic given my middle name.
However, whatever happens after death can't be much worse than this.
I'll sure be finding out soon enough.
Too bad I can't tell you about my experience with death then.

Anyway, this is my goodbye book, I suppose. So please, make sure to send the letters in this book to everyone mentioned. Or burn the whole book. It's not like I will ever find out if you did.
Is that enough of an introduction?
I only have two more weeks left. Well, that's as much of the time I grant myself.
I wouldn't know how much time on earth I have left. And I'm not here to find out. My life will end in two weeks because I decide to.

"Jesus, Lily!" A very angry Winter calls from my room door. She is interrupting my precious time writing my goodbyes.

If only I could be mad at her for it. Winter has been my best friend since freshman year of college. More or less a good one. We happened to be roommates, and as fate takes us, we remained roommates up until senior year. Good thing now is though, we no longer share one room. We have separate ones, with one living space, a shared kitchen and one bathroom. It's not too bad.

Unfortunately, Winter is a self-centered person. She only cares about herself. And if she does "care" about someone else, it's only up until she can turn it all about herself again.

"Have you seriously been in bed all day?" she asks, staring at me with wide eyes. My room is dark since I never bothered to open the blinds. And I also never really bothered to get up to get dressed.

"I have." Not that it's any of her business. "Is that a problem?"

"You're twenty years old, a senior in college. You shouldn't spend all day, especially not all Friday lying in bed," she tells me. "We're going to the hockey game in an hour. Our school's team is playing against Yale!" Winter flips on my ceiling light, causing my eyes to squint close for a moment. *Maybe it is darker than I had realized.* "You look horrible, Lils."

"*Gee*, thanks, Winter."

When I manage to open my eyes, I am greeted by a pair of blue ones staring back at me. Winter is standing at the foot of my bed, her red hair curled perfectly into beach waves. She even put on makeup. Not that it surprises me. Winter is *always* ready to get out of the house. Well, or dorms for that matter.

"Please don't tell me you forgot." Her eyes are staring right into my soul. It's unbearable. Seriously, if Winter lays eyes on someone when she's mad, you'd wish you were dead. But then again, I do wish I was dead. Maybe that's why I don't mind it.

I think I can't judge Winter's eyes too much, I have always had some kind of hatred for blue eyes. It doesn't have a reason, I simply never really trusted blue-eyed people as much as I could trust brown-eyed ones. Perhaps it's because dark eyes are more interesting to me than lighter ones.

Darkness has always been in my life. It sort of makes sense that dark eyes seem more trustworthy to me when all I've known my whole life was the dark. The mystery it brings and, as weird as it sounds, it brings me comfort.

"I didn't forget," I lie. "I just don't feel like going anymore."

Despite my wish to die and my incapability to stay happy for longer than an hour, I love going out. Every now and then, that is.

It's nothing compared to Winter. She goes out every single day. Not that it's something bad. And go her for being social.

It's just not for me. But I do love going out, until my battery runs out and I lose interest in leaving my bed for the next couple of days.

"Then why aren't you dressed up already? It's Aaron's big day! Scouts will be there, and God knows, maybe he will get an offer to go pro after graduation!" She's way too excited about that.

Though, it's nice knowing one of Aaron's ex-girlfriends still truly cares about him. She always has. But I also understand why Aaron got sick of her.

I have no idea what to say.

Winter knows I struggle with depression, but she doesn't know how deep it goes. She thinks I take some medication that plasters a smile onto my face and makes me happy again and that's about it.

"I just lost track of time. But I will get ready right now."

Winter nods in approval and leaves my room.

I will continue this later. Winter urges me to go to a hockey game.
I love hockey though, so that is fine.

Lily

As promised—*kind of*—I force myself off my comfortable bed and walk over to my dresser. It's all I could fit into this tiny room with a bed and a desk.

I quickly grab a pair of blue jeans, a white, long-sleeved blouse and a beige sweater vest.

After changing into something more suitable for a hockey game, I walk over to my desk and take a seat. Since Winter is taking way too long in the bathroom each morning, I converted my desk into a half makeup table and half college-work table.

Another good thing, I don't have to leave my room if I ever get ready.

I quickly cover up my dark circles under my eyes and add some concealer onto areas that need covering. I don't usually work with foundation, because I have no idea how not to make it look cakey.

At last, I'm adding some mascara and I'm ready to go.

I don't want to leave my bedroom, but I don't have much of a choice. If I don't go to this game, Winter will never forgive me. And neither will Aaron.

"Look at you!" Her mouth stands wide open as her eyes scan my body. "You're so beautiful!"

I know she is lying. Winter made it her own personal job to always tell me I'm beautiful, ever since she knows I'm depressed. It's like she thinks I believe I'm too ugly for this world.

I'm fully aware that I am not. I am depressed, not insecure about my facial features.

From our friend Mia, I know that Winter secretly thinks I look dead ninety per cent of the time she sees me. Which is why I hate Winter's *pity* compliments.

"Thank you," I say and give her a small smile. It's a fake smile.

I usually fake a lot of smiles around campus all day so nobody would ask if I were okay.

"I do hope I get to go down on Aaron again. Jesus, I miss him so much, Lils." I cringe at her statement. But she is my best friend, so I guess I have to listen to her boys-talk.

"I'm sure he would let you in a heartbeat."

"Don't know. He's been pretty cold with me today, and he refuses to talk about it." Her usual happiness darkens the room so suddenly. I hate when she is upset, takes me down right with her.

"Well, you two are separated. Maybe he just doesn't feel like talking to his ex about possible struggles," I remind her. Just that this reminder reminds me of something: Aaron has just as much of a shitty day as I do.

She lets out a long sigh as she walks up to me, wrapping her arms around my neck.

"I just wished I could help him through his heartbreak," she cries out in a thick voice.

Somebody have mercy on me, please. I can't deal with tears. Not with my own. Not with anyone else's.

"His parents split up, and according to him, they're still fighting over it."

"It's not that unusual that parents split up, you know."

"I know, Lils. Your parents are separated as well, and they do fight too. But it's Aaron we're talking about. He is perfect. His life should be perfect as well." I roll my eyes. Luckily, she can't see it because we're still hugging.

For a short moment I want to remind Winter that life sucks and everyone's problems matter. But to Winter, there are differences. She doesn't want to see that no matter how deep the water someone is drowning in is, drowning stays drowning.

To Winter it has steps, and if someone has "bigger" problems than the other, the one with less severe problems shouldn't whine about it. Not in front of the other person at least.

But then, Winter does speak to me about her boy problems. More specifically, Aaron problems. The ones I don't want to hear of.

"We should get going. I don't want to miss a second of Aaron's sweet ass." I make a gaging sound right after those words leave her mouth. And she laughs. "Ah, maybe we'll even see Colin. I'll make sure to set you up for a date with him. He's ridiculously hot, not as hot as Aaron, obviously. But he's single, inked and is just as dark-humored as you are."

Dark-humored. I am a depressed being, making jokes about my death to cope. Maybe they're not too much of jokes since I actually do want to die.

Her arms leave my body, and she immediately walks over to our coatrack, getting her and my jacket for tonight. Clearly, we're in need of one. Not because it's the end of September, but because ice rinks are cold, unless you're the one on the ice.

For some reasons, the cold just disappears when you're on it. Probably because of the movements. No, definitely because of movements.

Actually, I have no idea why that is. I'm not much of a physics girl. I don't understand most of it, so I ignore it.

Back when I used to skate still, I was never cold, which is how I know movement keeps warm on the ice.

Now I don't skate anymore. Not because of college and all the assignments, but because I lost my motivation to do what I loved doing.

Chapter 2

"well now I know that I'm the fuel and she's the spark"—Wildfire by Seafret

Colin

"First game of the season," I announce to my teammates. It's not like they're not aware of it. Of course they know. But I guess it's my job as the team captain to say a few words before every game.

The room quiets down. No other sounds but breathing is to be heard. It's weird. Usually, this group of dorks is loud as hell. A little silence doesn't hurt anyone though.

"It's the last season for all of this year's seniors. It would be a shame if they graduate without a last win." I look around the locker room. Every single pair of eyes is on me. Half the guys are still half naked from being mid-changing, but neither of us cares. "This game will determine how good this season will go for us." Not really, but you know, everyone has their superstitions. "After last season's defeat at the Frozen Four finals, I think we all have enough rage to rock this one."

A loud roar comes from my teammates. God, they're so annoying sometimes. They couldn't even think of anything better. Other teams cheer or have a special saying, but no, my team roars like a lion.

Come to think a catchphrase such as *"Nine, Nine"* from that TV show *Brooklyn 99* would be great. Maybe like a *"Trews!"* you know, pleasing our college since it's called "St. Trewery University" *Okay, no, that's just as stupid as roaring.*

"And to all of our new freshman," I continue, looking directly at the handful of newcomers. "Best of luck proving yourself worthy for the St. Trewery hockey team."

The St. Trewery hockey team has been one of the best college hockey teams in the New York State for as long as anyone can remember.

"Now that we have a new coach, I think you guys have a pretty good chance to impress him."

"Or not," one of my teammates laughs. I immediately shoot him a death glare. One of our many unspoken rules is and will forever be: *Never ever make fun of your teammates. And never ever doubt they can make it.*

Teammates should respect one another. And I find it pretty important to keep that up. I don't need my team hating on each other. Every single one here should know that we've got each other's backs. If one falls, we all do.

"I'm just saying, man. Coach Carter is a tough nut to crack. He's only coaching us because he is not coaching the pros at the moment. Why ever that is."

I roll my eyes at Aaron Marsh's comment. Aaron is my closest friend of all those douchebags. He's been stuck with me ever since freshman year. We somehow ended up renting a house together.

And the house right across from ours, two of our teammates decided to move in to. We share one garden. Neither of us minds. And neither of us cares that the other two guys hang more around Aaron and my house than at their own. Still, we're all referring to the other as "roommate," though technically we're not. Just Aaron and me, and Grey and Miles. The four of us are inseparable.

Aaron is a fit guy. Not only fit, but he also has a brain. He is ridiculously smart, and we all hate it. Not that I don't refer to myself as smart, but this guy, *damn*. I think he's majoring in Architecture. Actually, I *know* he is. He certainly knows his way around math.

"Yeah, Coach Carter is going to be the death of us," another teammate says. *Miles*. He is one of those filthy-rich kids that get anything they want. (So am I, thanks to my father being an NHL hockey coach).

Miles is a lot to take in, a lot to deal with. Lucky for my father, he knows his way around an arrogant hockey player.

"Enough now. Coach Carter will push us all to our limits, we all know that. But it's what the team needs," I tell them. "He will have pity on some of your asses though." Laughter erupts.

"You mean, he will have pity on *your* ass," Miles corrects, raising his eyebrows at me. Of course they all know Coach Carter is my father.

Normally, my father is coaching the New York Rangers. But he doesn't want to be away from his family, more specifically, from Eira, my younger sister. Eira is sick and before he would regret travelling the world with his team instead of being with his daughter, he decided to take a step back for a while. Hence, he is now coaching us.

However, my father coaching us doesn't mean he will go easy on me. In fact, I think I will be the one he will go the hardest on. He always has been hard on me.

I ignore Miles's comment. "Now," I speak again, "get your asses dressed and let's crush Yale!"

Another round of roars echo through the room. But this time, it's a really great spirit. Maybe a roar isn't so bad after all. This roar got something.

WE CRUSHED YALE. 5-0, that's what the huge scoreboard reads when the last second of the timer runs out and a loud, ear hurting tone shrills through the arena. People jump off their seats and cheer for my team. Other people, probably Yale fans, have their heads hidden behind their hands.

I'd be lying if I said winning isn't one of the best feelings ever. Because it fucking is.

As the team captain, I feel obligated to skate over to the Yale hockey team, their team captain more precisely, and have a quick word with him.

I go tap Anderson on his shoulder blade as I approach him. "Good game," I say, he nods in agreement. At least they're good losers. But before I know, his team is skating off the ice and leaves. Not that I care.

"DUDE! FIVE TO FUCKING ZERO!!" Miles cheers, yelling through the arena. Loud "*Woo's*" stream through my ears, followed by a ton of "TREWERY!" cheers over and over again. Damned if that doesn't boost my ego.

"Off to the locker room!" Coach Carter claps his hands to get our attention.

He taps everyone on their back as they pass him, telling us how good of a game this was. But then he also says we could do better. I'm the last one to leave the ice, the last one to approach my father.

"You've done a great job there, son," he speaks, giving me a fatherly hug. "You make me proud." *Yeah, right.*

I do have a great relationship to my father. He has never been anything but nice to me. He has always been supporting me, celebrating every victory. But he pushes me over my limits. Not that that's a bad thing. It's just too much sometimes.

One time, I was about sixteen years old, he pushed me as far as to vomit on the ice during practice. He made me practice with his team. It was an honor to be there. But I was sixteen, not even close to those guys' age. They had way more experience. They had way more training than I ever had. And sure enough, my stomach couldn't take it anymore and I was emptying my guts on the ice.

Being mortified after that would be an understatement. I wanted to sink into the floor, die right there on the spot.

I'm sure my father is proud of me. I mean, what kind of jackass father wouldn't be proud of their child's victory. But hell, he lives his life through me. He could never go pro himself thanks to an injury, but I can. Unless I fuck up and get an injury like he did. I sure as hell want to go pro, it's always been a dream of mine. I was maybe three years old when I was on the ice for the first time. Of course I couldn't do much then, but my father insisted on taking me with him as he went to coach his team.

When I step into the locker room, my team is out of control, roaring like they don't care if they lose their voices, singing, dancing in victory. I can't help but laugh at these dorks, but then I join them, cause to hell with silliness. We fucking won.

I strip off my hockey gear and quickly throw on some sweatpants and a t-shirt.

Instead of taking a shower as I would normally, I will be going back out there. I just need to get rid of the protective gear first. I don't care if I fall and hurt myself. I'll be alone on the ice anyway, so nothing too severe to worry about.

Maybe trying to get faster on skates without the hockey gear is a stupid idea, but it's a start, so I'll take that.

"Where are you going?" Aaron asks when I head toward the exit of the locker room, clearly not having my stuff with me.

"Just going to skate for a while. You know, getting some extra training," I tell him. He nods slowly, then shrugs and waves me off. It's not like I owe him an explanation, but I also know he thinks I'm off to fuck someone. "Seriously, just some skating," I say, even pointing at my feet.

"Didn't say you weren't." He laughs. "Don't stink up the whole rink. We've early practice tomorrow."

I flip Aaron off with a grin on my lips and walk out of the locker room, my back heading out first. The second the double door closes, I turn around and walk toward the ice rink.

I'm pleased to find the arena empty. It's an oddly calming silence, one that is good for improving skills. I grab the AirPods case from my sweatpants pocket and stick the buds into my ears, opening my music app right after. I press play on my favorite playlist, only to find out that my sister added some songs when I last visited.

My ears are filled with *Get Into It (Yuh)* by *Doja Cat*. I don't bother switching the song though. Eira loves her, and whoever Eira loves, I shall love too. My sixteen years old sister would be mocking me right now if she heard the song I am listening to. Fortunately, she isn't here right now.

Only seconds after I step onto the ice, I come to realize that I am not alone here. Sure, my teammates are still in the locker room, or shower room, or anywhere back there. But I am not alone *here*.

Blonde hair catches my attention. Someone is sitting on the seats right on the opposite side of where I'm standing. Their head is lowered, and doesn't look above the railing, which makes it pretty hard for me to identify that someone. I skate closer. So close that I am now standing in front of *her*, still on the other side of the tempered glass.

I knock onto the tempered glass, hoping that will catch her attention. It doesn't, she's in her element. Usually, I would just shrug it off and go back to do my thing, but her body is shaking slightly. I think she might be crying.

The blonde girl is holding a notebook in her hands, and she is writing something into it. Judging by the few wet stains on the paper, she most definitely *is* crying. *Someone can't take the loss of their hockey team very well.*

Being raised to care for vulnerable people, I tug back my ego and get off the ice. Fortunately, there is an exit right next to where she is sitting. At least I don't have to make an extra effort walking all around the rink in skates to get to a crying girl.

She doesn't even notice me when I walk up to her, nor when I sit down beside her. I remove my AirPods from my ears and put them back into the case, then go to take hers out of her ears. Well, one of them.

Green eyes meet mine. Jesus, her eyes are the most beautiful shade of green I've ever seen. She has a few freckles on her nose, spreading over her cheeks and forehead. It suits her and reminds me a lot of someone else I know.

Her eyebrows find together. She is frowning at me in confusion. Can't blame her though.

"Are you okay?" I ask. Clearly, she is not. Her face is tear-stained, which means my assumption about her crying was correct. She nods but doesn't use her voice to confirm. "I don't think you are, blondie."

She doesn't say anything.

"What are you writing about?" Maybe that is a bit forward, and obviously private as she slams the notebook shut and sets it down onto the seat beside her.

"Congratulations on your victory," she speaks. Her voice is sweet and calm, I think I just fell in love with it. That sounds silly, I admit. However, I want her to talk more.

I thank her wholeheartedly, though I'm not sure *she* means it. "Sorry your team lost."

Blondie chuckles quietly, but I'm not sure if it is an ironic chuckle or a "*great, now leave"* one. Perhaps both. "I'm attending St. Trewery, Colin. I wasn't here for Yale." *Oh, fuck me.*

"You know my name," I note, somewhat bobbing my head. For a short moment I wonder if she stayed here because she was hoping that maybe one of my teammates would meet her here and she would get laid.

"You are kind of Trewery's big star, you know." She shrugs unapologetically, giving me a slim smile. Not even a genuine one that reaches her eyes. No. It is a pity smile.

"So, who's your favorite?" I don't think talking to her about what I saw would be such a great idea. So, hockey it is.

"Aaron Marsh," she says with no hesitation. I must look like I've seen a ghost, because she starts to laugh, looking at me with an awfully intense stare, I would back off if she didn't seem all nice.

My hand finds the spot over my heart, my mouth opens as I pretend to be butt-hurt by her favorite hockey player choice.

Aaron is good. He has mad skills; I can't blame her for liking him. And it's not even that, Aaron is *fine*. Even I can say this guy does not have issues getting it. Not only because of the tons of girls he brings home every week.

"Sorry, blondie, but Aaron doesn't do girlfriends, otherwise I would link you up."

She freezes, but shortly after, she fakes some gaging sounds before breaking into even more laughter.

"I'm good, thank you very much."

"Not into hockey players then, huh?"

"I'm not into Aaron specifically." I don't miss the disgusted tone in her voice, but I don't dare asking her about it. "He dated my best friend for a while before breaking her heart." At least she offers me an explanation anyway. Though, I don't believe her.

"Aaron isn't the dating type. So, I call bullshit."

"Aaron totally is the dating type. He just doesn't date anymore because Winter and Aaron have this on-off thing going since freshman year. But I bet he told you all about it. Aaron adores you." I wonder how she knows that. I mean, Aaron and I sure are pretty damn close, but there is no way she knows that for sure.

He did tell me about Winter and their relationship though. Roughly.

"So, what's the deal with you and Aaron?"

"There's none. I just hear a lot about him from my best friend." Again, I don't believe her. But I don't have any other choice, this girl won't talk.

"You know my name, so it's only fair if I get yours too," I demand. But she shrugs and gets up from the seat. Without saying anything further, she walks away. She. Walks. Away. From me. *Ouch.*

I watch her leave, and once she is around the corner, I notice a mint green notebook lying on the seat. She forgot her notebook, *dammit*.

Maybe I should go after her. Only so she gets her book back, but she is too far away already. I can't possibly catch up with her while wearing skates. I could yell out her name, but I don't know it. Let's pray I will find her on campus, that way I can give it back to her.

The mint green notebook is staring at me, screaming "read me." I know I shouldn't, but c'mon, as if I could keep this book with me for what? Days? And not look inside at least once.

I allow myself a quick look, just trying to see if I find any indications as to who she may be, but then I'm hooked.

Dear whoever reads this,

I have no idea how I am supposed to talk about me. Maybe this will just be a way of me expressing what I felt while writing this. Maybe not.
You see, I don't ever speak about my past. Come to think it's a habit of my mother's that I picked up along the way. She never speaks about what happened, but I think it's just what I needed back then.
I.

Want.
To.
Die.
I'm not afraid of death. In fact, I think it will be quite peaceful. For me at least.
I won't have to deal with all those feelings anymore.
I won't have to deal with the pain anymore.
I won't have to deal with the people causing the pain anymore.
I won't have to deal with the constant cries and long nights anymore.
It will all be over. How much better could it get?
I used to be afraid of death, but I can't be afraid of it anymore. What awful thing could there possibly be? I could be dead. But that's the whole point, isn't it? Maybe I will remember my life on earth, have an afterlife or continue to live as a spirit. But even if that's not the case, it's the best-case scenario. I don't want to remember me.

Lily

I stare at those two pages. Two whole pages of the girl I found crying. *Lily.* Two pages on which she speaks about death as if she's been fantasizing about it for way too long already.

Two weeks. *God dammit.* This girl is giving herself two more weeks to live. I hope she's joking. But to hell with that. It's a really bad joke.

When I first found the book still lying on the seat, I thought she left it on purpose. But I highly doubt that now.

There is no way that she ever wanted anyone to find this before she… what? left?

I turn the page to see if she wrote any more. She did. I want to read it, but I know I shouldn't. This is her battle, her thoughts. But how am I supposed to ignore a cry for help like this?

I remind myself that this isn't a cry for help. It's a goodbye.

If only I knew more about her. Where is she from? Does she have any other family members that care about her? Who are her closest friends? Literally anyone I could inform about her condition.

She needs help. But if she wanted it, she would ask for it, right?

God, does she know she needs help? She for sure does. I mean, someone doesn't just want to die for funsies, right?

The next page is the beginning of a letter. One of the letters she mentioned before. It reads "*Dear Ana,*" I wonder who Ana is. Maybe her roommate. Does she live at the dorms? Maybe Ana is her best friend. No, that was Summer. Or Winter? I don't care, it was a season.

Maybe Ana is her sister. I have no idea who Ana is, but she must be close if she is getting a letter.

I try to stop myself from reading any further. This is private. I shouldn't read it. It's not meant for my eyes.

But Lily needs help.

Instead of reading it myself, perhaps I should hand this notebook over to the counselor. *What do I do?*

Dear Ana,

I am so sorry.

Nine Days

I am sorry that I never gave you a chance to be more to me.
Dad told me you always wanted a big sister. You always wanted a sister that would help you out, give you great advice when it comes to boys. Teach you how to do makeup when you're old enough. You wanted me.
But I didn't want you.
That sounds awful, I know.
I have to be honest with you, Ana. I hated you. For as long as I can remember
I wanted you gone, because you had what I didn't; My father.
You got to see him daily. You got to have a loving father that would protect you, love you, be there for you. But he was my father too, you know.
My brother got to experience it along with you. But I didn't.
I couldn't hate him for that, but I could hate you. Because you weren't my family.
Dad isn't your father, not biologically at least. But he is mine. And yet, you still got more of him than I did.
I was so jealous. I think I still am.
But it's time that I forgive you for getting what was mine. It's not like you had any say in it anyway.
Ana, I want you to know that all my hatred never had anything to do with you. I feel awful for letting it out on you.
Whenever I would visit, I never paid you any attention because you got enough from the man that was supposed to be there for me, not for someone else's kid.

You were so young when you came to this family, you could not have known what it did to me. I knew I shouldn't hate on you for it. But I did.
And I am so utterly sorry for it, Ana.
Maybe we get to be sisters in another life. Because, despite what I told myself all these years, I like you.
You are a part of my life. Maybe not as big as you wished you'd be, but you are. And I love you, Ana. I really do.
I loved you from the first second I saw you.
I'm sorry I couldn't be a better sister to you. But I will make it up to you in another life. I promise.
And Ana, please don't ever give up on your dreams. I know you can make it far. I will watch over you and protect you from this day forth. I will smile with you, laugh with you, cry with you. Be the big sister you've always wanted.
Too bad I can't physically be with you for it. But I will be there. Every step you take, I will be there.

Lily

Yeah, I should not have read this.

Lily Reyes is writing her goodbyes in a notebook. In. A. Notebook. The one that she forgot here. In an arena for everyone to find.

I jump off my seat, quickly skate over the ice to the other side to get back into the locker room. I have to find her. I have to give this notebook back to her and find someone that can help her.

Standing outside of the locker room, I hear laughter coming from inside. That means some of my teammates are still around. Honestly, I thought they would all be gone by now. I have no idea how long I've been gone, but I assumed longer than for anyone to still be around.

"Yo! That was a short skate," Miles says while he's struggling to put on some pants. His hair is still damp from his shower, and I just bet he didn't bother enough to dry off his skin before trying to slip into his pants.

Fuck it, right? "Do you know a Lily Reyes?" I ask him. Miles shrugs and shakes his head.

"Never heard of her. Is she hot, though?" I roll my eyes at his question. I'm not up for this talk right now.

"Reyes? I've heard that last name before," Grey Davis—the last dude I "share a house" with—informs me. "I think she is in one of my classes."

"Which one?"

"Not sure. I don't pay much attention to people, you know that." That's true, at least in some ways. Grey isn't much the people-person. He sure doesn't mind being around people, but he tries to avoid them as much as possible.

"Nah, you don't pay much attention to *girls*," Miles mocks, winking at his best friend. He slaps Grey on his back, then goes to stand on the bench.

I let out a deep sigh. Whatever is about to come out of Miles's mouth can't be anything good.

Miles mocks people. He's an arrogant ass and uses anything to make stupid jokes at all times. But that's the thing with Miles. No matter how silly and immature he may be, he's the most loyal friend anyone could get. And he would never use anything that's no-go topic against someone.

"I have an announcement to make." Miles holds his hand up, pretending to hold a glass when he says, "I think our team captain has a little crush. That would be a first."

Grey pulls Miles off the bench, shaking his head disapprovingly.

"I need more information than a name, Princess," Grey says. He raises his brows in anticipation, waiting for the ultimate description on my behalf.

Okay, maybe Miles is the one hoping for the greatest description, not Grey.

"Uh, she's blonde and has green eyes," I tell him. "A few freckles, and she's cute, I guess."

"Ah, now that narrows it down." Grey laughs and shakes his head. "We need a little more than that, Colin. Why don't you just call her and ask for a date already?" Just when I thought Grey would be more mature than Miles. He is, by far.

I wish I could do that. But I don't do dates. "I don't want her that way." I shrug. "She forgot her notebook in the arena, I just want to give it back to her."

"Who even writes in notebooks these days?" Miles asks, walking away from Grey and me. He is back by his locker, gathering his stuff.

"What are we talking about?" Aaron comes walking into the locker room with just a towel around his hips. He is always the last one to exit the shower room. For some reasons, he has a hard time showering with anyone else in there. Well, anyone but the three of us. Grey, Miles and me. But the other guys, he prefers to stay away from them.

I get that. Some of the guys are dicks. Kaiden Callahan once took a picture of a teammates dick and sent it to our team group chat…and possible girlfriends. It was a dick move, but Zachery didn't take it too badly. In fact, Zac winked at Kaiden and proceeded to pose, making Kaiden take even more pictures.

Like I mentioned before, this team is…different.

"Lily Reyes," Grey fills Aaron in. "Forgot her notebook in the arena. Our princess here wants to give it back."

"I can do it, if you want," Aaron offers. That's weird. Aaron never does anything for a girl, not since his ex-girlfriend fiasco anyway. Winter, was it. God, of course. Aaron knows Lily. He was dating her best friend after all.

"It's fine. Do you have her number so I can hit her up or something?"

Aaron furrows his eyebrows. Something about his expression screams "*discomfort.*" He doesn't like the idea of me hitting her up. Maybe their relationship goes deeper than I thought. "Don't think she would want you to have it."

"Look, she mentioned you in our short conversation. If y'all are dating, then you can gladly give the notebook back to her, and I promise I won't try to start things. But then you should know something," I tell him.

To my surprise, Aaron does the very same fake gaging sound as Lily did. It catches my attention. So something did happen between them already, and neither of them is proud of it. But he also doesn't jump onto the opportunity to find out what he's supposed to know of.

"I take that as you guys aren't dating," Grey speaks for me. "So what's your deal then. Having a crush? Long lost enemy?" That gets a snicker from me. Lily seems like she has a few of those. I mean, her not-really-sister seems to be one of those. Then again, Lily did apologize for treating her wrongly. So maybe Lily isn't the type to make enemies.

"Nah, neither. Just not my type."

"Marsh, if Carter thinks she is cute, she is totally your type," says Miles, chuckling.

Aaron eyes me. Disgust is written all over his face, but there is more. Something he doesn't want to talk about. Clearly Lily is a topic he does not like to discuss, and I respect that. But if there is some kind of relationship between them, maybe he should know about her condition. "Is she an ex-girlfriend? Someone important to you?" I ask. Aaron shakes his head and walks away from us.

He stays in the room, but I suppose he is getting cold.

"Can't really tell you guys the deal with her. But we're not a thing, nor will we ever be, trust me on that. But don't you dare touch her, dude." His voice is strict, still has the slightest amount of discomfort in it.

I shouldn't push him any further. But to hell with that. Aaron Marsh just openly admitted on not being with her, yet he doesn't want me touching this girl.

Something is off, and I will find out what it is.

Chapter 3

"there's just too much that time cannot erase"—My Immortal by Evanescence

Lily

"Fuck!" I curse under my breath. I can't believe I forgot my notebook at the arena. I must have left it on the seat when I put it as far away from Colin Carter as only possible.

I have looked through my entire room already. It's not here. And it's not in the living room either. *Because it's at the hockey arena.* This can't be happening. To hell with my goodbye book.

It's only a matter of time before the school's counselor comes marching in here, making me see yet another shrink. Or worse, sends me off to a mental hospital. Can he do that? I mean, he's just a school counselor after all, and I am twenty years old. I have a say in what's happening to me, right?

My phone chimes. I'm not up for company right now.

Aaron: You forgot your notebook. Why the hell did you take a notebook with you to a hockey game?

Oh God. Of course. I should have known Colin wouldn't be able to keep his mouth shut. Does Aaron know what I wrote inside? No, he would have called me, stopped by personally only to push me off a building himself.

Lily: Homework. Do you have it?

I couldn't possibly tell him the truth, right? I'm praying he won't open the notebook and read it. God, he would actually tell my dad. Or worse, call the counselor and get me into a mental hospital. *Dang it*.

Aaron: Carter has it. What's going on between the two of you anyway?

Lily: Nothing, Ron. We just talked for a moment, then I left. Forgot the book, apparently.

Aaron: Mkay. You up for a coffee? We should really catch up. I don't have the notebook, but maybe I can get Colin to tag along.

I consider it for a second. But Colin most definitely looked inside. He even asked me about what I was writing before, no way he didn't look into it when he got the chance to. Which means, if he comes, Aaron will find out.
Though, why would Colin even care what I wrote about? He doesn't know me. He shouldn't put his nose into my business.

Lily: Coffee sounds good. Colin not so much. Just take the notebook with you, will you? And don't look inside, please. It's private.

Maybe telling the only guy that ever truly cared about you not to look into something private is the wrong thing to say. But I know for sure Aaron would not invalidate my privacy unless it's one hundred per cent necessary.

If he's smart enough, he will look inside. It wouldn't change anything about the way I feel about life, but it could potentially force me to stay alive a bit longer.

Aaron: Kk. Meet me at Claire's in ten.

Claire's is the only place he should not have chosen. It's always crowded with tons of college students. Granted, it's the only coffee shop close to campus. There are a few up in the city, but why would anyone go there when Claire's is literally a five-minute walk from campus?

I didn't plan on leaving my room again for today, but I guess meeting up with Aaron won't be too bad. I always loved catching up with him. And I always have a good time whenever we're together. It's like I forget all my pain for a moment. He makes me happy, so why wouldn't I grab a coffee with him?

Okay, maybe Winter wouldn't like knowing I meet up with her on-off boyfriend. But she doesn't know half the truth, so I don't really care.

Aaron is late, as always. But I can't blame him. I'm not sure if he is still at the arena or went home. If he did go home, it will take him at least fifteen minutes alone to drive down here. Not sure why he wanted to meet up at Claire's then.

He lives on a college student street. Well, it's not really a street for college students, other people used to live there too. But with every year the overpriced houses were rented out to college students. Eventually the families got tired of the noises, the constant parties and fights, and moved away.

"Can I get you anything, Lily?" Mia, a good friend of mine asks.

"Yes, uh, could I get a Chai Latte and a black coffee, please?"

"Coming right up." Mia writes down my order, gives me a smile before walking away.

Good thing I know Aaron's order by heart. Literally anywhere. I know what he will order, even if we have never been there before. It's not only coffee shops. It's any Café or restaurant we go to.

"I am so sorry, Lily. Carter refused to give me the notebook, so I had to fight for it." Aaron sounds out of breath. He takes a seat across from me and slides the notebook over the table. "I've got it anyway."

"Thank you, Ron." I take the notebook and slip it into my purse. "You didn't read it, did you?"

"What? You think I want to read about your sex fantasies? No thanks."

Relief instantly sweeps through my body. I give Aaron a weak smile, but eventually this weak smile turns into a genuine one. I don't know how he does that, but just his presence makes me feel so much lighter, so much happier.

"How are you, Lils?"

"Stressed, I think. You know, tons of assignments and stuff." I allow a chuckle to cross my lips. I don't feel like talking about me, I never do. So I need to change the topic. Fortunately for me, Aaron loves talking about himself. "Oh, Winter mentioned scouts watching you today."

"Yeah." At first, he tries to hold back his smile. But I know Aaron too well. I can read him like an open book, and he knows it. The corners of his mouth twitch, and soon enough he is grinning like a toddler. "I'm not supposed to talk about it, but I got an offer from the New York Rangers." He sighs. "Nothing *too* official yet cause…well, NHL rules and such but…"

"Seriously?!" I'm so proud of him. He worked so hard for this, almost all his life. "That's huge!" I say excitedly.

"I suppose."

"Quit the modesty, Ron." He laughs and shakes his head at me. "You're never modest about anything. Then this happens and suddenly you don't want to rub it in my face?"

"It doesn't feel the same anymore." *What?*

"What do you mean?"

Before he can elaborate, Mia is back with our drinks. She sets them down at the table and glances at me with jealously. Yeah, jealousy. I know that look on her face. On any face, actually.

I'm surprised Mia is jealous. She usually stays as far away from any jock as humanly possible.

Aaron isn't bad looking. His blonde hair and green eyes are really pretty, along with the freckles that decorate his face, some would say he is an 11/10.

I, however, never fell and never will fall under his spell. For obvious reasons.

Mia turns on her heel and leaves as fast as she came.

"Skating just doesn't feel the same anymore when you don't do it with me." *Here we go again.*

I used to skate a lot. I was a figure skater, even did competitions. I loved it more than anything. Aaron and I used to meet up every Sunday to race one another. I have always been faster than him, and I can do more tricks than he can. It was refreshing, playfully competing with the guy you wish nothing but the best for.

For most of my life, I was excited to meet him Sundays. I loved our skate-dates. Though, they were never dates, and it is kind of weird that I refer to them as such. *They're not dates. Never were.*

Eventually my depression got the better of me and I gave up on skating. I made up excuses to Aaron as to why I couldn't show up. I never told him the real reason. I know he would have understood, he would have dropped everything to be with me and make me feel better, but I didn't want him feeling bad for me.

So I lied. Told him mom wouldn't allow me skating anymore. She was too afraid I could get seriously injured and die. He didn't question it one bit.

"Aaron," I say quietly. I hate that he's affecting my own feelings this much, by being upset only.

He feels bad because skating was both of our passion since forever. Skating was an escape to me, until it wasn't. "You know mom wouldn't be happy to know I started again."

"I can't believe she would do that to you. I mean, she knows how much skating means to you. She knows how much you love it." And now I feel guilty. I hate lying to him. But I can't tell him the truth. Maybe I will tell him someday. *In his letter, for instance.*

"She doesn't know we're still in touch. Actually, she doesn't know we have ever been in touch. I think she would officially replace me with another daughter," I say, he chuckles but agrees with me. "I can't believe she never even tried to reach out to you, Ron."

"Well, no offence, but I don't want her in my life anymore anyway. Liz has been the mother I've never had for as long as I can remember." Yeah, Liz Marsh, Aaron's new mother. The very same that broke off my parents' marriage. But, hey, my father loves her, and she sure loves him, so I am happy for them. And for Aaron.

"You had mom up until you were five," I remind him.

"Almost five," he corrects. "But yeah, I guess. And then she pushed me away like I never mattered in the first place."

Sixteen years ago, our parents decided to split up. And as it is, everything gets split in half when a divorce doesn't go through peacefully. The house had to be sold, the money for it got split in half. Every single one of our belongings; sold and the money split in half.

Their children. Split in half.

They thought, "*good thing we have two kids, twins even. Makes it easier.*" My father got one, and my mother one.

"Lily is staying with me. She is a girl. She needs her mother. You can take the boy," she said. I was only five, but I remember her words like she said them yesterday. It was a knife in my heart. *"I don't allow her any contact to you or Aaron. And Aaron may never get in touch with me either. This is your half now, your commitment. No going back."* I think I've hated her for years after that.

But I was five, well four but soon to be five. I didn't understand what was going on. All I knew was, I would never see my brother ever again.

Jokes on my mother, my dad is a decent guy. He wanted me in his life, and he wanted to be part of mine. So before he left, we made a deal. Aaron and I would meet up every Sunday at the ice rink in town. I told my mom I had new skating lessons every Sunday. It was my first ever big lie. And I regret nothing.

So every Sunday, dad would meet me there, together with Aaron. We would skate for a while, then grab some food before he took me back to the rink so my mom could come pick me up.

When I grew older, I used to lie to my mother about where I would spend the nights. I would tell her I was going to a friend's house, when in reality, I went to stay with my father and Aaron for the weekend. These were the most fun weekends I would experience.

And my mother never found out about it.

I have no clue why my mother never questioned my new skating lessons. Or why she never wanted to come inside to see if I was actually meeting my Coach. But I am not mad about it.

If she did figure it out, I wouldn't want to know what she would have done to my father.

"Do you think she ever regrets not keeping me in her life?" Aaron asks. A small amount of words, yet they have my heart breaking. The answer is no. Mom never regretted turning her back to her son. She never even gave him one more thought after that day. She didn't keep pictures, didn't speak about him to me, didn't even mention him to other people.

When someone asked how many children she had, she had not more than one daughter. Aaron wasn't even worth mentioning.

"No." I know this will hurt him, but I can't keep lying to my brother. He's a sweetheart, he shouldn't hold onto her when she clearly has no intentions seeing him or inviting him into her life. He deserves better. Liz is better…to him.

The doors to Claire's open. Usually, I wouldn't pay attention to who's entering but when the same muscular figure from the ice rink enters, I can't help but stare.

He is here. What in the world is he doing here?

"Marsh!" Colin yells out. Aaron's back is turned to Colin, but he has a great view on me. And he uses it. His eyes are locked with mine. He doesn't seem like he knows anything. Colin Carter just gives me the very same smile he gives everyone else. The star-smile. The I'm-oh-so-much-better-smile.

Colin walks up to our table, his eyes still on me before he takes a seat next to Aaron. His hand finds the back of Aaron's neck, grabbing it, giving it a squeeze before he lets go.

"What's up Lilybug?" Colin nods his head at me. *He read it*. I just know he did. Colin didn't know my name before, so he checked if there was one inside the notebook. Hence, he figured out my name, read the rest, ratted me out to Aaron and now… what now? He's here. Why is he here? And why isn't my brother yelling at me for wanting to die?

"Lilybug?" I raise my eyebrows at him. He nods. "Seriously?" Another nod. Aaron is laughing. Of course he is laughing, as so is Colin.

"Would you prefer it if I called you *little lady*?" he asks.

"How about Lily?"

"No can do, Lilybug."

I let out a sigh. And to avoid his intense stare, I am now looking at my fingers underneath the table. I'm playing with the ring on my left ring finger. That only ever happens when I get nervous. Why am I getting nervous?

"Hope I'm not interrupting your little coffee date," he speaks, annoying me.

Aaron groans, closing his eyes to calm down, taking a few deep breaths. I just know he is trying his hardest not to grab a knife and stab Colin with it.

"No date, dude. She's like a sister to me."

I *am* his sister.

"So what's the deal then?"

"What's there to be?" Aaron asks in return.

We both agreed on never mentioning that we're siblings. Though, if someone looked at the both of us a little longer than just a second, I'm sure it's obvious that we're twins. We look ridiculously alike. Fortunately, I have the more feminine genes. And I'm way shorter than Aaron. Probably by a whole foot. Not a clue how that happened.

Aaron and I only agreed on never saying a word because we don't want to risk our mother finding out we're attending the same college. We did the same back in high school, and elementary. My father made sure my mother would never find out.

"Are you like a thing?"

"For fuck's sake, Carter," Aaron cusses. "Lily and I are not a thing, and we won't ever be a thing."

"So then what the hell is going on between the two of you? You told me I can't touch her, so there must be something."

Ah yeah, that's the big brother I remember. Aaron never wanted any of his teammates to *"get in my pants"*—his words, not mine. At least not after that one disaster back in high school.

He has always been protective of me. Always made sure the guys I've been with weren't some criminals.

It used to be so difficult for me to even be with someone because whoever I was interested in, he was never putting up with Aaron's expectations for me.

Which is why the only guys I've ever dated were fictional.

"Just leave it, would you?" I demand.

Colin's eyes meet mine. He looks bemused. I know he has something on hand that will ruin my life. Or more my way out of life. Maybe I should watch my mouth around this dick.

"Fine, so then I don't see a point why I can't fuck her," Colin speaks, his eyes never leaving mine. Aaron presses the palms of his hands to his face, stroking them down his face with another groan.

"Alright then. No girlfriend shit you have with her, but exclusivity, got it. I will stay away." Colin winks at me and gets up from his seat. He makes his way over to another table and sits.

I'm not even surprised when I see that the table he just took a seat at wasn't an empty one. Colin Carter is now sitting with two brunettes. *Maybe brunette is his type*.

"Your friend is gross," I tell Aaron. He bobs his head in agreement, watching Colin flirt with yet another girl. "But so are you. You do the exact same thing."

"We're not going to discuss my sex life, Lils."

"Not discussing it. I'm stating a fact."

"Whatever. Tell Winter to come over later," Aaron says and gets up. He pulls out some money from his back pocket and places it onto the table. "I need a good fuck after this."

"*Ew*, Aaron!" He laughs as he walks away.

"LILY, I MEAN IT, Aaron hates me!" Winter complains, frustrated. And like the dramatic person she is, she does a perfect dramatic fall onto my bed, with the back of her hand pressed to her forehead and everything. *She is such a drama queen.*

"Aaron doesn't hate you. He just has a bad day," I reassure her. I'm not sure if Aaron ever truly loved her. I wouldn't blame him if he didn't. Winter is a lot to take in.

"But I should be the one he wants to talk to, Lils." *Yeah, if they were dating, perhaps.* "He never talks about himself. He doesn't even want me meeting his parents. It's so tiring."

"Then why do you stick around? You're always jumping onto the next opportunity to fuck him. He calls, and you start to run."

"I love him. You wouldn't get that, but I do think he loves me too." Tears rolls down her cheeks.

"Love shouldn't be that much work, Winter. If you have to fight for him loving you, then maybe it's not supposed to be," I tell her.

She stays quiet. The only sounds coming from Winter Varley are the sobs from all the crying.

Winter ends up falling asleep on my bed. I don't mind it though. My bed is big enough for two people. And to be honest, I could use some company for once.

Chapter 4

"breathe in, breathe deep, you know that's all you need"—Chariot by Jacob Lee

Lily

IT'S BEEN TWO DAYS SINCE I LAST RAN into Colin.

It could have happened yesterday, but I refused to go out with Winter. Which was a good decision because Winter ended up in—*surprise*—Aaron's bed.

At least I had the dorm room to myself. I could fill my notebook without any interruptions.

To my surprise, Colin did not inform the counselor about my condition, at least no one tried to reach out to me yet. Maybe he didn't read the entries after all and just looked for a name. Or maybe he asked his friends if they knew who this notebook belonged to. But that could not have been the case, I just recently bought it. No one would have known.

"Twelve more days," I mumble to myself as I write another entry. "Twelve more days and this will all be over."

Today is another one of my down-days. But that's the case on most Sundays. I would much rather be at the ice rink and skate with my brother, but I can't. Not because my mother wouldn't allow it. Hell, she wouldn't even have a say in it if my lie were to be true. But I haven't been on the ice for good three years.

I'm sure I can still skate, but I don't want to start loving something again. Not right before my life comes to an end. It's just not worth it.

Dear whoever reads this,

I can't stop thinking about skating.
Ever since Aaron mentioned it on Friday, I can't stop thinking about how good it felt.
I can't stop wondering if it would still feel this good.
Would I still feel like floating when I step on the ice?
Would I still lose track of all my surroundings when the sound of classical music streams through my ears as I go through with my program?
Would I still feel as light as a feather when my skates glide over the frozen water?
Would it be the same?
Aaron got an offer from a hockey team. He doesn't seem too happy, but I know he is. It's what he has wanted all his life.
I'm so proud of him. But I wish I could see him rank up with every new hockey season. Unfortunately, I will not make it this far. It is getting too much.
You should have seen the sadness that overcame him when I told him I will not return to skating.
Let me tell you this:
Aaron and I had this dream. It's silly, but we were determined to make it come true.

Aaron Marsh, the superstar hockey player. He's on the ice, playing against whatever team is on the agenda. And then, it's one of the breaks. I would get on the ice and entertain the hockey fans while they wait for the game to continue.
I would skate and have fun.
I would have loved this.
We both would have.
It's such a shame that it won't be happening.
But, hey, at least I am determined to go through with my suicide plan.
Okay, this needs a better name.
My unalive journey 101.
Sounds just a stupid.

Lily

"Does this need reasons why I want to die?" I ask myself. "Probably," I answer myself. Yeah, I talk to myself, so sue me.

What if Aaron finds me first and reads this book? He would want to know reasons behind all of this.

I rest my head in my hands. I can't imagine how devastated my brother will be when he finds out that this notebook was the beginning of my ending and he held it in his hands before. When he finds out that with just one look into this book, he could have saved my life.

But it wouldn't have. I would find a way to die, even if he found out in advance. This whole thing here, breathing, it's getting too much for me. My body doesn't want to be here anymore, neither does my soul. I'm tired. *Oh, that's a good thing to mention.*

So I start to write again. And after that I start another entry. And another. And another. Until it's time for the second letter.

The next letter will be even harder on me than Ana's was. I was never close to Ana, but the next person, I owe my life to him.

Dear father,

If you're reading this, that means I've died.

Jesus, that's the lamest way to start a letter. Ever.

Don't worry though, I am not suffering anymore. (I hope) I used to. When I was still alive. Right in the moment when I am writing this letter to you.
Dad, I need you to know something.
I'm thankful for you. Truly, I am.
You gave me a family when I needed it.
You didn't give up on me when mom wanted you to. You know, the same time she gave up on my brother.
I am so thankful that you gave Aaron a better mother. Liz is perfect. She is everything Aaron needs to be happy.
So, thank you. Thank you for giving my brother a chance to see me. Thank you for giving him a chance to have a better family than I did.
But most importantly, thank you for sticking around. You know, it's usually the dads that leave the family. According to some of the "hilarious" internet user. But that wasn't you. You, dad, you were my hero. You are *my hero.*

*You stuck around when you shouldn't have. At least that's
what mom wanted: you gone.
But you stayed. You stayed for me. You made me happy.
You made my childhood less gray.
There's no other way to say this, dad.*
You are my hero.
*You were my chariot, urging me to become courageous
and determined to take life into my own hands.
You were my savior when I needed you the most.
It's ironic, I know. You couldn't save me from my pain.
You couldn't save me from my suffering.
You couldn't save me from committing.
But dad, that is not your fault.
You did nothing wrong. You were always there for me.
You always cared.
This is a battle I lost. A battle against myself. There was
nothing you could have done to prevent it.
I love you, dad.*

Lily

Just when I finish writing the letter to my father, the door to the dorm room opens. I hear giggles coming from the living room. It sounds like Winter's, but she is not alone.

"LILS!" *Yup, I can now confirm, it's Winter.* "COME GET DRUNK WITH US!" The hell I will. It's Sunday. I have classes tomorrow. I won't get drunk on a Sunday night with my best friend and whoever her company is. She knows better than to ask me such thing.

The door to my room swings open in a swift move. It's so fast, I barely even see it until I hear the *thud* it creates when the door slams into my desk. Let's pray my door didn't get any damage from that.

"Mia told me she saw you with Aaron last Friday." A completely drunk Winter stumbles into my room and takes a seat on my bed. Her makeup is smudged all over her face. It's everywhere but where it's supposed to be. She looks awful.

That's a new thing to say because Winter Varley always looks flawless.

"We ran into each other at Claire's," I lie. "Told him to stop playing with you."

"I call bullshit, Lily." Of course she does. Just like everyone else at this college, Winter has no idea that Aaron and I are related. "He is totally cheating on me with *you*. My best friend. You're not supposed to screw guys I'm in love with."

I debate telling her the truth, but Winter has a big mouth. She talks. She loves listening to gossip, and she loves gossiping. If I told her Aaron is my twin brother, she would lose her shit and tell the whole school. Actually, she would probably print it onto a banner and hang it up by the main entrance.

Truth is, sometimes I wish people knew. Whenever someone sees us together, they immediately assume we're dating. The disgusted looks I get from that are painful. It's not like it should bother me much, but it does. Either they see me as the biggest whore in history, or some bitch that stole their man. Though, Aaron doesn't do dates, and they should know that.

Either way, looks can hurt. And I think people seem to forget that. Not only words cut deep, looks do too.

"Believe what you want, Winter. I'm not up to discuss this. Aaron and I are *friends*. Not ever going to be more than that. If you think your *ex*-boyfriend is cheating on you, then maybe that's a you-problem."

Winter lets out a gasp, covering her mouth with her hand. She looks at me as if I just told her to kill herself.

"You know what, Lily Reyes"—she shoots up from my bed, crossing her arms in front of her chest—"go fuck yourself!" I don't bother reacting to that. She doesn't even give me a chance to do so.

The next thing I know, an angry Winter is storming toward my door. She grabs the door handle, pulling it after her as she leaves my room.

But right before she leaves the room completely, she turns around and looks at me one more time. "I liked you, Lily. But you're such a bitch. Maybe you are better off dead."

Ironic, isn't it? I believe the exact same thing. I *am* better off dead. And here's proof that not only I believe so.

But the worst bit, even if Winter, my best friend, is mad at me. As a friend, you don't tell the other person they're better off dead. In fact, you don't ever say those words to *anyone*.

Wishing someone to die is not okay. Not ever. No matter how deep your hatred goes. It's never okay to wish for someone to die.

Who knows, maybe they're like me and wish the exact same thing.

And who knows, maybe they will actually go through with it.

Like me.

And oh-so suddenly, I feel like I'm *Hannah Baker*, and Winter is my thirteenth reason why.

Chapter 5

"if love is what you need, a soldier I will be"—Angel With a Shotgun by The Cab

Lily

MY FILM DIRECTING CLASS STARTED TWENTY minutes ago. For some reasons my alarm decided not to go off this morning, which now makes me late for class.

A great way to start my Tuesday.

I've always hated being late for class. Back in high school, I would skip the entire day if I were late.

The looks when you walk into the classroom too late scream far more than "*judgment.*" They're filled with arrogance, like any person that was there on time thinks they're something better.

People will pay attention to me. Attention that I do not want nor need.

I know the second I open that door and walk inside, people will look at me.

They will look at me and think I'm trouble. They will think that I am some wrack that can't even set an alarm to be on time.

It shouldn't even matter to me, not right now, *not ever*.

I'm late, so I shouldn't waste any more time thinking about being late. Instead, I should just walk right into the classroom.

Fortunately for me, someone else is late as well.

Unfortunately, that someone is Colin Carter.

He smiles at me as he stands beside me. He looks down at me, grinning like the smug superstar he is. The grin he keeps on his lips is disgustingly charming. He has a beautiful smile, so much can I admit.

"Hey there, Lilybug," he greets me. "Since when do you have film directing?"

"Since forever. You would know that if you paid more attention to your surroundings, Carter."

Colin snickers and grabs ahold of the door handle. I inhale a sharp breath. *Yup, this is totally going to be the death of me, emotionally*.

"You okay?"

Why does he care?

Probably because he wants to make fun of you for wanting to die, I tell myself.

But the real reason shows soon enough.

My breath is out of control. It's quick, and I feel as though my lungs don't fill with air. It's painful. My lungs start to hurt. I'm hyperventilating, aren't I?

Of course I am.

I place my hand over my heart as I stumble backward until my back hits one of the walls. I slide down to the floor. My chest rises and falls so quickly, I can't even see it. But fuck, it hurts. Every breath hurts and yet I don't feel the air coming into my lungs.

"Jesus, Lily," Colin says, a hint of worry sounding through his voice. He approaches me again, kneeling down. He takes my hand in his. "Breathe," he tells me. *No seriously? Thanks.* "You're okay, nothing is going to happen."

"Would you—" air gets caught in my lungs, but it still doesn't feel like I have enough oxygen in my body to breathe properly "—shut up."

The feeling of death is streaming through my veins. Not that it's something bad. I want to die after all. But not like this. Not at school with superstar Colin Carter watching me.

I feel tears run down my cheeks. Great, now I'm crying in front of the asshole that stole my notebook. Or somehow gave it back to me. Either way, he read it.

My whole body is shaking. My mouth is dry, and I can feel the headache build up. For a moment I'm praying death won't actually feel this way.

No, Lily. It's going to be peaceful. Remember that.

Nope, fear takes over my body. Not the fear of death, fear of the pain. I don't want any more pain, *please*.

"Lily, try to calm down." He speaks calmly as he lays my hand down onto his chest. I can feel his chest rise and fall under my palm. He is taking slow and deep breaths that I try to mimic.

His hand covers mine. Our gazes locked as he counts from one to eight, inhaling. Not once does he break the eye contact with me.

We hold our breaths for a short moment, then he counts again as we exhale. Colin is repeating this exercise for a little while until I find it easier to keep up and my body begins to relax.

Only when my body stops shaking does he release my hand. I immediately pull it away from his chest. For the first time, I acknowledge the worry in his eyes.

Is Colin Carter worried about me? Why would he be? He doesn't even know me.

Despite my body slowly calming down, I still find it hard to breathe, hard to feel the air fill my lungs.

"Thank you," I mumble weakly.

"Wait here, don't move, okay?" I nod. Like I was going to do anything else. And just like that, Colin leaves and disappears into Professor Meisner's classroom.

By the time Colin returns, my breathing is almost back to normal, but I still feel drained and more than exhausted. Every muscle in my body feels sore, like I've worked out for hours.

My head is spinning, throbbing in pain. There is no way I will make it through the day without breaking down again.

And that's just another reason for me to die. My own body hates me. My own body wants me beat down. I can't fight this any longer.

"We're partnered up for a project," Colin informs me. He grabs my hands and helps me up on my feet. "You're off for the day, Lilybug. No way in hell will I let you attend classes like that."

I chuckle at his way of phrasing this. "No way in *hell*," I repeat to myself, but he hears it. "You do know I will be there soon, right?" I know he knows.

"You won't." I'm not sure why *he* is so convinced of that. "If anything, you will get send straight to heaven for fighting against whatever makes you want to die."

"Colin," I say in a whisper. He is still holding me up. I'm glad he is, because I doubt I could stand on my own. My panic attacks aren't normally this bad, but for some reasons they chose today to intensify. "You know we can't be partners."

"None sense, Lilybug." There it is again, the smug grin of his. "Even if you decide to kill yourself, it will only benefit me."

"We aim to please, Carter." I offer him a weak smile. I know he is joking. Well, it would benefit him. When I die, our assignment will automatically be graded with an A. "But there is no 'even if' and 'decide', Carter. It will happen. I've made my mind up already."

Colin doesn't respond to that. He walks us out of the building, leading me right toward his car. Of course he owns a Tesla. I knew he was rich. I mean, his father is a hockey coach from the NHL. His family is probably bathing in money.

"I assumed you'd be more into sports cars. Saw you owning an Audi R8, or some Lamborghini."

Colin snorts, pressing his lips together. "I am. The Tesla is my father's but I'm in use of it most of the time. My hockey bag barely fits into my BMW, the Tesla has more room for it."

I nod, suddenly feeling like an ass for assuming, even though I was right after all.

"Got my BMW for my twenty-first birthday, didn't even buy it myself. I feel like a spoiled frat boy for never using it."

I grip onto his arm a little tighter, trying to keep myself up.

"Where are you taking me?" I clear my throat. "I live in the dorms."

"I know, Aaron told me. But you're coming with me." The hell I am. This guy can't just kidnap me and take me home with him. I'm not one of his puck bunnies.

"Aaron will chop off your head if you touch me," I say with confidence.

"Aaron will also murder me when I tell him I knew you wanted to kill yourself and I didn't let him know what was going on with you. So either way, I will die." He's not wrong. I can see Aaron throwing Colin out of the house they share because of it. "Gives me a chance to haunt you in the afterlife."

"Fuck you, Carter."

"You want to?" He looks at me with lust, I think. No one has ever really looked at me like he does. It's like he is staring into my soul, but with this desire to undress me. Or he is undressing me already, mentally.

"No thank you."

"You're a tease," he tells me. "Now get in the car." Colin opens the passenger door for me and helps me inside. It's not like I need help. Maybe I do. I mean I can't even stand without feeling like I'm tipping over.

Once I'm seated, Colin closes the door and jogs over to the other side. However, once he's inside the car, he doesn't start the engine yet. He just stares at me for a moment as if he's trying to get me to talk. But I'm not speaking.

He takes the lead. "Do you actually want to die, Lilybug?"

I play with my thumbs, looking out of the window, hoping to come up with words to say. I end up nodding an answer.

There is no way I could explain what he read otherwise. It was as clear as a cleaned window. The words "I want to die" are unmistakable. There is no way anyone could interpret them differently to what they say.

"Why?"

"That's none of your concern, Colin."

Colin's lips form a straight line. He knows he shouldn't get involved in my business, and I'm sure he regrets every second of him reading what I wrote. But he did. He read it, all of it. I'm sure once he started, he couldn't stop. And now here he is; stuck with his best friend's suicidal sister.

I've never referred to myself as "suicidal," though it's obvious that's just what I am. A suicidal wreck.

"How come Aaron never mentioned you before?" he asks, changing the topic. Another topic I would gladly stop talking about altogether. Not just with him, with anyone. Aaron and my relationship it nobody's business.

"There is nothing to mention. We're friends. I'm sure you, too, have friends you don't speak of."

"Sure, but they're all dudes, mostly. But I don't care about either of the female ones as much as Aaron cares about you. I mean, Lilybug, he forbids me to touch you. That's not exactly 'we're friends' kind of behavior." He is right. It's not. Aaron is my overprotective, by two minutes older *twin* brother. But Colin doesn't know that.

He starts to drive, accepting my lack of enthusiasm to answer his questionnaire about my family tree. Just that he doesn't start driving toward his house. I know where he lives, and I know how to get there. The direction he's taking is not the one to go with.

"This is not the way to your house," I let him know. He snickers. "Where the hell are you taking me?"

"Relax, Lilybug. You're coming home with me." What does that mean? His *home* is in the other direction. "I need to see my sister. And since I can't leave you by yourself, you're coming with me."

"I am not going to meet your family, Colin!" Now I'm furious. Is he sick or something? I won't meet his family, it's weird.

"Too bad, you are. My father isn't home, because he is coaching *my* hockey team in a bit. My mother is probably at work as well. So it will only be Eira, Reece, you and me."

"Still. It's weird."

"Why would that be? Friends can meet the other's parents, right? And my siblings aren't even my parents, so it's not weird at all." He is smirking. Thank God he is looking at the road because I know this smirk is to die for. I've seen it on pictures and videos on Instagram before, even on the college website.

Colin Carter is everywhere. He takes everyone's breath away in a heartbeat.

I bet it's doing his already through the roof ego nothing but *good*.

The guy that breathes off of other's breaths.

Good an hour passes and we're finally in New York City. Well, literally. Not just the state. St. Trewery is located in New City, New York. Our college is actually only a one-and-a-half-hour car drive away from Manhattan.

I have never been here before. Never had the chance to go. Dad always promised that he would take me to Manhattan someday, but we never got to do that. My mother would have somehow figured out where I was at. I couldn't possibly tell her I was going there with friends. She's a control freak. She would have asked all of my friends if that was true.

I'm surprised she never questioned my sleepovers back then. Glad she didn't, still surprised though.

I want to get out of the car as soon as it comes to a halt, but Colin stops me. We haven't been talking for the majority of the time during the car ride, which is why I'm quite surprised when he chooses now to speak.

"Lilybug," he says in the softest tone I've ever heard him speak in. It's almost flattering.

Looking at him, I feel as though my breath gets caught in my lungs. It should be illegal to look this good.

I mean, he is probably six foot three. Colin is a tad taller than Aaron, and Aaron is six foot two. My knowledge of Colin's height is completely based off of my brother's.

Colin's hair is long, but not too long. The top half of his hair is rather long and fluffy, the curtain haircut. Truthfully, I was never a fan of this haircut, but it suits him. A lot.

Colin has blue eyes, the color I don't trust, but for whatever reasons, I could picture him with dark eyes.

Don't even get me started on his body. He is muscular. I think that's what most of these hockey players are. Colin's jawline is literally as sharp as a knife. I'm sure if I touched it, it would cut me, despite it being physically impossible.

On top of that, he looks good in a suit. I've seen a couple of pictures before.

Though to be fair, other than the suit, Colin Carter only ever wears black and white, maybe some dark blue if he feels silly. Mostly some black cargo pants and any wider shirt.

The only color I've ever seen on him is red. But that also *only* because of his hockey clothes.

But it suits him. It suits his body, even when his muscles go lost under his baggy shirts.

Colin has quite a few tattoos decorating his arms. I'm not sure, but I would say his chest is tattooed as well. Assuming, because he has a tattoo on his neck going down to his chest, I haven't actually seen him bare-chested before.

I'm also not really planning on doing that.

Anyway, his seemingly dark and broody appearance doesn't suit his bubbly personality all too well. Another assumption. I can't judge his personality yet. For me to be able to do so, I would have to know him a little better. But he seems…okay?

What's there not to like about Colin Carter? He is pretty damn handsome. And apparently, he even cares about suicidal girls he doesn't even know one bit.

"I have to warn you of my sister." It's always just a couple of words that can bring you back to reality. He sounds serious, sad even, if I'm being honest.

"Why would you have to do that?"

"My sister has been diagnosed with…" he trails off. I can see the gloomy cloud rising over him. "She's sick at the moment. She has a fever. But that's not what I have to warn you of."

The cloud vanishes as fast as it came.

"Eira is talkative and cheerful, way too happy sometimes. I don't think you would like that much." Although he doesn't seem upset anymore, his voice says differently.

Colin may be good with plastering model-like smiles onto his face, but he certainly can't hide pain in his voice.

"She talks about death a lot. In a good way, like you do," he tells me. "It's scary."

"I don't think death is scary."

"It is for everyone that doesn't want to die."

"Your sister wants to die?"

There's a light twitch on his face. Like I just hit some kind of nerve that I should not have.

Why would he phrase his sentence like this when he doesn't want me thinking this? What else am I supposed to think?

Perhaps he just wants me to talk to another suicidal person in hopes that it will change my mind.

Just like he can hear my actual unspoken question out loud, he answers me. "I took you here because I want you to be here, Lily. Eira isn't suicidal. She's just not thinking badly of death."

I want to ask why he said "everyone that doesn't want to die" then. It doesn't make much sense otherwise, maybe it does in some ways. But before I get the chance to ask, he speaks again.

"Just, please don't talk about death. I really don't like that topic. It makes me uncomfortable."

"Colin, in case you didn't notice. I don't speak about me wanting to die. Neither do I talk about the pain I feel." I think I said too much. I have never said this out loud, not even to myself. It has always just been on paper.

The pain I feel, four simple words that just make it real.

"I didn't think you would. I also want you to know that I didn't take you here to reconsider. Death is off-topic today, for you and Eira."

I have known Colin for four days. Knew of him before that, but we only started talking on Friday.

Not even that. We had like three conversations. And for some reasons I come to think he is anything but the asshole I imagined he would be.

Colin leads me inside the huge house, or mansion. It's definitely a mansion. Everything looks so much cleaner than back at my house, although I wouldn't consider my childhood home "dirty." Maybe it just appears that way because of the literal marble flooring this house has. It's so shiny in here, I think I might need sunglasses.

"Don't worry, not every room looks like this," Colin utters with a slight chuckle.

This entry way is bigger than my bedroom back at home. Of course I am amazed.

I feel like a celebrity walking the red carpet here. Just without the red carpet and camera flashing.

And without the celebrity status.

Colin gets ahold of my hand, intertwines his fingers with mine and leads me upstairs.

My heart beats a little bit faster as I come to realize that this floor doesn't just *look* like I could slip on it. It is a whole ass slipping trap.

But, hey, at least if I do slip, fall down the stairs and die, I would have died on expensive flooring.

"What, you don't have an elevator?" I tease jokingly.

"Don't get ahead of yourself, Lilybug. You haven't seen half of this house." He squeezes my hand lightly. "Eira is in her room, and this is the fastest way to get there." There are more ways to get to her room? I'm officially blown away.

Though, I'm wondering why Colin only comes here to see his sister. He mentioned someone named Reece possibly being here. Assuming it's his brother, why wouldn't he want to see him?

Colin leads me down the hall once we reach the first floor. He doesn't even give me a second to breathe. And I really need that intake of oxygen.

He approaches a white door, lets out a heavy sigh before magically throwing a smile onto his face and opens the door. And for some reasons he is still holding onto my hand.

His grip tightens even, as though he's nervous. Kind of like he could use some more comfort than I do from my panic attack earlier.

Why is he acting like this?

"Sweet chicken nuggets, COLIN!" A brunette girl screams in excitement. She looks just like Colin, that I have to admit. Eira is utterly stunning.

She holds her arms out for him, and finally, he releases my hand and walks right over to his sister's bed. He picks her up, twirling her around a couple of times before laying her back down. She giggles. It's an adorable giggle she has.

I feel totally out of place. I shouldn't be here. I don't even know this girl. Colin took me here without asking if that was okay with me.

It is not okay with me. This is his family. I shouldn't meet his family. I'm not his girlfriend, and I'm sure that's one of the first questions we will get asked by his family members.

It always is.

"Colin." Eira inhales a sharp breath. "*¡Dios mío!* Is that a *girlfriend*?" She asks all excitedly, pointing at me. *Called it.*

I press my lips together into a thin line, trying my best not to roll my eyes. I'd die before I'd ever develop feelings for Colin Carter.

When Colin's eyes meet mine, there is something odd in his gaze. Like he is trying to tell me that he has to lie to his sister for her own good.

Or maybe I'm over analyzing it and he just knows that I won't ever have another boyfriend.

He looks at me with sympathy, just like he does a lot of times when he lays his eyes on me.

If *I* were to answer, I would say no. I would tell her the truth. And maybe she should know nothing but the truth.

When the opposite words of mine leave Colin's mouth—"*She is*"—a sudden rush of anger bolts through me like fire, burning on my skin.

Colin Carter is as much of a liar as I am. Just that I lie about my happiness, and he lies to his sister about his relationship status.

But when Eira lets out an almost to unbearable shrill shrieks. I start to believe she wishes for him to be in a relationship. For whatever reasons that might be.

Even if she wishes for Colin to be in a happy relationship, he shouldn't lie about it. Colin and I are neither happy together, nor in a relationship.

"Don't just stand there. Come over here," Eira says to me. She is so energetic, I can barely wrap my head around it. But I suppose Colin did warn me about it.

With as much as respect I could say this, Eira looks awful. She is pale and looks like she would break any second. She is still beautiful with no doubt. But her, what I assume is a flu that she has, clearly rules over her body, and it shows. Yet, she still has energy left to be happy and cheerful.

I admire that about her.

As she wished, I walk over to her bed and take a seat on it. The space right next to Colin will have to do. And if it couldn't get any worse, Colin takes my hand in his once again, stroking his thump over the back of it.

"Tell me everything about you," Eira demands. She wears a huge grin on her lips. It's the same one Colin shows most of the time.

Eira is such a copy of him, which makes me wonder what their mother looks like.

I know for a fact that Colin doesn't look much like his father. Sure, he has some features, like the same nose, same hair color. I'm not sure if he got the eye color from his father though. To be fair, I don't pay much attention to the new hockey coach.

"I wouldn't know what to tell you," I reply in all honesty. It's the truth. Even if I wanted to open up to her, I wouldn't know what to say.

"What's your name? Let's start there."

Colin chuckles at his sister's eagerness.

"Well," I begin, "my name is Lily." *This is awkward.*

"I love it. I'm Eira, but I'm sure Colin has mentioned that before." He has, but I don't say that out loud. I prefer to let her do the talking. "When did you two meet? Are you also a senior at Trewery? Do you have a favorite color? What's your favorite animal? Do you like hockey?"

Why is she asking so many questions?

Since my brain consists of two brain cells in total when it comes to social situations like these, I only remember two questions. "I do like hockey, and I am indeed a senior at St. Trewery."

To my luck, Eira doesn't repeat the other questions she asked before and just moves on.

I listen to Eira babble about literally everything and nothing at all. For the next thirty minutes, she tells me all about how Colin used to take her skating with him when their mother wasn't around. She mentions something about their mother never liking the idea of Eira being on the ice because her bones have always been pretty breakable.

Somehow we're all laughing at that, but I'm not sure why. It's not necessarily funny.

I also find out that Eira is 16 years old. She spent her birthday at the hospital, it was also the day she decided to go home and spend the rest of her life where she thought she belonged.

I don't question her words. Teenagers talk a lot of nonsense, I know I did back when I was 16. I figure going with Eira being a bit overdramatic is the safer option.

"Eira?" A voice shouts from down the hall, only moments before a knock appears on the door and it swings open.

"Ay, Colin. I had no idea you were stopping by this early." A woman, I would assume around forty-five, steps into the room, looking a bit startled. Her hair is blonde, but it's obvious that it has been bleached before. Okay, it would not be too visible if her roots weren't dark. I'm assuming she had no time to get a touch-up.

Mrs. Carter has a heavy and distinct accent when she speaks.

"I didn't know I was coming yet until I was," Colin says, shrugging with his shoulders.

"Mamá!" Eira does a little excited dance. "This is Lily, Colin's *girlfriend*." Just when I think this couldn't get any worse with the fake-dating scenario, it does.

"*¿Novia?*" Mrs. Carter is surprised, but I can't blame her. Colin could never have mentioned me before. And judging by what his mother said, I'm sure he comes to visit quite often. "When did that happen?"

Without opening his mouth, Colin is conveying his mother the message he should have told his sister. And how do I know that Colin is basically telling his mother that he isn't dating me? She nods and drops the question like she had never even asked it.

I'm unsure of how this is even possible. Does mentally conveying a message require a special bound with the other person? If so, I certainly don't have this with my mother.

"It's nice to meet you, Lily." Mrs. Carter holds her hand out to me. I shake it carefully. She offers me a smile, which I return. Good thing I mastered the fake-smile skill a long time ago. "Are you guys staying for lunch?" she asks Colin.

"We would love to, Mamá," Colin answers immediately. I'm not even hungry, but I guess that's on my agenda now.

"*Eso es adorable*. I will start cooking then. Do you have any allergies I should know of, Lily?"

Humans, I almost blurt out, but I manage to hold myself back. "I don't, but thank you for asking," I say, giving Mrs. Carter a sweet smile. "Actually, Mrs. Carter, can I help you cook?"

She seems stunned for a moment, but then a huge grin appears on her lips. *They definitely get their smile from her.* "I would be delighted."

"So, what are you getting in exchange for playing Colin's girlfriend?" Mrs. Carter asks just as we walk into the enormous kitchen.

I chug down a giggle, not wanting to be rude by laughing at her question. My answer would most definitely be "*a headache.*"

"Nothing. I didn't even know I was playing his girlfriend up until he declared me as such," I answer. Figured the truth is always a great way to go.

"I can't believe this boy sometimes." I can tell she wants to laugh, but just like I did, she holds it back. "Colin never brought someone home with him." *Just great. Now there are expectations.*

"Really?" I do hope I don't sound disinterested.

"Really. I never thought he ever would. Figured hockey would always be more important than meeting someone."

"Well, if it makes you feel any better, Colin and I are just friends, and I am not sure there would ever be anything more between us," I tell her. I mean, I can't possibly tell her that Colin and I would never be a thing because I will be dead in the next ten days. But regardless of my death, I don't think I'm Colin's type. And without my *unalive journey 101* we would have never even gotten in touch in the first place.

"He is a good guy, you know." She rests her hands on the countertop. "I know, every mother says this about their sons"—*not mine*—"but Colin truly is. He comes to visit Eira every single day. Colin and her were always really close. When she got sick, he even refused to go back to college. He wanted to drop out only so he could be around more."

That's weird. It's just the flu, I assume. Colin never confirmed Eira having the flu. He did say she is sick though, with a fever. It will be over in a few weeks, at most.

And once again I am proving to myself that talking to mothers is not for me. I never know what to say. Especially not to Mrs. Carter.

I offer Mrs. Carter a weak smile. Not because I don't know what to say, I sure don't, but because I believe I shouldn't have anything to say.

"I thought you wanted to start cooking and not tell Lilybug all about your awesome son." Colin's voice echoes through the kitchen. He makes his way to the refrigerator, opens it and takes out a small orange juice box.

Correction, he takes out two of them. After closing the refrigerator again, he walks over to me and hands me one of the orange juice boxes. "Hope you like orange juice," he says with a smile.

"And I thought you were staying with Eira," his mother replies. She is searching through some cabinets until she finds a pot to fill it with water.

"She got tired and wanted to sleep for a while."

Mrs. Carter doesn't say anything to it. I think it's nothing new for Eira to get tired easily. But even when Mrs. Carter doesn't say a word, her face speaks for her. She is in pain, but why? There is no way Eira would walk around dancing while having a flu.

"Lily, *cariño*, would you be so nice and grab me some noodles from the pantry?" If I knew where their pantry was, sure. "Colin can show you where it is." Seems like Mrs. Carter is great at mind-reading as well.

"Sure." Just like that, Colin leads me out of the kitchen toward the pantry.

I'm not even surprised to see that everything is so organized in here, with nametags and all the fancy mason jars. They have probably ten to fifteen different kinds of noodles in here, all tagged with their names.

"Now, which ones?" I ask Colin. He laughs like he has no idea either. "Well, I can't just take spaghetti's when your mother cooks lasagna."

"She's making lasagna?" he asks.

"Not a clue, and that's what I'm talking about." *Point proven.* "Well, she did take out a pot, so I think it won't be lasagna."

"Lilybug, I have no idea how to make lasagna. Do you really think I would have given that pot even just one thought?"

"I always thought everyone knew how to make lasagna," I tell him. All I get in response are a few fast blinks. Like he is trying to make sense out of what I just said. Maybe he feels like I called him stupid. If so, he can gladly feel that way, because I did. "What's your favorite kind of noodles?"

"I don't know, Lilybug. The normal ones?"

I'm laughing. I am actually and genuinely laughing. I'm wondering how he does that. It's like Colin Carter is naturally funny. But what he said wasn't even meant to be.

Does stupidity come with a clown costume?

"Please tell me you know noodles vary in taste depending on their kind." But to my horror, he shrugs.

"They all taste the same. They're all made of the same ingredients, so there is no way they taste differently." Now it's my turn to stand there just blinking at him. He can't be serious, can he?

Not willing to continue this conversation, I decide on Penne noodles. They're one of the more basic ones, can't do anything wrong with that. Taking them from the shelf, I walk past Colin and make my way back to the huge kitchen.

Colin follows me, and before I can enter the kitchen, Colin grabs onto my free hand. "Give me two weeks, Reyes."

"Two weeks for what?"

"To show you that life isn't as bad as it may seem at the moment." *This can't be happening right now, can it?* "Give me two weeks to show you that there is more to live for, more to be alive for. Give me two weeks to make you fall back in love with life."

Chapter 6

"but if you never try, you'll never know just what you're worth"—Fix You by Coldplay

Colin

LILY DOESN'T EXCHANGE A SINGLE WORD with me. Not at my parents' house, not when I drive us back to campus.

I get that Lily doesn't want saving. She made up her mind, but that's just one more reason to let me try, right? She could spend her last days drowning in assignments and emotional pain, or she could give me a chance to make her last days bearable. I just want to try to bring a smile to her face.

Even when her world has been painted gray, she should never stop believing that there is more to life than pain and sorrow.

I'm sure she used to believe it, at least I hope she did, but clearly, she hadn't gotten the chance to see it.

Eira always talks about how the universe will rip you out of your current life-adventure because you're no longer needed. But in exchange for that it will give you another adventure to live through.

I never believed in all that. I never believed in the theory of a soul always staying and just wandering into other bodies to collect as much experience as possible.

Technically it makes sense because a body contains energy. And since energy doesn't go lost, it'll have to go somewhere after death, right?

Maybe this whole theory is more common to believe than I could imagine.

At least that would be one of the less horrible ways to think about death.

I think Lily wants that too, leave this life to start another life because she thinks what her current one has to offer is too much for her to take.

If we go with that theory, then Lily is forgetting something.

She would not have been put into this life, into her situation if the universe didn't know she would be able to take it.

Lily needs to start believing in herself. But most importantly, she needs to see that beyond all the pain lies beauty.

Not one beautiful thing comes without a bad part. It's what *yin and yang* taught us. Bad comes with good, and good comes with bad. It's just a matter of time for the good to shine through, or the bad to fog up the place. Nothing ever comes for free, but nothing ever stays unrewarded either.

Lily is *yin* in this scenario. She is in the dark, fighting through pain. She can't see that *yang* is about to come. She can't see because her world is gray and fogged up.

So if there is a chance that I can be her light shining through the darkness, that I can be the *yang* to her *yin*, I have to try.

But I will not accept someone throwing their life away just like that. Not without trying to help.

Lily might not want my help. Hell, she might even think I'm crazy for caring. I know it's not any of my business. But I can't just let her go through with it. Someone needs to show her what she will miss out on.

I was lucky enough to never have to deal with anything Lily is dealing with. I will never understand what it is like to feel the way she does. What it is like to look forward to the day they die.

But I can try and give her a helping hand out of her misery.

I roll up at the dorm parking lots and turn off the engine from my car. Even if Lily doesn't want to speak to me, there is no way I would let her be by herself today. Or any day until she agrees to my offer. Or at all for that matter.

"Unlock the door," she demands, trying to get out. But I don't. The doors stay locked. At least until she agrees. "For God's sake, Colin. Open it."

"Fourteen days, Lily. Give me fourteen days. That's all I'm asking for."

Lily lets out a heavy sigh and falls back into her seat. She doesn't look at me, doesn't speak either. She just stares ahead toward the building entrance in front of us.

She is fidgeting with her fingers. I'm assuming that means that she is getting either uncomfortable or nervous. I've seen her do the same back at my parents' house whenever my mother asked her a deeper question.

"What do you have to lose?" I ask. "You want to die. So what does it matter if you give me two weeks to try and make you reconsider? Either I will convince you, or you will die. But when your mind stays the same, you at least had a good time before death."

"Who says I would have a good time?" Her hands turn into fists. "I'm not the type to go big, Colin. I don't have the energy to go out every single day. And besides, I gave myself two weeks left to live. That was four days ago."

"Give me ten days then. I can work with that."

Beautiful green eyes look back at me with something mad in them. Something that screams for me to leave her alone. But I can't.

"I need my off days, Colin. Sometimes even just attending classes gets too much for me. Imagine what ten days of constant going out with someone I don't even like would do to me," she says. "That wouldn't be a good time, it would be torture."

"Give me nine days then. You will have an extra day to do all the drowning in self-sorrow on your last day."

Lily looks out of the window, her head leaning against the glass as she lets out a heavy breath.

"I don't even know you, Colin," she says after a good minute of silence. "How would I know that you don't want to murder me?"

"Well, if I did want to murder you, I don't think you would be mad at me. After all, you want to die, don't you?" That gets me an ironic chuckle, easing into a sweet, innocent laughter.

Lily has a beautiful laughter. Probably one of the most sincere and sweet laughs I have ever heard. It's not too high-pitched, not too low, and it's not fake either. When she laughs, then she does because it is genuine.

Sure, Lily fakes smiles, but who doesn't? No matter how hard she tries with faking a smile, she can't fake a genuine laughter.

And this was hers. Sweet and adorable.

"And besides, when you get on a plane, you don't know the pilot either, yet you trust them with your life, don't you?" She nods. "When you take the bus to go somewhere, you don't know the driver, yet you place your life in their hands and hope you get to your destination without getting in an accident, right?" Another nod. "You don't have to know me to trust me."

"Colin," she breathes out my name. "Why would you want to do this?"

"I even volunteer to make sure everyone gets their letter when you do end up dying," I offer, ignoring her question. "Just give me those nine days, Lilybug. You have nothing to lose."

"I have nine days of my time to lose," she objects.

"Wrong," I disagree with her objection. "You wouldn't do anything but write in your suicide book—"

"I named it my *unalive journey 101*," she corrects, interrupting me.

"Fine. You would only write in your *unalive journey 101*, stupid name by the way, and cry to some sleazy rom-com."

"Wrong," she mocks. "I would cry to dramas and eat pints of ice cream."

"Same thing."

Lily narrows her eyes at me. She takes a short moment to think before letting out a groan.

"Fine. You have nine days. Eight, because I count today as day one."

"I can work with that." I unlock the car and step out of it. Lily does the same.

In all honesty, I would have liked it if she'd let me open the door for her, but we're taking it one step at a time.

Now I only need to find nine awesome things to do with Lily. That shouldn't be too difficult.

I just hope my father doesn't decide to add even more ice time to my schedule. If it were up to him, he would have the team at the arena from Mondays to Sundays during all of their free time. Luckily, the school says no to that.

I follow Lily into her dorm room. She isn't too happy about me sticking around, but I also don't really give a damn.

"What do you even want to do here?" Lily plops down onto her bed, frees some space for me by simply throwing books and papers onto the floor. "Sorry, no energy to tidy that up."

Although she claims for her room to be a complete mess, it's not too bad in here. Aside from the books and papers she just threw onto the floor. Or her desk that is crowded with brushes, makeup stuff and more books, and her chair that is overflowing with clothes.

I feel the urge to pick the stuff off the floor and lay them onto her desk, but I don't want to upset Lily, so I don't. Instead, I take a seat on her bed and make myself comfortable.

And with comfortable I mean, lie down with my head on her mountain of pillows. I rest the palms of my hands on the back of my head, and just relax.

Her bed is actually pretty damn cozy. I never thought the number of pillows and stuffed animals—*mostly frogs*—Lily owns would be anywhere near comfortable, but they are.

I might stay here forever.

"We have a film directing project to work on," I remind her. "Told you about it."

"Right. When is it due?" She picks up a notebook from the floor, then grabs a few pens from the nightstand and lays them on her bed.

"We should be done filming by October 7th. It has to be completely done, with cutting, voiceover et cetera by October 15th," I let her know.

"Great, so I will still be alive for finishing the filming part. Sorry to dump the cutting and voiceover onto you."

I did the math as well. Today is September 28th, that means ten days from today would be October 8th, meaning she will still be alive by October 7th to finish the filming.

I can work with that.

What she doesn't know, I will cut the video while filming. I want it to be done for her to see still. Because what she is also not aware of, I picked the topic "*Life and it's beauty*" for us.

I plan on filming her process. The process of Lily Heaven Reyes falling back in love with life. How she goes from misery to seeing the beautiful parts.

Perhaps it doesn't exactly hit the topic I chose, but then again, it does.

Not one assignment sheet states that we can't portray the bad and turn it into something beautiful. Not one sentence in the requirements *or* tips section for our project states that beauty is only within flowers and sunshine.

Beauty is also within the darkness. It's within misery and solitude, even if it's masked.

And I will not only show our film directing class that life's beauty is found in everything, but I will also prove to Lily that there is beauty within *her*, and her life.

"Just let me do all the work. I'm a video production major after all. I just need you to be the actress, okay?"

"You are? Cause so am I." She looks stunned for a second, but she shakes it off flawlessly a second later. "But if you do all the filming, what the hell am I doing? I can't just act. I'm not an actress. And I am certainly not a drama major."

"Just trust me on this one. You have no dialogue. Nothing to act out. I will just record you randomly throughout our nine days and maybe have you send me some voice notes for a voiceover." She doesn't seem convinced. It appears Lily doesn't like sitting back, and she doesn't like working on a partner project when the parties work isn't equal.

"Lilybug, it's just a video project. Nothing too heavy. And besides, you will be dead before this project is officially due. So relax, it's not that deep."

But it is. Because this project could either show that Lily Reyes fell in love with life again or lost the battle. Either way though, this video book will end with a moral to learn from. Which would check off point one from the assignment checklist.

LILY AND I ARE SITTING on the couch in the living room when the front door suddenly opens, and a young woman tumbles into the room.

I pause the TV, not wanting to miss even a second of what's playing. Lily made me watch Grey's Anatomy with her. I've always hated this TV show. Not that there was ever a real reason behind my hatred. It's a great show, but it's just not for me. Or so I thought for the most part.

But now that Lily makes me watch it, I come to realize that I might actually like it.

"Lily, I am so sorry," the redhead speaks as she walks into the living room. The living room is the first room that's coming into view when opening the front door, but for some reasons, Lily's roommate still takes a bit of time to find her way in.

"Jesus, Winter. Are you drunk?" Lily raises from the couch and walks over to Winter. *So that's Winter*. "It's 4 p.m., your classes just ended, how are you drunk?"

Winter starts to cry. I consider leaving. I shouldn't be here when Lily's best friend walks into their dorm, crying like someone just ripped her heart out. Maybe someone did.

Yeah, I definitely shouldn't be here for that.

But I don't want to leave Lily.

"Come here, sit down," Lily says, leading Winter over to the couch where I'm still seated. I don't dare moving. Truth be told, I am afraid I might get yelled at for being here. So if I don't move, maybe Winter won't see me. *Yeah, right. Cause this is some action movie featuring dinosaurs.*

"Aaron broke up with me," Winter cries, falling right back against the couch as Lily sits her down.

"You weren't even dating, Winter. He can't break up with you when you're not a couple." Lily speaks in a soft tone not too sound as though she was making fun of her best friend.

I am most definitely not welcome here right now. I should leave.

Yet I stay seated.

"He said he loved someone else," Winter speaks through gritted teeth. Suddenly, she sits up straight. Her attention is focused on Lily, so I assume she doesn't even notice me. "We both know this *someone* is you."

I don't agree with random girls most of the time, but Winter does have a point. The way Aaron cares for Lily, there has to be something going on between them.

Aaron never insisted on giving anything back to any woman, unless it would get him some sex in return. He also never told me to keep my hands off someone unless he had a soft spot for her. So clearly, Aaron and Lily are hiding something.

But then why wouldn't Aaron try and stop Lily from committing suicide? Does he even know Lily is suicidal?

"For the millionths time, Winter. Aaron and I are not dating. And to think you believe we are…it shows your trust in the both of us. I told you so, and I know Aaron did too."

I finally decide to leave. This is a conversation they should have in private and not with me, the best friend of the guy in question, being around to hear their conversation.

As soon as I get up from the couch, a hand grabs mine. I turn around for a second as I did not expect anyone to try and keep me from leaving. But I'm even more surprised when I see that it's Lily who is holding my hand.

She looks up at me with brooding eyes. Anxiety gleaming on her face. Her grip on my hand tightens.

Lily doesn't want me to leave.

"Stay," she mouths, followed by a pleading expression.
Certainly can't say no to this.

"Oh my God." Winter spots me right next to Lily. She is still holding onto my hand. "You've got to be kidding me. Now you're cheating on Aaron!?"

"I am not. Jesus, Winter. You really think I am some kind of homewrecker, don't you?" So much to best friends. I doubt a best friend should act like Winter does.

"I don't, Lils," Winter denies Lily's assumption. "You're my best friend. You know I would never think of you like that."

"You just did."

"I didn't mean it." She sure did though. "Why is Colin here then?"

"We're friends," I speak for Lily. "Friendships between boys and girls are a thing, you know."

"Is this why you keep seeing Aaron? So you can see Colin?"

Lily's eyes move from mine to Winter's and back. "Yes," she lies. "Aaron is helping me get close to Colin." She lets out a quiet groan, rolling her eyes when Winter isn't looking at her, because she is looking at me now.

"I totally got her to confess her feelings for you, Colin. Now you will have to confess yours too."

"I didn't hear any 'I love you's' so that was not a confession," I say, praying Winter will just drop it. This situation just got really awkward, and I have no idea where this is going to lead to when it doesn't stop soon. "I can give you some advice, though, Winter."

"That would be?" Of course that has her intrigued, looking at me with anticipation.

"Drop those feelings for Marsh. He is not into you. And I'm pretty sure he would have mentioned having feelings for Lily to me. He doesn't have the time for commitment at the moment. Just leave it, move on and be happy."

To my luck, I no longer have to participate in this conversation after that because my phone chimes. I wouldn't care who texted me, because whoever did, they just saved my ass from girl-talk.

Aaron: Celebrating my birthday this Sat. so drop any other plans you might have, bro.

Speaking of the devil.

Colin: What makes you think I would drop my plans for you?

Aaron: We're flying out to Vegas and get married, dude. No way you won't attend your own wedding.

Sometimes I don't understand this guy. He has the weirdest fantasies. I am honestly afraid to even question whatever he just texted. I don't think I want it to make sense.

It doesn't even matter. I do have plans this Saturday, and there is no way I would drop them.

I don't think Lily would like to tag along to whatever Aaron is planning. There is no way in hell that Aaron didn't plan something stupid. But I am certainly not going to let Lily be all by herself watching some boring rom-com all day and night long.

But I could ask her if she is doing anything, maybe that would solve things.

"Lily?" I say. She is in the middle of arguing with Winter. I wonder how I didn't hear them. I am standing right beside them both, and yet I heard nothing.

"I am leaving!" Winter shouts as she storms off. "You're the worst best friend ever!" *What happened?*

"Don't get pregnant," Lily yells after Winter.

Winter stops and looks back into the room. Shortly before she would shut the door behind her, she starts to laugh, flipping Lily off.

Unexpectedly for me, Winter comes running back toward Lily, hugs her and then disappears.

I don't understand women. I don't think there is ever going to be a time I will.

"You said my name," Lily states. "My actual name. You didn't call me Lilybug."

"It's weird for me too," I admit, though, I know I did it before. "But Lilybug, I have a question."

"And I suppose even if I don't want you to ask, you will ask anyway." She sits back down on the couch, pulling onto my arm so I would do the same.

She has a point. Even if she didn't want to hear my question, I would ask. "What are you doing on Saturday?"

"You tell me. It falls into your nine days radar." She shrugs like she truly thinks I am planning out her entire days now.

"Lilybug, I don't make decisions for you. You can have plans. I will only ever take a couple of hours from your days. Mostly evenings because I have hockey practice. And believe it or not, I do have plans as well."

"Alright. I planned on visiting my mom for a little while. Probably go see my dad, too, but that is unlikely."

"Why would that be?"

"Why did you ask me what I was doing for my birthday, Colin?" She is dodging my question. But I'm okay with that.

There is no other way around this. "It's Aaron's birthday, so would you mind if I took you to his party with me?"

"I know it is." She sighs heavily. "As your date?"

"Sweetheart, we're basically a couple by now," I utter. "You sure will be my date, Lilybug."

"Aaron wouldn't like that."

But sweetheart, I don't care what Aaron thinks, I want to voice, but instead I say, "I will talk to him." She snorts in disbelief. "Here, I will shoot him a text right now."

I hold my phone visible for Lily as I open the chat with Aaron, shooting him a text message.

Colin: Have plans to marry Lilybug instead. Can I bring her?

I figured Lily wouldn't be too happy about the way I phrased it, but I did not think she would beat the hell out of me. But that is exactly what she is doing.

Lily slaps me. Once. Twice. I lose count of how many times her palms come into contact with my arm before I eventually stop her. I grab her wrists and hold her steady to the point where she can no longer slap me.

Her face is so close to mine, I can feel her hot breath roll off my skin. Her lips are so close, it would only take me a slight leaning forward to touch them with mine.

She stares into my eyes, then down to my lips. I smirk when I notice where her eyes keep wandering to.

But that's when she snaps back to reality. "He will murder you, Carter," Lily informs me. "And he will kill me right with you."

"Aw, so you do want us to haunt earth together as spirits." She rolls her eyes, yet a smile tugs at her lips. I think I'm growing on her. She certainly is growing on me.

Man, today is our first official day of hanging out together. The first day we've truly talked, exchanged more words than five and she's already got me wrapped around her finger.

What the…?

"Fuck you, Colin." Now if that's not some invitation.

"I think we should get to know one another a little bit better first. But you could give me a kiss."

Her jaw drops. I can tell she is trying to find words to say, but somehow can't articulate herself properly. So she just stares at me in shock, blinking.

"The hell you get. I'm not kissing you, dumbass." I guess she found her voice after all.

I can't help my laughter that follows. She is too much fun.

The way her eyes are trying to express rage, but she is too confused by what I have just said is the most adorable view I have ever seen. No, the most adorable confusion I have ever witnessed.

Her nose scrunches up when she processes information she did not expect, that much I came to learn about her. And she is speechless a lot of times. Or maybe she just never expected me to tag alongside her, so that is why she has a hard time processing *my* words.

"Did you just give me a really cute-ass pet name?" I pout at her.

"I called you a dumbass."

"Like I said, a cute-ass pet name."

Lily shakes her head doubtfully, being speechless once again.

That's a 1:0 for me, Lilybug.

Aaron: Fuck off, dude. I told you to stay away from Lily.

Looks like Aaron truly doesn't want me hanging with Lily.

Should I listen to him? *Totally.*

Do I care? *I certainly should.*

Am I going to continue to speak to my Lilybug despite his demands, and risk my best friend chopping off my head for betraying the bro-code? *Most definitely.*

"I told you Aaron wouldn't be too happy about it," Miss know-it-all says. I forgot she could still look at my screen and read my texts.

"Maybe I would back off if I knew why he wants me to stay away. You two aren't dating. The both of you made that pretty clear. Tell me what the deal is, Lilybug. Just so I can ogle you without feeling guilty." All this is getting totally weird.

Not a single guy acts like this about their friend unless he thinks the dude wanting to be with the girl is a total dick. And even then, most guys don't even really care. Unless there is a way deeper meaning behind all this.

"Tell me, Lilybug." I give her the most hopeful and pleading eyes I could come up with. "*Please.*"

Aaron: You can bring her. But if I see you touching her just once, I will have to chop off your hands.

Doesn't that just prove my point?

Lily's silent treatment tells me that she won't budge, so I will have to find another way to get the information out of her. "When did Aaron and you meet?"

"A long time ago." *Seriously?*

"Alright. Who was your first boyfriend?"

"First grade, he was fictional. Just like every other guy. Why is that relevant?" She narrows her eyes at me. "Who was your first girlfriend, Colin?" Lily questions in return.

"I never had one." I shrug. I'm not ashamed of it. I could have had some before, but I just didn't want one.

None of the girls that were throwing themselves at me piqued my interest in that way. I sure did other things, but I never wanted to go any further with it.

I was kind of telling myself that I would know if she was the right one. Like, it would just click right away. We would get along right when we meet, and that would have nothing to do with sexual tension.

Aiden used to tell me that's how it works.

Kind of like with Lily.

"That's boring," she says.

"Did you know Aaron in high school?" I ask, she nods slowly. "Was he your first boyfriend? Fuck, maybe even your first time? No wonder he is so protective of you."

Lily sighs, but it turns into a groan. "Like I said, I never had one." Her head falls back into her neck for a moment before she turns her attention back to me. "He is my brother, Colin."

Now, that's my time to be speechless. I blink at Lily as I try to wrap my mind around her words. *He is my brother, Colin.*

It can't be. They don't even share the same last name.

Aaron never even mentioned her. I know of his siblings, even met them. Well, Ana, I met her. Aaron did mention having another sister, he said she attends some college at the west coast, which is why she's never around.

I remember her letter. Lily was talking about a sister that isn't her sister. The one that "stole her father." Lily mentioned a brother. She said he had their father, but she didn't.

Oh God. Did their parents split them up? Who does that?

"My parents," Lily says. I believe she can read my mind. Or was I thinking out loud? "They did split us up. Aaron got to live with my father, I had to stay with my mom. We weren't allowed to be in touch, but my dad kept in touch with me anyway. He gave me a chance to keep my brother in my life. Our mom never found out."

"I'm sorry, Lilybug." My mind is running marathons. How could I have not noticed the similarities? "Aaron and you, you're twins?"

"Did you look at Aaron and me?" She chuckles. "We look identical. Almost."

"Why the hell didn't you just say so right away? No, instead you're letting me babble all about how you fucked your *brother*."

Like I said, I knew Aaron had another sister, other than Ana. Though, whenever I accompanied Aaron home and the topic of his other sister came up, all they ever told me about her were basic information. Like her attending some college outside of the state of New York, somewhere in Los Angeles. Or that she is two years younger than Aaron.

So basically, they dished me some bullshit. Unless it's true, there is another sister and Lily is a third long lost one. One that happened to never have been mentioned before.

Emerson Marsh wouldn't neglect his children like that, I hope. He never appeared to me as the type of father that would just disappear out of his children's' lives.

"Yeah, that's a nasty thought," she agrees. "Aaron and I agreed on never telling anyone. The more people know, the more likely it is for our mom to find out."

"God, that means it's also *your* birthday this Saturday!" I make a mental note to buy a present for her. "You guys are almost twenty-one years old. I don't think she can do much about it."

How am I only registering this information now? She mentioned it like five minutes ago.

"Colin, it's always just been me and my mom. Sure, I had my dad every Sunday, and when I was older, I stayed for a weekend once every six months. She pushed her own son away because my parents are both egoistic. Neither of them wanted the other to have just one tiny bit more. So splitting up the children it was. My dad wasn't supposed to be in touch with me, and my mom was denied any contact to Aaron," she tries to explain. "She thinks my dad kept his promise. But he didn't. Imagine what she would do when she finds out my father had both me and Aaron, and she just got me."

I don't dare saying anything. I don't think I can.

What Aaron and Lily's parents did is awful. How could anyone just separate their children like that and then decline to stay in touch with the other?

I'm wondering if that's where Lily's depression started. I mean, a divorce can be traumatizing for children. And Lily certainly didn't just lose her home that belonged to both of her parents. She lost her brother as well.

I have always been close to my sister. And ever since Reece was born three years ago, I have quite the bond with that little guy as well. Sure, it's not as deep as it is with Eira, probably due to the age gap, but I couldn't imagine what it would be like losing that bond.

And to be completely honest, I always thought twins have an even deeper bond than "*normal*" siblings. Which, in my world, would mean Lily Reyes lost the other half to her, the day her parents decided to fight against one another.

"Carter," Lily speaks quietly. "You cannot tell Aaron about my condition. You need to promise me you won't say a word."

Chapter 7

"if only you saw what I could see, you'll understand why I want you so desperately"—*What Makes you Beautiful by One Direction*

Colin

I MANAGE TO RECORD A FEW—ABOUT two or three-seconds-long—videos of Lily.

We are talking all evening long, mostly about the fun times she's had with Aaron and her father without her mother's knowledge.

She calls these Sundays their skate-dates. She also admits that it sounds inappropriate, but she doesn't really care about it too much.

While she is talking all about her memories, it is quite easy to catch a few shots of her expressions. Mostly sad ones, but not *only* sad ones. But that is just what I need.

The happy ones would come soon.

Before I can portray the happy side of life, I have to make sure I capture the ugliness. That being sadness.

Though, even sadness has its glory.

Lily's face lights up like hundreds of lanterns in the dark when she speaks about skating and how she was supposed to take her competitions seriously but never did.

As it appears, figure skating might have been her passion, but she'd much rather do it for fun than be bound to contracts and such.

I love listening to her talk, love watching when she smiles at memories and laughs when she remembers how she felt in these moments. She looks so…carefree. So calm. Even when a tear rolls down her cheeks every now and then, looking like these memories are painful to think back to.

When I get home around 10 p.m., I am lucky enough not to bump into Aaron. I'm not mad at him for not telling me about Lily, but I sure do love to pretend I am.

IT'S ONLY 5 IN the morning when I come downstairs to get some water from the kitchen. As surprising as it is, Aaron is sitting on a barstool, his elbows propped on the island counter and his head resting in his hands.

"You good, Ron?" I ask as I enter the kitchen.

His head immediately shoots up and he looks at me. I grab a new bottle of water and lean against the closed refrigerator, waiting for an answer.

"Lily told you." *She sure did.*

"Yeah, I kind of pressured her into telling me. I'm sorry." I really am. If I had known the background behind their we're-going-to-keep-being-twins-a-secret pact, I wouldn't have disgusted her into telling me. But I couldn't have known. "I won't say a word. You know I wouldn't."

"I know." Just like Lily, Aaron lets out a heavy sigh. Ever since I know they're related, I began to see it in their habits as well.

Aaron sighs a lot when he is frustrated. So does Lily.

Lily has this one special stare that leaves you feeling intimidated. Aaron has the very same.

And don't even get me started on their facial features. Their eye colors? The same shade of green. They have the same nose. Their hair color is identical as well. Both of them have freckles.

The only major difference is that Lily has a bigger bottom lip and it's more curved than Aaron's. Her cupid's bow is more defined than his. Aaron's lips are slim.

And perhaps the fact that Aaron has a *way* bigger ego.

Now I actually do want to kiss Lily though. I was joking yesterday but thinking about her lips makes me want to try them.

"Now I get why you don't want me to touch her," I say, hoping it would somehow get the dark cloud over Aaron's head to disappear.

"Look, Colin," Aaron starts, "if you're genuinely interested in my sister, go for it. I know you wouldn't treat her like shit. But I don't want you using her for sex, okay? She's my sister. I don't want her sleeping with half the team like some puck bunny."

"Was that the okay for me to get in her pants when I want a relationship with her as well?" I tease.

Since it's still dark—and I didn't bother turning on the ceiling lights—I don't see the cloth Aaron throws at me coming. As luck would have it, it's just a cloth, could have been something worse—a lamp, for instance.

"You disgust me," he says, laughing. "Why are you up so early anyway?"

"Taking your sister out on a date."

"Dumbass. You completely ignored all of my '*keep your hands off of Lily's.*'"

"Funny. Your sister calls me the exact same name. Just sounds way cuter when she says it." Did I mention that I love teasing Aaron?

"It's five in the morning. Where are you taking her?" I doubt it's a question. He is demanding an answer.

So Aaron *is* the overprotective kind of brother.

"Not sure just yet," I lie. Of course I know where I am taking her, but I wouldn't want him to spoil it for my Lilybug.

I wonder if she's awake. Probably not. Wouldn't hurt to shoot her a text though, right?

"Can you send me her number?" I ask Aaron.

He snorts. "You're taking her out on a date, and she didn't even give you her number?"

Technically it's not a date. But I can't tell him that.

Perhaps I should tell him about her *unalive journey 101*.

But she made me promise I wouldn't.

But she's suicidal. That's enough reason to break a promise, right?

"In my defense, I was out for sex. Apparently, I can't have that without declaring her as my girlfriend. So, send me her number, please?"

The ceiling light turns on as footsteps approach us. Aaron and I both turn toward the sliding glass door that leads to the porch of our backyard.

"What the hell are you guys doing up this early?" A perplexed Grey leans against the wall to kitchen.

Aaron crosses his arms in front of his chest, lifting his eyebrows. "We could ask you the same."

"I have a visitor," he answers with no hesitation.

"Oh, who is it?"

"Some guy from my psychology class. Don't think you know him." *Sure*.

Aaron narrows his eyes as he analyses our best friend's face and body language.

That's something he does a lot. He analyses people when they don't provide him exactly the kind of information he expects. "So then, if you have a guy over, why are you here and not over in your house, in your bedroom, cuddling up to Mr. psychology class guy?"

"Because he is asleep, and I am hungry." Right. The house across from ours lacks of groceries. Not because they don't have enough money to buy some, but because they're twenty-one years old guys, being busy with assignments, Hockey, and sex partners.

It's not like Aaron or I go grocery shopping regularly, but we at least have something to eat here at all times.

A wrinkle appears on Aaron's forehead, he licks his lips then lies his hand flat on the island countertop. "Are you guys like, just friends? Friends with benefits? Exclusive? In a relationship?"

Grey chuckles. He shakes his head slowly, looking away from Aaron and me. His cheeks are slightly flushed.

"So it's serious, huh?" I note, bemused by Grey's reaction.

"I think so, yeah."

"That's awesome, dude! We got to celebrate," Aaron throws in with a cheer, clapping his hands before jumping off his seat. He walks over to Grey and takes him into a very manly embrace.

And with manly I mean he hugs him like a guy would hug his girlfriend. With the butt cheek squeeze and everything.

"You're so weird, Marsh." Grey somehow gets out of Aaron's embrace and takes a few steps back. "By the way, you could have told us you have a twin sister."

Aaron stands still. His voice vanishing as if he never even had one in the first place. And the color is draining from his face.

It's obvious that Aaron doesn't like talking about Lily. Or more their relationship to the other. But from what Lily told me, I think I understand both of their reactions.

I bite my tongue, not wanting the laugh that's lingering in the back of my throat to come through. Despite the fact that Aaron tried to hide Lily from us for three years, even having a great reason for it, it's still hilarious how his ass just got busted.

"I should go," I say, walking out of the kitchen to go find my car keys.

"You're not off the hook, Carter." Grey stops me. "You have a thing for Ron's sister. Good luck with that. If she's only a tiny bit like him, you will definitely need it."

Even if she wasn't anything like him, I'd need it.

"Got to get going, assholes. See you later at practice." To Grey, I only reply with a lopsided smile, followed by a lazy wink.

Five minutes later I'm out of the house, sitting in my car when my phone chimes. It's a message from Aaron, I know because he has a special notification tone. He actually sent me Lily's number.

Thank God he did. I thought I might have to fight him for it.

I click on her contact info and decide to shoot her a quick message. If I'm lucky, she's awake. If not, I will have to call her to wake her up.

Colin: Hey, Lilybug. Your favorite boyfriend here. You awake?

I can hear her groan in my head. I just know a groan will be the first sound she makes after reading my message to her.

And the thought alone makes it worth it.

Lily: I am now. Thank you, dumbass.

Lily: And you are not my boyfriend, Carter. You're my unalive delayer.

Suddenly I am really glad I waited a couple of minutes to see if she would respond. I like her energy. I actually like that she doesn't admire me like all these other girls do at Trewery.

It's refreshing. Such a shame that she doesn't see how much of an awesome person she is. And I mean, even I can see it after five days of knowing her.

Colin: I'm not a plane that comes with delays. Nor am I the Deutsche Bahn that is never punctual. I'm making the rest of your days better. I don't add time onto it.

Though I wish I did.

Lily: Why did you ask if I'm awake?

Colin: We're going out. Get dressed. I'll be there in about fifteen minutes.

Fifteen minutes later I arrive at the dorms. Lily told me I should wait outside but I don't like listening to what she has to say when it comes to spending time with her.

I fear she might trick me. If I wait outside, she will probably never even come out. Which leads to me knocking at her door until she opens it. And when she does, I wish she didn't.

Lily didn't get dressed. In fact, she is still in pajama shorts and a thin tank top. I assume she went to sleep like that. She is also not wearing a bra, which brings up fantasies I do not need at the moment.

"I told you to wait in the car," she snaps.

"You didn't even get dressed yet. I said I would be here in fifteen minutes. It's been twenty and you're still not done."

"I'm tired, Colin. I don't want to go out. It's not even six in the morning yet." She lets out a quiet groan as she opens the door wider, allowing me to come in.

"Don't kill the mood, Lilybug. You'll love today." I walk inside, following Lily into her room. She takes a seat at her desk—the clothes that laid there just yesterday now spread all over her floor—while I lie on her bed.

"I won't kill the mood. I'd kill myself instead."

I sit up in a heartbeat. A sigh escapes me as I look into Lily's eyes through the mirror. "You have to stop saying things like that."

"Why? It's the truth."

"I don't want to hear you talking all about your death. The one that most likely won't happen," I tell her. I'm pretty convinced that she will end up wanting to stay alive after these nine days.

Okay, I'm not convinced. I'm hoping she will want to give life a second chance. Being positive is the key.

"I most likely will end up dead by October 8th."

"Lilybug, you're underestimating my power to make you fall in love with me first."

She snorts and drops the brush she was holding. "You wanted to make me fall in love with life, not you," she reminds me.

"But if I'm your life, it's two in one." I'm joking. I don't plan on making Lily fall in love with me. Making her feel loved will be enough for now.

"Keep on dreaming, Carter." Lily continues to freshen up her face. She looks beautiful, but she also did before she put some makeup on.

"Gladly." I lean back on her pillows, relaxing. "Your brother told me I can get in your pants. He literally gave me the go for it."

"He did not. Stop kidding yourself."

"He sure did. Aaron loves me," I argue.

"Whatever. We won't ever go there. Now close your eyes so I can get dressed."

"Or I leave my eyes open and watch you," I suggest. But before she could come and beat me up again, I grab the next best thing to keep my eyes busy with.

The next best thing being her suicide book. Correction, her *unalive journey 101*.

"Do you mind if I read this?" I ask. "After all, I promised I would make sure your people here get their letters after your death. I will read it no matter what."

"Go ahead. But don't you dare comment on it."

Like I would ever do that.

Actually, I could see myself doing just that. Comment on every single phrase I do not agree with. Phrases like "*I want to die*" or "*This is my goodbye*" or "*I will be dead.*"

Dear whoever reads this,

I begin to read. But I can't help myself.

"Why do you always put 'Dear whoever reads this,'?" I ask. "You should exchange it with 'Dear Colin Baby.'"

"That sounds awful. I will just leave it." Of course she would ignore my question. But I guess I can imagine why she wouldn't address this to one specific person.

Colin Carter is an asshole.
I planned on spending my two remaining weeks writing my goodbyes, and my thoughts along the way to death, but instead I am stuck with an ignorant and stubborn jock.

"I'm not sure what I'm supposed to think of that," I comment, in spite of Lily's command not to. "I am *not* an asshole."

"You so totally are."

"Am not," I tsk. "I'm an amazing guy with only the best qualities to ever exist."

He won't even accept a simple no.

*He demanded to show me that there is more to live for.
Now guess what?
I will have to spend the next couple of days at his mercy.
Nine days, to be exact.
I caved in and gave him nine days to prove me wrong.
He won't manage to do that.
My mind is set on dying.
He can show me whatever he wants, it won't change a thing.
But I guess he is right.
Why would I spend my last days on my own when I can spend them with some stranger that offers me a good time for free?
I certainly hope he won't make me pay for anything.
I mean, I don't even want to be there in the first place, so he might as well pay.*

I start to laugh.

*I wonder if these days count as dates.
Isn't that what dates are all about?
Two people go out, go on adventures, eat at a way too expensive restaurant, do stupid things. And just have a great time.
But if that counts as such, does spending time with a friend count as a date as well?
A friend date perhaps?*

"Lilybug, you're my girlfriend now. They sure are dates," I inform her, joking.

Only a second later I am getting beat up by Lily's stuffed animals.

Well, she is beating me up with one of them, but it's basically the same thing.

"I am not your girlfriend, dumbass."

"That's too bad. I planned on a few dates we would go on. Like, stargazing, or wine painting. Maybe even take a swim course together," I joke.

"*Aw*, doesn't Trewery's superstar know how to swim?" She pouts at me with big eyes. "Does he only know how to skate?"

"Oh, I thought you didn't know how to swim." And once again she beats me with that frog stuffed animal. I think I will be naming him *Sergeant Froggo*. He wears an Army outfit, so might as well go big or go home with the name. "Stop beating me. You're hurting Sergeant Froggo."

"Sergeant-who-now?" She bursts into laughter as she falls down on the bed beside me. "That's not his name."

"I'm pretty sure it is. He looks like one."

"His name is Kermit."

"Way too basic. It's Sergeant Froggo now," I utter. "Now let me continue to read. It's getting interesting, sweetheart."

I wouldn't know. I've never been on a date before.
Not a real one at least.
Anyway, the next letter will be dedicated to Winter.
I know, Winter is a lot to take in.
She isn't very nice most of the time.
And yes, she is such a drama queen.
Oh God, Winter, if you're reading this right now, I am sorry. But you know it's the truth.

But despite her urge to cause drama, she has been my best friend for a while now. I couldn't live with myself if she didn't get a goodbye letter.
That's ironic, I won't even be alive to witness her reading it.

Lily

You're so wrong, Lilybug. You will be alive. You will be happy again. I promise.

Chapter 8

"don't worry, I promise you'll be fine"—*Fee Time by Ruel*

Lily

COLIN AND I TAKE ON A TEN-MINUTE car drive.

We find ourselves on Long Clove Rd, currently hiking up a hill.

If I had known I'd be hiking this early in the morning, I would have stayed in bed. Though, I doubt Colin would have given me a choice.

Who am I kidding? I don't have a choice but to follow him wherever he wants to take me. I agreed on these nine days. It would be such a bitch move to back out now.

And besides, Colin doesn't seem to be half as bad. Maybe he will be a great company for my last days.

I'm just worried I might grow on him like he's starting to grow on me…kind of.

Colin is still an arrogant ass. One I'd much rather punch in the face than have as my unalive delayer. But it would be unnecessarily cruel if I grew on him, and he lost me to death.

But then again, he kind of put himself in this position. I didn't ask for him to "help me." I don't need his saving.

"Great, so it's six in the morning and we're sitting on a blanket on top of a hill and now what?" I speak in a sort of annoyed tone just as Colin makes me take a seat on a blanket he brought.

"You're so anti-romantic." He laughs to himself. "We'll be watching the sunrise."

"I always hated watching sunrises," I let him know. "I never understood why it would be so magical. It's just the sun that rises. Nothing special."

"Wrong." Colin takes a seat next to me. "Sunrises are beautiful. A new day arrives. It's a new beginning. Each morning, with every new sunrise, you get the chance to start something new."

"I'm not superstitious."

"Lilybug, this has nothing to do with superstitions. It's simply a new beginning. View the sunrise as whatever you please. See it as a moment of carelessness. The second you can see the sun rise and the sky starts to show itself in all its glory, close your eyes and wish for something you truly desire. For instance, a painless day."

"That doesn't make any sense."

"Fine, let's just wait until the sun is rising, then you can stand by the edge and scream from the top of your lungs. Release all of your anger from the past years. Let the pain from yesterday leave your body. Grant yourself a pause, just until the sun is up and then you can come back to reality," he offers, I think?

He takes my hand in his, laying them down on his crossed legs.

"This is so ridiculous, you know that, right?"

"Feel free to give me feedback once the sun is up." Colin flicks me that perfect grin of his before turning his face away to look over the dark city.

I have no idea when the sun would start to rise. I never paid attention to it before, and yet I'm somewhat excited.

Honestly, I have always viewed sunrises as something stupid. Sure, it's the beginning of a new day. But I never understood what would be so interesting to see.

People go watch sunrises and sunsets every single day and enjoy it. I never believed they could be interesting. I mean, it's just a huge fireball showing on the other side of the globe. Nothing too spectacular.

"Lilybug?" Colin's soft voice streams through my ears.

"Yeah?"

"Tell me something about you that you've never told anyone before."

"I want to die," I answer with no hesitation. It's true. I have never told anyone about it. Nor did I ever really say it out loud before.

"Something I didn't already know."

"I have a weirdly shaped birthmark."

His eyebrows rise, lips pressing together as he waits for me to elaborate, but I don't. "Well, if you're not going to tell me what it is, don't even bother mentioning it."

"It's too embarrassing."

He rolls his eyes. "Fine. I'll find out eventually. Give me something else then."

"You go first," I say.

Let's be honest. I have no idea what I am supposed to tell him.

"Okay." He exhales heavily, and although it's still dark, I can see the fog in front of his face rise into the air. "Two years ago, when Eira had been diagnosed with leukemia, I tried to bribe the doctor into taking extra care of her."

"You were nineteen when you tried to bribe a doctor to find a better cure for cancer?" I question. Then suddenly I realize: *His sister had cancer?*

"To be fair, I am not a doctor. And I never really had to care about all that. I have always been healthy. I have never broken a bone, not even had a sprained ankle. And I play hockey. Always have. So that's quite the miracle. I never put too much thought into anything medical. I was so stupid. And I was eighteen still."

"I am so sorry about Eira, Colin. She doesn't deserve this."

He shrugs. "Yeah. It's alright though. She's Eira. I mean, Eira thinks beyond everything. She is excited to die because she believes that the universe wants her to start a new adventure. No, *needs* her to go on a new one."

That is actually a really beautiful way of thinking about death.

"Is she dying?"

"Nah." He dismisses my question. "She's cancer free now."

"Did you think she was going to die?" *Why am I even asking?*

"Sure did, for a while. I never wanted to accept it. I mean, she's my sister. I don't want her to die. But I came to accept that I can't do anything about it. And crying about it now won't give her more time either, if she were to die." He lets out a painful sigh. Something is off. "Good thing, she is cancer free and won't die yet."

I need to change the topic. I doubt Colin wants to continue speaking of his sister's death. And I'm not sure if I should be wanting to carry this conversation on either. "I used to think the moon is made out of cheese."

Colin snickers. "Everyone thought that as a child. Give me something deeper."

I think about my life for a second, letting every event run through my mind before admitting, "there was a period of time in which Aaron hated me."

"I don't believe you." His head turns toward me, his eyes landing on mine. He isn't expressing any kind of anticipation, but at the same time it looks a lot like he's desperate for me to enlighten him.

So I do.

"Our dad got married to another woman. Her name is Liz, but I'm sure you knew that already. I didn't take it very well. But I took it even worse when I found out that Liz has a daughter. Ana. She was only three when she became a part of our family. Aaron and I were eight. I was so jealous of her."

"Oh, I read the jealous part, sweetheart."

"Yeah, I know you did," I say, rolling my eyes. "Aaron loved Ana right from the start. He played with her at all times. And well, I only had my mom. She never gave me any other siblings. When I went to see my dad and Aaron, Aaron only ever wanted us to play with Ana. Which led to me getting mad at him. Eventually my jealousy got so bad that I didn't even want to look at Ana anymore. I would do cruel things to get attention. I even cut Aaron's cuddle-blankie in half."

Colin gasps. "No way, Lilybug. You can't just do that. That's some real trauma you caused Aaron!"

I laugh. The kind of laughter I didn't allow myself to let out for years. It gets so much, I start grunting like a pig while inhaling. And those piggy-grunts only make me laugh even more.

I don't pay much attention to what's around me. But when I catch Colin smile at me, I feel this weird tingle in my stomach. Probably a sign I'm about to vomit.

Colin Carter has smiled at me before, but it was never like this. Never with admiration. I think maybe he is proud of himself for making me laugh like that. But even if I'm overanalyzing this whole smile right now, I don't care.

I don't care because laughing feels good.

Feeling a hand come in touch with mine, I immediately stop to laugh and look down to Colin and my hands. He is intertwining them, holding mine closely to his as our fingers interlock. His thumb brushes over my skin in soft strokes.

Colin isn't looking at me, but I'm watching his side profile while he stares straight forward over the city.

He is really handsome. But that wouldn't even matter to me. Colin has a loving soul. Even although I'm still sure Colin Carter is a complete asshole and is just good at hiding it from me.

He cares for people he doesn't even know. And I come to believe that maybe if I weren't going to die, I could see him in my life as someone more than just a friend.

I can't think like this.

My time is almost over. I have only eight days left. I can't fall in love now. Not that I was going to fall in love with Colin. We've only known each other for six days, and our relationship didn't start off too great.

Colin could potentially be a great friend. Maybe even turn into my best friend if we had more time.

That's what I'm talking about. A great, deep friendship.

The only reason Colin is here with me right now is because I want to die. And he wants to show me I don't.

But I do want to die, and no matter on what adventures he takes me, my mind won't change.

"Look," he commands, pointing toward the horizon.

A few lights in New City are turned on. It's not as bright as I thought it would be at 6:30 in the morning. I thought more people would be awake, more lights would light up the city, but I was wrong.

And I was even more wrong to say that sunrises are nothing but a waste of time.

The sky turns into all the colors I could only ever imagine it could turn into once then sun starts to rise.

The darkness diminishes, and it's as if the ocean could catch on fire and turn into something completely new. As if a pool with the deepest blue water cleans up and appears golden from a source of light shining on it.

Something completely odd and yet something everyone needs to see.

There is no sign of darkness left as the huge ball of fire rises on the horizon, spreading warming gold and purple color throughout the sky in every direction imaginable. The clouds gleam like dusty pink cotton candy in front of a work of art that is the sky.

It's breathtaking to see the sun painting the world's sky in all its glory.

Colin gets up from the floor, pulling me up once he stands. He walks us to the edge so we're just standing there, watching the sun rise.

"Do it," he whispers. "Scream, shout, let out your anger and frustrations."

I allow myself to look at Colin in shock. He said I could do that, but I didn't think he would actually want me to.

"Think of the sky as your pain and scream at it."

"You're crazy," I tell him with a chuckle.

"I can live with that." He turns and lifts my face up to the sky. "Now, Lilybug. Scream." He takes a few steps back, granting me more space.

And then it comes over me. The anger I feel for never being good enough. The frustration I feel for longing for a better life that will never come. The pain I have felt for years from the separation my parents took over me and my family.

So I scream.

I scream from the top of my lungs, letting all the anger and agony from my past leave my body.

He was right. It's refreshing. It feels good to finally let it all out.

It's like being at the gym and lifting 220 pounds at the bench, then finally getting rid of the weight. The satisfaction that comes through when you realize you carried so much weight like it was a feather. You feel lighter when it's gone and only then do you realize how heavy it was on you.

The weight is lighter on me. I know it's not gone. It will never be gone. But it still feels good to get rid of it for a moment.

Tears escape from the corner of my eyes as I calm down and stop screaming. I'm not crying, but I kind of am.

I always thought crying only happens when your heart is aching from all of the pain you feel. Never did I think you could cry from relief.

When I turn around to look at Colin, I see him putting away his phone.

Assuming he just recoded my entire outbreak of anger doesn't sit right with me. I wonder what our project is all about. He won't tell me anything.

Despite the unwell feeling of assuming that Colin Carter has a video of me screaming on his phone, I don't really care much.

"Thank you." I thank him wholeheartedly, walking closer to him.

Colin opens his arms for me, allowing me in for a hug.

I hate hugs. Or I used to until I'm in Colin's embrace. His arms wrap around me so gently, yet firm enough, accompanied by so much protection, I feel like he is trying to convince me that he is my armor now.

And boy do I feel safe in his arms.

The side of my face presses against the front of his shoulder as my arms wrap around his torso. I feel Colin's hand stroking through my hair, and his other hand drawing circles over my back.

It's soothing.

A few more tears roll down my face as I realize that I won't get to experience moments like these anymore. At least not many.

But that's all right. I will savor them and if I do remember my life before my death, I will come to think back to these moments with a smile on my face.

Suddenly I'm way more excited for the next seven days with Colin. I can't really count today anymore. He's chosen the early morning as his time of the day, so I don't think I will see him much for the rest of it.

We're just standing here, hugging for a whole while until I eventually pull away.

Colin cups my face with his hands, caressing my cheeks ever so lightly by sliding his thumbs over my skin. It sends shivers down my spine.

For a moment I believe he wants to kiss me, but I know that's not the case. So, as quick as the thought enters my brain, it vanishes from it as well.

His eyes are staring into mine. A gentle smile is tugging on his lips as he watches me.

"You're really beautiful, did you know that?" He speaks softly. Something in his voice seems odd. Usually he's all cheerful and chirpy. But this time he is gentle and jovial.

If I read Colin correctly, he doesn't like being vulnerable. So telling me about his sister, about how he felt when he thought she was dying—and acting like anything but Mr. tough-guy—must have been pretty difficult for him.

"Thank you," I say, offering him a small smile.

Colin tilts my head up, his index finger under my chin as he does. His face moves closer to mine until his lips brush over my skin.

He places a kiss to my forehead, slowly.

My heart beats faster. So fast, I can feel it beating inside of my chest. My stomach seems to be turning upside-down, but this time it's not from feeling sick. Maybe I do feel sick, but a different kind of sick. A kind of sick that doesn't sit right with me.

It's like a flutter in my stomach, like someone was tickling me from the inside.

It's nerve-wracking, a feeling—a *flutter*—I have never felt before.

Please remember this when you're dead, Lily.

When he pulls away and goes to collect the blanket he brought, I feel empty again. Like something inside of me feels lost without Colin by my side. I hate that I feel this way.

I shouldn't feel this way. I shouldn't want Colin. I shouldn't because it's not fair to him.

But I do anyway. I want Colin, even just for one night. I want to feel his lips on mine as much as I hate the thought as well.

I hate wanting him.

How did this happen anyway?

Colin was nothing to me when we met. Actually, he was a pain in the ass. I didn't want him around. I didn't want him to show me the beauty of life.

Yet here I am, longing for his lips.

I think it's because he's the only guy that ever truly paid attention to me. He's the only person that is trying to save me. Of course it has my hormones go crazy and give me wrong signals.

Colin isn't nice. Not once did I hear someone refer to him as a good person. He is an asshole. He's still the same superstar that so much as nods into a girl's direction and has her undressed a second later.

But despite all that, he seems nice enough for my brain to mistake his newfound kindness for something else.

"No, I swear Miles was staring at me throughout all of finance," Carina tells us. With us I mean my friends and me.

As I would every day, I spend my lunch break with my friends in the cafeteria. The four of us are sitting at a table, currently listening to Carina Rico's fantasies about Miles King.

After attending St. Trewery for a while, I figured that a lot of women at this school have a thing for the hockey guys.

They're all ridiculously hot, I give them that much. I used to think being hot is a requirement to start playing hockey here. Obviously, that's not the case.

Still Miles King seems to be getting the most attention.

Miles has a couple of tattoos, not as many as Colin (I think). I'm actually not sure how many Colin has. I've only ever seen his arms and neck covered in single tattoos, I wouldn't know if he has some on his chest or back as well.

Miles, however, I know he doesn't have many.

Simply for having tattoos and a pretty face, Miles King is getting quite the attention. For no reason, so I believe.

Okay, maybe for a reason. His abs are more defined than any I have ever seen before. And then in combination with the few tattoos on his arms and chest is to die for. But he sure is missing the dark hair.

But that's not everyone's type. I guess there is more that attracts girls to Miles like food attracts pigeons.

Maybe it's the fact that he's a hockey player.

I wonder if girls are just as crazy about Colin as they are about Miles. The thought irks me, but it's not my business anyway. I shouldn't care.

"He was just looking for the next girl he could fuck," Mia says unfazed. She's one of very few women here that wouldn't sell their soul to the devil for Miles King's existence. "Honestly, Miles is just disgusting. Just like the rest of them."

"He's not disgusting just because he has a more active sex life than you do," Carina defends her beloved Miles.

"Sure not. But do you see me fucking two different women in a time span of five hours?" Mia asks.

"Stop trying to talk him bad, Mia. Just accept that he is ridiculously hot."

"Sure, I can do that. Doesn't mean I want to get laid by him."

"I don't want that either. Well, I do. But I want him as my boyfriend as well," Carina cries out quietly.

Carina is as much of an emotional wreck as I am. Just that she is emotional when it comes to people. More specifically guys. She gets attached to a guy because he gave her two seconds of attention.

Before anyone can save her from it, Carina has planned her wedding with said guy. Only to get frustrated when said guy doesn't even want to be with her or pays any more attention to her.

"Now shut up, he's here!" She squeaks, staring as Miles and three of his teammates walk right into the cafeteria.

Every single voice in this room mutes. If a pin were to fall down, everyone would be able hear it. That's how quiet the room goes once the jocks make their entrance.

Aaron walks in next to Miles, followed by a black-haired guy with a three-day beard. He is just as muscular as everyone else of them. And tall. I would guess about six foot two, a tad taller than Aaron, though not too much.

Since Colin is the last of the four jocks entering, I assume the black-haired guy is Grey, the other not-really-roommate.

Thanks to Aaron, I know that he is living in a house with Colin, yet Grey and Miles sort of live there too but not really. At least they get their food intake from my brother's house in the morning, and whenever they're hungry.

Aaron didn't shut up talking about Colin for the first two months of freshman year. He mentioned Miles a couple of times before as well. And it's not too surprising to know who Miles is.

But Grey? *Hell*. He's been mentioned. I just never saw him around before. I don't think he is around a lot.

My friends—*and I*—watch the guys walk over to the line to buy some food. They're goofing around, ignoring the eyes that are solely on them.

I always thought stuff like this only happens in teen movies. But being here right now, witnessing it myself makes it pretty realistic.

Trying to get my friends back to talking, I ask a question, but it stays unheard. Clearly they're too focused on the hot guys that are buying food, the same way every single other person in this cafeteria did before. Apparently when jocks buy food it's automatically more interesting.

"Miles looks so good in his clothes," Carina says. If my eyes aren't playing any tricks on me, I could swear she is drooling.

"He's wearing jeans and a shirt. Just like 98% of the other guys here," Mia points out. She is right. Miles doesn't stand out too much. Aside from his height.

"What do you think are they talking about?" Carina is questioning, still watching as Colin starts to laugh and Aaron shakes his head after an obvious eyeroll.

Then Colin slaps his hand on Aaron's shoulder blade before he starts to walk away. Toward the tables.

"I think Colin found himself another victim," Mia jokes, taking a sip from her apple juice.

Winter and I turn back around to face Mia and Carina, turning our backs to the guys. I'm glad the fascination about the hockey guys only ever lasts a couple of minutes before life continues to go on. I wouldn't be able to sit through this until they eventually leave again.

"You're partnered up with Colin for your film directing class, aren't you, Lily?" Mia asks. I just nod a reply. "Poor you. You probably have to do all the work."

I don't. In fact, I am the one not doing anything. But I can't say that out loud. Fortunately for me, I don't have to. The second I try to speak, Carina gasps seconds before I feel arms wrapping carefully around my neck.

"Hey there, Lilybug," Colin whispers into my ear before I feel his lips brush my skin. This time he plants a kiss onto my cheek and not my forehead.

His arms loosen around my body, then eventually disappear completely. Taking a look toward my friends, they all look as equally shocked as I feel.

Thinking Colin left, I'm dumbstruck when he is taking a seat right next to me. Or more half under me.

The second he is seated, Colin tugs on my leg and places it over his so that the bottom half of my leg is dangling between his. At this point he might as well have pulled me right onto his lap.

"You didn't eat," he says, pointing toward my full tray. He is right. I'm not hungry, but I promised Winter I would try to get something down. It just never happened. I was hoping that maybe if I let it sit in front of me, I would eventually grab something from the tray and eat it. It didn't happen.

"I'm not hungry," I tell him. "What are you doing here?"

"Keeping an eye on you." He shrugs like there is nothing wrong with the way he just phrased this. In front of my friends. "The guys are coming as well. Hope you girls don't mind," he says to my friends.

Of course they don't mind. It's good for their reputation on Campus.

Their presence will give Carina a chance to speak to Miles.

I'm not so sure about Mia. She usually stays away from the sport guys. She believes they're all arrogant assholes that only care about themselves.

Winter probably won't like it too much either. I got her to block Aaron's phone number. She needs to heal and stop dreaming about a perfect relationship with him. It won't happen. We both know it won't.

"Of course not," Carina replies with excitement.

Only a few moments later the other three guys approach our table. Luckily, the table is big enough for eight people to sit at. Well, it gets a little tight, but it fits.

Aaron sits next to Colin, Miles and Grey on the opposite side of their teammates.

Unfortunately for Carina, Miles doesn't sit next to her. But that's good for him. Poor guy wouldn't be able to eat in peace with her next to him.

"So, you got not only one, but four hockey players wrapped around your finger now?" Mia snorts bemused, looking at me.

Mia isn't the only one snorting. Aaron does the exact same thing. But I bet for a whole different reason.

"Just me. We are a package deal though, so they will have to do some good deeds for her too," Colin answers for me. I wish I was faster with answering questions. "That sounds dirtier than intended."

My friends start to laugh, as so do Grey and Miles. Aaron, Colin and I stay quiet. I understand why Aaron doesn't laugh at the awful phrasing. He has the same reason I do. But why doesn't Colin laugh at his own words?

"Stop taking so much space for yourself," Aaron says, pushing Colin closer to me, if it gets any closer, that is.

Bemused, Colin presses his lips together into a thin line, then grabs onto my other leg—the one that is still free from his body—and pulls it over his leg as well. Shortly after that I'm seated on one of his thighs.

He moves a bit closer to Winter, giving Aaron a bit more space. He seems grateful for the space but pissed that his twin sister is currently sitting on his best friend's lap.

Colin seats me sideways, though, I think if I sat with my back against his front, it would get super uncomfortable in a short while

Colin holds me close to him. One of his hands is resting on my hip, his thumb tracing the outlines of my panties through the thin layer that leggings offer.

Since I don't know where else to place my hands, I decide to just rest them on my thighs. Just that that's exactly where Colin's other hand is lying. *How did I not even notice that?*

Aaron almost gags. I just have to look into his face, and I know what he thinks.

"No way, you're an actual thing then?" Miles asks, looking Colin and me up and down.

"Don't think so, Miles. Carter isn't even trying to eat her face right now," the guy, that I'm still assuming is Grey, speaks. His voice is deeper than I thought it would be.

"Is this what guys do in private?" Mia asks. "Do you guys watch your friends making out?"

"Making out?" Miles laughs. "I have full on sex tapes from these guys on my phone. I watch them every evening before going to sleep." He's trying too hard to appear serious, forcing his face to stay expressionless. It only makes the mocking joke more obvious. And maybe because he won't stop laughing at himself for his hilarious lie.

"He's joking," Grey confirms.

"So? Do I get an actual answer?"

"We don't watch the other making out," Miles says. "But at some point, you just know your best friends. That includes knowing how they act around—and with—girls they just want to fuck, and girls they want for more than a quick thing."

"Yeah," Aaron agrees. "You can't tell me you don't know when, let's say, Winter wants to bang or when she wants a relationship." He eyes her, she looks back at him with a mad frown.

If looks could kill…Aaron would be six feet under right now.

They continue to talk, but I can no longer concentrate because Colin Carter is stroking his hand up my body. So high that it's eventually crawling under my sweatshirt and tracing over my skin.

Chapter 9

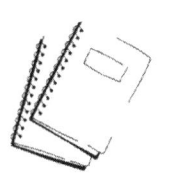

***"you kept breathing but stopped living"*—Birthday Cake by Dylan Conrique**

Lily

Dear whoever reads this,

I've had another panic attack today.
It was worse in comparison to the one I've had yesterday.
They're getting worse with every day, but I don't know why.
I've occasionally had panic attacks since I was younger, but recently they're so much worse.
They're so much more intense.
Maybe it's fear? But I wouldn't know where that would come from.
I'm not afraid. Not of death anyway.
I'm afraid that I won't want to die anymore. I do, as of now, but what if Colin manages to convince me to stay?
I don't see it happening, but what if?

When he touched me today, my body reacted a way I never thought it could.
I felt warmer. I felt like the ache in my heart got less because he was around.
But that's not right. It can't be right.
Colin is Colin. (Sorry because I know you will read this, Colin).
Perhaps I am afraid of feeling altogether.
I didn't plan my life further than October 8th of this year.
I don't have plans for my future.
I don't know what I want to do after I graduate college.
I don't know how to live.
I don't know how to smile, how to laugh, how to be happy.
But Colin makes it all look so easy.
He knows what he wants to do after college.
He knows how to be happy.
He knows how to live.
But I don't.
I will never know.
And it scares me.
I'm scared that if I stay, I will only continue to live in misery.
That's why I can't stay.
I don't want to stay.
I can't feel the pain anymore.
It's getting unbearable.
I can't fall asleep with dry eyes, and I can't wake up with them either.
I'm always crying.
Always, except when I'm with people.
But even when I am with people I cry sometimes.
And now I'm crying again. Perfect.

Nine Days

The pain is back.
I don't want it to come back.
Make it go away, please.
I can't do this anymore.
I keep telling myself that it's only nine more days. Eight if you don't count the couple of hours I will be alive on day nine.
It's way too far in the future.
I should have just done it right away instead of giving me more time for this stupid unalive journey 101.
Fucking ridiculous.
I am so fucking ridiculous.
My chest is hurting, Colin.
My heart is in pain.
I can't take this anymore.
I want to leave, but I want to stay for you.
I want to stay so we can have more of these fun days together.
It's only been two days.
But it's been two days I have enjoyed more than the twenty years I've been alive so far.
We didn't even experience anything exciting. Just spending time at his parents' house, then watching TV in my dorm room.
But he made me enjoy it.
And today was amazing.
I like sunrises now.
They're beautiful.
And a new beginning.
Today was a new beginning.
But it won't last forever.

Things aren't meant to last forever, that's why I'm okay with saying goodbye to Colin soon.
He will continue to live happily.
I know he will.
He is Colin.
But I wouldn't.
I would cry. And cry. And cry some more.
Colin would leave me when he convinced me to live.
I won't fall for his trap. Or his marvelous blue eyes. God, I hate blue eyes.
My heart is still hurting.
It's painful.
I am so tired of fighting.
Isn't it funny how people look into your eyes every day, and yet they never see that you're about to cry? That you're holding back tears?
Can you imagine how exhausting that is?
Can you imagine how painful it is to be feeling drained and pretending to be the most cheerful person all day?
Until you're on your own, lying in bed, finally able to break?
Whoever reads this, please know I am hurting.
I'm not feeling the kind of pain that goes away with some Advil.
It's not some kind of pain a doctor can make disappear.
Sure, I have my medication to help. If only they were helping.
Every single one of my days feels like I'm falling apart.
I spend every day picking up the pieces that fall throughout the day and glue them back together. But what's once broken can't be whole anymore.

No matter how much glue I put on my broken pieces, I will never feel whole again.
Every single day I am begging the crying creature staring back at me in the mirror to just hold on for a little while longer.
Begging myself to stay strong.
I keep telling myself that it will get better.
I've been telling myself that for years.
It's never gotten better.
So you tell me, what do I do?
Do I continue to live in pain? Continue to feel like nothing makes sense anymore. Continue to shatter my own heart by allowing me to have hope, only to get disappointed again.
Or do I give up?
Do I end my pain, my suffering and move on to another dimension?
A dimension where I don't have to feel this way.
Where I don't have to cry myself to sleep.
One where people don't tell you "Well, if you're upset, you have to know what it's about."
That's another thing that I hate.
When I do say I don't feel well...I don't always know why.
Actually, I barely know why I don't feel okay. I just don't feel okay, accept it.
But people tell me I need to have a reason.
I don't.
But it's hurting when they tell me that. It makes me feel unworthy, stupid...like something is seriously wrong with me.
They don't understand me.
They don't want to understand me.

No one does.
So, tell me:
Do I stay, and continue to feel worthless, or do I leave and pray to God I will be happier wherever I land?

Lily

Chapter 10

"I'd do anything for my bippity-boppity-boo?"—Find My Way To You by Miles Parrish, Shalom Margaret

Colin

ONCE THE LAST CLASS FOR TODAY IS OVER, I head home. I can't wait to take a good nap. Today has been exhausting. All this studying and thinking about Lily is exhausting.

I'm not even too sure if I'm more worried about Lily killing herself any moment, or her staying alive and cutting me off.

It's definitely odd.

But I don't think too much of it. Lily is a great friend to me. Maybe I would even consider her my best friend at this point. Which is weird because I already have three of those. One being her twin brother, who—*if I'm being honest*—is my favorite of those three dorks I call my best friends.

Something about Lily is refreshing. And it irks me that I won't have her around for too much longer anymore. That is if I fail to convince her.

The second I arrive at home, I make my way to my bedroom. I don't have much time before I have to leave again.

My father has the team come to the arena for practice at 4 p.m., if I'm late, he will probably have me take on an extra hour of practice. He wasn't all too happy that I skipped on yesterday's practice hours. Luckily, when I told him that I was visiting Eira, he seemed less mad.

I know I shouldn't use my sister as an excuse to skip practice, but it wasn't even a lie. I did go see her.

But to be honest, despite what I told Lily, I did want her to meet Eira. I was kind of hoping it would mess with Lily's head.

I'm aware of how shitty that sounds.

I have no idea what suicidal people go through. I don't know what would make them happy, or even reconsider wanting to commit for just a second.

It was probably a really selfish and dumb thing to do. I admit that.

Telling her the crap about Eira and her fascination with death, if it brought just a tiny bit of doubt to Lily, I will be pleased.

Unfortunately, I can't read Lily's mind, so I won't ever know if she thought about it. I won't ever know if she doubted her decision, even if it was just for a second. Apart from my wishful thinking, Lily doesn't even know half of the truth.

We haven't spoken ever since we bumped into one another at the cafeteria. Okay, "bumped into one another" might be an understatement.

Lily ended up sitting on my lap for good an hour before she had to leave for her next class. Not even going to lie, I was pretty disappointed when she left.

Thinking of her reminds me of something. I have this other *thing* planned for today. I'm aware that I took her out this morning already, but she technically only gave me eight days instead of nine, so I get an extra date today.

Who am I kidding? I don't have anything else planned, I just want to make sure Lily doesn't die even earlier.

Colin: Meet me at the arena at 6. I'm taking you out.

Lily: You already did. Your time is over for today. Save if for tomorrow.

Colin: I had less time yesterday, meaning I have more time today.

Lily: I'm not getting onto the ice.

I chuckle. She's so adorable, thinking I wouldn't get her back on the ice eventually. Lucky for Lily, that is not my plan for tonight.

Colin: Why? Can't skate?

I know she can skate. I've read it in her journal before.

Lily: You hit the nail right on the head there, dumbass.

Colin: Well, don't worry then, Lilybug. I'm an excellent skater. And so are you, liar.

Lily: Aw, forgot you read my unalive journey 101. But seriously, I don't skate anymore. I have evolved a rational fear for ice skating.

Colin: Liar. I'll let it slide for now, if you come to the arena at 6.

Lily: Fine, whatever. Do I need to dress up?

Colin: Hm…Yes. Wear my jersey.

Lily: Nude, got it. Don't forget protection. x

I need a moment to remember that I have to breathe. Not for a minute have I imagined Lily being this bold. Like, I knew Lily could be…different. But bold like this? Never did I see that coming.

"CARTER, WE HAVE a surprise for you!" Zachery yells with as much enthusiasm as he can offer, just when I enter the locker room.

A surprise from this team can't be good. They don't do surprises. And if *we* do plan on a surprise, it's never something good.

Which means, I'm positive that whatever they've planned to surprise me with, it's more likely going to be a punishment. *Oh sweet baby Jesus.*

"Take a seat, captain," Parker Griffin, our goalie, says. I choose to obey for my own good. These guys are capable of anything. And I mean *anything*.

"We spoke to the Coach before. He is in on this, so there is no need playing the dad-card," Aaron informs me, speaking loud enough for the entire team to hear. It wouldn't even make a difference if they hear a thing or not, they are all in on this.

Judging by the grins on their faces, I'm even more certain now that this is more of a punishment. I've suspected it before, but now I'm one hundred per cent convinced I will end up losing a body part after this.

"You didn't show up for practice yesterday," he continues. "What was so important?"

I don't hesitate to answer. "My sister."

My team knows about Eira and that she used to have cancer.

This team is like a second family to me. We're all a little crazy and do call the other out for dumb shit. Sometimes we even throw insults into conversations. But we're holding together like chewing gum holds onto the bottom of a shoe.

That said, it's either all of us, or none of us at all. Like I said, we're a package deal. The whole team.

Sure all of us have their little groups. I have mine. But that doesn't mean the rest of the team doesn't belong to the package.

"You skipped practice for your sister?" Aaron makes sure he got that right. "Not mine?"

The team starts to laugh.

Ever been seated in front of twenty-one other guys and they're just laughing at you? Me neither. Up until now.

"Ana isn't exactly the age-appropriate girl for me. She is only sixteen."

"But Lily is age appropriate. She's twenty, almost twenty-one." Kaiden winks at me with a nasty grin on his face. I'm just going to assume Aaron finally admitted to him having a twin sister. I suppose it was long overdue anyway.

I also assume that Aaron threatened to cut off the guys' junk if any of them let the word out to any other student.

I clear my throat, not knowing how to say anything back to Kaiden.

"You remember the unspoken rules, right?" Aaron takes over again. "Unspoken rule number one: Skipping practice for a girl will not stay unpunished."

"It's an unspoken rule. How would I remember it?" I question. "And I didn't skip for Lily. I actually went to see Eira."

Of course I know how I am supposed to remember a rule that has never been mentioned before.

These "unspoken rules" aren't too unspoken.

I made them up. And they're actually all written down in a notebook. Twenty-five *unspoken* rules in total.

They're not getting talked about, but everyone knows them. When I first got voted as captain, I made sure we had some rules. I figured we needed them because the captain before me didn't care one bit about the team. It was all about him and winning.

I wanted a team that actually sticks together. One that would take care of the other, be there for one another.

So I made up some rules.

Every teammate got a list to learn by heart. They called them the "teammate requirements." Most of the rules were jokes at first. Rules like "don't ever jump into a pool at a party on your own" weren't meant to be taken seriously. But the team took them seriously. Meaning, we'll go by them.

"Oh, I know," Aaron says, chuckling. He undoubtedly spoke to Lily before all this, to get proof that I was with her.

But that means he also knows we were with Eira. "But what about rule number ten?"

Unspoken rule #10: Teammates' siblings are off-limits.

"Oh, fuck you, Marsh," I snap. "You gave me the go, remember?" And besides, I'm not even dating Lily. We're not a couple, or ever going to be one. I just want her to stay alive and realize life is worth living.

The problem is, I can't tell him that.

"You're a complete asshole, but I know you will be good to her." Aaron offers me a slim smile before he turns back to grinning like the devil. "But you will have to face the punishment anyway."

"Alright, beat me up already."

Another round of laughter breaks free.

Whatever they think my punishment should be, clearly beating me up does not measure up to their expectations.

"We figured you could use a wardrobe change." The grin on Aaron's face widens, as so do the ones on the other guys' faces.

This can't be good at all.

"Just so you know, Coach signed in on this," Aaron reminds me.

Only moments later, two of my teammates hand me a piece of clothing each. Grey hands me a white cropped top that looks like it's going to be way too small on me. Zac hands me a tutu fitting to it. A white tutu that I will be freezing my ass off in.

But these aren't the highlights yet.

When Grey and Zac step back, Aaron comes into vision. He is holding a pair of white fairy costume wings in his hands. I know they're from a fairy costume because these belong to my sister.

"You guys know I will most definitely break a few bones or die from the cold, right?"

They shrug. All of them. They're just shrugging and then burst into laughter like this costume is the most hilarious thing ever.

It is. I have to admit to that. If I weren't the one in the hot seat.

"Come on, Princess Fairytale, get dressed," Aaron says, swinging a wand around before bopping the tip of my nose with it. After that he makes his way to his locker as quick as possible.

The laughter never dies out. In fact, with every piece of clothing I strip out of, my teammates find it more and more hilarious. And by the time I'm only in my boxers and have to put on the *great* costume, they're all dying of laughter.

But I don't back away from a challenge, so I squeeze myself into the way too tight clothes and try to present them as manly as possible. When that doesn't work, I decide to go with unleashing my inner princess. Or fairy for that matter.

Does that make me the Fairy Godmother now?

I mean, I'm the team captain in a fairy costume. That definitely makes me the Fairy Godmother. Now, where's my Cinderella?

Just when I think their laughter couldn't get any worse, it happens.

"Someone take a picture of this!" Grey yells, bringing his hands to his mouth to mimic a megaphone.

I give Grey the finger but embrace my photogenic genes and pose for some great ass pictures, being fully aware that these dumbasses will post them all over the internet later today.

But, hey, what's a team without some fun shit like this, right?

"Since we don't want you to get hurt," Kaiden begins. He walks over to me, his hands hiding behind his back. "We made sure you have a helmet." Kaiden brings his hands upfront, showing me the helmet they prepared for me.

It's a plain white helmet, fitting to the white cropped top and white tutu. But what's new is the paper crown glued right on top of the helmet.

"Why, thank you, guys. This is awesome!" I take the helmet with pride and put it on, continuing to pose for more pictures. "Wait, did I get some awesome new skates as well?"

"Do we look rich or something?" Aaron asks.

"You do, actually." It's sort of the truth. Aaron Marsh doesn't look too rich, but what even defines "looking rich?"

What I do know, his family sure as hell has money. His father is a medical lawyer. And his mother, what I know now is his stepmother, is a cardiothoracic surgeon.

"Fuck you, man."

"I would, but I have your sister for that," I lie.

Aaron tenses, his hands balling into fists. For a second I think I've gone too far, I probably have, but he doesn't act out. His lips form into a thin line like he is thinking about what to say.

"She's not sleeping with you," he ends up saying. "I would know. Winter would rat you out to me."

"Not unless Lily doesn't talk to her."

"Winter would have to unblock you first, bro," Miles throws in. The other guys stay quiet, choosing to chuckle every now and then, instead of getting themselves some ass whooping.

"Yeah," I agree, "what's going on between you two anyway? Is it officially over?"

"It's been for a while. She just didn't get the memo." Aaron rips off his shirt, being completely unbothered by this conversation. "She's a great fuck, but nothing for long-term. She's too giggly and dramatic."

"Sure saw the dramatic part," I admit. "You do know she is driving Lily insane, right?"

"Well, Lily is twenty years old, she can handle someone like Winter."

"I doubt that," I mumble inaudibly.

I put on my skates, grab my hockey stick and leave the locker room together with the rest of the team. I'm sure I won't make it out of here without tons of bruises today, but that's alright.

I'm just praying I will still have every part of my body working by the end of today's practice.

"Colin!" Coach Carter exclaims. "Get your ass over here!" By the sound of his voice, I start to doubt this was approved by him. He is upset. I know he is.

I quickly skate over to my father, keeping some distance between us in case I have to run for my life.

"I suppose you weren't in on this then?"

"Oh, no, I was," he laughs. "Got you the wings. Eira wants a picture as proof you actually wore them."

"Of course she does."

"Colin, you need to promise you won't run away in a minute," he says in a soft tone. It's scary. My father barely ever speaks like this. Only when he has bad news for me.

It's not like Tobias Carter is a bad guy. My father has his moments. He's a great father, and he's been my role model for as long as I can remember. At least when I was a child.

But he also has his aggressive moments. He lets his anger out on the ice though, never on people around him.

Except for his team, that is.

When Tobias Carter is in a bad mood, he tortures his hockey players. That means more intense practice.

"What happened?"

"Your mother had to take Eira to the hospital earlier," he says. "She is alright. Well, as alright as it gets given her state. They let her go back home, but she can't have many visitors these days."

"So you're saying I can't come home to visit her anymore?"

"God, no. Do you know your sister? She would rip our heads off if we no longer let her favorite sibling come visit her."

"So then what are you saying?"

"She won't make it to the game on Friday."

"Jesus. You could have just started with this and then elaborate instead of giving me half a heart attack," I tell him.

"I know you hate it when she can't come to your games—"

I cut him off. "Dad. All that matters is that Eira's condition isn't getting any worse. We can't risk her losing her life. It's bad enough as it is. You really think I would get upset about her missing out on my games, when these are infection catcher?"

He offers me a slim smile before turning me around and slapping his hand between my shoulder blade, dismissing me.

"We're starting off with warm-ups!" He blows his whistle to signal the beginning of practice.

My father urges us to do a way longer warm-up than ever before.

Usually we do some stretches for a couple of minutes, just to get our blood flowing, maybe shooting a puck once for the sake of it. With no goalie. But not this time. Coach Carter has us skate up and down the ice for an hour straight, as fast as we could possibly go. And if we are too slow for his liking, we have to repeat it. Over, and over again.

As two hours pass, most of the guys are sitting on the ice, protesting to go any further. We're working on shooting the puck "the correct way." For some reasons, our goalies choose today to not let even just one in.

See, if this was a game against some other team it would be good, great even. But not letting us, their own teammates, shoot these damn pucks into the goal when we're already close to dying on the ice just sucks balls.

And since the team fails to get even just one puck into the net, Coach Carter continues to push us. "You won't get out of here until all of you goaled at least once," is what he said half an hour ago.

Another hour later, half of the team wants to escape and never step foot on this ice ever again. Or any ice.

"Fine, you go drink something, stay hydrated, and then get your lame asses back out here!" he yells, dismissing us for only five minutes at most.

I watch as my teammates skate toward the exit, running to get some water into their system. I stay on the ice. At least until I catch the same blonde hair, I've seen at the very same spot five days ago.

Lily is here.

"What time is it?" I ask my father.

He checks his phone, saying, "5:42, why?"

"Permission to say hello to someone real quick?"

I watch my father look through the arena, trying to find that *someone* I want to say hello to. When he finally spots Lily, he chuckles, then gestures up and down my body. "You sure you want to say hello to *her*, dressed like *this*?"

"Lily has seen worse days," I say, giving him pleading eyes. If they work for Eira, they should work for me too.

Spoiler: They don't.

"Stop the puppy-dog eyes, kid," he laughs. "You want to go pro, Colin. You can't just leave the ice for some girl."

"But she's not just *some* girl, dad." It's the truth. Lily isn't just someone to me. She's way more than that.

"Two minutes."

I don't waste much time and immediately skate over to the exit on the other side of the ice and run toward Lily. While running, I figure it's a great idea to take off my gloves. These gloves don't allow me too much movement. Or I just want to feel her skin on mine. Either way, I'm okay with taking them off for now.

She doesn't seem to notice me until I'm standing right in front of her.

"Nice outfit," she compliments falsely, biting onto her bottom lip to stop the laugh from slipping out. "You owe me a shirt."

I suck in a sharp breath. "This is yours?"

And finally, the slightest of chuckle slips out from Lily's throat.

She nods. "Aaron called me earlier and asked if I had a cropped top that I don't care about."

"Traitor."

"I like it. This costume suits you."

"Does it now?"

"Don't you have to be on the ice?" Lily asks. "Your teammates are gawking."

"Let them. It's not like we're doing forbidden things here."

"What would that be?"

I don't response. Instead, I look at her. Lily is the kind of person I could look at all day and never get bored. She is unbelievably pretty, but that's not even the point. I just like looking at her for some reasons.

I take Lily's hands in mine, stroking over her knuckles. She has a few bruises on them. I wonder where she got them from, but I don't ask.

"Aren't you cold?" Her green eyes staring into mine. She looks concerned for me, it makes my heart melt.

"Not so much. The moving keeps my body pretty heated."

She responds with a sigh. "Right."

I know Lily used to figure skate. But I don't understand why she stopped when she still loves it.

"I should be out in half an hour. I have to take a shower after practice, but I will hurry up, I promise."

"You certainly need the shower, Mr. Stinky."

"I do. Practice ends in ten minutes. You will wait until I'm back, right?"

"No."

I raise my eyebrows at her. She has to wait, I won't accept anything else. Lily looks away from me, her eyes fixed on my teammates that are probably pressed against the glass to see as much as possible. *Nosy asses.*

I take off my helmet, needing to plant a kiss to Lily's forehead. It has become a move I like to do. At least when it comes to Lily.

Nine Days

"Colin! Get your ass back here!" I hear my father yell, but I refuse to pay him any attention just yet.

"You hear that, dumbass? Your presence is needed on the ice," Lily says.

"Too bad. Because I'd much rather be here with you." I place my index finger underneath her chin, resting my thumb on it at the same time as I tilt her head up for me. I lean down, and just like I've done it before, place a slow and tender kiss onto her forehead. Her skin is warm against my lips, somehow filling my body with an amount of heat I've never felt before.

When I pull away, I notice Lily biting down onto her bottom lip, trying to hide her smile. She fails miserably.

I stroke my thumb over her lips, freeing Lily's bottom lip from her teeth. "Don't hide your smile. It's too pretty to keep it hidden," I whisper.

"You have to go. Coach Carter will get mad."

"He's my father. He will get mad either way."

"Yeah, but this is *your* place, Colin. You belong here. In an arena, playing hockey. You do want to go pro, right?" I nod. "So you should use all the ice time you can get and improve."

"Are you saying I'm bad at what I'm doing?"

"Not at all. But there is always space to improve," she speaks softly.

"PRINCESS FAIRYTALE!" One of my teammates yells. Most likely Grey.

Lily laughs. "I love your new nickname."

"My new nickname is Fairy Godmother. I won't accept anything else," I tell her.

"That's even worse."

I grab Lily's water bottle into my hands and take a few sips. She doesn't seem to mind it. Even if she does, I wouldn't care.

"Not when you call me that." I wink at her and tilt her face to the side. Lily's cheek facing me now.

I bend down just enough so I can kiss her cheek, but Lily has other plans.

My mouth is an inch away from her cheek when Lily turns her head, facing me. "What are—"

Our lips meet. It's totally unwanted and accidental, but I don't want to move away. When her soft lips meet mine, I no longer think about who is around us. All that matters to me is Lily. Lily and her lips that are connected to mine. The same lips that send tingling sparks through my body, multiplying the heat that rose inside of me a minute ago by five.

This is a new feeling for me. I never felt this electricity running through my veins when I kissed someone.

I've heard this could happen. I've read about it, but never experienced it myself. Especially not with such a kindergarten-kiss like this.

Yet it's more than feeling excited. It's more intense, more breathtaking in a different way.

It's *more*.

Everything around me doesn't exist. We're not in a Hockey Arena. We don't have all twenty-one of my teammates, plus my father, watching us kiss.

It's just Lily and me. Two *friends* kissing by accident.

But then why don't I want to leave her lips?

Why do I want to pull her in closer, taste her on my tongue? Why do I want to feel her closer, kiss her harder, deeper?

As much as I loathe having to pull away, I know I have to.

This was an accident. It wasn't supposed to happen. Lily and I weren't supposed to kiss. We're friends. Friends don't kiss.

Her cheeks are flushed when I look at her again. I hope this won't change anything now.

She is clearly embarrassed. I hate that she is.

A part of me is hoping that she felt the same tickles run down her spine, intoxicate her body with me like mine got intoxicated with her. At the same time I am hoping this meant nothing to her. Because if it did, it will complicate the "dates" I've planned.

Are these even considered "dates"?

I'm aware of me joking about all this a lot. I call her my girlfriend to her face sometimes, when I know she is not.

What does this mean? Why do I even really care if she dies or not?

Sure, I care now that I know her better. But why did I care right from the start?

I just bet this is all because of Aiden. He made sure I cared for people, not let myself get lost in fame and money. But Aiden and Lily are two completely different people to me. She wasn't my business, Aiden was. I made her mine to care about, and now she's too important to me to stop.

I want her alive. I need her alive. I need her to breathe, to live. I need her to be here, with Aaron, with her family and friends.

"You'll wait, right?" I repeat my previous question, needing her to tell me she won't run away now.

She clears her throat, looking down to the floor, avoiding my eyes. "I, uh, sure."

"Lily." I sigh. "We didn't mean for this to happen. Let's not make it weird, okay?"

"It's not weird. We're cool."

Something tells me she is lying. She is still avoiding my gaze.

I quickly look toward the ice, seeing my teammates mocking me for what just happened here. Griffin does the basic making-out with oneself move. Aaron is rolling his eyes at me. Grey is smiling like an idiot, knowing me only too well.

Allowing my eyes to wander over to my father, I see him smiling at me knowingly. It's the same smile Grey gives me, just that it's so much more powerful coming from the man I owe everything to.

He waves me off, telling me I'm free to go.

I grab onto Lily's hand, pulling her off the seat. She lets out a shriek but shuts up when I drag her after me. She only starts to protest when I step onto the ice.

"I'm not going on the ice," she says with a warning tone. "Colin, I will bite you."

"You do that, Lilybug." I scoop her up from the ground, holding her up shortly before throwing her over my shoulder and begin to skate over the ice.

She is screaming for me to let her down, but I'm not. Lily doesn't want to touch the ice, so I won't let her touch it. Not yet anyway.

My teammates are catcalling over what is happening. The knowing "*ooh's*" and "*ahh's*" escaping their mouths when I pass them tell me that I will regret this sooner rather than later.

It is definitely a challenge to skate with someone hanging from my shoulder. But it's manageable. Though, if she keeps on pinching my ass, I might drop her.

I swear, Lily Reyes has some strength in her fingers. I always thought Eira was good at pinching me, but Lily tops it all.

By the time I reach the other side of the ice, I swear I will have a bruise on my ass cheek.

"Colin, let her down." Aaron steps in my way, stopping me from moving. Aaron is the only one protesting. The rest of the team is either wooing for me, or just ignore me skating over the ice with a pretty hot girl swung over my shoulder altogether.

"Not going to happen."

"Let me down, Colin!" Lily screams, pinching me once again.

"Fine, you want to walk over the ice in your shoes?" I start to let her down, pulling her back over my shoulder to the front before she eventually stops me.

"Let me down when we're back on *not-ice* territory."

"That's what I thought." I allow myself to chuckle, then make my way to the exit closest to the locker room.

Aaron is still watching me, I can feel his eyes on me, following my every move. I can't blame him. If some guy did this to my sister, I would have beaten him to death. Probably not to death, but close to it.

"No girls in the locker room, Colin!" My father yells after me. It has always been forbidden, I know that. The locker room is the teams' private space. All of our belongings are in there. And well, it's just in general for *us*, not some visitors. But regardless, there's another reasoning behind the "no girls" rule. It's a simple and obvious rule.

No girls, because every hockey player at this school is something different.

But the rule also relies on the name "Zachery Bloom."

I step off the ice, turning my attention toward my father for a slight moment. My hand stays locked in position around Lily's wrist. If I let it go now, she will run away. I won't risk that.

"No bad intentions, dad," I say loud enough for him to hear me. "I promise!"

Chapter 11

"I think I found a flower in a field of weeds?"—
surrender by Billy Talent

Lily

"I'M NOT FIVE, COLIN," I HAVE TO REMIND that douchebag of jock. He is dragging me into this—not at all—nasty locker room. And even worse, he pushes me into a shower cabin, locking the door so I couldn't get away.

For some reasons Colin believes I will run away if he lets me wait outside.

He is right, of course, but I don't want to boost his ego even more. He can't know that he is already pretty good at reading me like a book. And besides, it scares me that he can.

Colin strips from his clothes, stepping into another shower cabin. The one right opposite of where he holds me prisoner. Thank God for the shower cabin doors that cover just the right places. Well, I wouldn't mind seeing a bit more of his torso. I sense this guy being muscular, who wouldn't want to look at that?

And like I somewhat expected, Colin Carter has tattoos on his chest as well. His tattoos aren't connected. They're more like a ton of tiny, sometimes a little bigger, alone standing ones.

"You're not," he agrees, to my surprise. "But Lilybug, I saw the embarrassment flash in your eyes after the kiss. Knowing you, you're about to bail when I give you the chance to. No way in hell will I let that happen."

Did he have to remind me of the kiss? It's bad enough that I actually enjoyed that silly thing. It wasn't even a good kiss. A middle-schooler could share a better kiss with someone if they tried to.

Colin and my lips touched for about two seconds, maybe five. It wasn't some deep shit. And it was totally involuntary. He wanted to kiss my cheek, not my lips. If I hadn't moved my head, this would not have happened.

But I also kind of wanted it to continue.

Now all I feel is embarrassment and regret.

"I wasn't going to bail." I cross my arms in front of my chest. "This kiss meant absolutely nothing. I was embarrassed, but only because it was so surprising. And surprisingly bad, too."

"Totally agree with that one," he says. "Shared better kisses in my life before." Damned if that doesn't evoke something inside of me. It can't be jealousy, that I know for sure. Anger, maybe? Or maybe it *is* jealously.

How would I know? The only times I've ever felt jealous was connected to anger. So I suppose it could be both after all.

"Not the worst either," Colin adds after a short while.

He looks at me over the partition door. His arms resting on the top of the door while his chin lies on his arms. Colin offers me a charming smile, winking when I finally meet his gaze.

"What kiss could have possibly been any worse?"

"Middle school. My very first one."

"Oh my God. You weren't born as the asshole with an ego through the roof?" I ask, raising my eyebrows at him in surprise, though, most of my "surprise" is fake.

He grins at me. "Didn't say that."

"Your very first kiss was bad," I remind him. "Meaning you weren't always good at your own game."

"It's not my own game, Lilybug." He shrugs. "Kissing was a thing way before I was born." Sometimes I really do hate this man. "And I sure was great. She wasn't." There he is again. The asshole deep inside of him.

"Of course, it's always anyone but you."

"Precisely."

I narrow my eyes at him, about to open my mouth to talk when I hear voices. Voices that grow louder with every second. "I don't want to be here for the sausage-party," I tell Colin.

Grinning, Colin grabs a towel and wraps it around his waist before exiting his shower stall. He walks over to mine and unlocks it. For some reasons this arena, locker rooms included, is the fanciest ice hockey arena I have ever seen. These showers are lockable. I'm talking full on *passcode* needing locks.

But that's not even the highlight yet. They have Wi-Fi in here. Like they would actually need it. Surely no one has access to it, except for the hockey team, of course. But this arena still has so much more to offer, I couldn't even count it all if I wanted to.

- 149 -

"About time." I push his arm away when he tries to grab me, making my way to the exit of the shower room.

"I wouldn't walk out there without me going first, unless you do want to run into that, what did you call it? Sausage-party."

I sigh in defeat. He is probably right. I mean, he knows his team better than I do after all.

I am certain these guys don't care about running around naked in front of the other. They're basically family. Anyone can see that.

Colin walks out first, followed by me so close behind, I bet he can feel my breath on his muscular back.

Is it weird that I want to touch him? That I want to trace my finger along the lines of his tattoos? Most definitely weird.

"Any of you naked yet?" Colin asks, coming to a stop. I bump into him, gasping as the cold of the water still covering his body hits me. "Lily's here."

"Put your dick away, Green!" I hear someone yell, followed by a round of laughter. "You too, Simms!" A moment later, the same guy speaks again. "You're good, Carter."

Colin grabs my hand, turning to face me just to grin at me, he then leads me back into the locker room where the guys are getting changed—or undressed.

"Would it hurt you to leave your chicks outside?" A guy with reddish hair asks, chuckling as he walks past Colin and me. "You know the rules, big guy."

"Fuck off, Simms." Colin flips Simms off. "Ignore Jackson, he's the main asshole."

"Ignore Colin," Miles shouts from the other side of the room. His hands are giving the illusion of a megaphone around his mouth. "*I* am the main asshole!" At least he is being honest. I can't help a chuckle from slipping out.

Colin leads me to what I assume is his locker. "Take a seat," he says, motioning to the bench on the opposite side of the locker he just opened. I do as I'm told, not really feeling comfortable with at least eleven pairs of eyes staring at me.

I don't dare looking around the room, so my eyes stay focused on the floor in front of me. That is until someone takes a seat beside me, swinging his arm around my shoulders.

"Please tell me you will continue to lead him on just a while longer," Aaron whispers into my ear. I'm sure he's eying Colin as he waits for me to answer. When I don't, he tells me why he hopes that. "He's got it bad, Lils. Everyone can see it. And it's hilarious."

He does?

That's not good at all.

Unfortunately, yet also fortunately in this situation, Aaron loves to mess with me. So I refuse to believe his words. Back in high school, Aaron used to tell me a lot about some guys "having it bad" for me. It was never the truth. Turns out, Aaron went through the rebellion-puberty-phase at that time. He was messing with everyone around him.

But he's not a teenager hitting puberty anymore. He's a grown man. More or less grown with his almost twenty-one years of living.

From the corner of my eye, I notice the towel from Colin's hips fall down to the floor. I know he dropped it on purpose to get dressed, yet it's still weird.

With just one look to the side, I would catch his bare ass staring at me. A sight I'm intrigued to see, yet I'm also not really interested in that. He can show his ass to some of those puck bunnies, I'm sure they would enjoy the sight.

"Anyway—" Aaron clears his throat as he stands up from the bench "—have a great evening with Carter." With that said, Aaron makes his way to the shower room. So do most of the other guys.

Strange, he once mentioned hating the more-or-less private showers.

It is pretty scary being the only girl among twenty-two guys. If Aaron and Colin wouldn't have been here, I'm sure my mind would have played through some horror scenarios.

At least now it's only Colin and I left…and maybe one or two other guys.

My eyes stay focused on the floor again, not sure if it's safe to look up yet. It should be, Colin had enough time to at least put on some underwear. My gaze remains where it's one hundred per cent safe anyway.

That is until Colin bends down and his face sneaks into my vision.

"You there?" he asks bemused, waving his hands in front of my face.

I must have been in some kind of trance because I don't remember Colin speaking to me before this. At least I snapped out of it eventually.

"I sure am." I follow his figure up as he straightens his back. "I just don't want to be there."

"Lilybug," Colin sighs, trailing off into a groan, lifting his face to the ceiling. "Okay, this is only the second day. Give me some more credit."

"For what?" I ask. I'm pretty sure a wrinkle appears on my forehead as I frown.

"Trying. I have so much more planned. You don't even give me a chance to prove to you that you will enjoy our time together."

"I can enjoy the time I spend with someone and still want to die," I say, whispering. "Can we talk about this elsewhere?"

He nods. "We're going to a bar tonight," he informs me.

"Hell no. It's Wednesday. I have classes tomorrow," I protest.

"So do I, Lilybug. Some fun won't hurt. It's not like you have much to lose anyway."

"Fine. One hour, then you'll take me home."

HE TRICKED ME. We're not going to a bar, Colin takes me home with him. Which only makes it worse. I'd much rather be at a college sports bar called *Brites* than spend a whole evening at his house.

"You can go upstairs if you like," Colin says, walking off toward the open kitchen. "My room is the first door on the right."

"I don't want to go to your room." I tsk, following him into the kitchen.

"Aaron's is the first door on the left, opposite of mine, maybe you want to examine his stuff instead."

"I can live without knowing his dirty secrets. Thank you," I speak dryly in response.

Colin beams an innocent smile at me, leaning against the kitchen counter. "I have three options for you. Option 1: We order pizza. Option 2: We're cooking together. Or option 3: I make some sandwiches."

"I'm not hungry."

"Well, sucks for you. I am, and you haven't eaten anything today. So you will eat if you want to or not."

"Is that why I'm here?" I ask. And how the hell does he know I haven't eaten anything? Is he stalking me?

No, he wouldn't. He's just attentive, I suppose.

It's weird suddenly having someone keeping an eye on you after years of not having *anyone* care one bit. I mean, sure, Aaron always cared about me, always asked how I'm doing…but he never paid too much attention to me. Not that he has to.

"You're here because I want you here, Lilybug." There is a pause, but he also doesn't continue speaking. Colin changes the subject. "So, choose one."

"What kind of sandwiches?"

"I guess cream cheese with jelly. I loved it when I was little, it's one of the only things I know how to make."

"Cream cheese with jelly?" I repeat, wanting to make sure I got that right. He nods. "Why?"

"Don't tell me you've never tried it."

"I haven't, but I guess I will," I say, whining.

"So you're just hating on great food without ever having had it before?" He fakes a gasp, holding his hand over his heart.

"I'm not really a jelly fan," I admit. "I also never had a peanut butter and jelly sandwich. I just don't like it."

"Then why would you choose the one option with jelly?" he asks, pushing himself away from the counter.

"It's the cheapest option." I raise my shoulders in a shrug.

Colin exhales a long breath. Kind of like he is trying not to say some really stupid words.

His eyes remain glued to mine, even when he walks over to me. He grabs me by my wrist, forcing me to follow him upstairs.

"We're ordering Pizza," he informs me as we step into his bedroom. It's big, and tidier than I expected. Definitely tidier than my room.

My floor is decorated with books, papers and clothes, his is free of *decorations*.

"Colin," I start, but stop myself before continuing. How do I tell someone I barely know that I can't afford Pizza anymore?

I already donated most of what I had to charities when I decided I don't want to live any longer. It's not like I was going to need it anymore.

"I'm paying, don't worry." He looks at me with a huge question mark on his forehead. "You're my guest."

"I don't like people paying for my food."

"So then, what is it? You don't like Pizza?"

"No." I chuckle. "I do. I just can't afford it these days."

"How?" His eyebrows draw together. "That sounds superficial, I know. But it's Pizza? And I know your family has money."

"Wrong," I tell him. "My father has money. Ergo, Aaron lives the rich life. I, on the contrary, live off of $450 a month, which is more than enough, usually."

Colin looks at me in shock. He doesn't move, doesn't speak, doesn't even breathe, I think.

I get it though. Colin grew up rich, he was born into the fancy life. And I believe his allowance is higher than what my mom makes monthly.

"My mother is a middle school teacher. She has like, what? $4000 per month?"

"That's not too bad." He pauses. "You're here on a scholarship?" Another pause. "Oh God. I sound like an arrogant jerk, don't I?"

With lips pressed together into a thin line, I not slowly. "Pretty much."

"I'm sorry," he says. "I didn't mean to offend you or anything. I'm genuinely asking, though. Are you here on a scholarship?"

"No, Colin. I keep getting the amount I pay for tuition send to my bank account monthly. It's from someone I don't know, but I'm assuming it's from my mother. She used to feel bad for me taking on two jobs to pay for it myself. The next month, payments came in from a name I don't recognize. I think she's working a second job to pay for it herself. She would never admit to it, which is why I never asked. I kept one job for some money to live off of but quit the other. Now, a week ago I quit my only other job as well because I really don't need it anymore." *Oversharing much.*

"So, if $450 usually works just fine, how come you can't afford Pizza?"

"Donated all I had left to a charity."

"Well, that means Aaron will pay for our food." How does this come out of whatever I just said?

I know I am bad at math, but this equation doesn't add up.

"His details are still saved in my phone from yesterday. He won't mind."

"Bullshit. He will. It's his money."

"Lilybug, this household here doesn't know 'it's his money,'" he tells me. "I'm pretty sure Aaron once bought a whole new bed for himself using my card."

"You guys are weird." And I stand by that.

Chapter 12

"be my friend, hold me"—Breathe Me by Sia

Colin

"Colin!"

I guess I'm awake now.

"What the hell, Aaron." Aaron is standing by my bedroom door, leaning against the doorframe. I struggle to look at him as my eyes still have to get used to the light.

"It's eight in the goddamn morning!" he yells, stepping into my room. "You've missed morning practice!"

Oh shit. Not again.

"You could have woken me up, you know."

"No." He fake-gags. "I preferred not walking in on you and my sister."

"Walk in on me and Lily?" Right. She stayed the night. Took a lot of convincing to do, but she stayed.

It was already 11 p.m. when she wanted to leave because she was tired. But we were in the middle of a movie marathon. With that I mean she made me watch *Twilight*. Apparently, it's very educational.

It's not.

All I learned is that a way too old Vampire guy falls in love with some way younger human girl. It's not exactly what I would consider interesting, but Lily could ask me to watch *Titanic* five times in a row and I would do it.

"Dude, you know Lily and I aren't actually dating, right?"

"You're not?" Aaron takes a seat by my desk. He stares at me dumbstruck, waiting for what? confirmation?

"We're not. We're just hanging out, as friends."

"Friends my ass." He lets out one loud laugh, crossing his arms in front of his chest. "When I came back home last night and wanted to ask you something, you were all cuddled up together. That's not exactly screaming 'friends.'"

"Cuddled up together?" I repeat. I don't recall being cuddled up to Lily.

Aaron shrugs, leaving me sort of clueless. "She's downstairs, by the way, making breakfast for all of us."

I sit up, narrowing my eyes at Aaron.

"Chill, Lily loves to cook. Neither of us asked her to." Once again, he chuckles. He turns in my chair, facing my gaming setup. I don't usually play games, I don't have much time for it, but I never got rid of it either. "Miles is totally digging her. It's so annoying."

Now that gets more of my attention than anything Aaron said before.

In less than a heartbeat, I'm standing on my feet, finding myself sprinting downstairs. No way in hell will I let Miles King get close to my girl.

She's not even *my girl*. But to hell with it anyway. Lily doesn't need Miles clinging to her ass.

"MILES!" Even I'm surprised by my tone. I never scream at my friends, ever. Except on the ice, but that's a different kind of screaming. It's not filled with anger…mostly, anyway.

Lily is standing in front of the stove, wearing nothing but a t-shirt that is only roughly hanging over her ass. She is swaying her hips to some music. And, of course, Miles is enjoying the show.

I love that guy, but if he dares touching what's mine, I will have to cut off some hands.

She's not yours, I have to remind myself. I ignore my own reminder though. She is mine, for a long as she is alive.

"Good morning, captain never-showing-up," Miles greets me. "That's going to be another day of the fairy costume."

"Like I care," I snap.

"Someone's a bit grumpy."

"Fuck off." I make my way over to Lily. She is making pancakes. It smells delicious. But to hell with food right now.

"Be so kind and take care of these for a moment," I tell Grey as I scoop Lily up from the floor, throwing her over my shoulder.

She yelps, hitting her hands against my lower back, telling me to set her back down. But I don't. Instead, I carry her back upstairs into my bedroom.

At least I don't have to deal with Aaron right now. He was smart enough to leave my bedroom.

I set Lily down on the floor once I closed the door behind us. "Stay right there," I say in a strict tone, walking toward my closet.

"You're not my father, you know."

"Aware of that." I look though my clothes, trying to find anything she could wear. "There is still no need for you to shake your ass in front of Miles. Not like that."

I take out one of my hockey jerseys, knowing they will be way bigger on Lily than the t-shirt she is wearing.

"Jealous?"

"Furious." I put her arms up once I'm standing back in front of her, pulling the jersey over her body.

"You can't be mad at Miles for being there."

"I'm not," I tell her, still feeling my blood boil. "Miles is like a brother to me. I would share anything with him. Anything but you."

"You don't own me."

"I don't," I agree. "Doesn't mean I appreciate him gawking at you."

"He wasn't gawking," she protests. "Miles is actually fun to hang up with, you know."

"Jesus, Lily!" I brush my hands through my hair in frustration. "If you want to fuck him, just ask him. Trust me, he will be in your pants in a heartbeat."

I expect Lily to freak out on me. But she isn't. I know I went too far with saying what I had, yet she doesn't seem mad.

"Can you take me home?" Lily sounds…upset. Her voice trembling, and when I look at her, she's quivering.

Is she afraid of me now? *What have I done?*

Panic streams through my system. I don't want Lily to be afraid of me. "Lily," I say quietly, sighing. She looks at me with fear in her eyes. It breaks my fucking heart.

"Colin, please. I want to go home."

I FOLLOW LILY to the dorm rooms, walking her inside. I don't want to leave her just yet. We haven't exchanged a single word after she told me she wanted to go home.

The tension between us has never been this thick. It's almost painful.

At least she doesn't complain when I walk her inside.

"I'll see you in class then, huh?" I offer her an awkward smile, she returns none.

"Yup." Unlocking the room door, she steps inside but she doesn't close it yet. "Are you not coming in?"

"Do you want me to?"

"I don't know," she admits, awkwardly. It hasn't even been this awkward after our involuntary kiss.

"I should go then," I say. "You're not sure if you want me here, that's an obvious 'leave, Colin.'"

"Colin, I like your company. But this is awkward, and I hate it."

"I'll see you in class," I tell her. "Oh, you like coffee, right?"

"I do," Lily answers. The confusion is written all over her face. I don't blame her. It is an odd question.

"I'm taking you coffee tasting later."

She starts to laugh, leaning her head against the door for support. "I've heard of wine tasting, cake tasting, even soup tasting. But never once did I hear someone say, 'I went coffee tasting.'"

"It will be fun, trust me."

She has a point though. Coffee tasting isn't something a lot of people do. Might as well be a one out of one thousand situation. But driving around the city, going to taste every coffee the café has to offer sounds like fun. And like a lot of caffeine.

Caffeine aside, we will find the best coffee in the city. That way Lily and I can have a spot. *Our* spot, with the best coffee.

That being said, I say goodbye to Lily and leave to get back home.

I need to take a shower before classes start. And I need to call my father to beg for forgiveness. Okay, I don't have to beg for it. All I really have to do is tell him why I missed morning practice.

I could so easily tell my father about Lily. Tell him what she is going through. He would excuse me for the rest of the week, maybe even the next as well.

But given that Lily is suicidal, he would try to contact her parents. And I can't have him do that. Lily would murder me.

Chapter 13

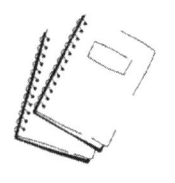

"it kills me how your mind could make you feel so worthless"—Before You Go by Lewis Capaldi

Lily

Dear whoever reads this,

Colin is taking me coffee tasting in a short while.
I don't even know what I am supposed to wear to that.
Do I dress up? Wear sweats and a baggy shirt?
It's complicated. Frustrating even.
I still have his jersey. I might wear it. It smells like him, I like it.
To think that Colin does this to show me that life is worth living is also frustrating.
Today's morning, he seemed so mad at me, or Miles, perhaps. Either way, he was jealous. I know he was.
But that's scaring me.
What if Colin likes me more than I thought? (That can't be)
This can't happen. I can't do this to Colin.

*He deserves better than a suicidal girlfriend.
We're not even a couple, and I still think he deserves better than me.
He still wants to save me.
It's only day three. I should have more faith in him. But I don't even want to believe in saving.
Imagine how embarrassing it would get.
"Oh, I will stay alive, thank you, Colin."
"No worries."
And then we're both going separate ways.
Forever.
Awkwardly stare at the other from across the room.
Awkwardly nod a hello.
Awkwardly say congratulations at graduation.
No, thank you.
I couldn't even continue to live if I wanted to.
Even if he shows me there's more to live for, the pain would still be there.
I don't want to die because I don't think there is more to life, but it's the pain that makes me want to leave.
I don't want to continue to feel empty.
I don't want to be numb anymore.
I want to feel joy.
I want to feel love; be loved and love someone.
But I can't.
It's all...numb.
Nothing but nothingness.
I know there are people that love me.
Like Aaron and my dad. Even Ana and Liz.
But it's not the same love I desire.
It's not the same love that makes me act like a little girl.
It's not the same love that makes me lose my mind.*

Nine Days

I've never felt that kind of love. I have always been too numb for it, I suppose.
And now it's too late.
No one could love me back to life. I can't even love myself back to life.
I can't expect anyone saving me when I can't even save myself.
I'm like a ticking bomb.
I can explode any second, destroying everything and everyone around me.
Not with an outburst of emotions. But with my death.
My family will be devasted, I know they will be.
But I don't care.
That's the part that irks me the most.
I don't care that I will hurt my family with my death.
And Colin?
I bet he will be sad. Or so I kind of hope he will be.
He devoted nine days of his life to me.
Nine days of showing me why I should stay alive.
And he will lose.
He will wonder if this is his fault.
I mean, he knows it's not.
But we all know what this is going to do to him.
He will wonder if he could have done just one thing differently, taken me to one other location to save my life.
But he couldn't. Colin, you couldn't.
This is about me.
I want to die because I can't live with me being me.
I can't live with me.
I can't live with my emotions, or the ones that are left.
I used to be so good at sleeping.
And now I can't even do that anymore.

It's tiring. Really.
My thoughts are killing me. Literally.
I can't stand this anymore.
I am not that strong.
I fought this for so long.
I took so many medications to fight it.
Nothing helped.
Nothing is helping.
I want to leave.
Please just let me leave.
Dying in vain doesn't sound so bad when you see the positive side.
I won't have to suffer anymore.
I will be a free soul. No more crying at night.
No more pain.
No more numbness.
I finally found a way out. I am no longer trapped.
And I will never be gone.
I will always be around, watching over the people I love.
That's what one says, right?
Spirit world sounds peaceful.
Wandering around as a spirit, doing some mischief.
That sounds lovely.

Lily

Chapter 14

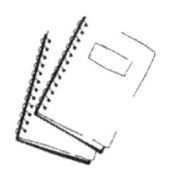

"I'll bring you coffee with a kiss on your head"—Say You Won't Let Go by James Arthur

Lily

"Nope, this one is nasty!" Colin spits his sip of coffee back into the cup.

I laugh. This is the fifth coffee he has done this to.

Since we're taking these coffee's to-go, nobody ever sees Colin's hideous way of tasting them. To his own luck. If the staff member were to see the way he spits his coffee back into the cup, I'd assume he'd get banned from the coffee shop in no time.

We've already been to six cafés. I, for my part, liked four of them. They weren't the best, but I also had worse coffees before.

Colin, on the contrary, he hates every single one. Except for the very first coffee we've tried.

"I like it," I tell him.

Colin made up two rules. *"Don't drink too much"* and *"we're only buying one coffee per café with the same amount of milk and sugar."*

It makes sense. We have at least ten more cafés to visit, and I would prefer not dying from too much caffeine intake. That would be a sad way to go.

It definitely is a waste of money and coffee anyway. I hate that. Colin promised he would take the cups home and serve them to the guys though.

I wonder if he will give them the ones he spat in as well. It certainly would be hilarious to know my brother drank a coffee that contained Colin's spit.

Disgusting, but hilarious.

"How? This one is even worse than the one we had before."

"It's not," I protest.

"It is, Lilybug."

"I would try it again, but I prefer drinking coffee without saliva in it."

"I just saved your life, you're welcome."

Colin starts to drive again, making our way toward the next destination.

"Who's your favorite musician?" I ask in need for this silence to be gone.

I usually don't mind silence. And the one between Colin and me isn't awkward. But ever since today's morning it's just weird. But so is talking.

Yet I still enjoy his company.

And although I have to admit to this coffee tasting being completely unnecessary and stupid, it actually is quite fun.

"Don't think I have a favorite. However, I do listen to *Chase Atlantic* a lot," he answers.

My eyebrows raise without me being able to control it. "I really can't picture you sitting in this car while vibing to *PLEASEXANNY*," I laugh.

Colin shakes his head and throws his phone into my lap. "Connect it with my car and open my playlist, I'll show you."

My mouth stays open and for a moment I just look at him dumbfounded. He tells me his passcode and eventually I do open his music app. He has five different playlists. The very last being titled "Alone-Time."

"Seriously?" I click onto the playlist only to find it filled with Chase Atlantic songs.

I hit play and *Falling* starts to play. And so suddenly, I'm spending the next four minutes watching, laughing, while Colin is pouring his heart out, singing along to the lyrics.

At some point I join in, now going with a duet. I don't even care that I can't sing.

When the next song comes up, we're both laughing.

"Aw, shit," Colin mutters under his breath. "I could go for some McDonalds."

I look out of every window, trying to figure out how the hell he thought of food.

Turning the volume down, I say, "I don't like McDonalds."

"God dammit, Reyes!" He is shocked, much to my amusement. I'm sure if he wasn't driving, he would look at me with those huge blue eyes, boring into my soul. "Tell me you're kidding!"

"Not kidding."

"Aw, hell." He exhales a deep breath. "Like, nothing that they have on their menu?"

"Nothing at all," I admit.

"How?"

"I don't know. I personally just don't like the flavor."

"The flavor of burgers?" he asks incredulously.

"No, but their sauces. And I don't like their consistency. It's weird to me."

"McDonalds is a lifesaver," he objects. "Not only is it affordable, it's also good for its price."

"So is KFC."

"So, you like KFC but loathe McDonalds?"

"I've never been to KFC before," I admit, laughing awkwardly.

The car stops at a red light. The second the car comes to a hold he turns, eyes on me, holding a gaze of irritation and uncertainty.

"Have you been living under a rock?" His mouth stands open, not for one second does he believe me telling the truth.

"Some people prefer homecooked meals," I say, avoiding to look at him. I find it much more appealing to look at trees right now.

"Alright."

Colin and I are walking into the next café, diner fits it better. It has a retro touch to it, I like it. It has the typical black and white tiled floor. Red seating booths, and red chairs for normal table seats. The front bar has white tiles and red countertops, fitting to the red and metal barstools.

I never even knew New City had a diner like this.

"I love this," I say under my breath. My eyes wander around the room, taking in the stereotypical movie ambience this place brings.

And I truly feel like I'm in some kind of Hollywood romance movie. The only thing missing is the cold and rainy weather while it is also dark outside.

I certainly have the guy of someone's dreams here with me.

All this is so mesmerizing to me. I don't even realize when Colin takes a seat at one of the booths. All I do is stand in the middle of the diner, staring around myself like a fool.

But when I snap back to reality, I see Colin videotaping me. I don't even question it anymore. I know he needs those for our project that I have no knowledge of.

"Excuse me?" A black-haired young woman taps onto my shoulder. "I love your outfit."

Her hair is straight, but one can see it's been straightened and that's not its natural state. She has beautiful eyes, dark and mysterious. I feel like this girl right here is someone trustworthy.

But then again, I tend to trust brown-eyed people more.

"Oh, my God. Thank you." A smile appears on my lips. Compliments about outfits are the best. "I love yours, too."

The girl is wearing a white, skintight, satin dress, showing quite the amount of cleavage as well. It's beautiful, with no doubt. But I personally wouldn't wear this to a diner. A club for sure. But hell, she can pull it off.

The white of her dress glows on her skin, and it's absolutely stunning. *She* looks absolutely stunning.

My outfit, on the other hand, is completely boring compared to hers. I did decide to wear Colin's jersey. Why? I don't know. I was hoping he would comment on it, think it was adorable. But he didn't, much to my dismay. And I paired it with some black leggings and sneakers.

So like I said, nothing fancy. I wonder why she likes it.

"You're a hockey fan?" she asks, flashing me a big white smile.

"I guess I have to be," I say, shrugging. "My brother is one of the hockey players at St. Trewery U." I have never said that out loud. Well, if you don't count telling Colin that Aaron is my brother.

"For real?" Her eyes widen in shock. "That must be exhausting."

I decide to just offer her a slim smile. I never felt like Aaron being a hockey player was exhausting. But then, I also didn't exactly grow up with him. Perhaps Ana thinks differently.

"What's your name?" I ask instead of answering.

"Kya Young," she says, smiling. "What's yours?" I feel like starting another possible friendship isn't something I should be doing. But Kya seems genuinely nice.

"Lily Reyes," I answer. "Are you here all by yourself?"

She lets out a sad sigh, then plasters a smile back onto her face. "I am. I had a date, but he stood me up."

"Such a dick," I say. "You can eat with Colin and me if you want." I point toward Colin. I doubt he would mind.

"I prefer not to tag along on someone else's date."

"This isn't a date." I laugh. "Colin and I have a bet going. We're just friends."

"So that's why you're wearing Colin Carter's hockey jersey, huh?" She smirks, raising her eyebrows. "But…we can exchange numbers, hang some other time. I'm sure we will see each other on campus, now that we met."

"You're a St. Trewery student?"

"Yup. I study architecture," she answers. "I'm not sure why I attend some classes. Our construction technology professor only has eyes for Aaron Marsh."

These are a lot of information to give to a stranger.

"I swear, she grades him A's for his looks."

I look over to Colin, only to find him staring at me. He has this questioning look printed on all over his face.

Kya and I end up exchanging numbers. She doesn't stay to eat with Colin and me, like she said she wouldn't.

I guess, if I didn't have this huge plan of my death right in front of me, I would actually love having Kya as a great friend of mine. She seems like a hell lot of fun.

Kya leaves after hugging me goodbye like we've known each other for years.

"Seems like Kya likes you," Colin says as I take a seat across from him. I blink at him like I'm in some sort of trance, trying to make up a story as to how he knows her. Every single one I could think of ends up with them having dated at some point in life.

I hate that I even think about it. I shouldn't care.

"She's stopping by at my parents' house every other day, tutoring Eira." A smile tugs onto his lips as if he knew being in the dark about their relationship bothers me.

Colin's hand reaches over the table, lying on top of mine, giving it a reassuring squeeze. A surprisingly comforting squeeze I never knew I needed.

"Lilybug." His voice is raspy, kind of as if he's fighting the urge to spit some words out. I wonder what words those would be. Then a low guttural sound comes out of his throat, throwing his head back into his neck.

"What's wrong?"

He appears to have some internal conflict going on. He adjusts his head, his eyes flickering between mine, my lips and our hands.

"What the hell are we doing?"

"You're trying to make my life less miserable for the amount of time I have left." I offer an awkward smile. Truth is, I have no idea is going on.

Ever since that accidental kiss at the arena, there is this certain warmth in my chest whenever I look at him. I feel safe around him. But to hell with what that could mean.

His head bobs, chuckling as he tries to find words to say. He's as much at a loss for words as I am.

"Maybe we should stop," I suggest, pulling my hand away from underneath his. At least I try to.

Colin's fingers wrap around my hand, digging into my skin until it is almost painful, keeping my hand from leaving his.

"Stop what?" He doesn't even acknowledge his hand squeezing mine. "Stop trying to get you to see a more colorful world? Stop trying to pretend that I don't want to kiss you? Stop trying to ignore that I'm hard as a rock right now, only because I am touching your hand?"

I gasp. Jesus, how can he say stuff like that so casually?

"Stop playing with me. That's not funny."

"I'm not joking, jeez."

This has definitely taken a turn I wasn't expecting.

Colin was supposed to pretend he could make me fall back in love with life. He was supposed to give me a couple more good days, not complicate it with some attraction.

"Just forget it," he says, withdrawing his hand from mine. "You're right. It was a bad joke."

Damned if that doesn't burn in my lungs as I suck in a sharp breath. He was joking, dammit. How does one joke about...that?

Just in time, a brunette waitress approaches us. I'm glad she does, otherwise I would have probably started to cry.

"What can I get for you today?" she asks in a sweet tone, holding her notebook right in front of her. Her name tag reads "Miriam." She looks friendly, but also kind of like she is about lose her shit.

And despite her friendly appearance, I can't help but notice the hungry look she beams at Colin. He doesn't even acknowledge it.

"Not a clue, can you recommend anything?" Colin looks up from the menu, but he doesn't look at her. Instead, his eyes are on me.

"Would you want something light, or something for a bigger hunger?" She's looking at me this time. Clearly she got the hint that Colin wasn't going to pay her any more attention.

"Not sure what he prefers, but I would take something lighter."

She beams a smile. "Sure. How about the Chicken Salad Croissant?" she suggests, then proceeds to tell me what it is made of.

"Sounds good. Also, could I get a blueberry-cheesecake muffin?" Miriam nods, writing down my order. "Colin?"

For the first time since Miriam approached us, he looks at her, allowing himself to appear friendly enough. "Do you have burgers?"

"Yes, but our menu is small. We only offer three different ones."

"What's the best one?"

"I would have to say the Hickory Burger."

"Great." Colin fake-smiles. "I'll have one of those. And I will take fries with it."

Miriam nods and writes down our food orders. "Would you like something to drink?"

Colin and I are both quiet. His eyes are back on mine, boring holes into my soul. At least until he cracks a smile.

"We'll have a water each. And one coffee, two packs of sugar and about"—he holds his thumb and index finger up to Miriam—"this much milk."

In an attempt to fight my laughter, I bite my lip. It doesn't help much, because a chuckle still manages to escape from my throat.

This one little chuckle triggers Colin to the point where he breaks out in laughter as soon as Miriam leaves. Which then causes me to laugh.

Chapter 15

"so go and break up my relationships and break my fucking heart"—PLEASEXANNY by Chase Atlantic

Colin

"You're not coming inside?" Lily asks as I walk her to her dorm. I just stand by her door, watching her as she steps inside, not even attempting to follow her in.

This is giving me a really bad feeling of déjà vu.

I shake my head. I can't go inside. If I do, I'm not sure I will be able to control myself for much longer.

Today has been such a fun day. Tasting a million coffees doesn't sound like too much fun, but it sure is.

Lily and I even ended up declaring that Retro Diner as our new favorite. It may be half an hour away from campus, but their burgers are totally worth it.

We were supposed to find the best coffee in the city. And we did. Lily and I didn't even need to drive around to find a better one. We both knew the coffee we shared at the diner was a total winner.

Okay, maybe the burger was what convinced me to vote for it, doesn't mean the coffee was bad. The Retro Diner has a great coffee. It's not watery, not too strong either. It's perfect. *So are the burgers.*

And besides, it looks pretty damn cool. Not only does it make you feel like you're stuck in a time machine. Or as Lily phrased it "makes you feel like you're in a Hollywood teen romance movie," it is freaking awesome.

I don't think I will ever be able to go there without taking Lily with me. This is what "having a spot" means, right? A place you share a really great memory with someone else with.

If so, then this is totally it.

I wonder if Lily will write about it in her journal. Never mind, she only writes about her bad emotions and why she wants to die. Why she *will* die, apparently.

Lily still insists on me saying "when you will die." She refuses to let me get through to her. But then again, I know nothing about dealing with suicidal thoughts, nor depression. Maybe this is just what comes with it.

Anyway, after we left the diner, I convinced Lily to come back home with me. I promised to let my friends try the coffees after all, so they wouldn't go to waste. And much to our amusement, I didn't tell any of them I spit in most of them.

They were cold, so even less drinkable than before.

Lily went nuts with laughter when Aaron took a sip from my least favorite coffee. The very one I spit into not once, but twice. Had to get the taste out of my mouth somehow.

When he said, "It's not even that bad," even I lost it. Not going to lie, hearing your spit tastes "not even that bad" is a real ego boost.

"Why not?" Lily sounds disappointed.

"I will regret it." I slide my hands into the pockets of my jeans, slightly lifting my shoulders before I let them drop down.

She cocks an eyebrow at me, not understanding.

I hate this. I hate that I can't just walk up to her like; "Hey, let's fuck" as I would with any other girl at a party. If I do this with Lily, not only would she throw me out of the window, so would Aaron.

But that's not even what scares me. What scares me is her reaction, how she will act the next few days. I'm afraid things would get weird.

I can't help my groan as I try to come up with a great reason. "Lilybug." I run my hands through my hair, tugging at the ends of it, frustration streaming through my system.

"Have I done something?" Concern sweeps through her voice like wind sweeps through the air.

"It's what I haven't done," I answer, only confusing her more.

"What haven't you done?"

"Aaron warned me." My voice is soft and euphoric, yet I sound tired, uncomfortable. Even I can hear it. "I shouldn't have gotten so close to you."

"Why not?"

Maybe I should be straight forward with her. It's so early in our friendship, but I also can't lose time. Our days are numbered, at least until she comes to her senses.

"Because now I can't stop thinking about your lips." I storm past Lily, walking inside her living room. I grab onto her wrist on my way in, pulling her after me.

I have never felt like this before. I have never been frustrated because I wanted a girl, and yet here I am. Lily being the only person running through my mind, especially in times when she shouldn't.

We're entering her room. I practically push her inside, locking the door when I follow her in.

I try to breathe like a normal person. Try to control my urge to jump her, press my lips to hers and kiss the hell out of this woman.

"Are you okay?" Her sweet voice streams through my ears like classical music, flowing, easing my nerves.

I don't answer. I don't even react at all. All I do is stand, with my back pressed against her closed door, inhaling deep breaths, exhaling even deeper, longer.

I can't fucking do this anymore.

And then she steps closer. With every step she takes I feel like the air is getting thinner. *I can't fucking breathe.*

"Take one more step toward me and I will have to pinch you up against the door."

She freezes. "Colin, what the hell is happening?" She demands an answer I cannot provide her with, sounding louder and austere.

My behavior is freaking her out and I can't even blame her. I would be freaked out as well.

Uneasiness rises inside of me. God, she is so beautiful. How have I never seen her before? We've shared some classes for years. How have I never laid eyes on her?

She takes another step closer, clearly ignoring my warning from just a second ago.

"Lily, I mean it."

"So pinch me against the goddamn door. As long as you're talking to me, I will take it." She comes closer to me, making it even harder to breathe.

"Tell me something depressing," I beg. "Talk about your death."

Lily snorts a laugh, coming to a hold right in front of me. Her head tilts back enough so her eyes can meet mine. The hope and amusement in her green eyes have me melt on the spot.

"You think it's depressing that I want to die?" Then she corrects herself, "That I will die next week."

"How could I not?"

Her hands come in contact with my chest, blood rushing right to my groin. Summoning a slight gasp from me as her hands stroke deeper down, her fingers keeping track of ever curve of my muscles.

"Then how come you want to talk about it now?"

I look up at the ceiling, not being able to look into her eyes any longer. She's got me trapped, and she knows she does. The grin on her lips gives it away.

I try not to concentrate on her hands that are skimming over my abdomen, finding their way to the hem of my shirt before slipping right underneath. Her skin on mine makes this room appear so much hotter than it is.

Fuck this. I am in *hell*. This is fucking torture.

"Now, would you look at me, Colin?"

I can't. There is no way I won't just slam my lips right onto hers when I look back into those breathtaking green eyes.

Ever since that accidental kiss in the arena, her lips are all I can think about. It's never been like this for me. I've kissed tons of girls before, and never had one stupid, *accidental* kiss make me feel… *desperate*.

Just breathe, Colin.

"No?" Amusement dances on her tongue. "Would you just kiss me already?"

My head falls, eyes landing on hers, my breath officially taken away from me.

Did she just say what I think she did?

Lily is biting her lip, smiling softly.

I swear, she wants me dead.

"I can't."

Disappointment draws over her face.

"I will go way beyond kissing."

"Is that a challenge?"

Nope, I'm done for.

I grab onto one of her wrists, pulling her hand out from underneath my shirt and place it down right over the bulge in my pants.

She sucks in a sharp breath but doesn't withdraw her hand. Instead, Lily moves her fingers, adding just a slight amount of pressure as she rubs over my hardening— *covered*—erection.

She smirks up at me knowingly, moving her hands closer to the button of my pants.

"Unbutton my pants and I will no longer keep up the nice guy. Because I will have to fuck you disrespectfully," I warn.

"You can't even kiss me, Colin."

I firmly grip her nape with one hand, pushing her hips against my body with the other.

My lips cover hers, proving her wrong.

Her hands are warm when they press against my abdomen, once again discovering every inch of my abs. My heart beats rapidly, not wanting to realize this is happening. But it is happening.

I take control of the kiss, deepening it by pressing her just a bit closer to me, if that is even possible.

My tongue darts across my lips, dipping inside her mouth as I taste her. She tastes like coffee and pomegranate, her chap stick flavor, I assume. And so much like Lily.

I love the taste of Lily now. I could only ever downgrade from it. No one could ever measure up to her ever again, now that I got a taste of heaven.

Pulling away, I push her back just enough to bring space between us. Enough space that'll keep me from doing worse, from going further than this.

Even this is a step too far. Kissing Lily, I mean. Her lips are off-limits, as so is her body. *She* is off-limits.

God dammit, she wants to *die*. She's not planning some vacation for a short while. No, she wants to be dead.

I cannot get anywhere near more people with one foot in a grave. I've had plenty of those in my life.

And yet…

Lily grabs onto the chain around my neck, pulling me close to her. Her lips gaze mine, never quite connecting our lips.

Honestly, *fuck it*. One night won't hurt.

"You make it so hard to breathe," I whisper. I don't let her speak and just press my mouth back against her soft lips. Her tongue brushing mine as I claim her.

She moans into my mouth, enjoying this as much as I do. *I hope*.

I slide my hands down her body until my they reach her wrists. Taking them in mine, I turn us around, pressing Lily's back against the door. I pinch her hands up over her head with one hand, using my other to hold onto her waist.

"You taste so good, you know that?" I say close to her ear. My tongue comes into contact with her skin, trailing wet kisses all down her neck, sucking and biting on the tender skin until light red spots appear. Not dark enough to leave marks by the end of this.

Except for one or two maybe.

Her mouth opens slightly, eyes only half-opened.

"Colin," she says in a breath, arching her back away from the door as I press my erection into her stomach.

Deep down in my head, I know this is wrong. I know we shouldn't do this. We shouldn't cross the invisible line that neither of us ever really drew.

But for my own sanity, I need to pull away.

"Lily, we can't," I speak, my voice hoarse and I bet I sound out of breath. "I can't do this."

"Colin, make a decision. We can either do this or watch a movie." She looks at me with disappointment, though I guess she understands my hesitation.

No, I believe Lily is thinking this is about her, that I don't find her attractive or something like that. But the truth is, I'm more afraid of myself if I go too far with her.

I've never feared going too fast or too far. I've never feared sleeping with someone. But I fear sleeping with Lily.

I know myself, and I know I've never been more attached to someone like I am to Lily. I know her for less than a week and I can't stop thinking about her. I can't let this happen, because otherwise, I might never get her out of my system.

And if she does die, by then I will be so attached to her that it will rip my heart out and I'll die with her.

"Please," she begs, "make a decision."

Please, someone cut my head off with a Guillotine.

I slide a hand down my face, blowing out one quick breath.

Attaching my lips back to her skin, I kiss my way up her neck, over her jaw, right back to her lips.

Releasing Lily's hands, I pick her up. She immediately wraps her legs around my hips, her arms swinging around my neck.

"You sure you want this?" I ask, pulling away from her lips for a second.

"Whatever happened to disrespect?" *Yeah, I don't think it's going to happen.*

"A guy can fuck you in all sorts of ways, and still make sure you actually want it."

"I want to see those 'all sorts of ways,'" she says, smirking.

"We might need a repetition then." I carry Lily over to her bed, setting her down onto her feet.

"Who said this will be a one-time thing?" *Fuck me.*

Sliding down Lily's leggings, she steps out of them, pushing me onto the bed. She sits down on my lap, cupping my face as she forces her lips back to mine, kissing me passionately, her tongue tasting mine. She is revealing a new side of possessiveness to me I never thought she would have.

Her hands roaming over my body like she is examining me. Now discovering *every* inch of muscle and skin I have to offer with hot freaking touches that send bolts of electricity down to my cock.

As her hands travel down to my pants and she's about to undo them, I have to stop her. Not because I don't want her hands on my dick, but because I fear losing myself way too quickly when she does.

For some reasons her hands are affecting me more than anyone's ever could. Just a soft and tiny touch of Lily's and I'm a goner.

I grab onto the hem of her—*or more like my*—jersey, pulling it over her head in a swift move.

"Aw, fuck." I move my lips over her hot skin, kissing up her cleavage, over her collarbones back to her lips.

I found a new addiction for my lips. That being: attached to hers.

Her fingers are clinging to the material of my shirt, tugging on it as she pulls it over my head, throwing it across the room. She takes a moment to look at me, skimming over my upper body like she'd never seen it before.

"I think you need to work out a bit more." She traces the tips of her fingers down my chest, stopping at my abdomen. "Wouldn't want my new sex-buddy having less abs than my brother."

She's joking, I know she is.

"Jesus, can we not talk about Aaron right now?" I laugh.

"Only because you've asked so nicely." She beams at me, placing her hands back onto my jawline as she kisses me.

My hands reach behind her, unhooking her bra. Sliding the straps down her arms. I curse out once again. "Fuck, you're so beautiful."

Her cheeks flush. I already figured out that she doesn't take compliments very well, but fuck it, I will compliment the hell out of this woman.

Because. Lily. Is. Fucking. Gorgeous.

"Quit the admiration. You promised disrespect."

"Reyes, for fuck's sake." I stroke the pads of my thumbs over her nipples, feeling as they harden a tad more. "Fuck the disrespect. You're too breathtaking."

Lily places her hands on top of mine, laying them down right onto her breasts, giving them a squeeze with my hands.

Hint taken.

I let my hands skim over her breasts, squeezing them, rolling her nipples between my fingers, hearing a few whimpers coming from Lily.

"Absolutely stunning," I whisper, kissing down her body until my mouth covers one of her nipples. My tongue darts out, softly gliding across the hardened nub. She lets out a moan, hands tugging firmly onto my hair.

I know this shouldn't happen because this is totally going to complicate the next six days.

Chapter 16

"she's headin' for something that she won't forget"—
Night Changes by One Direction

Lily

COLIN SEAMLESSLY SWITCHES OUR POSITION, pulling me from his lap as he lays me down onto my bed.

He pulls out his wallet from his pants, taking out a plastic wrapper and laying it down on my nightstand.

Colin tugs on my underwear, sliding it down my legs, leaving me completely exposed to him.

I watch as his head tilts back, letting out a long groan, sliding his hands down his face. "I'm going to break you."

"Don't flatter yourself, Fairy Godmother." I chuckle.

But I think he might be right. The second he pushes his pants and boxers down, standing in front of me just as naked as I am, a gasp escapes my throat. Much to his delight.

He chuckles at my reaction, crawling on top of me, leaving a trace of kisses, beginning at my stomach and ending with his lips back attached to mine.

His kisses are to obsess over. The best kisses I've ever experienced. Hot, with passion and lust. They're seductive, possessive; not too much tongue and not too sloppy.

His hand tracing down my body feels like fiery bits from hell caressing the spots he is touching. Stingingly hot, yet he touches me with such gentleness. It is almost disrespectful.

Gasps and moans escape from me when he cups my pussy, slipping his fingers through my folds.

"Ah fuck, Lilybug." He can feel how embarrassingly wet I am. "This is hot." His voice deepens so suddenly, sounding a lot raspier than usual.

Pleasure flows through me like pop rocks, prickling through my body, tickling on the surface of my skin when Colin pushes a finger inside of me.

I like that he's not quiet. It's encouraging me to take on the challenge to be louder than he is.

I can't believe that he barely touched me yet and I'm already this wet. It's truly embarrassing, but Colin seems to like it.

"I need to taste you." His voice is hoarse as he speaks quietly against my lips.

He lifts off me, and it'd be a lie if I said I don't feel lonely with some of his weight no longer pressed on top of me. But that thought quickly vanishes when Colin pushes my legs further apart, placing a kiss to my pussy.

"Oh, *God*," I gasp. "Colin."

He kisses me again, then he decides to add his tongue, gliding from my core to my clit, eliciting moans from me. I feel him vibrating against my skin like he's humming something. But if he is, I either can't hear it because he's too quiet, or my head is too busy processing and savoring every touch, every stroke of his tongue, *everything*.

Just when I'm about to tangle my fingers into his hair, Colin stops and moves over to my thighs.

Colin kisses the inside of my thigh suspiciously long and only moves in a half circle, sucking, biting.

"Are you giving me hickeys?" I ask somewhat breathlessly. I wonder where my breath went.

"I might," he mutters, and I feel him smiling against my skin.

Honestly, so be it. It's not like anyone would see my inner thighs anyway.

And then, Colin lifts my hips, my fingers gripping into his hair as he presses his tongue back against my pussy, pushing past my opening, licking up until he sucks at my clit. With his tongue back inside me, he hums again—a satisfied hum when I moan out his name.

Two of his fingers trace around my entrance before he inserts them, making it harder for me to contain myself. Groans and pleasure filled cries travel over my lips, filling the room with sounds.

I want to kiss him, feel his lips back on mine, but I also want him to continue working my body the way he does.

"Colin." My voice is barely even a whisper anymore at this point. I moan out louder, he mumbles something unintelligible against my skin, continuing to suck on my clit as his fingers push in and out of me.

My body feels hot, as though I was running a fever but without actually feeling bad. In fact, I feel *good*. Great even.

"You like that, sweetheart?" His voice is deep, hoarse, filled with lust.

My back arches, leaning my head into the pillow, pressing into it as my grip tightens in his hair, completely messing it up.

"*Please*," I beg, whimpering.

I pull him up by his hair, praying it's not hurting him. Luckily, he just smirks at me, hovering right back over my body.

I don't even care that his mouth and parts of his nose are covered in my wetness, I need to feel his lips on mine.

And so I do.

With my hands on his nape, I pull his face down to mine, possessively forcing my lips onto his, working my tongue against his.

Panting, I tell him, "I want you inside of me." He chuckles softly, reaching his arm over to my nightstand.

"What if I want you to come on my tongue?"

"Oh God, no."

"No?" he snickers. "But you're fucking delicious. I could eat you all night long."

"Colin," I groan, sounding desperate.

I'm not quite sure when or how he put the condom on, because the next thing I know, Colin is stroking the tip of his cock against my entrance, magically summoning more of my moans.

It's like I'm one of those singing birds, calling for a potential partner. Just that my vocals aren't bird chirps, but gasps and groans that give away my satisfaction.

He slams inside of me rapidly, causing both of us to groan out loud—though, I'm sure I was gasping more than groaning. Him groaning from pleasure, me gasping from pain.

But I don't mind the pain. Not at all. I heard it could hurt, so I guess I was prepared. Mostly, anyway. It's not like it'll hurt forever.

Stilling for a moment, he looks into my eyes as if he could tell this hurt me, waiting for some different kind of reaction on my part.

But when I don't react, he starts to move, pulling out of me only to slam back inside just as fast as he did the first time. Only this time, he doesn't just go fast, he is also rougher, pushing into me that tiny bit deeper.

"*Fuck*," he groans. "You're so tight."

Rough, deep and fast strokes that send my body to a whole other dimension.

One after the other, Colin lifts my legs up, wrapping them around his waist, making me cry out in pleasure as his cock hits *the* spot

"Is this okay?" he asks, looking into my eyes. I nod, not being able to form any logical sentences. Or a simple *yes* for that matter.

I try meeting his thrusts, lifting my ass, but strength fails me when he plunges into me over and over again.

His lips are claiming mine like he's meaning to keep them to himself forever.

I don't think anyone has ever made me feel this good. Colin certainly knows how to work his body and mine along with it. It's scary. Truly scary how he knows exactly when to go rougher, when to go faster, when to slow down and when to add his fingers, circling my clit.

As my moans grow louder, cries becoming more frequent, Colin doesn't stop kissing me. He probably tries to mute me, or at least silence me down, but I doubt that's working. I don't mind his lips on mine, though.

He holds my arms above my head using one hand, not allowing me to continue touching him. It's frustrating, I *want* to touch him. I *need* to touch him. I need to roam my hands over his body, feel the curves of his muscles, feel *him* tense under my touch.

"Lily," he breathes against my lips, pushing into me just that tiny bit harder.

I'm secretly praying Winter isn't at home. She can most definitely hear everything, not only the bedframe rocking against the wall, but everything else as well.

"That's right, sweetheart," he praises. "You're taking me so well."

Colin rubs my clit a bit faster, adding more pressure, thrusting into me faster until I reach the point of oblivion he's been working toward to.

"Oh…*God*." I dig my nails into his skin, at least as much as it's possible with him still holding them up.

"No," he says in a strict tone. He grabs my chin, pressing his finger into my skin.

My eyes jump open, not knowing what the hell I did wrong.

"You're going to look me in the eyes," he demands. "I want your eyes on mine when you come, with my name rolling over your lips. I need you to see who's fucking you, sweetheart. Who's making you feel good."

So he meant *disrespect* in a hot way.

He proceeds to thrust inside of me, his eyes looking into mine deeply, watching me as I reach my climax, reaching a state of oblivion I never thought I could.

It's so much more intense than doing it to myself.

I cry out his name, seeing, but not really acknowledging the satisfied look on his face when he gets just what he demanded.

Colin pulls out of me, turning me over, sticking my ass up only to slam back inside of me. He doesn't even give me a second to come down from my orgasm, only rocks my world right through it.

I feel him squeeze my ass cheeks, picking up the pace as he proceeds to plunge inside of me.

His grip tightens on my ass causing me to yelp out in pain. I'm surprised when I find the pain arousing.

The longer and deeper he pushes in and out of me, the closer I get, again. That has me question whether or not all those women claiming to fake it each time are being honest.

Or Colin just knows how to do it right.

I wonder if Colin fights back his orgasm, wanting me to come again before he does. His stamina-game certainly seems strong enough for it.

With his hands on my hips, forcing my body to meet his thrusts, he hits this very sensitive spot inside of me over and over again. The very same that has me cry out his name with all the strength I have left.

"Lily," he grunts throaty, his voice hoarse, his hands moving up to my waist, pushing me against him.

The sweat on my body starts to drop down.

At this point I'm a panting mess, barely able to breathe correctly. It truly feels like I have forgotten how breathing works.

At least I'm not the only one that feels this way.

Colin is panting as well, cursing, groaning, fingers digging deeper into my skin.

Until he stops, only softly riding out our satisfaction as we both reach our orgasms.

I can feel my wetness dripping as he pulls out of me. I tip over, landing on my stomach. I don't want to move, too exhausted from Colin's godly cock.

I barely have enough brain cells left to acknowledge Colin pressing his lips to the back of my shoulder. Only when he says, "it's a heart," do I realize. "You have a heart-shaped birthmark."

That I do, apparently.

"It's cute, Lilybug. Not embarrassing."

"Wish I felt the same about it." I speak into the pillow, still not able to move.

"Get up," Colin then commands, already standing next to the bed.

How the hell does he have the strength to move his body after *that*? I mean, he was here, too. He was doing more work than I did. How isn't this man exhausted?

"I don't want to."

"You do want to." In a matter of seconds, Colin pulls me off the bed, scooping me up with his arms and carries me out of my bedroom—disposing the used condom into my trash can—then walks us into the bathroom.

It seems like Winter isn't here, it's certainly way too quiet for her to be around. But I'm glad she isn't, because Colin fucking Carter just carried me five steps out of my bedroom and into the bathroom. Naked.

He sets me down on my feet, plants a tender kiss to my nose then grabs one of the towels hanging next to the sink.

"Do I need to tell you how to take care of *your* body?" He looks at me with sincerity in his eyes. "Go pee."

"Not with you here."

"You do remember the part, just a couple minutes ago, when I made you scream my name as you came?"

"Mhm," I hum in response. Still doesn't mean I can pee with *him* being here.

He lets out a sigh in defeat as I don't budge. But he doesn't complain. He simply wets the towel he just ripped off the towel holder and stands back in front of me.

His eyes scan my body as if he's taking one last look, burning the image of my naked body into his brain. But then he kneels down in front of me, pushing one of my legs up, resting it on his shoulder as he starts to clean me.

Yup. Colin Carter is cleaning up the mess he made. Or more like *we* made. He certainly has a sweet side to him.

How does a guy so sweet and respectful have such an awful reputation?

Not that he has a bad one, it's just…girls complaining about the sex experience they've gotten. It's never about the sex itself, apparently that's mind-blowingly-amazing. I can totally agree to that now. But according to half of the sorority sisters, he's never been gentle or nice to either of them afterwards.

Clearly, I can't say the same.

Colin has been taking care of me ever since we started this nine-day journey three days ago. Surely in different ways, but it's still considered "taking care of someone," right?

"Can I—" he stops himself from continuing. He stands back up, walking over to the sink to wash out the towel.

"Can you what?"

"Stay just for a little while longer?"

I freeze. Not because I don't want him here, because I let myself assume he would stay the night, especially after what we did.

"You can just say no, Lilybug."

"Oh," I sigh softly. "I do want you here, Colin."

He smiles at me. "Good, because I wasn't planning on leaving anyway." He presses his lips to mine one last time and then walks right out of the bathroom.

As I return back to my bedroom a couple of minutes later, Colin is lying on my bed. He is wearing sweatpants, a pair he definitely wasn't wearing before. And for some reasons, my bedding is changed as well.

"How long was I in the bathroom for?" I ask, checking the time. Not that it makes sense since I have absolutely no idea what time it was when he carried me into the bathroom in the first place.

"I think about ten minutes." Colin holds his hand out toward me, pulling me in when I take it.

His arms wrap around me, holding me close to him. He brushes my hair out of my face placing a gentle kiss to my temple.

He traces his index finger along something on the crook of my neck, chuckling "I love this," he whispers. "Guys better stay away from you now."

"You gave me a hickey?" My eyes open wide in realization. How have I not seen that in the mirror?

"You're just blind." *How does he always know what I'm thinking about?*

"But I'm not."

"You sure as hell are."

"Colin, people will think I'm in a relationship. This can't be happening," I tell him.

"Why not? First of all, you certainly are *mine* now. And it gives me a great excuse to drop a few assignments by throwing in the 'my girlfriend just killed herself' card."

"Gee, thanks. At least now I know you're only here to get A's more easily." I roll my eyes, trying to escape from his embrace.

"Lilybug," he chuckles and rolls us over, lying on top of me this time. He is using my goddamn boobs as his pillow. "In case you haven't figured it out yet, I'm here to help you stay alive. I don't want you to die."

"Well, but I do want to die."

"That's alright. I won't be selfish and tell you that 'think about your friends and family' shit. Or even add 'but I'm so deeply in love with you, stay for me.' I just think it would be a shame to throw your life away."

Everything he says leaves my mind and all I remember is that one tiny part. *I'm so deeply in love with you.* I know he is just joking and still my stomach turns upside down.

Not sure if it turns because that sounds good or bad.

"I will never understand how you feel. But Lilybug, I can try and help you understand that you're not alone. I can try and make the pain bearable. You're such a wonderful person. I couldn't live with myself knowing you've died, and I didn't even try to keep you from it," he says, stroking his fingers through my hair.

As much as I'd love to believe him, nothing could ever change my mind. But instead telling him once again that I don't want his saving, that I *want* to die, I say, "so that's why you want me to be yours then?" I raise my eyebrows at him. "You want me to be your girlfriend so you can—what? Have professors grade you with more care because you've lost someone you 'love.'"

"I never declared you as my girlfriend."

"You said I'm yours. It's the same thing."

"So it appears, huh?" I can feel him smirk against my breast as he nuzzles into me like I *am* a pillow. "You're mine to spend the next six days with. Mine to convince how amazing life can be if you let it."

These are going to be six very interesting days.

A sudden warmth creeps into my chest, storing the words "you're mine" scarily close to my heart. I shouldn't feel this way. I shouldn't be wanting to jump around like a toddler, screaming, laughing with happiness.

But I want to. Because Colin Carter calls me his. And *he*'s lying on top of *me*, his arms are wrapped around *me*, not around someone else.

I'm getting way ahead of myself. I'm more of a mission for him. A challenge, if you will. Someone to play with until I die. There are no hard feelings. No commitment.

The room quiets down, the only sounds being heard is heavy breathing, though neither of us seems to be falling asleep any time soon.

"Do you mind if I give my sister a call?"

I don't care, but I do wonder why Colin would want to call his sister at eleven at night.

Reaching over to the nightstand, he grabs his phone. He pulls me against him, still wanting to keep me close. Then he swipes through his phone, landing on his messenger app, giving me quite the opportunity to skim over his last texts. Fortunately for my own sanity, he clicks on Eira's chat and dials her number before I get to hurt my own feelings.

Not even sure why the thought of Colin messaging a couple of other girls bugs me. We're not involved in any other way but this nine-days arrangement.

Nine Days

"Please tell me you were awake," Colin says shortly after Eira picks up the phone. I don't hear what she answers, but I take Colin's relief as she was awake.

"No, *enana*, I just didn't manage to stop by today." So, he does visit his family every single day? That's impressive. I haven't seen my mom in good a month.

Though, to be honest, my mother and I haven't been quite that good for one another recently anyway.

"You know I would never do that." God, I hate only hearing one half of conversations. "*Uh, claro. Dame un momento, ¿sí?*"

Colin gets up from the bed in a heartbeat, the phone clamped between his shoulder and ear, walking through my room, picking up clothes.

"Are you leaving?" I ask, drawing my eyebrows together.

Colin shakes his head at me, mouthing, "*not yet*."

"*No, esa era Lily.*" He walks over to me, sticking my arms up into the air, pulling the same jersey from earlier down my body.

"Give me a second, would you?" He laughs as he sits down beside me, holding the phone in front of his face just when the camera turns on, revealing a pretty tired looking Eira Carter.

She shrieks in excitement when she sees my hair in one corner of the screen. "Lily!"

I sit up, leaning against my bedframe.

"Colin won't stop talking about you, you know that?"

Colin shifts awkwardly. Through the screen I see him giving Eira a warning look. She ignores it though.

"He won't?"

"Yup. Just yesterday he was all like 'she's so gorgeous.' If I recall correctly, he was drooling as well." *Drooling?* "He has like a million pictures of you on his phone."

He does? I know he takes videos of me occasionally for our project, but pictures? Maybe they're needed as well. I wouldn't know, Colin doesn't tell me anything about our project.

"Anyway"—I need this conversation to be about anything but Colin and me—"how are you feeling?"

She still doesn't look much healthier. If I'm being honest, she even looks a tad sicker to when I met her two days ago.

"Just great." She smiles wryly. "Time's just getting tougher."

And then Eira proceeds to tell us about her day. How their mother took Eira out for dinner earlier and her going back to school for a couple of hours. Colin doesn't seem too excited about the news, but I wouldn't know why.

School is normal, she at least has to get homeschooled at her age. So why isn't he happy about it?

Half an hour later, Colin ends the phone call and gets up from the bed.

He kisses my forehead, gathers his belongings and marches out the door. He doesn't even say goodbye, he just leaves like the total asshole he is.

Chapter 17

"it could be nothing cause nothing lasts forever"—Like Strangers Do by AJ Mitchell

Colin

"You fucked my sister!"

Everyone's head turns, pairs of eyes stare at me like I'm some kind of performer on a stage. It physically hurts to feel the eyes of my teammates on me.

I'm used to hundreds of people watching me play on the ice but having a good number of guys from your hockey team stare at you like you've committed a crime sucks balls.

"You literally gave me the green light." I turn to face an angry-looking Aaron. He's just walking into the locker room.

Half of the guys are already on their way to the shower room, washing off the scent of victory sweat.

We've had another home game up until a couple minutes ago, and we won. I thought the team would be in a good mood after our victory, but one of us clearly isn't.

Though, why is he only yelling at me for it now? Lily has been walking around with that hickey on her neck for the entire day.

Granted, she tried to cover it, not even I could see it in film directing earlier.

"I didn't think you would actually do it!" Aaron yells, not caring that the other guys are present. I won't even hope for backup from those guys.

Fucking your best friend's sister can never end well, in spite of having the go. I should have known better.

In all honesty, I was a dick afterwards. I should have stayed the night. I should have slept next to her, woken up next to her the following morning. But I chickened out.

Common sense kicked in. Lily and I are *friends*. We aren't supposed to have sex.

It's not like I could change anything about the way I feel about Lily.

"Remember the part when you said you'd know I'd treat her right?"

I wait for Aaron to approach me properly, but he doesn't walk any closer. I guess it's because he doesn't want his fist to end up in my face.

Truthfully, I don't think I would even fight back at this point. Only thinking about one of my teammates touching Eira in the slightest has me want to vomit.

But then again, Aaron gave me the okay. It's not like I went behind his back…anymore.

Aaron inhales deeply, slowly, calming his nerves. "Dude, she's my fucking twin sister."

"Well aware of that." If he wants to evoke some kind of guilt inside of me, he's not doing a great job. I wouldn't regret sleeping with Lily for anything. At least for his satisfaction. I don't regret it, but I kind of do anyway. It's…complicated.

"We almost have the same face. It's like you fucked me."

And now he's exaggerating, crossing an obvious line.

"How do you know about it anyway? I doubt she walked right up to you and told you."

"She didn't," he says irritated. "She has a damn hickey on her neck, dumbass. That couldn't have been done by anyone but you." I swear, the vein on his neck is about to explode.

"I'm not even trying to deny it was me. But now that you mentioned 'others'…would you rather it being some other guy hitting it off with her? Like one of the frat guys, for example?"

"Fuck off, Carter. She's not supposed to be with any guy."

"Ron, your sister is almost twenty-one years old. She's old enough to make decisions."

"Aaron," Grey speaks calmly, placing his hand onto Aaron's shoulder. "What is your problem? I hate to take sides, but you did tell Colin it was okay. Bitching about it now is just a dick move."

Aaron exhales deeply, steadying his breath—*again*—as he tries to control his anger.

"At least tell me she's not just one of many," Aaron demands, looking into my eyes with anger burning in his. I swear, if looks could kill, I'd be lying on the floor and kissing death hello.

"She's not," I answer with no hesitation. "You really think I would do that to Lily? Fuck her for one night and then disappear?"

"Yes," he snaps. "Like you do with every other woman."

"Did you at least stay the night?" Miles asks.

I should have. But I couldn't. I'm afraid of my own feelings. Lily and I have gone way too far with this already, I can't let this go any further.

My friends know that I usually send the girls home right after doing it. Or I sprint out the door without looking back. And never do they hear from me again.

But it's not like those girls don't know that I won't stay. I always make that clear right from the start.

It's just that Lily is different. She is *more*. And definitely means way more to me than I'd like.

"I didn't." I'm incapable of lying to these guys. Perhaps not incapable given that they have almost to no clue what's going on in my life most of the time. "I stayed for a while and then left.

"I don't believe you," Aaron spits out with an amount of venom I've never witnessed in him.

I fucked up big time with him.

Without saying a word, I take out my phone from my locker, unlocking it then going straight to dialing Lily's number.

She picks up on the second ring.

Aaron is watching me, still having his angry eyes focused on mine. He doesn't move, doesn't even change his expression for a second.

"Colin?" Lily's sweet voice comes through the phone. Somehow just hearing her voice makes Aaron's madness seem less mad to me.

"Lilybug, where are you right now?" I ask. I know she has to be around here somewhere.

"Same bench you found me at the day we met. Why?"

"Okay, stay there, will you?"

I quickly change my footwear. Not waiting until Lily could respond, I hang up the phone and jog over to the other side of the arena, ignoring the fact that someone—most definitely Aaron—is following me.

I need to see her.

When I see her blonde hair only slightly above the railing—which means she is either on her phone or writing in her journal—I experience instant relief. Not even sure why.

Lily stays seated as I approach her, but when I do stand in front of her, her head tilts up for her eyes to meet mine.

"Congratu—"

I guide my lips to hers, kissing her gently, yet also rough enough to draw out a soft moan from her throat.

I didn't even know I needed this kiss until my lips are covering hers.

I also didn't know I was going to kiss her until I find myself doing so.

"Thank you," I say as I pull away from her lips. "For the congratulations I didn't let you finish voicing."

"You're welcome."

Looking over Lily's shoulder—down to the seats—I notice her mint green notebook lying on one of them. Before she has the chance to forget it again, I grab it.

"What are you doing?" she asks with confusion written all over her face.

"Holding onto this in case you accidentally leave it here again."

"I won't."

"Sure, Lilybug."

She smiles lightly, carefully swinging her arms around my torso, pulling me into a hug.

What I thought was going to be a cute and friendly hug, quickly turns out to be an attempt to murder me as her iced-cold hands find their way underneath my jersey.

But I don't budge. I don't because if I did Lily would no longer be hugging me. I happen to enjoy her almost to never happening hugs a little too much. Even more than I like her mouth pressed to mine.

Never mind. I love her lips more.

"Are you ready for day four?" I ask, swinging my arms around her as well, pressing her closer into my chest.

"Depends. Where are you taking me?"

"We'll go visit Eira for a bit and then I'll take you somewhere to let out your aggression."

"I'm not aggressive." She looks up at me, pouting.

"Alright, we'll leave that for tomorrow then." I kiss her forehead. "Rollerblading it is."

"No," a voice from behind me snaps. "She can't do that. She isn't even allowed to skate on the ice."

I look down at Lily, raising my eyebrows. I know for sure she is allowed to but just doesn't want to. Or more like her depression won't let her.

"What if I promise that I won't let her break her bones?" I ask nicely, or fake nicely.

I mean, come on, Aaron is overreacting right now. I understand that he's pissed. I would be as well. But he has to get over it already. He was the one telling me to go for it. If he hadn't said it, hell, I don't think I even would have continued seeing Lily for those nine days.

That's not true. I definitely would have continued to see her. Daily.

"*Her* mother is going to chop off your head."

"Oh," I gasp. "I think it's time for me to meet your mother," I say to Lily. "She will love me. I know your dad does."

"Dude, seriously?" Aaron groans, shaking his head in disapproval.

"Deadly serious," I tell him. "Your dad loves me."

Maybe it's a bit overexaggerated. Not the part with Aaron's father loving me. Not to brag, but he once called me his son. But the part where I said Lily's mother would. Mothers usually hate me…except for my own.

"Aaron"—Lily's voice is harsh—"you're not seriously mad at Colin, are you?"

Aaron doesn't answer, he chooses to go with the silent treatment. *If he won't answer, she won't keep asking.*

Just that this is Lily we're talking about.

"Answer me."

"You wouldn't understand it, Lily." Once again, Aaron brushes his hands through his hair. "You don't have a younger sister to protect from guys."

"Even if I did, Aaron, it wouldn't be any of my fucking business. It's not like you don't know Colin."

"Exactly!" he yells. "I know Colin. I know who he's been with before. How shitty he treated every single one of those girls before you."

I mean, he has a point. I haven't been really gentle with any of those girls before. But Aaron also knows that I do treat people I like well and truly care about them.

I can't blame him for being mad. I wouldn't have hesitated punching him in the face if he touched my sister, no matter how good I know he'd treat her.

"Cool. But you clearly don't know what he did last night. You don't know how he's treating me, Aaron. He isn't mistreating me in the slightest. If anything, I am the one doing crap to him. I'm pulling him down with me, not the other way round."

I don't want her to say it like that. It's not true. Lily is not pulling me down. In fact, Lily is breathing air into my lungs. I thought I would be the one showing her how beautiful life could be. When in reality, Lily is the one showing me what I will miss out on once she is gone.

"You're not pulling him down." Aaron's eyes switch between Lily and me, uncertain of who to look at. "But I'm afraid you won't be able to handle what *his* life will bring, Lily."

"What's his life going to bring?" she asks. "He's made me happier than every Sunday we've spent together on the ice, Aaron. In just three days."

I watch as Aaron's face drops. I'm not sure what it is: amusement, more anger, shock, astonishment, maybe even happiness? It's not clear. But it's something.

"Colin managed to make me feel more alive in three days than I've ever felt for almost twenty-one years. You can't seriously be mad at your best friend for making my life better."

I'm not sure if Lily is lying to Aaron, saying all those things to make him feel better, or if she truly means those words. I want them to be honest words. I wish for them to be true, not because that's a damn ego-boost, but because I want Lily to be happy. More than anything.

Aaron settles his eyes on me, saying, "If I hear her say anything but good stuff about your relationship—" he pauses, focusing his eyes over to Lily for a moment before they travel back over to me. "—I will have to throw fists at you, Carter."

"Totally understandable." Just that Lily and I aren't even in a serious relationship. I think. I did, technically, claim her as mine, that's because she is. I'm not letting anyone touch her, but that's because I want to protect her from even more darkness.

"Now that we got that out of the way, we're celebrating our birthday at Brites."

"We are?" Lily frowns. "Does that mean I can invite people?"

"It's a bar. Anyone can come."

"You do know the more people come, the more *you* will have to pay, right?"

"I'm not paying for everyone's drinks." Aaron taps my shoulder a couple of times. "I can't afford that, unlike this guy here."

"Sorry, I'm just paying for my and your sister's drinks."

"Jackass." He starts to walk away. I did tell him I would pay for all of the drinks if that meant I wouldn't have to get him a present. God knows what I should buy a guy that already has everything.

"Love you too, bro." Aaron flips me off. Turning back to Lily, I find her laughing, muffling it down by pressing her face into my chest. "Hey, you have no right to judge."

"I'm not. But maybe you should date my brother. Seems like he got quite jealous over us 'being together.'"

"What do you mean?" She pulls away from the hug, raising her brows like me not understanding is equal to the world ending. "Aaron and I have been in a relationship for years. We're basically married."

"Figured." Lily takes her notebook from me, sliding it into her handbag. "Do you really think you should meet my mother?"

When I said it's time for me to meet Lily's mother, I did say it only to make my intention clearer to Aaron. Meeting parents is a big deal, I guess.

However, Lily met my parents before as well.

She knows my father because he is the hockey coach at our college. And my mother happened to be home when I took her with me to see Eira.

I never truly intended for my parents to get to know her.

"I'm your personal chauffeur, Lilybug. You said you wanted to pay your parents a visit tomorrow, so we'll do it together," I say. "Ergo, I will meet your mother."

"Isn't that kind of weird though? I mean, meeting my mom is a big deal, sort of."

"Nothing weird about showing me off."

Lily starts to laugh, punching her fist into my arm.

Chapter 18

"I'm happy that you're here with me, I'm sorry if I tear up"— death bed (coffee for your head) by Powfu, beabadoobee

Colin

> *"Dear Winter,*
>
> *If I'm being honest, it's quite the miracle that you're getting a letter from me.*
> *You've been my best friend ever since freshman year, which makes it a shame that it took me a good amount of time to find words to say.*
> *You knew I wasn't doing well. You heard me cry, scream when the pain got too much. But not once did you walk into my room to ask if I needed your comfort.*
> *I sure as hell would have said no, but knowing you were there for me would have—"*

"LILYBUG, YOU CAN'T WRITE THAT," I say, interrupting Lily as she reads her letter to Winter out for me.

We've been on the road for twenty minutes and Lily is still figuring out what to write. I mean, from what I've witnesses, Winter cares more about herself than anyone around her. It's truly a shame that Lily doesn't know what to say to her so-called best friend.

I can't blame her though.

"I don't know what to tell her. All I've got is to tell her how much of a shitty friend she can be."

"She's been your best friend for years, there has to be something good about the time you've spent with her." I stop at a red light, finally being able to properly look at my Lilybug, even if it's just for a moment.

Lily shakes her head no. "Whenever Winter tries to listen to my complaints, she ends up down-grading me. You know those people saying 'Oh, well, my hamster died this morning' when you tell them someone close to you passed?"

"Not exactly with this example, but yes."

"Winter is one of those." Lily sighs. "She tells me to stop whining about feeling depressed because I 'cry for no reason.' She tells me to stop whining about how horrible I feel because there are people out there having it worse."

"Alright." I pinch the bridge of my nose, trying to find words to say. "How about, instead of babbling all about friendship, you just thank her for being a *great* friend and then say something like 'I just didn't feel like breathing anymore, lol,'" I suggest, knowing it's total bullshit.

At least it gets me a laugh from Lily. A cheerful, happy laughter that fills my ears like music.

"Might just throw in a few 'lmao's' as well."

"Exactly."

"Okay, let me try this again."

Another good twenty minutes pass until Lily starts to read out what she's written, again.

"Dear Winter,

Our friendship had been quite the amusement park, wouldn't you agree?
I don't think I've ever had a friend anything close to what you are.
You're cheerful, kind, a literal party girl; always one the move.
You showed me that spending time all by myself—at all times—isn't what life is all about."

"Hold up," I have to interject, "*she* showed you this? I'm pretty sure I did."

"It's all I could come up with, Colin." She lets out a frustrated groan, falling back into the seat like she's just been liquified.

"Alright. Proceed."

"You dragged me out into the world, showed me that there is more to life than having my nose stuck in some textbooks.
Unfortunately, this life wasn't for me.
I'm nothing like the party person you are, Winter.
I like being on my own.
I like spending time alone, be at home, cuddled up under my blanket while watching Legally Blonde for the hundredths time.
Sometimes I wish I could be more like you.

Carefree and always on the move. Jumping right into another adventure. Going out to clubs and start twerking at the next best guy I come across.
Though, if I'm being honest, I probably wouldn't just start twerking at some random guy.
Let's keep this a bit more realistic, okay?
I wish I could be more outgoing and happy like you are. You always seem to know exactly how to suppress your madness, deal with grief and sorrow.
But sadly, that's not me.
I can't deal with the pain I'm confronted with. I can't deal with the solitude, the isolation I force upon myself for the sake of others.
I withdraw myself from people so I wouldn't annoy them with my awful feelings.
And it's getting too much to take on.
It got too much, Winter.
I can't do this anymore, which is why I took the precautions I did.
Taking my own life.
This has nothing to do with you, but everything to do with me and my feelings. I hope you understand that.
I'm just writing you this letter so you can hopefully find closure, knowing this isn't about you.
Maybe we get to see each other in another life.
Until then, I wish the best for you.
I wish for you to become the greatest actress you've wanted to be for so long.

Lily"

"I mean, it's definitely way better than your first attempt," I tell her, offering a slight shrug.

"It's awful," she groans. "Most of this is a lie."

"Well, but would you rather leave with telling her how much you despise her?"

"No." Lily connects her phone to my car, allowing herself to put on some music. She doesn't even ask if that's okay with me. But let's be real, I don't care.

Lily could steal my car and drive it into the nearest lake, and I wouldn't even get mad at her. Not because she's already dealing with way too much, but because I think it's almost incapable for Lily to do anything that would truly upset me to the point where I would be mad at her.

Those feelings scare me. It scares me that one person can make me feel so many different things all at once when I've spent the last years avoiding to feel at all.

Lily makes me happy without even trying to. Seeing her smile and hearing her laughter warms my chest in all the ways I refused to believe was possible, and I don't know why.

But what scares me the most is the thought of her dying.

"WE'RE STAYING here tonight, if that's okay with you," I say to Lily as we walk into my childhood bedroom. She stands in the middle of the room, looking around dumbstruck.

I know I've been living in luxury all my life—and I'm grateful I never had to worry about anything—but something about Lily's stunned expression irks me. *Not that I can blame her.*

"Do we leave early enough so I can see my parents tomorrow?" She turns to me, the stunned expression drained from her face with nothing but Lily's typical emptiness left.

She always looks at me like all the life has been sucked out of her. Like there is not a single spark left. But that only ever happens when we're alone. Whenever we're out in the open, with people surrounding us, Lily looks the happiest of fake happiness I have ever seen. But then, when she does have a great time, for instance when I took her to see the sunrise, honest euphoria takes over her.

It's like a switch sometimes. A pretty confusing construct, but I'm here to figure her out. Here to find out what makes that switch turn until she gets to feel all the excitement in the world. What makes her feel more happiness than she could ever imagine.

"We're leaving at eight," I tell her. "You just need to tell me where your mother lives."

Lily chuckles, falling down onto my bed. "Alright, Mr. Stinky." Lily sits up, watching me as I walk over to my desk. I can feel her eyes on me, burning into my skin. "My dad comes first. I'm sure you know where he lives. My mother lives in Wesley Hills."

"Can't believe you have me chauffeuring your ass around the whole world."

"It's not the whole world," she laughs. "And I can take the train, you know."

"Lilybug, I'd rather sit days in a car to drive you wherever the hell you want to go than have you take the train."

It's not a lie. I will gladly be her chauffeur. Not only because that gives me more time with her, but also because public transport seems dangerous. All those strangers and creepy people. She could be groped at, or even worse. No thank you.

Chapter 19

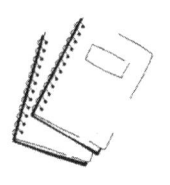

"but listen, pretty lady, you don't have to be alone"—
Baby Don't Cut by Bmike

Lily

AFTER SPENDING THE NEXT TWO HOURS in Eira's room, Colin decides that we're no longer going out tonight. Which is fortunate because I don't really feel like going on any more adventures today anyway.

I've already been at the arena watching a hockey game today. And now I spent most of my energy socializing with Colin's younger sister.

I'm drained. Even if I wanted to go roller skating tonight, I wouldn't have the energy for it. So I'm glad he called it off.

Eira went to sleep, or more like fell asleep mid talking. I already thought she didn't look too well last night but seeing her now—*in person*—she still doesn't look better. If I had to judge, she looks even sicker now.

Reece, Colin's three years old brother is currently waiting for Colin to read him a goodnight story. It's already

10 p.m. and Reece was supposed to be asleep hours ago, but as toddlers are sometimes, he was way too energetic to fall asleep. And now that he finally grows tired, Mrs. Carter asked Colin to read him a story.

While I wait for Colin to come back to his bedroom, I continue to write in my journal. It's nothing too spectacular anymore. All I manage to talk about is how my day has been and how tired I am now.

And then I suppress the urge to babble about Colin. Recently he's the only thing I can think about writing. I always start off by writing about how I feel, and then I drift off to my day and end up with how amazing Colin is. Which irks me. A lot.

I don't want to find Colin amazing.

He sure is a great guy. And the more I get to know him, the more he's growing on me. But I don't want him to grow on me. Even worse, I'm afraid I'm growing on him.

Colin has been looking at me all evening long. Not the same way he used to. He has never looked at me like I was some broken glass that needed some extra strong glue to be put back together. But he also never looked at me like he was...I don't know, getting used to me being in his life? The scary and exciting kind of being in someone's life. The one that fills your chest with heat and fears loss because it would end in a heartbreak.

Or maybe that's just me and I'm overanalyzing again.

The door to Colin's bedroom opens hastily. "Come with me," he speaks without even stepping inside of the room. I jump off the bed—not even questioning his command—and follow Colin through the mansion. He leads me to the top floor, right outside to the balcony. From there, Colin lifts me off the ground and tells me to get on the roof. Once again, I don't question him and do as he says.

Moments later, Colin and I are both on the roof of the building, sitting on the slope as we're watching the stars.

We're sitting in silence, feeling the cold night air brush over our skins. Or at least it's cold for me. I am freezing. Colin doesn't seem to mind the cold.

Would have been nice if he told me where we were going so I could have brought another jacket with me. I am wearing a thin jacket, but if I had known we'd be sitting on the roof, I would have stolen one of Colin's thicker ones.

As I begin to curse Colin out in my head for having me freeze, he suddenly lays a jacket over my shoulders. The one he has been wearing this whole time.

"Thank you," I say in a soft tone, no longer feeling the desire to cuss him out.

"Lilybug, can I ask you something?" I just shrug. "Why have you been wearing your jacket all day long?"

"Cause I'm cold," I lie. Though, right now it's not a lie. I am freezing.

"All day long?"

"Yes."

"I don't believe you." His eyes bore into mine intensely. It's intimidating. "Tell me the truth."

I remain quiet. Colin might be the only person in my life knowing about my wish to die, but there is no reason for him to care about any of my other problems.

"Lily, there's no reason for you to lie to me," he says, his eyes still locked with mine. "When did you do it?"

"What?"

"Don't play dumb, Lily." I have recently discovered that I hate it when Colin calls me Lily. Not only have I gotten used to my new nickname, but whenever he calls me Lily, it's more of a warning, sign of strictness and seriousness.

I hate it.

Taking a deep breath, I sigh in defeat. "After you left. It's not what you think, though."

Colin grabs my hand in his. Starting at my wrist, he slowly works his way up, pressing the tips of his fingers against every inch of clothed skin. Until he presses one wrong spot, right on the back of my arm. The very spot that has me wince in pain as he presses into it.

He watches my face, analyses every reaction, every bit of pain that displays on my face as he presses against it again to make sure this wasn't just a one-time reaction.

"Cold, my ass," he mutters almost inaudibly, dropping my arm. "Cut or burn?"

"Does it matter?" He nods just once, continuing to look at me madly. "Burn."

He sighs, bobbing his head lightly as he processes what I said. Or he tries to come up with words to say. I wouldn't know what is going on inside of his head.

"Why?" is the only thing he questions. I was prepared to be yelled at, not asked for a reason why.

"I didn't know what to do, Colin." I was frustrated when he left, and I don't even know why. Colin had every right to leave after what we did. He wasn't obligated to stay all night, especially not since we're supposed to be nothing but friends. So, why is a good question.

"Okay," he says breathy. "Here's what we're going to do."

Colin reaches into the pocket of his jacket that is still lying over my shoulders, pulling out a lighter. He hands it to me, not even giving me a second to question him before he begins to speak again. "Whenever you feel the urge to hurt yourself, you're going to call me."

"What?"

Colin holds his hand up, stopping me from speaking. "You're going to call me, and I will be right there." He inhales deeply, shakily. It's like he has no idea what to do. Like the thought of me hurting myself truly doesn't sit right with him at all. "You're going to hold that lighter to my arm, not yours. You're going to burn my skin instead of your own."

"Colin"—fear takes over me—"I'm not going to hurt you."

"You will," he says, grabbing my hand in his. He flicks on the lighter using my fingers and holding it close to his skin. Not close enough to burn him yet though. "You can have a death wish all you want, but if you're going to hurt yourself, you'll hurt me too."

"I can't." Tears begin to build up in my eyes, slowly rolling down my cheeks.

"You'll hurt me either way. Might as well use my body for it right from the start."

"I couldn't do this to you, Colin," I cry. "I couldn't hurt you like that."

And that's when I realize.

His words linger in my head, repeating in a loop. *You'll hurt me either way.* I am hurting him. Right this second. Right in this moment. I'm causing pain over the guy that had done nothing but provide me with happiness.

It's been four days. Four silly days and he's done nothing but bring light into my life.

And here I am hurting the guy that tries to be my savior.

I shouldn't have agreed to these nine days. I shouldn't have let him into my life. I shouldn't have allowed this to happen.

God, I am so stupid. How could I have done this?

How could I do this to him?

Colin is the only person to ever truly care about me, and I messed it up. I am hurting him.

"How can you say this, Colin?" I ask through tears. "Why do you do this to yourself?"

I pull my hand away from his, letting the lighter drop on the roof. Luckily, it's not one of those that keep the flame lit even when no one is pushing the button anymore.

His hands gently caress my jawline, thumbs stroking along the skin beneath my eyes, removing the salty tears. "I'm not doing anything to myself, Lily."

"You're here with me. You're putting yourself through hell to save me. It's only going to destroy you."

"So let it destroy me."

"No." I try to slide down the slope, wanting nothing more but to go to sleep and forget this awful encounter.

It's a coping mechanism I've evolved throughout the years. Whenever I want to avoid something, I go to sleep. It started when my mother began to drink. When she came home from bars late at night, barely able to make it up the stairs without passing out on them. When she was drunk throughout the days too, yelling at me for not cleaning up after her.

But I can't do it now. Colin is holding onto my body, not letting me move an inch.

"I want nothing more but for you to experience less pain. I don't need you to be one hundred per cent happy. No one ever is. You're already living with so much pain, one that I will never understand. But I can make sure you're not adding more to it." He sounds sincere, like he actually means what he says. And I can't help but want that as well.

Colin makes everything sound easy. He makes life sound exciting. But I've seen the ugly part of life. I know that no matter how good something sounds, there is *always* an ugly side. A side that's not worth staying for the pretty one.

His hands are back on my face, cupping it, forcing our eyes to stay on the other's. "I have five days left. You'll be staying those days with me."

"I'm not."

"You are. You'll be staying with me and Aaron. They all agreed on it already. Well, Aaron said he would only agree if you stayed in his bedroom and not mine."

"They all?"

"Excuse me? You think I would get around moving a pretty girl into my house without asking my roommates—that aren't my roommates—for permission?"

For the first time in felt like way too long now, I chuckle. Chuckling or laughing around Colin is almost a habit. He always manages to make me smile. So when I haven't been laughing since we stepped onto this roof, I began to miss it.

When did I start to miss laughing?

"I won't share a bedroom with my brother."

"Don't worry, I kicked him out."

"You did what!?" I ask a little too loudly. I'm sure Colin's parents could hear it down on the patio.

"I'm kidding," he says. "I told him that I'm old enough to have my girlfriend spend the night in my bed."

"I'm not your girlfriend."

"But Aaron doesn't know that. And now all we have to do is make sure he won't find out."

"Grey knows," I let him know. "I bet he can sense it."

Colin groans, making me laugh. "He sure can." Another groan follows. "But Grey knows how to keep his mouth shut. How would you know Grey 'can sense it' anyway?"

"He seems like a smart guy." I lift my shoulders, shrugging. I have never really had one conversation with Grey. Except for the one at the cafeteria two days ago. "And even if he can't, I'm sure Izan knows and told him."

"Who is Izan?"

"Grey's boyfriend?" I draw my brows together, not wanting to believe that Colin doesn't know about this. "He's the captain of the soccer team?"

Colin blinks hastily at me. "No way."

"Yes way."

"How do you know that?"

"Izan told me." Colin's expression falls, I'm not quite sure why.

"You do have quite the number of friends for someone who supposedly hates being around people."

"Believe it or not, I used to have a way better best friend than Winter," I tell him. "Sofia and I were inseparable. Though, perhaps not enough because after she moved away, we weren't able to stay in touch."

"Who's Sofia?" A little fold appears between his eyebrows.

I smile at the memory of her. "We used to skate together all the time. We were partners. Up until we were eight. After that, she had to move away as her father had to move for work. We tried to stay in touch for like a month or two, but at the age of eight, you don't really have the attention span or many possibilities to stay in touch with someone that's six hours before your time."

Colin bobs his head. "I'm sorry you had to lose her."

"Besides, I don't hate being around people." I shrug, choosing to avoid talking about Sofia. Even after all this time, talking about her makes me want to cry. "I just have this social battery thing going. I can only ever spend so much time around other human beings until my battery runs out. And then I need time to recharge."

"Well, you need a better charger then, because we will be going out tomorrow. And the day after that. And the day after that."

"And apparently I will be living with two guys for the next five days."

"One of which is your brother." Colin taps my nose with his index finger. "And I have awesome plans. Like…annoy the hell out of him."

"How?"

"Easy. I just fuck you in the kitchen."

"No." Though, it might be exciting. "We can't do this again, Colin."

"¡Colin, deja de ser raro!" A voice, sounding so much like Eira's, just with a far stronger accent, yells from the patio beneath us.

"Let me have a private conversation with Lily, thank you!"

How much of this conversation did his parents hear?

"Did you tell them about…" I trail off, not wanting to continue in case they could hear me.

"No." He shakes his head before lying down on the roof, only propping his head up with his hands. "Lie down, Lilybug."

I have to be honest. Lying on a rooftop has never been on my bucket list. And this truly can't be hygienic, but I've already been sitting here for almost two hours, might as well lie down then.

"Lilybug?" he speaks softly, calmly. "You know it's never too late to ask for help, right?"

I let out a deep breath, one that says I've been holding my breath for a little too long.

"I don't want help, Colin. I want my pain to go away. I want nothing more but to never have to feel the way I do ever again."

"And you think committing suicide is just going to have it go away?" It's a relatively stupid question.

"I wouldn't know. But it's better than to stay alive and never find peace," I admit.

His head turns, he's now facing me and no longer the sky. "Explain it to me."

"Explain what exactly?"

"How do you come to that decision? Wanting to die, I mean. There are so many other options, yet you choose to go with death. Help me understand why."

Another wave of air escapes my lungs in a hurry. "Okay." My voice is quiet, low. "Do you remember as a little kid, when the TV wasn't playing a show or anything at all. It only had this logo move from side to side and you were desperately waiting for it to hit the corner?" He nods.

"You were getting so frustrated when it took a little too long to reach the corner," I say. How am I going to explain this properly, enough to make him understand? But at least Colin doesn't seem like he's confused. In fact, Colin looks like he's truly trying to understand.

So I continue. "Now imagine being that logo. Imagine you wanting to hit a corner, that corner being relief, happiness, no more having to feel the pain from hurtful words, from betraying, separation and more. It might take a while to get there, right?" He nods again. "But what if you never get there? Imagine you're spending all day watching that one logo move to reach one of those four corners and not once does it hit one. It's frustrating. And you've only been watching for one day. Now try watching it for years on end, and it never once hits the spot. The frustration never stops, it grows and gets more with every passing day it doesn't reach its target. Eventually you're going to give up on expecting it to happen. You grow tired of it. You stop hoping, you stop wanting it because you give up. It's not happening."

"That's what my life feels like, Colin. I've been waiting to hit the corner for years, it never happened. Not even one time. I give up."

Colin starts to point up to the sky, and speaks in a soft voice, "Those look like a giraffe eating a lion." *He's changing the topic.*

"What the hell?" I don't see it. How could I? There are way too many stars to make out which ones Colin has put together in order to get a giraffe eating a lion.

"No, seriously. Just look close enough." Colin pulls me closer to him until my head is only a fist away from his.

With a swift move, Colin rolls me on top of him, my front pressing to his.

"Can't see the stars when I'm facing you instead of the sky."

"No need to look at the stars when you can look at the sun," he says, offering me a smug smile. I knew this guy was in love with himself, but God, someone scratch at the surface of his ego just a tiny bit, *please*.

"You know, I knew Aaron had another sister, other than Ana." Oh okay, he's trying his hardest to stay away from more death-talk. "No one ever mentioned your name. All I got as information about where you were was 'at some college,'" he says. "And they told me you were like two years younger."

"More like two minutes," I mutter.

"They also said you had brown hair and blue eyes."

"Now, that's just rude. They know I hate blue eyes."

"I have blue eyes."

"Yeah, and I hate them," I lie. Somewhere along the way I somehow found comfort in Colin's eyes, even though they're light blue.

Colin chuckles at my unreasonable hatred for blue eyes. It is unreasonable, I know that, so I don't mind him laughing about it.

We spend a fair amount of time just looking into the other's eyes, not speaking, not even exchanging one single word.

Until a question pops up in my head.

"Colin?" He tips his head up. "Why do you call me Lilybug?"

A small grin creeps up on his lips. Colin's arms close around my waist in a hug, even though we're still lying on the roof.

"You know the meaning of ladybugs? Good fortune, true love, innocence…needing to make the right choices in life."

I know of the first three meanings. Never have I heard of the last one.

"It's said that when you encounter a ladybug something positive is about to happen. It's supposed to resemble that even the gloomiest days will be brightened. And well, your name is Lily. The lily is a beautiful flower with yet another deep meaning. Mix that with ladybug and what do we get? Lilybug."

I'm not quite sure what I'm supposed to make of that.

Thankfully I don't get to speak because Colin checks the time on his phone, smiling.

"Happy Birthday, Lilybug."

Before I could thank him, he presses his lips to mine, allowing the unwanted butterflies in my stomach to awaken. Again.

Chapter 20

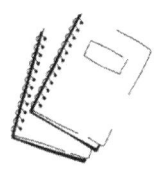

"the world would break us out we weren't wrong"—and by EDEN

Lily

AFTER SPENDING THE MORNING OF MY birthday with Colin's family, I'm relieved to finally be at my father's house.

I adore Colin's parents. His father is much nicer than I imagined he would be. And his mother has such a kind soul, I adore her even more than little Reece who wouldn't stop babbling about *Paw Patrol*. That kid loves his animated animals that go out for rescues.

And Eira, where should I begin? Eira is amazing and truly funny. Despite having caught a flu—that is supposedly not contagious—she is joking around and enjoying every bit of life she's been given. Eira is so energetic, I wonder what she is like with more strength and less flu in her body.

His family even went as far as to gift me a couple of things. These people don't know me one bit and yet they all ended up having a present for me.

I didn't even want to accept them.

Eira gifted me a designer dress. It still had the price tag attached to it.

Mrs. Carter, who I'm supposed to call Elena, gifted me a pair of new high heels, expensive ones. Mr. Carter added a new purse, fitting to the shoes. Reece drew a couple of pictures for me. I like his pictures the most of all the presents. Mainly because he didn't pay for it.

I didn't want all those presents, neither did I ask for them, and they were a total waste of money. Nonetheless, I am grateful for them.

And Colin, well, he insists I get my present from him later tonight. That's totally not freaking me out.

"Good morning there, dimples," Colin greets Ana when she comes downstairs to get breakfast. Her hair is still messed up from sleeping, she's still in shorts and a tank top, indicating that she'd just woken up.

And judging by her flushed cheeks when her eyes meet Colin's, she doesn't seem pleased by seeing him.

"Morning," she mumbles as she walks past him, heading straight to the coffee maker.

"She's always cranky in the morning," dad tells me, like I didn't know that already. To be fair, I never stopped by in the mornings. The only times I've come over to visit was late in the evenings. Yet I still know Ana isn't a morning person at all.

"Oh my God," Ana breathes. "Lily!" Her excitement to see me throws me off. I've never been nice to Ana, yet whenever she sees me, she acts like I'm her favorite person. "Happy Birthday!"

"Thank you." I don't offer more than a slim smile.

"Where's Aaron?" Ana eyes Colin with caution. Of course, she knows Colin as the guy being her brother's best friend, and somehow that annoys me.

"Not sure, home, probably."

"Then why are you here?" I'm not sure if Ana likes Colin a lot or loathes him to death.

"Meeting my in-laws."

My father laughing, covering it with a cough when he sees my serious face. Ana looks just as serious as I do.

She's a lot like me. Always serious when she doesn't like someone's comment. She won't even act like it was funny, just like I wouldn't. My father once told me she used to say she wanted to be just like me. I always dismissed that thought. Ana couldn't possibly like me, given how I'm treating her.

But despite me mistreating her for envious reasons, I like Ana. She's such a sweetheart and a genuinely nice person, always there when someone needs her. I'm sure she's a great friend to her people. Hell, she's a great friend to me and I never even gave her one reason to like me.

"That's not funny." Ana picks up the cup from the coffee maker, taking a sip. Apparently she likes dark coffee. No sugar or milk. Just plain coffee, right from the coffee maker.

"It's not," Colin agrees. "I am deadly serious. I'm getting married to my girlfriend tomorrow."

Ana's jaw drops to the floor, her eyes widening like there is a ghost across the room. "You're shitting me."

"Watch your language, Ana." Dad always disliked mature language. Cussing is a complete no-go for him.

"He's joking," I reassure Ana. "We're not getting married."

Ana visibly calms, letting out her breath as she shows her relief. I wonder why that's such a relief to her. Is the thought of me marrying Colin such a bad one? Is she worried he might regret marrying me because she knows I'm a horrible person?

"Who said I was getting married to you?" Colin looks at me, smiling. "I already signed the contract to marry Ana. Right Emerson?"

My father chuckles, shaking his head in disbelief. My father has never looked at me with such amount of amusement in his eyes. I wouldn't know if he ever looked at Aaron this way, I wasn't around much. But he sure didn't look at me like that. Not once.

My father was always proud of me. Always. After every new stunt I've learned on the ice, dad used to throw a tiny party for me the following Sunday. I really miss those days a lot.

Ana disappears upstairs, but comes back twenty minutes later, fully dressed and with a touch of makeup on her face.

She dressed up. Not like a normal Saturday morning outfit. No, I'm saying full on spending a night out kind of outfit.

"Where are you going dressed like that?" my father asks.

"Picking mom up from work." Ana grabs the car keys and puts on a jacket.

"Your mother has a car, Ana."

"She didn't take it."

"She did," my father says. I'm sure he knows whether or not his wife would need a ride home from work or not. "So, where are you going dressed like that?"

"Just driving around." She sighs and drops the keys back into the bowl by the front door. "Why can't I ever spend some time out alone?"

"You can. Just not dressed like that, Ana." I'm not blaming my father for calling Ana out on what she's wearing. Especially not when she only wants to "drive around." I mean, Ana put on a really short dress with high heels that end up brining her to my height. She straightened her hair, even put on red lipstick. And the cleavage from the dress is definitely way too much for a sixteen-year-old.

This outfit seems so familiar to me. Kind of like I've seen it before. Or worn it before.

"Go upstairs and get dressed. Properly."

"Colin likes it, don't you?" Somehow I keep forgetting that Colin is actually quite attractive when he's not riding high on his ego horse. Okay, even then he's this handsome guy girls tend to gawk at.

"It's too showy," Colin says without even looking at her once. His eyes remain on our intertwined hands, watching as his thumb brushes my skin ever so lightly.

"You like showy though."

"Says who?" He—*finally*—looks at Ana.

"You're dating Lily. She always walks around dressed like this."

Colin looks me up and down, frowning. He has every right to frown at me. Colin has never seen me truly dressed up, mainly because I haven't done that in two years. At least not in a short dress with a ton of makeup.

These days I prefer to fade into the background instead of standing out.

Self-hatred aside, I know I'm not bad looking. I'm aware of my curves, some girls would kill to have. I used to embrace them. But then I stopped because I didn't want any more attention than I've already gotten.

All I wanted was to be on my own, be forgotten so I can leave this world without anyone noticing.

"Never seen that on her." Colin shrugs, looking at me with a softness in his eyes.

Ana rolls her eyes as she storms upstairs. My father is about to go after her, clearly not tolerating Ana's behavior. But I stop him, going after her instead.

It's not like I have much to lose.

I knock on her door, waiting for her to let me in. But what comes instead is a "go away."

"Ana? It's Lily. Can we talk?"

"You never speak to me. You can ignore my existence now as well," she snaps. I totally deserved that.

"I need some advice."

"Get it from someone else." Her voice is quiet, suppressing tears. "Or ask your *boyfriend* for it. I'm sure Colin would love to hear you talk."

"I'd rather get some advice from my sister." I decide on cutting the word "step," knowing calling her my sister only would have her cave.

"Come in." *Called it*. I suppose this is my time to rectify my relationship with Ana before my death. Personally, not in form of a letter.

I walk into her bedroom, finding Ana sitting on her bed, crying. Closing the door behind me, I make my way over to her, taking a seat across from her.

"Ana," I say, almost whispering. "What is going on with you?"

"Nothing." She groans, knowing I will continue to ask until she spills out the truth. "You. That's what's wrong."

"Me?"

"Yes. You're the perfect daughter. Everyone always praises you. I'm living in your shadow and you're not even around."

I had no idea. All this time I thought Ana is the favorite. I mean, my father sure loves me, I know he does, but ever since Ana was in the picture, everything is always about her.

"And now you even got Colin." She takes a few deep breaths, toning down her anger. "You weren't even supposed to know each other. And you keep lying to me, Lily. You need my advice, on what? How to steal my whole life?"

"Actually, I wanted to say I'm sorry." Ana's eyes dart toward me in shock. There is no going back now. "I know I haven't been the nicest to you. I was jealous of you. You just came and stole what was mine. You stole my family, not that it was your fault. But I made it yours," I speak slowly, calmly.

"You've got all the attention from my father. You got to grow up with the man that was supposed to help me grow up. You even got to see my own brother more often than I did. I envied that. So I made it my own personal mission to hate you."

And then we spend the next twenty minutes talking about how much I've messed up ever since Ana is here as well. How messed up it was of me to hate on a little girl, one that couldn't even comprehend what was happening when she first got here.

I apologize a couple of times, but each time Ana tells me to stop apologizing and goes straight to hugging me.

And just like my father and Colin told me, Ana does look up to me. I don't quite understand why, but it feels good to know.

"So, you like Colin, huh?" I offer a slim smile. Having a crush on someone you can't have sucks. And having a crush on Colin Carter can never end well. I've witnessed more girls crying over this guy than I've seen planes in the sky.

"No." Ana denies it, but when I raise my eyebrows at her, she admits to me hitting the nail right on the head.

"You know he's a bit too old for you, right?"

"It's just five years," Ana says as her cheeks flush. "16 and 21 sounds wrong, it won't sound wrong anymore when it's 20 and 25. Or even 18 and 23."

"Well, good luck stealing his heart. You will lose a lot of nerves to get through his ego."

She laughs, but it quickly dies down. "He loves you."

"He sure as hell doesn't."

"You did see the way he looks at you, right?" Ana's eyes light up like the Eiffel Tower.

"How does he look at me?"

"The way I've wanted him to look at me for a while," she says, but I don't quite understand. "Like he's in love with you."

Chapter 21

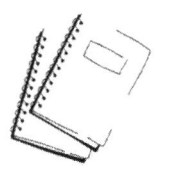

***"I've been looking for love, all I'm finding is pain"—
Shawn Mendes by Seth Bishop***

Lily

Dear whoever reads this,

*I'm not quite sure how to feel about today.
I'm excited, but I also fear what's about to happen.
Colin is going to meet my mother. My mother will hate him. I've never admitted this before, never even thought I would have to eventually...but she hates me.
She truly hates me. It's the last thing she told me a month ago when we fell out. But she hated me way before that already.
My mother always acts like she loves me so much around everyone, but when it's just the two of us...she hates me.
She's scaring me. She's hurting me.
But Colin scares me more.
Ever since that one night we've spent together, when he made me feel like I could mean more to him (moments*

before he ruined it by leaving like I was just another woman on his list), I fear him.
He kisses me sometimes. And when he does, I feel like a toddler being excited for candy. I feel every single butterfly in my stomach explodes. Not even those silly butterflies can take it anymore.
You know, ever since I could comprehend words anyone said, my parents taught me a lot of things.
Like "stay away from cigarettes and pills. There's a chance they'll kill you."
Or "never tag along with a stranger. They might kill you."
Whatever it is, it's always the same ending. It's always ending with my death.
And that makes me wonder; why would anyone want to live when all there is in the end is death?
I mean, sure, we're all destined to die eventually. But why put ourselves through the pain of life when it could all end so much earlier?
But then I think of Colin…
suddenly the pain doesn't matter anymore. It's still there, I feel it, but he makes it bearable.
And I'm scared he might succeed to convince me.
(Although I don't see that coming)
But my only reason to stay would be him.
Colin Carter would be the only reason for me to stay alive, and that's such a stupid reason.
I'm not alive for anyone but myself. In the end, anyone can backstab you. Anyone can crawl underneath your skin and cause so much more pain than you've ever felt before. And I fear Colin would be one of those kinds of pain.

He's not a bad person. But I'm sure he would leave me. And staying alive for someone that's going to leave me doesn't sound too appealing.
I will end up dead either way. Either before he has the chance to break my heart, or after he's done it.
I choose to avoid the heartbreak.
Anyway, that's not all I wanted to say today.
Although this day started off quite good, I just know it will take a drastic turn. And it frightens me.
I feel empty, yet I have to put on a smile so Colin—who's sitting right next to me while I'm writing this—won't ask about it…about me and my feelings.
I don't feel like talking about my numbness. It's truly unbearable.
I want to cry. But I know I can't.
So I will have to put on my big girl pants and just pretend. Like I do every day.

Lily

BEFORE WE ARRIVE AT MY MOTHER'S house, I need to finish writing the letter dedicated to her.

I'm not sure I have much to tell her.

I love my mother. She's been great to me. The best even. At least until she wasn't anymore.

I could never forgive her for tearing our family apart.

She knows I blame her for it. I've given her plenty speeches about how much I hate her for bringing nothing but misery into my life.

I have only ever told her that when I was mad at her for something else. Like…when I wanted to go out and she wouldn't allow it. I've always had the same excuse.

"You're a horrible mother. You tore my family, my life apart and now you won't even let me go out with my friends."

She hated it. I know she did. I know it was wrong of me to do that, it was wrong of me to continue to throw it against her head even after years. But I was mad. I *am* mad.

Yet I still have one chance to apologize to her for it.

In form of a letter.

I can't face her and tell her any of it, I know she wouldn't even let me finish my sentences.

I even doubt she will read the letter. My mother doesn't care about me anymore. Not one bit. And I'm only visiting her because I will be dead next Friday. No matter how this meeting will turn out, I need to see her one last time.

I love her. I do. Which makes it really difficult for me to let her go. To say goodbye to her. I know she won't be too sad about my death; not even sure she will care at all.

So I write her a letter, stating how sorry I am. How awful I feel for holding a grudge when all she wanted was to be loved just as much as my father was…by Liz. Apologizing for being the brat she always said I was. Apologizing for not being good enough.

My parents both cheated on one another. They've never been in love, regardless of being married. Their marriage was nothing but platonic and only used for finance profits.

And probably because they had two children together.

By the time I finish writing the letter to my mother, Colin and I arrive at her house. Now the only letter left is Aaron's.

"I bet she will hate me." I notice Colin's hands shaking, so I take them in mine, kissing his knuckles.

We haven't made whatever we are official, and we aren't going to. But the both of us know that there is more to *us* than just friendship. Friends with benefits, perhaps? That's what it is, right? Friends that fuck and kiss occasionally? We haven't even had *that* talk.

"She will love you," I assure him, but Colin doesn't seem too convinced. Neither am I.

"Did you ever take a look at me?" *I sure have*. "Every mother on this planet tells their daughters to stay away from me."

I chuckle. He sure has a point. Colin doesn't look like he has any good intentions with anyone. And before I knew him just that tiny bit better, even I thought he was a bad guy.

Not like in a sexy way. Well, he sure is handsome. But I mean, a genuinely bad person.

I hate myself for falling into the trap filled with stereotypes whenever someone has a couple more tattoos. And I know my mother will judge him for those, probably won't even give him a chance to prove that he's a great guy.

"We'll just be staying an hour. I can't be around her for too long anyway," I tell him as we approach the front door. We stop and Colin's eyes are on mine almost instantly.

I wish I could describe the way he looks at me. It's sweet and I feel the respect he has for me portrayed through his eyes. But there is something else to it. Something I can't name. Words are failing me.

"Why is that?"

I sigh, debating whether or not he should know the cold and naked truth. "She's not really fond of me." It's not like he won't witness her hatred in less than two minutes.

Colin studies me, studies my words like he is trying to find one bit of false information in them. But he can't, my mother truly doesn't like me.

"Colin, she's the only person I had. She was a great mother to me. But she wasn't always nice to me. I wasn't nice to her either. We've had our difficulties, a lot of arguments and hatred. She was relieved when I moved away for college."

Technically, I could've stayed home for college. I could have taken the bus or my mother's car to get to class every day as our house isn't too far away from campus. But I wanted out.

He blinks. Once. Twice. Never saying a word. He just looks at me and blinks like he's waiting for me to continue. Like he is expecting me to say that it's all better now. But it's not.

"She is slobby. I've been handling the household most of the time. I cleaned after her. I was more of a mother to her than she was to me. Not right from the start. It started when I was around fifteen," I explain. Colin remains silent. "I said a lot of hurtful things to her back then. So she started to dislike me, I guess. She would have never said it to my face, but I could feel the disconnection."

"Alright," he says, almost whispers.

Moments later we're seated at the kitchen table. My mother smoking her cigarette while looking at Colin like she's never seen another human before. She eyes him with disgust.

I knew I would be wrong about my mother liking Colin. She doesn't even like me, so how is she supposed to like him?

I feel Colin stiffen, especially now that our fingers are interlocked. He doesn't speak one word. All he does is look at me then back at my mother.

My mother didn't even bother wishing me a happy birthday when we came inside, nor does she make any attempts to do so now.

I could swear she was about to…until the second she noticed Colin next to me; my mother turned into a brick—emotionless and cold.

"So that's your boyfriend?" my mother speaks with revulsion.

"Yes." *No.*

"I see." She blows smoke out in my direction, knowing very well that I hate when she does that.

I don't care about her smoking. It's her own body, she can do whatever the hell she wants. But that doesn't give her the right to force me to passively smoke along with her.

At least Colin seems to feel just as disgusted by the smoke. He tries not to let it show though. I, on the other hand, I'm coughing, waving my hands around in order to free, not only my sight, but also to clear the air I'm inhaling from smoke.

"And you're an athlete?"

"I am," Colin answers, offering my mother an awkward smile. I bet he wishes he'd never come.

Now that Colin met my mother, I'm sure he will tell Aaron that it's not worth getting to know her. It'll make it easier on my part because then I won't have to talk too much about our mother in his letter.

"Like Aaron then," my mother says. I almost choke on the air while Colin gasps.

She has never even mentioned Aaron's name in sixteen years. Never said it once. Whenever I tried to speak about him, my mother would push the topic away and tell me to stop thinking about him.

So how the hell does she know Aaron is an athlete? And why would she connect Colin to Aaron?

Colin looks at me, eyes filled with fear. He has no idea what to say, and neither do I. I have so many questions, yet I don't know where to start asking.

"I know you will be together tonight." Now it's my time to stiffen up. "Celebrating your big birthday together."

"Mom"—*I need answers*—"how would you know that?"

"Don't be silly, Lily," she chuckles. "You've been seeing him for way too long. I know you have. Why do you think did I start disliking you?"

"Because I was misbehaving?" Damned if her openly admitting to disliking me doesn't sting in my heart. I mean, she has before…a month ago, but I thought that was the heat of the moment and it just slipped out.

"You were," she agrees. "Your father knew what he signed you up for when he kept in touch with you. We had very little rules, and here he was breaking every single one of them."

I'm not sure if my mom mentions all this now to scare Colin off, or if she's just fed up with me. Either way, I'm kind of glad she finally says it out loud, meaning it. Hating me, I mean. It will make leaving this fucked up life a ton easier.

"You're so much like him," she says, smiling. It's a devilish smile. If Colin wouldn't be here with me, I'm sure I would be running out of the door right now. "And your brother, he's just as arrogant as I imagined he would be. With his rich father, the rich stuck-up stepmother. You're both little shits."

I want to cry. I want to rip my heart out right at this moment, tear every organ out of my body until I pass on to another dimension.

My mother has officially ruined my birthday for me.

"With all due respect, Mrs. Reyes, Lily is amazing. She's a really great person. And so is your son by the way. Maybe you should try finding flaws in yourself and not the children you've abandoned." I only roughly pay attention to Colin. I'm more focused on suppressing my tears. I won't cry in front of my mother. I won't.

"I didn't abandon Lily. I am a great mother. I have always been good to her. I let her live here for many years."

"That doesn't make you a great mother. In fact, it makes you an even worse one. You had no intentions keeping Lily close to you, so I would assume by the way you're speaking about her. The best thing you could have done was to give her away to her father. To someone that would have made sure she'd be happy."

Colin stands up from his chair, lifting me up to my feet as well. He tightens the grip around my hand as he looks at me. His other hand places down onto my cheek, wiping underneath my eye. *A tear must have spilled over. Dammit.*

"Lily is suffering from what you've caused over her. She is handling so many things, stuff you would know of if you only paid a little more attention to your own daughter. And yet here you are, telling her that you dislike her. On her birthday."

"It's not my fault she can't care for herself."

Words could never express what it's like to admire the woman that gave birth to you, and she treats you like a waste of space.

She hasn't always been like that, maybe that's why I'm still holding onto her. Even now.

"I gave her everything and she threw it away for a guy that cheated on me."

"It's not like you didn't cheat on dad!" Dear God, please stop these tears from wanting to spill over. I can't do this today.

"Your father is a piece of shit. Just like you and your brother!" She slams her hands onto the kitchen table.

Colin and I haven't even been here for fifteen minutes and she's already about to break the next window. I can sense it.

It certainly wouldn't be the first time that she'd break one. I know if this doesn't stop soon, she will throw something at the kitchen window until it breaks. And for what? So she can run after me with a few broken glass pieces and threaten to kill me with it.

Colin takes a deep breath as he pulls me out of the kitchen, forcing me to leave this house along with him.

I'm glad he decides we're leaving. I don't want to be here for another minute.

"You shouldn't have been born, Lily!" My mother shouts right before the front door slams close. I can still hear her scream and throw things around, breaking furniture, even through the closed door.

She doesn't come outside. She doesn't want to make this right. She won't apologize, I know she won't. I also know that this is the last thing my mother will have said to me before I died.

You shouldn't have been born, Lily.

How much hatred does a mother need to have inside of her to scream this at her child? How much pain does she have to be in, in order to make her daughter feel this miserable?

A lot, I assume.

She's not feeling any better than I do, I know that for sure. Only a broken soul can react this way. I don't blame her for wanting to hurt me. She's trying to deal with her own problems. She's trying to deal with her own pain.

Doesn't mean it wounds me any less.

But now that the door is closed and it's just Colin and I left, I let the tears slip free. I allow myself to break, allow my tears to run down my cheeks, allow my pain to take over my body.

No matter how shitty my mother treats me, I will never stop craving her love. I will never stop wanting her to be in my life. She is my mother. I know that sometimes relatives can cause you more harm than anyone, but I still love her. She hurts me like no one ever could, and I still love her with all that I have.

"I'm sorry you had to witness that," I say quietly, tugging onto Colin's shirt. He doesn't answer. All he does is wrap his arms around my body, pulling me close to him.

He doesn't care when my tears wet his shirt. He doesn't care when some of my mascara stains it, or when I start to cry so much, I can barely breathe.

He just stands there with me, hugging me so tightly that I almost feel okay. Almost like my mother didn't just tell me that she wishes I was dead.

But she did say that. And he heard it. And he now knows where I get these thoughts from.

"Lilybug." His voice is a whisper, filled with concern and sympathy. I can hear how sorry he is for me. But I don't want him to feel sorry for me. I don't want his pity.

"Can you just drive me home?"

"Can I take you somewhere else first?" Colin pulls away from the hug, looking at me.

His hands remain on my body. He's holding me by my waist, gently moving his thumbs over my body, looking so deeply into my eyes, I could melt. I would melt...if I didn't believe there was almost to nothing left of me.

"I'm tired, Colin. I don't want any more adventures today."

He nods, but then lifts his shoulders as he shrugs at me. "It will be good for you, I promise." I don't get to answer because Colin lifts me up from the floor and carries me over to his car, sitting me inside like I'm unable to do that myself.

My eyes follow him as he jogs over to the driver's side and slips into the car, starting the engine faster than I could blink. And just like that, we're back on the road, leaving my mother behind like nothing happened.

Fifteen minutes later, Colin stops in front of an older looking building. It doesn't have any signs, no indications that anyone lives there, but it doesn't look like an abandoned house either.

We get out of the car, his hand taking mine the second we're back next to one another. I like his hand in mine, or mine in his. It's a simple gesture, yet it offers more intimacy than I would have ever thought.

The longer Colin is holding onto my hand, the more it starts to burn. Not that I feel any physical pain, but it burns in my heart. It burns like a lit torch is being held right underneath me. The flame isn't hitting my skin, but the hot air still touches me.

Or maybe his touch appears more like the color yellow to me. A color so warm and powerful. It's the heat you feel when you rub your palms together. This kind of warmth floods through my veins when our hands link together. It's as joyful as seeing the little drop of water on top of grass, so simple yet so beautiful.

And that's what I feel in my heart when Colin is with me. It's what I feel when his hand is holding mine. Happiness. Warmth. He makes me *feel*, banishing my numbness for a short while.

Chapter 22

"when your eyes can't see, take your eyes from me. When you're lost and losing faith, I will be your saving grace"—Saving Grace by Kodaline

Colin

I DO THINK THAT LILY NEEDS THIS. She needs to let out her negative feelings, her anger, her frustration. Especially after what just happened back at her mother's house.

Lily doesn't speak when we're inside the building. She looks quite irritated even, like she doesn't know why I took her plate smashing.

I think it's self-explanatory, she doesn't seem to think so.

"Take this sharpie," I say, handing her a black sharpie. She hesitates at first, just furrowing her eyebrows at me. Eventually she takes it though.

I tell her to wait right where she's at, then walk off toward the reception to pay for a couple of plates. I make sure it's alright that we'll be writing on them. All the guy sitting at the front desk says is, "They'll break anyway. Do as you please."

He has a point. Still, I wanted to make sure it is okay.

I pay for a total of twenty-two plates, carrying eleven plates over to Lily, then go back to get the other eleven.

Lily doesn't help, but I also don't want her to.

Once all of the twenty-two plates are placed on the table nine feet away from a huge target sign, I only walk back to the reception one last time to get two helmets.

I put one on my head, then go back to Lily and put the other onto her head. She's confused, but I guess she has assumptions as to what this is about.

"You got the sharpie?" Lily nods once, holding it up. "Good."

I hand her an empty plate and take one for myself. She watches me as I write something down on mine.

Forgive me, Aiden.

"Who's Aiden?" Lily cocks her head to the side.

"Not too important." I offer a slim smile. I didn't tell her everything there is to know about me. Actually, I don't think I've ever truly told Lily anything about me.

And with no further explanation, I throw the plate at the huge red target sign with all of the anger I have inside of me. It smashes, splintering into tons of tiny pieces when it hits the wall.

It's a relief. I know this doesn't take away the naked truth and the fact that the problem is still present, but it does offer some relief. Even if it's just a short-term relief.

I turn to Lily, nodding for her to do the same. She thinks it's silly, so she doesn't want to do that.

"Do it anyway."

Lily shakes her head. "I won't write something down and smash a perfectly fine plate."

"They're all malfunctions. Have a few cracks already. They would have gotten thrown out anyway. You'll feel better."

Lily sighs, knowing I'm right. I wouldn't go as far as to say I'm always right…but I kind of am.

"Just throw one and see if it does something," I tell her.

Lily nods carefully, pulling the cap off the sharpie before writing something down. I would love to know what she is writing, but I'm not going to ask for her to tell me. If she wants me to know, she'll tell me.

Before I know, Lily is throwing the plate across the room, watching as it shatters into pieces. She falls down to her knees, sobbing again.

She's been crying ever since we stepped out of her mother's house, and it is breaking my goddamn heart. I don't want to see her tear-stained face anymore. It hurts me. But maybe crying is good for her.

I don't dare touching Lily, not right now. I want her to deal with her pain, feel the relief as the emotions she wrote onto that plate shatter.

So I'm waiting. Waiting for Lily to react. Waiting for her to say something, move, do literally anything. But it doesn't come. Not for the next two minutes at least.

"Why'd you get so many?" she asks, her voice so quiet, I barely hear it.

"Twenty-two, for twenty-one years of bullshit. And one for me, because I had to demonstrate how to do this safely."

She turns her head to look at me. A soft smile tugs on her lips, her eyes hopeful and filled with appreciation.

"That must have been expensive."

I shrug. "Not more than $30. It was a dollar for each plate, $8 for extra time."

"I'll pay you back."

"You will," I say, "by throwing those plates against the wall."

"Thank you, Colin." Lily stands back up on her feet, so I hand her another plate. She takes it and starts to scribble down another word, or a couple more.

She throws it against the wall with all of her strength, letting her tears just roll down her face as she lets go of her pain. For a moment at least.

"*I've never been more disappointed in you, Liliana.*" Her tenth plate reads. I wonder if her mother said this to her.

But wait a second; *Liliana*?

Why did she keep that from me?

I want to ask Lily about it, but I don't think this is the right time to ask if her first name isn't Lily but Liliana.

Maybe I'm imagining things. I mean, my heart is still aching for this beautiful blonde girl in front of me. It's still hurting from the tears that I see on her cheeks whenever she turns around and smiles at me. It still hurts when I see her red puffy eyes and her reddened nose. It still hurts when I hear her voice break as she screams when she throws the plate.

It still hurts to know that she's in pain.

"*Maybe I should have kept the other disappointment instead of you, Liliana.*"

Lily isn't writing down what she feels. She is writing down hurtful memories. Memories she wishes she doesn't have. Sentences that broke her world, ones she is now shattering, banishing from her life. Maybe for a just a moment, maybe forever. Who knows?

"*I don't want to see you anymore. Just leave. Leave or die. I don't care.*"

Lily is down to two plates. Her eyes lock with mine for a second when she takes one from my hands. She looks happier. Maybe not happy, but definitely lighter.

Like throwing these words against a wall and see her connected emotions burst into pieces lifted off some of the weight she's been carrying with her.

"Can I write down wishes?"

I nod. She can do whatever the hell she wants with those plates. She could have thrown them all at once for all that I care. As long as it's helping, even just for a little bit, I'm good with it.

"Good." She smiles and turns away from me. She won't let me read what she writes before throwing the plate against the target sign.

This time she's not crying when it shatters. She turns around, scrunches up her nose as she beams at me. "One more," she says as she takes the plate from my hands. But before she turns back around, Lily tugs at my collar, pulling me down to her enough to brush her lips against mine. "Thank you," she whispers and turns back around.

Kissing Lily is starting to feel natural. I could never get bored of it, and it's not like I fear kissing her anymore. If I want to kiss her, I do and I will.

She may think I'm only trying to protect her from more pain when I said she was mine. But that's not what I was talking about.

She is mine. Even if she dies, she's always going to be mine. I know this girl is special. She has a huge heart, loves with so much brightness. It's so sad to see that she wouldn't even see it herself.

So I'll be loving her. I'll love her until her last breath, and even after that I'll continue to love her with every breath I take. Even if I have to breathe for the both of us.

Lily throws the plate, but this time it's not breaking.

We're both looking at the plate with huge question marks over our heads.

Lily just threw a plate against a brick wall from nine feet distance, and it didn't break. What kind of dark magic is that?

"What the hell?" Lily laughs. "It was the most important wish." Her hands fall to her sides, her body slightly sagging in frustration.

"What did you wish for?" I ask. I would get the plate for her, if the area wasn't locked off for anyone but employees.

I see Lily's brain work, like she's contemplating on telling me. It can't possibly be that big of a secret.

"Your happiness."

"What?" I almost start to cough from swallowing in surprise.

"I was wishing for you to find a girlfriend that loves you unconditionally. Someone to be alongside you when I can't do that anymore."

I gulp, swallowing hard. Once. Twice. Probably a couple more times before I find my voice. "Why?" is all I can come up with. It's all I can get myself to say. My mouth is far too dry to bring words across my lips.

"Because I need you to be happy, even after my death. I need you to be okay. I want to know you found your happiness, Colin."

I inhale deeply. How do I tell someone who's suicidal that I've already found my happiness, and it will leave right when she does? How do I tell her that she is my happiness, that she is bringing light to my life? How do I tell her that she is my joy, everything that brings me satisfaction, that she is my euphoria…without sounding like I want her to stay alive for me?

"Better luck next time," I say, grabbing her hand in mine.

We're giving our helmets back to the guy at the front desk and say goodbye. The guy, who's name I think is Jeff—at least that's what his nametag says—seems a bit confused.

Can't blame him. He's watched Lily have a whole mental breakdown over plates and then she leaves with a huge grin on her lips while half her face is still covered in mascara smudges.

She still looks pretty though.

"I JUST DON'T GET IT," I say, munching on some popcorn.

When Lily and I got home, she asked me to watch a movie before we eventually have to get going for the bar. Of course I agreed.

I wouldn't have if she told me *she* was picking the movie.

Okay, I still would have agreed.

But now I'm stuck here, watching *Legally Blonde* because it's Lily's favorite movie. And I don't get it.

"What's there not to understand?" She is laughing at me. I don't like that she thinks I'm stupid, but at least she's laughing.

Luckily, it's the end of the movie now, meaning I no longer have to sit through an overly sexist representation of a rich girl, living on solely daddy's pockets.

Seriously, why do these older movies always have the rich teenage female main character dressed in pink? And only pink, like it's some sort of character trait of theirs. What if they wanted to wear blue? Not every rich girl loves pink.

"The ending," I say. "Emmet totally should've gotten with Elle."

Lily laughs...again. "Did you not read what it said on the screen by the end?"

"It's a movie. You don't do reading while watching a movie, Lilybug."

Lily rolls her eyes at me, shaking her head disbelievingly. "It literally said they've been dating for two years."

"Liar." I don't believe Lily. Okay, I do. But I know if I don't and rewind the part now, she will laugh again.

So I rewind the movie until the beginning of their graduation. We watch until—*who would have guessed it*—it says just what Lily told me.

"Oh, fuck me."

"Like, right now?"

My eyes shoot toward Lily with shock displaying in them. I was expecting another round of laughter. Maybe even her literally making fun of me. But I never saw *that* coming.

I feel my dick harden instantly.

In not even a heartbeat, I tip Lily over, her back meeting the sitting space from the sofa, and hover right over her. She lets out a breathless shriek as I press my weight onto her, though I make sure she can still breathe properly. Lily is just a tad dramatic sometimes.

"I'm always down to have sex with you, Lilybug," I say, grinning. "But are you down for it?"

Lily smiles at me mischievously, shrugging, not saying a word.

She is trying to kill me.

"I'll figure it out." That said, I trace my hand down her body, cursing her out in my head for deciding to wear jeans today. Jeans have to get unbutton first, only then can I slip my hand inside her pants. If she'd be wearing leggings it would be a lot easier. But I'm not going to complain…to her at least. In my head, I sure am complaining.

I unbutton her pants and reach inside, watching her gaze change from pure sweetness to pure lust. Her desire for me to get her off almost makes me come in my pants. It's ridiculously embarrassing.

Cupping my hand over her pussy, just slightly brushing over her underwear has Lily's breath shaky. And I am absolutely digging it.

She doesn't tell me what to do. She isn't telling me to stop, but she also isn't begging for me to touch her, *yet*. She is just letting me do what I think is right, knowing it will get her out of here satisfied.

I'm not saying my finger game is mind-blowing, but I'm pretty confident with what I do, and I know how to do it right.

I add pressure against her entrance, pressing her underwear slightly against her core, feeling the wetness slowly soak through the fabric.

Lily lifts her hips up, wanting me to go further than that.

So I slip my hand underneath her underwear, sliding my finger through her folds, coating them in her wetness. I dip one finger only slightly into her core before pulling it out and spreading the evidence of her arousal around.

She moans, wrapping her arms around my neck, pulling me down just a tiny bit more so her lips can brush over mine. I'm not fighting the kiss. In fact, I'm glad she is kissing me. I was craving to feel that sweet mouth of hers pressed to mine again.

Dipping fingers back inside of her, Lily's breath hitches, her hips shifting into my touch.

"Aw, fuck." The feeling of Lily has my head spin—A good kind of spinning.

All I want to do is rip off her clothes and fuck her right here on the sofa. I want—*need*—to feel her. I need to be inside of her. Right now.

But what I want more than to be inside of her right now is to please her. To listen to her whimpers, begging me to make her come. To hear her moan out my name when she does.

My fingers curl up inside her as I stroke the pad of my thumb over her clit, flicking it, slowly.

God, what I would do to taste her right now. Taste her when I suck on that clit of hers instead of massaging it with my thumb. Taste her on my tongue when I dip into her core, licking her.

But instead I have her lips pressed to mine. More or less so. Lily barely manages to kiss back. But instead of finding that annoying, it's a great way to tell that she's feeling good. That *I* am making her feel good.

And then, she starts to beg. "*Please*." Her mouth is open against mine, no longer kissing me but trying to.

It brings a chuckle to my throat, but I don't let it slip out.

I could continue to tease her, pull out my fingers and stop stimulating her clit. I can decide to be a tease or give her what she wants: an orgasm.

Since it's Lily's birthday, I choose the latter and give her what she is begging for.

Lily is panting, trying to steady her breathing, my hand still inside her pants when gagging sounds appear from the door.

I don't budge too much, knowing that's Aaron. Lily, however, is panicking.

She pulls my hand out of her pants, quickly zipping them up before hiding her face in the palms of her hands. She doesn't sit up, doesn't even move at all. All Lily does is lie there, hiding her face.

It's amusing, but I know I shouldn't find this funny. Lily is embarrassed, mortified—probably.

I sit up, looking into Aaron's eyes as I slowly suck off Lily's wetness from my fingers. He watches me with disgust written all over his face.

If it wasn't Lily lying on the sofa next to—*or behind*—me, Aaron wouldn't care. Truth is, I once fucked a girl right next to him. Like the good best friend he is, he pretended to be asleep until she left. He didn't care one bit. But this is Lily, of course he cares now.

"Did you just finger fuck my sister on our sofa?" It's a rhetorical question.

Lily squeals at his words, not wanting to hear him say this. Then she is finally sitting up, having found enough courage to face her brother.

Or not. Cause instead of facing him, Lily moves right behind me, wrapping her arms and legs around my torso and hides her face in my back. It's like she is using me as her own personal armor.

"No," Lily mumbles, yet at the same time I voice a "Yes." Lily slaps me for it, but I don't understand why. It's not like Aaron is stupid. He knows what he's seen, hell, maybe even heard.

"That's disgusting," he says through faked gags. "Can you at least try to keep this away from my eyes? Otherwise I will move out."

"Even better. Gives Lilybug and me more privacy."

Lily slaps her palm to my chest once more, tapping her forehead against my back a couple of times while groaning in desperation.

"Wait, you said Lily would stay for five days only."

"Yup. Still only five days."

"I don't want to be here," Lily groans out. Aaron laughs, shaking his head.

Even when Aaron stops to laugh, he still has a gentle smile on his lips. I'm not sure if it's there because he is happy for Lily that she found someone to use as her shield, or if he's just bemused by all this and plans on killing me tonight.

I'll go with the latter, taking a mental note to lock my bedroom door when we get back home from the bar.

"I'm so glad it's my birthday and we're going to Brites. I really need a drink after *that*. Or ten." Aaron makes his way upstairs, but I stop him, calling out his name. "What is it?"

"Happy birthday."

"Fuck off. But thanks."

Chapter 23

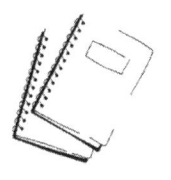

"even when it's do or die, we could do it, baby, simple and plain, cause this love is a sure thing"—Sure Thing by Miguel

Lily

I HATE BARS.

I hate that wherever I look, there is always some guy hitting on a girl, being just a bit too touchy.

And I hate that I'm seated at a booth with five hockey players, one soccer player and only one other woman.

But what's worse, Aaron won't stop looking at me with this weird look on his face. Like he is traumatized. I'm sure he is, cause even I am. If I had walked in on him doing something remotely close to that, I would have to go straight back to therapy.

"I thought you would bring your friends, Lily." Miles smiles at me with hunger in his eyes.

If I wasn't somewhat engaged with Colin, perhaps I would find that charming. A bit disrespectful, but at least I'd feel attractive.

This guy could have anyone. I'm sure he would just have to look into some girl's direction, and he'd find her in his bed in less than an hour. So why the hell is he looking at me like he wants to undress me?

"Stop gawking and drooling over my girlfriend," Colin snaps at Miles. I like that he calls me his girlfriend, but it's bad for my health. We're not actually a couple. But then again, my mental health isn't really alive anyway, so what does it matter?

Izan, however, he looks at Colin with suspicion. I knew this guy would look right through him. Izan is smart, ridiculously smart. And he is good at analyzing people.

He's the only other person that figured out I'm not doing too well health wise.

We had one class together back in freshman year, we immediately became good friends. We don't speak too often anymore as he is busy with his soccer team. And I'm busy with Colin, apparently.

Anyway, Izan figured out my desire to die way before I was sure of it. He provided some help for me, asked his mother to become my therapist. And it helped. For a short while at least.

Fast forward three years, I no longer go to therapy because "I'm doing better" and I'm actually going to die in a week.

Aaron is on his third beer, he hasn't been drinking anything else since we've got here. Apparently the "harder drinks" will get into his system after midnight. Up until then, he will stick to beer.

Colin isn't drinking anything alcoholic, neither am I. Colin's reason to stay sober is that he has to drive, which is true. He has to drive us home. And probably drag Aaron away from some girl's ass.

I, on the other hand, I just never had the desire to drink alcohol. I've always been too afraid that I would start babbling about me and my feelings.

Actually, I know I will do that. I was drunk once in my life, and all I did was cry and whine about my depression.

Nothing I would like to repeat.

"Since when are you guys a thing?" Izan asks, his confusion visible on his face. He crosses his arms in front of his chest, impatiently waiting for an answer that confirms his suspicion.

"Couple of days. Aaron wouldn't let me—"

"Nope," Aaron interrupts, holding up a hand. "I do not need a reminder of what I witnesses earlier."

Colin starts to laugh like getting caught in the act is completely normal for him.

"Excuse me, what did *we* witness?" Miles asks. For a second I'm mortified, thinking Grey and Miles were there as well. But turns out these guys just tell the other every little detail. So if Aaron knows something, the rest does as well. With the same amount of knowledge.

I think it's great that they have such a deep bond, yet I feel miserable. I feel bad because Colin keeps secrets from them. That secret being me and my condition.

And then it settles with me. When I die next week, Aaron will find out Colin knew. Colin will lose his best friend. He knows that's what's going to happen to his friendship after my death.

And yet he stays with you, Lily.

"I will not recall that, Miles." Aaron brings his glass to his mouth, chugging down his entire drink.

"But some hot information about Lily won't hurt anyone," Miles protests.

Colin warned me about Miles not having a filter. He warned me about Miles being the best at saying stupid things without comprehending what they might mean to others.

Supposedly, it's never meant in a bad way.

I want to believe Colin with that. Miles seems like a nice person. But he certainly acts like a teenager hitting puberty.

As I stare at him for a little while, I notice something odd about Miles. He gets nervous. It's as though the nasty guy he seems to be is just a barrier to hide whatever lies beneath.

"I will hurt you when you continue speaking of Lily like she isn't here," Colin says. His hands ball into fists but he loosens them shortly after. "Don't be like that Miles. Lily isn't some toy. She means a lot to me, and I promise you, I will break your nose if you continue that behavior around her or me. I'm not sure Brooke would like to see that."

And the butterflies are back. *Stupid butterflies*. Maybe I should refer to them as dragonflies, because nothing about this is good.

It stings my stomach like fire burns skin.

From the corner of my eyes, I catch Aaron smiling. I'm not sure what that smile is about, nothing funny happened. But it also doesn't seem like an amused smile. It's genuine, soft…a happy smile, perhaps?

Colin leans in closer to me, his mouth close to my ear as he whispers, "Let's go dancing, Lilybug."

I shake my head. If there's something I can't do, it's dancing. I can move on the ice like a princess, but dancing in high heels is impossible. It's even impossible in sneakers already.

He presses his lips to my temple, sliding out of the booth and pulling me with him.

I guess I'm going on the tiny dancefloor this bar provides.

"Colin, I can't dance," I tell him, but he just shrugs his shoulders at me. I'm not sure he heard me. The music is quite loud, and I wasn't speaking loudly.

"They're not even playing a good song, Colin." If he hears that, he heard what I said before as well.

"What do you mean?" He wraps his arms around my body from behind, resting his chin on my shoulder. "They're playing *Sure Thing*."

"That's not a song to dance to," I let him know. Clearly his ears aren't working, neither are his eyes. "No one is dancing anymore."

"So what?" He chuckles and pulls me right onto the outlined dance area.

Colin's hands remain on my body, along with tons of eyes that are staring at Colin and me. I mean, who's crazy enough to dance to a song that's not danceable to.

But what I've come to learn, Colin doesn't care about what other people think of him. He doesn't care who's staring at him. He just does what he wants and enjoys it with every beat of his heart.

I close my eyes, terrified to accidentally lock them with some stranger that's laughing at us. Though it doesn't sound like anyone's laughing. In my head they're all laughing anyway.

With Colin's hands on my hips, I start to sway to the rather slow rhythm.

Once the chorus comes around, Colin leans in closer to me, whisper-singing the lyrics into my ear. And once his voice streams through my ears, I no longer hear the whistles from his friends. I no longer feel the gazes of strangers on me.

All there is, is Colin.

He's all over my skin, under my skin. He is in me, intoxicating every piece of my body.

Colin has become my addiction. He is like a drug. I told myself "Just this once," one kiss wouldn't hurt. One kiss wouldn't mean anything. And then we kissed. And we did it again. *One more time*, it wouldn't hurt.

And now that "one more time" has turned into a constant repetition.

So as soon as the song ends, I tug on Colin's necklace, pulling him down until our lips meet.

My tongue slips into his mouth, not caring that there are people watching us. Not caring that Aaron is watching us.

Colin tastes like Coca-Cola and Colin, but fuck do I love it.

And—who would have thought—the butterflies are back.

The way his lips move over mine, how his tongue tastes mine, how his fingers press into the skin on my waist, it all has me melt into him.

In the moment of our kiss, all of my feelings for him sneak out, pouring all the attraction into it. I fear bursting into flames, that's how heated it gets when our lips interlock.

I want nothing more but to give him my heart. I want more time with him. But it's impossible. My time is running out, we both know that. We both know that I only have six days left, five if you don't count the day I die.

Suicidal thoughts aside for a moment, I do wonder if there is a chance for me. If there is a chance for Colin and me *together*.

But I shouldn't stay alive for someone. I should be wanting to live because I want to, not because I seem to be attracted to a guy.

I love Aaron, and yet I don't want to stay alive for him. I should feel the same about Colin, given that I'm only attracted to him and don't love him.

The next song starts to play and suddenly more people make their way to the dancefloor. It's getting a little crowded, but I don't mind because Colin's lips are still pressed to mine.

I found peace in his kisses. It's like, when my lips are attached to Colin's, I'm home. It feels right.

We might need to pause for air sometime soon, but I really don't want to. Yet, we both pull away anyway.

His forehead comes down to mine and he stares into my eyes. His have nothing but absolute admiration in them. And if there was more to it, he is good at hiding it.

"I love that dress on you," he whispers into my ear, then leaves a kiss right behind it.

I was going to wear jeans and a sweatshirt but changed my mind and ended up wearing a red, skin-tight dress. It shows off my shoulders and collarbones, and I guess I look good in it.

"Do you know the song?" I ask. Colin shakes his head no. "Me neither."

"You want to go sit back down?"

"No." I grin, intertwining our hands. Spanish songs always have the best rhythms to dance to. Or most of them do, anyway. "Can you translate it?"

Colin cocks his head to the side, smiling slightly, yet I can tell he's confused.

"I know you speak Spanish."

He laughs, shaking his head in disbelief. "Someone's a bit of a stalker," he says. "I've never told you."

"You call your mother 'Mamá.'" I raise my eyebrows at him. "And you occasionally switch to Spanish when you're on the phone with your sister."

Something passes within him, like a thought that doesn't quite want to settle. "I do?" I nod. "Really? I don't usually switch between language in front of anyone but my family."

"Why?" I find myself asking. But either he doesn't want to answer me or he's refusing to do so.

His eyes narrow at me, one side of his lips tipping up. "You don't really want to understand the lyrics to *Rechazame, mi sol*," He laughs and pulls me off the dancefloor.

He leads me back to the booth we sat at before, but we're not sitting down.

"We're leaving, sweetheart," he whispers into my ear.

I don't answer to that, instead I voice, "What does it mean?"

"What does what mean?" he asks in return.

"Whatever you just called me. I know you did call me something." But instead of answering my question, he grins and speaks to Aaron.

"You better not lose it." Colin's voice is strict as he lays his credit card on the table in front of Aaron. "I'm in need of it tomorrow."

Surely that's because of me. Because tomorrow is another day he will take me somewhere. I hate that. Well, I hate that he is spending so much money on me, not that we're spending time together.

He hasn't spent too much yet, I think. The sunrise didn't cost anything. The coffee's, however, they were expensive. God, it doesn't matter what he spent, he spent money on me, and I hate that.

"Why? Going on a date?" Aaron speaks with a sarcastic undertone. I'm still not too sure if he's happy or if he wants to strangle Colin.

Aaron has a glass with whiskey standing in front of him, which tells me that it's after midnight by now.

"Got to spoil your sister." That said, Colin turns back to me, smiling tenderly.

I lean in closer to his ear, saying, "I don't want to leave yet." I'm not even surprised when his eyes widen in shock and a spark of concern shines through.

Colin knows I'd much rather be at home these days instead of with a crowd. Although I appreciate his concern and the fact that he wants me to be comfortable, I do actually want to stay this time.

"You sure?" His hand places down on my lower back, a bit too low for Aaron's liking.

"God, would you stop this already?" Aaron groans, taking a sip from his whiskey. "I want to enjoy this night and not be reminded of what I've seen."

"Just grow up and you'll be fine." Colin slides into the booth, seating himself next to Grey. I slide in beside him.

Izan watches us all with knitted eyebrows. Only then do I realize that Aaron might have told his hockey team we're twins, but that doesn't mean Izan knows. I just assumed Grey told him.

"Aaron is my twin brother," I enlighten Izan, not wanting him to remain clueless.

Instead of being surprised, Izan covers his mouth in horror as his eyes travel from Aaron to Colin and back. *Does he know something I don't?*

"You broke the bro code *and* team code?" Izan then utters, aiming his question at Colin. His sudden courage aside, Izan still appears horrified.

"Not so much to break it. I asked for permission. Still got some beating." Colin shrugs like it's nothing.

"I didn't hit you."

"Guys, I have an idea." Miles sets his drink down on the table, bringing a much-needed end to this conversation.

I already saw the red and blue lights from police cars flash in front of my eyes. Seeing how I have to explain to an officer why my not-really-boyfriend and my brother started to beat the shit out of the other.

"Let's see who'd cave first, Colin or Aaron." *Excuse me?* "I bet Lily could never get Archer Kingston's phone number," he voices a bet.

Miles certainly has all of the guys' attention now. Every ear and pair of eyes is on him as he explains his "*amazing*" bet in detail.

I'm saying, me flirting with some guy named Archer and what exactly I should get from him. Seemingly, Archer is hard to get.

It is the stupidest bet I have ever heard. And the most dangerous for Colin and Aaron.

If the guy I'm being dared to approach as much to looks at me the wrong way, Aaron will have his fist in the guy's face. If he as much to breathes into my direction, Aaron will freak out. But so will Colin, I guess.

I'm not sure Colin cares much about me flirting with other guys. However, I am certain he might act as though it bothers him a lot.

Next thing I know, Miles points toward a really handsome guy, telling me to get started. I don't usually walk up to random bar guys, nor did I ever even try to flirt with one before. But I guess this is my time to learn.

I don't have much to lose anyway. Worst case scenario, the guy hates me and gets beaten up for it. Well, or he breathes and still gets beaten up... *He will get beaten up.*

Making my way over to the goddamn hot looking redheaded Archer Kingston, I take a seat at his table without asking. He blinks at me as if to ask why the hell I am being so disrespectful and just take a seat at stranger's tables.

"Hello"—my voice is thin and lacks confidence—"I'm Lily."

"Archer," he says, raising just one brow at me. "You need anything?"

"*You.*" I cringe at myself for this one, internally. Feeling at least seven pairs of eyes on me, two pretty intensely staring ones, I decide to shake off my fear and proceed to speak. "I was kind of hoping..."

"Cupcake, who are you trying to impress?" He barks a laugh, looking around the bar. "Your friends sent you over here?"

I shake my head no. *Not friends, my brother's friend.* "It's my birthday and I figured spending it alone would be a shame."

"Your birthday?" Archer doesn't buy it. Dang it, he *is* one hard nut to crack. So I take out my ID to show him my birthdate.

"Liliana," he says.

I roll my eyes. "Lily."

"Technically, your birthday is over by now," he says, pointing at his phone screen that says it's 12:23 a.m.

"Well, as long as I haven't slept, it's still Saturday."

Archer takes my hand, kissing the back of it. "It's nice to meet you, birthday girl." *Not so difficult after all.*

"It's certainly an adventure knowing me."

He chuckles, yet he doesn't know what I was referring to.

"How old are you?" I find myself asking, even begin to get touchier. I slide my hand up his muscular arm and back down, offering him a smile.

"Thirty-two." My face must have turned completely pale because Archer starts to laugh like I've bathed my face in baby powder. "I'm twenty."

I want to speak, but when I feel Archer's arm wrap around my waist, pulling me closer to him, my voice leaves my body. It just packed a suitcase in a whole second and left me.

He slides his hand up and down my side, then guides it deeper down until it's almost touching my butt. I don't say anything, I still can't. My voice is still moved over to Australia. Come to think my voice bought a one-way ticket.

"Are you more of a one-night kind of girl, or do I need to take you out on dates before you'd let me in your pants?"

Now that's straight forward.

I find my voice, which is surprising because I had all my money bet on it never coming back. "Let's discuss this after you gave me your phone number."

"She's got her eyes on someone." The deep voice appearing from behind me speaks grumpily.

"Carter." Archer nods up at Colin. "Don't think she's much into you when Lily here came to speak to me."

"You will have four firsts in your face in about two seconds if you don't remove your hand from my girl."

Archer looks at Colin's hands, saying, "You only have two" in the cockiest way I've ever heard.

"So it appears." Hands are being shoved off my body. I'm being scooped up from my seat, put back down onto my feet a second later. "But she has a twin brother with another pair of fists."

"You're babysitting for the bro?"

"Close," Colin says, sliding his hand down my body before it lands on my butt, giving it a squeeze. "She's my girl. Not just a date. My *girlfriend*." My stomach makes a little flip, tickling in excitement.

"And yet she started to flirt with me."

"Had a bet going." Colin's arms wrap around my stomach from behind, his lips pressing to the heart-shaped birthmark on the back of my shoulder. "Totally adored the way she was looking at you. With so much disgust, it almost made me hard."

"You're such a dick," Archer says, yet Colin understands something else…or just makes it something else.

"You're right, I have a great dick. And it'll be inside my girlfriend in about twenty minutes."

"Didn't need to know that," Archer speaks in a crotchety tone. His eyes meet mine, but this time they're not friendly and welcoming at all.

Congratulations, Lily, you just earned yourself your first enemy for life.

Colin pulls me away from Archer's table, but he doesn't lead me back to our booth. He leads me out of Brites entirely.

"We're leaving," he tells me in a harsh tone. There is no arguing. Even if I wanted to, I wouldn't stand a chance.

"You're jealous." That I do note. The little glimpse of green in his eyes gives it away.

"Heck yes I am, *mi sol*." Oh, okay. Let's make this easy then.

Colin escorts me to his car, opening the passenger door for me, waiting until I'm seated before he slams it shut. He jogs over to the other side of the car, and I watch him through the window. He looks plenty pissed.

For a moment I wonder how the hell Colin is so effortlessly hot. He isn't even trying to be, and yet he's the hottest guy I've ever laid eyes on.

And why the hell would he be jealous when he could have anyone?

"Clearly you weren't aware of it, but you're mine, Lily." The only words sounding through the car when Colin takes a seat. "I won't put a label on whatever we are because you'd run for the hills if I did. But if I see you flirt with another guy ever again, I will make sure he experiences afterlife earlier than you do."

Not sure if I should find that charming or if I should be afraid.

"Besides, I don't think any other guy would like to put up with a girl has one foot in a grave. One that *plans* to be dead in less than a week."

Damned if that doesn't hurt me in some ways.

Colin is right though. I have my death planned out. I know how I will die, when I will die, and who will find my body when I'm passed. It's all planned out. Nobody would put up with it.

Nobody but Colin.

Chapter 24

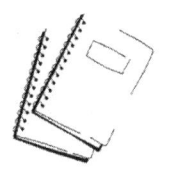

"cause you're the reason I believe in fate, you're my paradise"—Infinity by Jaymes Young

Lily

"Close your eyes," Colin orders as I sit down on his bed. "You're still getting your present, Lilybug. Even if it's technically not your birthday anymore."

"I don't want a present. It's not worth it."

"Shut up and close your eyes." So I do. It's not like I have much of a choice anyway.

Hearing as Colin rummages through his closet, the anticipation rises. I really don't want any presents, but somehow I'm still excited to find out what Colin came up with.

The sounds stop and I feel Colin's presence in front of me. "Okay, you can open your eyes."

And with his go, I do. I open my eyes, only to find Colin kneeling in front of me. For a moment I want to run out of this room. I want to leave and never return, but then Colin starts to laugh hysterically.

He laughs so much, he tips over and lies on the floor, holding his stomach as he proceeds to laugh to the point where no sounds come out anymore. I suppose he figured out what his position looked like.

"Okay, I'm sorry," he finally speaks, slowly sitting back up. "The look on your face, sweetheart...I should have taken a picture of it."

I debate slapping him. Maybe I should, he certainly deserves it right now. But I don't.

I don't because when I'm about to, Colin holds out a small gift bag for me. I watch him with suspicion as I take it. Though, besides my suspicions, Colin watches me with more intensity than I could offer. Like he is more excited for me to open this bag than I am.

Not being able to wait any longer, I open the bag and take out a small stuffed animal. It's a replica of the frog stuffed animal I have back at the dorms. But not only that, it has a chain attached to it.

Colin Carter got me a keychain. A *frog* keychain.

And I absolutely love it.

"Kermit will love this," I say, beaming a smile.

"Who the hell is Kermit? I thought we agreed on Sergeant Froggo."

"I never agreed to that."

"But I did." He grins, taking one of my hands in his. A second later, Colin pulls a small box out of his jeans pocket. "Don't think I just got you the mini Sergeant Froggo."

Before I know, Colin has put a bracelet onto my wrist. It's a thin silver bracelet, no charms, just one thin continuous chain. It's simple, and perfect.

"Colin," I say in a whisper, feeling tears building up. I'm not sure if they're happy or sad tears. Actually, I'm not quite sure what I am feeling at all.

I want to be happy. I am happy, I think.

Yet at the same time I want to cry because my heart is aching. Not the good kind of aching, like when it's aching from love. It's aching from emotional pain. Possibly because this one goddamn bracelet just reminds me that I will lose Colin very soon. Forever.

"It's perfect." I inhale a deep breath, looking up as I blink my tears away. "Thank you."

Silence falls over us, but it's not the uncomfortable kind. Colin is looking at me, watching me as I inspect his gift. I come to think it's the best gift I have ever received. Plain, modest and just perfect.

I mean, it's a simple bracelet. But *Colin* gave it to me, that makes this bracelet a million times more special.

"Lilybug?" I look up from the bracelet, meeting Colin's gaze. "Is Lily a nickname?"

I freeze for a moment. Not sure why. I'm not ashamed of my full name. I just don't like being called by it. The only person to ever call me Liliana is my mother, and she certainly ruined it for me.

Colin seems to notice my hesitation, so he takes that as an answer. "Your full name is Liliana?" Not sure if it's a question or a stated fact.

I nod, feeling my body start to shake. I *really* don't like being called Liliana. Yet when Colin says it out loud, it doesn't sound half as bad anymore. In fact, it feels welcoming and right.

"It's beautiful."

"You think so?"

He nods. "So, who started to call you Lily first?"

I chuckle at that, the story behind how Liliana turned into Lily connects with Aaron's incapability to pronounce words the right way.

"Aaron," I say. "He couldn't pronounce Liliana, for God knows what reasons. Bet he was just too lazy to say it. So instead, he called me Lily."

"He should have given you a better one."

"Thank you." I roll my eyes at him.

"Lilybug?" Colin gets up on his feet only to take a seat next to me on the bed. He lays one of his hands down onto my thigh, giving it a slight squeeze. "Tell me something I didn't know."

Again? I thought I've already done that before. Like, all the time, actually. I believe Colin knows me the best out of all the people knowing me. He certainly knows the more horrible things about me.

"I was a virgin."

His eyebrows draw together, head slightly tilting to the side as he is waiting for me to say I am joking. At least that's what I assume he is waiting for.

When he says, "before what happened?" I realize he is thinking completely different from what I meant. His tone is serious, no indications of amusement whatsoever.

Suddenly I feel stupid.

"Two, or now three, days ago, I mean."

He visibly calms, yet he still seems uncomfortable. His hand leaves my thigh, he is no longer touching me.

Colin stands up from the bed, walking up and down his bedroom while running his hands through his hair. I think I might have broken him.

He isn't saying one word, nor does he react when I say his name to get his attention.

Colin continues to pace around his room for approximately the next five minutes, ignoring my presence up until he finally turns to look at me again. "Why didn't you tell me that earlier?"

"Cause I wanted to avoid *this* reaction." And besides, it's not like what we've done wasn't consensual. I wanted to sleep with him as much as he wanted to sleep with me.

"*Fuck*, Lily." Another hand slides through his already messed up hair, tugging at the ends as he lets out a frustrated groan.

Opposite of what I'm expecting, Colin stays in the room and doesn't run away.

He walks closer to me, picking me up from the bed. My legs wrap around his hips almost instantly.

A cloud of his scent fills my nostrils. He smells nice. He smells like rosewood and fresh laundry. I think I might have found my favorite scent after all. *Colin*.

That's what it is, right? When a scent fills you up with warmth and increases the feeling of well-being, makes you addicted, wanting to smell it again, and again. That's when it becomes an ultimate favorite.

His hands lie on my ass, underneath the skirt of my dress, as he holds me up, his mouth capturing mine immediately. His tongue darts across the seam of his lips, dipping into my mouth.

My hands grip into his hair, stroking through his soft strands. Gently, I scrap his scalp with my fingernails until Colin lets out a throaty groan into my mouth.

"I'm going to give you a better 'first time,' sweetheart. Okay?" he speaks between slow pecks, carefully laying me down on the bed.

Colin hovers right over me, kissing my lips, then down my neck. When he reaches my cleavage, Colin sits up, sliding down enough to reach for my ankles. He undoes the strings from my high heels, setting them down next to his bed.

Then he starts to kiss his way up my legs, whispering compliments with every time his lips burn into my skin. With every kiss my body heats up. With every kiss a wave of anticipation gets send right between my legs.

When he's kissing up my thigh, Colin halts for a second, pushing up my dress enough to free my body up to my ribs. He doesn't remove it completely, so I take it upon myself to do it.

Since the dress is meant to be shoulder-free and my breasts aren't all too big, I'm not wearing a bra, meaning my chest is now completely exposed to him.

"You're trying to kill me, Lilybug," he says, looking into my eyes as he licks his lips like I'm the most delicious thing he's ever seen.

He tugs on my panties, sliding them down my legs, leaving me naked for him to look at.

"Aw, fuck," he groans. His head tilts back into his neck as he lets out a short blow of air before looking at me again. "Are you on birth control?"

I shake my head, not as an answer, but because his question catches me off guard. "Why?"

"Was hoping I could feel you without latex between us," he answers. "It's alright though. We'll stick to condoms."

He lowers his body over mine, reconnecting our lips. His lips are soft, and he doesn't taste like Coca-Cola anymore. His mouth is claiming me so possessively, if he weren't Colin, I would back off. But he *is* Colin, and he is claiming *me*.

"I am, Colin." He looks at me with uncertainty, so I elaborate. "On the pill."

"Then why'd you shake your head?"

"I was confused as to why you're asking. But I promise you, I am."

Flashing me a cocky smile, Colin gets off the bed and strips off his clothes fast enough to be back on top of me in no time.

Regardless of my arousal and how desperate I am for Colin, I can't shake the feeling that he only wants to sleep with me to feel better. His reaction when I told him I was a virgin still doesn't sit right with me. So I ask, "Do you feel guilty?"

Colin sits up. "Why would I feel guilty?"

"Because you took my virginity and weren't exactly gentle with me."

"Sweetheart, if I wanted vanilla sex then, I would have given you nothing but that. If you wanted it, you should have told me. And besides, you took it well. So, no, I don't feel even just one bit of guilt."

I want to speak and ask about his reaction, but all that comes out is a slight gasp when Colin plants a kiss to my pussy.

He hugs my hips, holding me down as his tongue explores the spot between my legs slowly. One of his hands glides up, resting on my breast, fingers pinching my nipple.

I love that he is so touchy. I love that Colin doesn't care for one part of my body only, instead, he makes sure to work all of it.

Feeling his tongue dip inside of me, I can't help the moan from slipping out. I cover my mouth with my arm, muffling my sounds. But when I do, Colin stops to please me and says, "No, stop covering your mouth. I want to hear how good I make you feel."

I don't think I've ever blushed more in my life. I am literally lying buck naked in front of Colin, and yet this comment makes me blush.

Once he sees my arm is no longer covering my mouth, he sucks on my clit, groaning when he hears my whimpers. My hips keep shifting until Colin digs his fingers into my skin to hold me still.

"Please," I beg. All this up-building tension is getting too much, to the point where I'm in desperate need to feel relief.

I can feel Colin smile against my skin. And for a short moment I want him to suffocate for it, but a breathing Colin sounds better than a dead one.

"I need you inside of me," I say with a husky voice, hands tugging at his hair in an attempt to pull him up. He doesn't budge though. All Colin does is chuckle and continue to work miracles with his tongue.

Not that I'm complaining.

As much as I love his tongue on my clit, I really do want to feel him inside of me. "I want to come around your dick, not on your tongue," I say, hoping so desperately that it'll change Colin's mind.

"Aw, fuck, Lily," he curses. "This is going to be over way too soon if you keep saying things like that."

"Colin, please."

He pushes two of his fingers inside of me while continuing to lick and suckle on my swollen clit.

His finger push in and out, the tips pressing against my walls, eliciting cries from my throat. Loud moans I didn't even know where possible to come out of me.

"You're going to come on my tongue, even if it takes us hours to get there. You got your way last time, I'm not missing out on it again."

His tongue is licking me while his fingers continue to thrust inside of me, curling up then pulling back out in a repetitive pattern.

I can feel my orgasm build up with every thrust.

Just when the tension inside of me gets so intense and I am forced to let go, Colin removes his fingers from me completely, sticking his tongue inside of me instead.

With his thumb on my clit, pressing, circling, I finally feel relief as I cry out in pleasure. Euphoria shoots through my body, tickling on my skin.

Colin reaches over to his nightstand, taking out a condom wrapper and opens it.

In a matter of seconds, Colin has rolled the condom down his erection. He then grabs a pillow from beside my head and lifts my hips like I weigh nothing, putting the pillow beneath me.

"Thought you wanted to feel me?"

"I do. But I'm not quite sure if you're lying to me or not. I certainly won't risk anything." That being said, Colin adjusts his cock to my entrance.

"I'm not…" I gasp, not being able to continue my sentence when Colin slowly sinks inside of me. With each light push as he eases deeper inside, I feel fuller. And once his full erection is inside of me, my body suddenly feels as though I'm completely filled up.

"Is that a promise?"

I only manage to nod my head when Colin starts to move his hips and his pubic bone rubs against my clit.

"I've never had sex without a condom before," he admits, easing out of me completely. He removes the condom, tossing it onto the floor and slowly sinks back inside of me.

That must mean something to him, right? *I* must mean something.

"Aw, shit." His mouth is back on mine, just kissing me without moving his hips. Not being able to wait any longer, I lift my legs and wrap them around his hips, pushing him just that tiny bit deeper.

A moan breaks out of me when he moves. Feeling his cock slide in an out of me sends my senses flying through the roof. I feel the urge to dig my nails into his skin as he makes love to me so fervently, I barely have anything left in me to function properly.

Cries of pleasure elicit from my throat with every thrust he takes on.

"Fuck, sweetheart," he moans into my mouth breathlessly. Doubt I've ever heard anything sexier. "You're going to be the death of me, *mi sol*." He thrusts into me.

Colin doesn't go rough with me this time. He keeps it all passionate and sweet, yet still hot and steamy. He has completely fogged up my mind, pleasuring me in every sense of way. Making parts of my body feel things, I didn't even know where possible.

"Oh God," I cry out, moaning.

His lips crash down onto mine, biting my bottom lip. His hips still, looking into my eyes with a stern look. "Say my name."

I blink. "What?"

"Say. *My*. Name."

"Colin, I—" He pulls out of me and slams back inside. I gasp.

"You see God around here somewhere?" I shake my head. "Exactly." He kisses me. Deeply. Possessively. "You're mine, Lily. I'm not even sharing you with God."

His lips claim mine like he means every word. And I believe him. I believe his words, his mouth.

Sweat appears on both of our bodies and pleasure rises deep within mine when Colin brings his hand between my legs. Fingers rubbing my clit, causing my vision to go dark.

And then, when he steals yet another orgasm from me (not that I'm complaining), Colin kisses me as he comes inside of me, mumbling the word "fuck" under his breath.

His forehead rests against mine. Panting as we're both calming down from our satisfaction.

I can smell him on me, his scent colliding with mine. I send out a silent prayer, hoping I will get to smell his scent wherever I'll end up after death.

His soft, yet swollen lips press to mine as he eases out of me. Lying down next to me, Colin pulls me close to him, resting my head down on his chest. I can hear his heart beating; fast and strong. His breathing is quick as well, but it calms with every breath he takes.

"I'm never going to do this with anyone else ever again," Colin says into the silent room. "It's only going to be you."

"Poor you."

"Indeed." Neither of us has to address this with more words. We're both aware of what we're talking about.

My death.

"Let's get you cleaned up and ready for bed, okay?" Colin says softly, lifting us both up to sit. "See, this time, we're even sleeping in one bed after. No more doing this all wrong." He stands, pulling me up to my feet right after.

As I stand, I feel something running down my thigh. Giggling when I realize what it is. "Colin," I say quietly. My voice is completely gone again. But not in the same way it was back at the bar. This time it's gone because I've been moaning it hoarse. "I think your cum is running down my legs."

He snickers, then tilts his head back in his neck and groans. When his eyes land back on mine, with a gentle touch, his arm traces down my body, bringing his hand to my thighs. With a bit of pressure against my skin, Colin slides his fingers up my thigh until he's touching my pussy. I spread my legs, letting out a gasp when his finger dip inside of me.

He leans down, mouth to my ear, whispering, "I might just do that again in the bathroom…but with my cock."

Chapter 25

"hearts break and hell's a place that everyone knows"—
Don't Be so Hard on Yourself by Jess Glynne

Colin

I'M NOT QUITE SURE HOW I'VE NOTICED that Lily isn't asleep, but I did.

We *both* went to sleep shortly after we came back from the bathroom, and now I'm pretending to be asleep while Lily is writing something into her notebook.

She's crying, and that's the only reason why I don't take that notebook away from her so she'd go back to sleep. Maybe she needs to write her feelings down on paper to cope. Or maybe not. But she certainly wants to write something into it, so who am I to keep her from it?

It also takes all of my will power not to wrap my arms around her right now.

All I want to do is press her against my body and hug the pain out of hers. But I can't. Not because a simple hug won't put her back together anyway, but because I think crying is good. As much as it wounds me, I think she needs to cry sometimes.

I think it might make her feel a little less heavy in her chest.

At least now that's she's busy writing, it gives me another look into her thoughts. She's still right next to me, allowing me a great view onto the pages.

I know I shouldn't look, shouldn't read what's going on in her head. But how else am I supposed to figure out what's happening?

So I read.

Dear whoever reads this,

I'm a mess.
A complete goddamn mess.
It's Sunday, October 3rd—5:30 in the morning—and I am sitting on Colin Carter's bed, crying, while he is sound asleep next to me.
This time it's not about him. It's all about me. My least favorite topic.
As soon as he fell asleep, I felt it all.
The pain.
The solitude.
The numbness.
I felt numbness.
How is that even possible? How can I feel something that's not supposed to be felt, because...it's numbness? How do I feel my heart breaking, and yet I feel nothing at all?
My mother wants me dead.

Nine Days

I knew she disliked me for a while now. But never did I think she would tell me to go and die. I thought, maybe she hates me, but she's my mother, she must still love me.
I was wrong. So awfully wrong.
And it hurts. It hurts so much more than I thought it would.
I've been wanting to die for quite a while. Turns out she wanted the same ending for me.
It's one thing when you want to die, but another when your own mother wants you dead.
But aside from my mother's wish for me to be dead...it's Sunday.
I loathe Sundays.
And yet today, I will have to plaster a smile onto my face and pretend I have fun all day long.
Maybe I will have fun. I always do with Colin. For some reasons, he affects me like that.
He makes me smile randomly. He makes me forget my pain.
But then he's not with me and I feel it all again.
Today will be torture.
I used to hate Saturdays just as much. You know why? September 24th, 2005, the day my parents decided they'd get a divorce. It was Saturday. The worst day of my life.
It's the day my mother pushed Aaron out of her life forever. The day my mother took my brother from me.
My parents' announcement to get a divorce was only half as bad. But what followed was the worst.
Ever since then...my depression got and still gets the better of me with every new day.

I was born with a genetic makeup, prone to depression. My parents knew that. And they've done everything to prevent it from developing.

At least until they split up and made all my happiness go away.

The doctors said it's possible that I'd never end up developing a mood disorder such a depression. But I did. Because my mother tore my family apart.

And now she wants me dead. And I want me dead as well. If it weren't for Colin, I'd probably be hiding in my dorm room right about now. I wouldn't have set one foot out the door, wouldn't have done anything but look at my ceiling and wish for the days to pass faster.

That's what I used to do a lot.

Spend time on my floor, looking at the ceiling for hours on end. The only other occupation was the music streaming into my eardrums. So loud, it probably could have led to hearing problems.

I really don't feel like going out today. But I will. For Colin.

Because seeing him smile warms my heart. And seeing him happy...it makes me happy.

I think he doesn't notice me watching him when he watches me.

Like on day one. When he was watching me instead of the sunrise.

I felt his eyes on my skin. It prickled everywhere.

He wanted to watch the sunrise and ended up watching me. It was one of the most magical sunrises I've ever seen, and yet I couldn't concentrate because his eyes were on me.

And when I screamed my lungs out, he didn't seem to find that weird. He didn't seem to be less intrigued to spend more time with me.

He watched me, filmed me for our project—whatever that is about—and smiled when I turned around to look at him. He. Smiled.

He smiled like he just knew I felt lighter.

God, please someone press my off button. I need to stop writing all about Colin.

This is my unalive journey 101. Not a "Colin Carter is such a great and freakishly hot guy" fan book.

And now that I've mentioned him, I might as well add another thing.

He is a nosy pain in the ass. Thinking I don't know he's awake and reads this right now.

Lily

I can't hold back my chuckle for that last sentence. "You think I'm hot," I note, now being able to speak since she obviously knows I'm awake.

"You know you are," is all I get in return.

"But freakishly hot?" I take Lily's notebook from her, not to read more pages, but to put it away. She tries to protest, until I have it in my hands. She stops trying to reach for it, kind of like she knows she doesn't stand a chance. "Today's going to be a rainy day."

"Seriously?" She chuckles. "You're talking about the weather to me?"

Yes, because the only other thing on my mind would be her tears and how I'm supposed to get rid of them.

I nod and pull Lily closer to me. "We're staying home today."

A quiet gasp leaves her throat. She stiffens up when she tries to come up with a reason as to why I wouldn't just take her somewhere indoors.

Which would be a great question, if she asked.

After reading what she'd written, how she's too exhausted to leave the house…I figured it might be the best to stay home—just the two of us—for a day.

I'm glad she's not asking. Telling her I want to stay home because she feels too exhausted to go—That feels like the wrong thing to say.

"Nothing planned?" she asks, narrowing her eyes at me. I don't think she's trying to come off as annoyed. I think she's trying to look into my eyes through the dark. I mean, it's not too dark, otherwise I wouldn't have been able to read her notebook entry.

"Before you agreed on these nine days, you said you'd need a day off…so this is it. It's going to rain all day and it's Sunday. You hate Sundays. So might as well spend it here and puzzle." If Lily was anyone but her, I'd probably had forgotten this minor information already. But for some reasons my brain just saves anything that has to do with Lily.

"Puzzle?" Her forehead creases—*I think*.

"Yup."

"Why?"

"Don't tell me you don't like puzzling, Lilybug." I pretend to be offended by that. "I have this amazing frog puzzle, you know."

"A frog puzzle?" She shifts, rolling right on top of me. Not that I care. "You do know I'm not into frogs, right?"

A shocked gasp comes from the depth of my throat. "You aren't?" Lily shakes her head. "Well, then why did I get you a frog keychain if you don't even like them? You're totally digging frogs."

"Colin," she laughs, "*You* got it for me. I didn't ask for it."

"You had Sergeant Froggo and many others before I got you the mini version of him. By the way, we need a better name for him."

"Kermit," says Lily with no hesitation.

"Still too boring, Lilybug. And I'm talking about Corporal Froggo." A few seconds of silence falls between us. "That's it: Corporal Froggo."

"I thought Sergeant?"

"God dammit, Lilybug. We're talking about the mini Froggo. You've got to pay more attention to me." I stroke my hand from the small of her back deeper down, resting them right on her butt. She doesn't tell me to remove it, so I keep it there, giving her butt a slight squeeze.

"You'd like that, wouldn't you?" My eyebrows rise. "More attention from me," she declares, tilting her head up just enough for her lips to collide with mine…almost. She's not kissing me, not even touching my lips with hers, but she's awfully close.

"Hmm." I slide my hand up enough to trace along the outline of her panties.

Lily isn't wearing any pants, only underwear and a shirt of mine. And I don't think I ever want her wearing anything else ever again—when it's just Lily and me, that is.

I can feel her breathing hitch when one of my fingers slides beneath the fabric, pulling on it before letting it snap back into place.

"Can I ask you something?"

She rolls her eyes. "Like you wouldn't, even if I said no."

"Okay, it might be a bit too deep given how early it is...but, how come you're good to have sex? I mean, I always kind of thought people with depression don't feel the desire to get intimate."

Her eyes widen instantly. I'm even sure Lily has a slight blush to her cheeks. It's adorable, the tint to her cheeks, I mean.

"Well, it's not the same for everyone. It sure can affect one person but the other doesn't have to show this kind of symptom. Depression in men, for instance, a sign *could* be self-medicating with sex and alcohol," she explains roughly. Though, I think I understand anyway.

"And to be fair, I didn't have the desire to sleep with anyone before you came along and were all kissy with me."

"I wasn't all kissy with you. I kissed your breath away," I object. "It was hot and steamy, and the best kiss you've ever experienced."

"It wasn't bad. But whatever helps you sleep at night." I swear, if she keeps downgrading our first—*real*—kiss, she might hurt my ego. "Anyway, Grandpa, you think we could actually have fun today with all the puzzling you've planned?"

"Depends. Will that include a great breakfast together?" I ask in all seriousness.

"You're hungry?" I nod, about to ask her if she's hungry when she gets off of me and stands up on her feet. "What do you want?"

"What do you mean?"

"I'll make breakfast. It's the least I can do for you letting me stay here."

"Lilybug, you had no other choice. I wasn't letting you stay at your dorm with all the shit going on. Even if you were to protest, you would still be here right now," I remind her. "You didn't ask to stay here, I made you."

She lifts her shoulders, shrugging. "You're fine with pancakes?"

"I would eat anything you made, simply because *you* made it."

"It could taste disgusting." Her eyebrows lift, a smile tugging at her lips. "Maybe you're allergic. Speaking of allergies, do you have any?"

"Coconut, why?"

"Interesting," she says, rubbing her chin like she is coming up with a plan to kill me. "I happen to have this amazing shower gel. It's tropical. I think it's coconut scented."

"You think?" I laugh, now being sure she is trying to murder me. "I've never smelled it on you before then."

"That's cause I didn't buy it yet. But I will."

"So you do want me dead, huh?"

She shrugs again, but this time she walks out of my room right after, leaving the door open.

I can hear her talk as she walks down the stairs, but I can't quite make out what she's saying.

I feel the sudden urge to check out who she's talking to.

Doubting it's Aaron, I get up from my bed, throwing on some sweatpants that I find in the depth of my closet and follow Lily downstairs.

"Good morning, Princess," Grey greets me as I come down the stairs. He's sitting at the kitchen island, holding some sports magazine in his hands. He's not even reading the damn thing.

"What are you doing here, Grey?" I ask like I wouldn't already know the answer.

"Grabbing something to eat, like I do every morning." His eyes move over to Lily, standing by the refrigerator, looking through it. "Turns out I'll be getting it served today."

And so suddenly another déjà vu pops up. Lily, half naked in my kitchen. At least this time it's not Miles gawking at her. Grey doesn't care one bit about Lily, and he'd never have any intentions getting into her pants. So I'm not worried about that.

"Where's Miles?" I find myself asking. I mean, I have to be sure he won't march in here and drool all over Lily's perfect ass.

Taking a seat right next to Grey, I rest my elbows on the island top and hold my head up with my hands, watching Lily.

"He's not in New City. Kya, Izan's sister, bumped into him last night and I think they drove down to New York half an hour later. They also had some other girl with them," Grey says, chuckling. Man, this guy knows exactly why I've been asking. He knows I wouldn't care one bit if Miles was around or not—if it weren't for my half naked girlfriend in the kitchen.

She's not your girlfriend, Colin.

"Kya is Izan's sister?" Lily turns around, her mouth wide open.

"Very much so. She's a year younger, so it's quite a miracle that Miles wanted to tag along with her."

"I thought she's a senior." Lily turns back around and starts to mix up some ingredients that end up being a pancake batter.

"She is," Grey confirms, "I think she skipped sophomore year in high school."

"Seriously? I wish I was that smart."

I snicker but try to cover it with a cough. Lily notices it anyway and shoots me her own perfectionated death-glare.

"Why wouldn't Miles go for younger girls?"

Grey and I sigh both at the same time. "He says he's afraid they might be too immature," I tell her, though that's not the truth.

To that Lily says Miles is the immature one. Grey and I both neither agree nor disagree.

Even though Miles is Grey's best friend, Grey knows how much of a pain in the ass our teammate can be. He experiences Miles's more-or-less immaturity more often than anyone else does, given that they've been sharing a house for three years.

Grey's words speak volume when it comes to Miles.

But to be fair, Miles was thrown into being an adult instead of maturing into one.

"According to Miles, every woman that's younger than him wants nothing but a diamond ring and his babies before they'd even gotten to know the other one." Grey looks at me, eyes narrowing as if to say I shall go along with it. "Or something like that," he mumbles, but Lily hears it.

"Maybe he's bonding with Kya to get your man, Grey." Lily turns to him, cocking her eyebrows with a devilish smile on her lips. "I mean, Izan would definitely be Miles's type."

Grey laughs, shaking his head. "Wouldn't even be surprised."

"However, I don't think Miles would be Izan's type. Izan has way better taste." Lily's voice is soft, sweet. I love when she speaks…if it's not about some other guy, that is.

Grey's laughter grows more hysterical and Lily joins in. I have no idea what is happening, but I don't like where this is going. Not at fucking all.

"I thought you'd have better taste than sir moody here, darling," Grey utters, speaking of me like I'm not even here.

I growl quietly, mentally planning how I'm going to murder him later tonight without getting caught. I'm sure Lily knows some ways. She seems like one of those girls listening to True Crime podcasts while getting ready for the day.

Grey sighs. "I doubt he left to actually get to know Kya though. He's most likely visiting Brooklyn. Kya was probably just driving him."

The sound of her name makes me wince. We don't talk about Brooke. Not to anyone but *us*.

"I heard that name before…Who is Brooklyn or Brooke and why wouldn't Miles drive himself?" Lily asks. Of course she would ask who Brooklyn is.

Grey shrugs, his eyes on mine like he knows he just fucked up. *He did.* "Miles had a beer or two. He doesn't drive with *any* alcohol intake. Not even half a beer, or just the teeniest sip."

Lily nods then turns over to me to get the rest of her question answered. I can't look at her. If I do, I'll spill things out like throwing up my guts after a drink too much.

I look at Grey in defeat. He shouldn't have fucking mentioned Brooklyn.

This is a test on his part, isn't it? Like "Would this dumbass keep quiet even when he's falling for a girl he's not supposed to fall for, and she is asking questions?"

No. No I would *not* keep quiet.

Grey looks at me with a warning in his eyes, but I ignore it. "Brooklyn is Miles's daughter."

Lily gasps, her eyes widen drastically. "Daughter?"

I nod. "She's four years old. They faced a few complications during Millie's C-section that had her end up in a coma. Millie died a couple days later."

Grey's eyes close as he takes a deep breath.

"Millie Scott?" Lily asks. I nod, though I do wonder how she knows her. "Seriously? She promised me she'd come to Trewery once we finished high school. She didn't even attend classes the last few months of it. Her mother told me she decided against college. I always wondered why her mother reached out to me and not Millie herself."

That's what everyone thinks. Neither her family nor Miles wanted the school, or anyone, to know as they all wanted to grief in peace. And since Millie didn't want anyone knowing she got pregnant at the age of seventeen, she stopped going to school. At least that's what Miles had told us.

"So where does Brooklyn stay when Miles is here all day?"

Grey licks his lips then says, "She's usually with Maeve, Miles's older sister, but stays here on the weekends. I told Miles I don't mind Brooke staying with us all week, but as he's still in college and plays hockey, he figured it was better for her. He also doesn't want to force her to his classes."

We all still believe Brooke would much rather be with her father, but it's his decision to make, not ours.

"You can't tell anyone, Lily," Grey says, the same look of seriousness he gave me before back on his face. "The only people knowing of Brooklyn is the team." *And I suppose Kya, now that Miles allegedly took her to see Brooklyn.*

I always wondered what I would have done if I was in Miles's position. What I would have done if the woman I loved died a couple days after giving birth to our child.

How Miles managed to somehow live through the death of his child's mother, and handle to be a single father at the age of eighteen…I will never understand.

And to make matters worse, Brooklyn looks so much like her mother.

"Princess, you're not getting your girl off enough." He taps his hand onto my back.

"Huh?" I'm not quite sure what I've missed and I'm also not sure I want to be enlightened either.

"That's not the problem, Grey." Lily sighs, setting down a plate right in front of him. "Colin is just…too extra."

"Excuse me?"

She ignores me. "He doesn't even know what he's doing."

Watching as Grey takes a bite from the strawberry-banana-pancake, snickering. I almost lose my temper. *What the hell is going on?*

Swallowing, Grey says, "I mean…did you look at him?" His head turns, facing me.

"I'm fucking gorgeous, thank you very much."

When Lily sets another plate down on the table—this time meant for me—I grab her wrist in my hand and pull her around the island. She ends up standing between my legs, facing me. She might be a bit surprised, but she's not complaining.

"*Mi sol*, you're going to have to enlighten me." Brushing my nose along her neck, I feel her shiver under my touch. Not a cold-shiver, a goosebumps kind of shiver. "What were you talking about?"

With my hands on her waist, I push her a tad closer to me, brushing my lips against hers. It's so natural. So wanted. So *needed*.

"You guys are bullshitting yourselves," Grey utters, fake gagging. Shooting Grey a stern and bewildered look, he cares to explain himself before I have to ask. "You may be able to fool Aaron into thinking you guys are a thing, but you can't fool me." A dirty snicker comes from deep within his throat.

"I told you," Lily says, hitting her palm to my chest.

Knowing Grey—and judging by the nasty grin on his lips—I know he knows better than to open his mouth about it. Especially because I know that he knows more about my feelings toward Lily than *she* does.

"Why's she staying here, Princess?"

For a moment I'm debating on telling Grey the truth. The whole truth. Not in front of Lily, obviously, but when I get a moment with him alone.

Grey knows better than to run to Aaron and rat me out. He also isn't the judgmental kind of guy. If anything, Grey would offer to help. Help me help her. He wouldn't go behind my back and get Lily the help she clearly needs.

Though, I'm sure he would ask why I'm not going behind her back and do so myself.

And if I had to answer that question…I wouldn't know what to tell him. Why *aren't* I doing that? Why aren't I dropping her off at some hospital, tell them what's wrong and have them help me get her the help she needs?

Maybe because I feel like I'd be betraying her if I did?

"Sex," I say, slipping my hands underneath the white shirt Lily is wearing. Grey cocks his head, his eyes boring into mine as if to call me out on even more of my bullshit. "I just want more time with her."

"You have all the time you need, even if she's not living with you." *If only you knew.*

"I wanted to stay, actually," Lily blurts out. I think she can sense my uncertainty. If she hadn't opened her mouth and spoke for me, I think I would've told Grey the truth right here, right now.

Maybe I do need someone I can talk to about her. About this. About Lily's situation. That person certainly can't be Aaron.

"I have a few problems with Winter. She's a pain in the ass sometimes. I'm sure you've heard of her. Aaron's ex-girlfriend." Grey nods. "Yeah, she's a lot to take in. And we just had this big fight recently. I don't want to be around her for a while."

I'm fascinated how easily these lies roll over her tongue. Not only this one with Winter. Everything. Her pretending to be alright all day long, plastering smiles onto her face, faking happiness.

In desperate need to change the topic, I pick up where we left off. "Anyway, tell me what you were talking about."

"You sat right here, didn't you listen?"

I shake my head no. "I was too busy planning Grey's murder, Lilybug."

"Why?"

Grey's eyes shoot toward me like he'd love to hear the answer. I'm sure he knows why, yet I tell *Lily* anyway. "He thinks I'm a bad guy."

"I did not say that," Grey defends himself. He did, though not using those exact words.

"You thought my Lilybug had better taste in men, meaning you think I either look bad, which we all know would be a lie, or I'm a bad person."

Lily smiles softly, her eyes never leaving mine even when Grey speaks. "I said you're moody."

I don't look away from her either. "I am not." Not when Lily's here. "I answered your question…now answer mine."

"I told Grey we're having a puzzle day."

"And you think that makes me 'too extra?'"

She snorts a laugh, shaking her head before pressing her lips to the corner of my mouth.

"No, but your bet to show her 'the world' in nine days does," Grey answers for Lily when she wouldn't.

I freeze, not knowing how to react. Did Lily tell Grey about her death wish? She didn't, right? She wouldn't do that.

A bet.

She said we were having a bet going.

God, how long was I in my head for, that I didn't hear a word they said?

"I'm sure you can join us?" Lily says her invitation as a question. I don't want anyone to be around us today. I told myself I would keep other people away from Lily for the day, and here I am failing before breakfast even really started.

"Maybe I'll join in later. I have plans with Izan." Grey winks at Lily, and for some reasons it makes my stomach turn. *Get your shit together, Colin.*

I shrug him off, turning my attention back to my girl just when she starts to yawn. Maybe she is more exhausted than I thought. Or maybe she just didn't get enough sleep.

"You didn't sleep much," I note, brushing Lily's hair out of her face. "If I recall correctly, not at all. What's going on, sweetheart?"

Her cheeks flush like she's embarrassed. Drawing my eyebrows together, I wait for an explanation that doesn't seem to come.

I hold her face in place with my hands, having both my hands lie on her jawline, thumbs gently caressing her heated cheeks. "Talk to me, Lilybug."

She sighs and proceeds to remain silent. It annoys me. Why wouldn't she just tell me what's going on? Is it because Grey is here? Insomnia maybe? But that wouldn't be embarrassing, would it?

Her eyes wander over to Grey, but when she sees that he most likely doesn't even care about her presence.

"I, uh"—once again her eyes drift over to Grey—"I can't sleep without Kermit," she admits. It's adorable, and definitely nothing she should be embarrassed about. Now I'm wondering if Sergeant Froggo isn't as new of a stuffed animal as I thought he was.

"You're so cute, you know that?" My expression softens as a smile creeps onto my face. I plant a chaste kiss to her lips before whispering, "I'll get him for you."

What have I turned into?

Never in my life would I have gone to get a stuffed animal from a girl's house just so she could sleep in peace—or at all.

What the hell are you doing to me, Lily?

Grey clears his throat and gets up from his seat. He takes his plate, thanks Lily for the pancakes he's gotten and leaves the house. I suppose he figured he shouldn't be around.

At least I'm alone with my Lilybug now.

"You really want to stay home all day?"

I nod, pulling her closer to me again. She had moved a bit while saying goodbye to Grey.

Only now do I notice that Lily smells like roses and sex. That brings a smile to my lips because I know exactly how that happened. I consider telling Lily about it, but I also don't want to freak her out.

"What are your favorite flowers?" I ask, surprised by my sudden interested in it. I've never really cared about giving anyone flowers, and I don't think I'll get some for Lily, yet I'm still interested to hear her answer. Not sure if that's because her name is Lily, and lilies are some type of flowers—and the fact I find it hilarious that she smells like a mix of roses and vanilla at all times—or if it's just pure interest in general.

"You're not getting me flowers." Well, now I certainly have to.

"Wasn't planning on. Just wondering."

"Don't laugh," she says, holding out her pinky finger toward me. I give her a quick frown of confusion before eventually hooking my pinky to hers and pinky-promise not to laugh. "I think lilies."

"You think?"

"I think I know so. I'm not sure. I don't know a lot of flowers, I just know my name is a flower, and I know roses. I know of dandelions, though I'm not sure if they count as a flower or weeds. And sunflowers, of course."

I chuckle, listening to her blabbing about different flower types for the next following ten minutes. Every now and then I get a bite from my now completely cold pancake, while also making sure she eats from it as well.

"What's your favorite color?" I then ask.

Lily lifts her shoulders, shrugging. "Mint green, I guess."

"Makes sense. I'll get you a mint green frog." I won't, but I might do something really stupid anyway.

"Colin?" Her voice is so soft, loving. I think her voice is the sweetest of sounds I've ever heard. Seriously, just listening to Lily talk brightens my mood. "Tell me something I didn't know."

"Playing my game now, are we?" I chuckle, pulling her in for yet another kiss. *Did I mention that I'm addicted to her lips?*

Feeling Lily smile against my mouth, I slide my hands down to her ass, giving it a squeeze. She yelps, laughing, slapping my chest just once.

"I had an older brother," I admit. I don't think I've ever truly talked about him before. Never wanted to really. I didn't even tell Aaron about Aiden. I've done well hiding my pain, hide the hole he'd left in my heart when he died.

But maybe it's time for Lily to understand why I'm doing this, why I'm wanting her to stay alive. Though this might be a huge mistake to let her in. Maybe the biggest even.

"Had?" she repeats to me.

I bob my head slightly as a nod. "He died when I was nineteen. Around the time when Eira got diagnosed with leukemia."

And then the fearful reaction I expected Lily's face to take on happens. Her eyes fill up with so much pity and horror, it wounds my heart.

"You once asked why I'm doing this," I recall, hoping she might remember her question. She nods. "I never answered your question." Another nod. "I let him slip away, Lily."

Her eyes widen, beautiful green eyes filled with nothing but horror. She takes a step back, or tries to. Fortunately, I still have my hands on her ass, so I can push her closer me again.

"Aiden couldn't take it. He said he couldn't watch Eira die, couldn't have her be the first one of us to go down." Lily stays quiet, listening only. I guess her mind is blocking me out, seeing me as nothing but a blur and some background music. But I started already, so I will continue. "He would leave hints, tell me how fucked up all this is. How weird it is that he's the oldest and yet our younger sister is about to die from cancer."

Lily shakes her head, not believing a word I just said. I can't blame her, not even I wanted to believe it two years ago.

"But she survived. She's all right, isn't she?"

I nod. "But two years ago it all looked a lot like she wouldn't make it. Doctors kept saying there's nothing they could do. And as painful as it might have been to my entire family, it hit Aiden the hardest." Looking away from Lily, I continue, "He has always been protective of Eira. And to think that his fourteen years old sister will die before him, he couldn't take it, Lily." I can feel old wounds reopen, tearing at the seams in my heart.

"He told me he wasn't going to let her down like that. He kept telling me that he won't let her be the first to die. I didn't think he would go and kill himself, but he did."

She gasps but still doesn't comment on it.

"I could have prevented it. If only I had taken him more seriously. If I had told our parents what he told me. If I had spoken to him about it…anything. It doesn't matter, but I know I could have prevented it if I had opened my mouth to my family. Yet I didn't take him seriously enough."

"You couldn't have known."

"I did know. Tell me how 'if one of us is going to die first, it is going to be me' isn't a clear indication."

Chapter 26

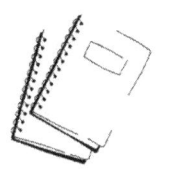

"if I can't be close to you, I'll settle for the ghost of you"—Ghost by Justin Bieber

Lily

HOURS PASSED SINCE COLIN TOLD ME about Aiden. I'm still in shock. But it all makes sense now.

It makes sense why Colin keeps sticking around.

He doesn't want to help me out of this hole of darkness for my sake, but because he thinks it might cleanse his soul. That it might cleanse his subconscious for letting his brother commit suicide when he could have prevented it.

Forgive me, Aiden. It makes sense now.

I still don't think Colin could have kept Aiden from committing. I understand he might feel guilty for not opening his mouth about it, for not taking his brother's words more seriously.

But this is just one more reason why Colin should not be sticking around me much longer.

He will fail again.

He will feel like he failed me, Aiden, himself all over again when I die.

I can't allow Colin to destroy himself like that. I can't keep being around him, allow him to show me a good time.

I don't want to see Colin hurting. And he will get hurt.

Yet at the same time, I can't stay away from him. I want him around at all times. I want to be with him, be in his presence. I want to talk to him all day long, even when I don't have the strength to speak anymore.

With Colin, I don't even have to speak. He's great at creating this comfortable silence to give me space. The most comfortable silence I have ever experienced.

And he makes me feel safe. He makes me feel good, gives me hope again.

Regardless, it won't last. The happiness, the feeling of safety…it won't last. He won't stick around for forever. He will leave as soon as he successfully convinced me to stay alive.

And yet I am thinking what if not? What if he will stay? What if all those kisses he's given me recently could be more than just…kisses? What if there could be more to us, and we never got to explore it because I died?

Fuck you, Colin. Fuck you for fucking with my head.

"*Mi sol*," Colin's voice comes through to me, so gentle and sweet, it causes my heart to melt. "The puzzle's not done yet." *Right.*

I also still have no idea what my new nickname means. He could be insulting me for all I know.

Honestly, I tried to translate it using a translator app…only to realize I would have to know how to spell it. So that backfired.

"Why did you want me to stay here?" I find myself asking, all the while looking through tons of green puzzle pieces.

"Had to keep an eye on you."

"I would have been good at the dorms."

"No, you wouldn't have been, Lilybug." He sighs heavily. "At least here I can look out for you. I can make sure you're not hurting yourself. And I get to kiss you all the time, so that's a bonus as well."

"You can stop doing that. The kissing, I mean." *Please don't.*

"No can do, *mi sol*. I'm addicted." Colin falls back against the sofa, holding his hand to his heart. He's looking at me with those mesmerizing blue eyes with nothing but happiness in them. There is a warmth in his eyes, one I couldn't put a label on if my life depended on it.

And then, like just thinking about my lips goes off like a bomb in his mind, Colin sits back up and pulls me in. His hands on my jaw, cupping my face as his lips press to mine.

It's nothing heated. No tongue. No lust. But it's sweet, sensual, loving. It's passionate, yet soft and gentle.

His kisses feel like feathers, but they weigh so much more.

His kisses warm up my chest, making my stomach fill with *dragonflies*. It's the best, yet also worst feeling in the world.

The best because I love feeling his lips on mine. I love feeling of yellow it brings to my body. I love the effect it has on my heart, even if it scares me. It feels natural. It feels like this is supposed to be. It feels right.

The worst because it scares me. His kisses scare me. I get lost in them. They're captivating. Mesmerizing. They're powerful, strong. He's got me hooked, making me lose all of my self-control.

And just like that, like my body is being controlled by a switch, I no longer have the strength to even puzzle.

Once the thought of Colin being heartbroken over my loss—*not because he lost me but because he failed again*—settles in and the anxiety I get from his kisses…I'm no longer even remotely strong enough to do a simple task.

I can feel my heart breaking. I can feel the strength leaving my body. I can feel the emptiness creep up on me once again.

My hands begin to shake, dropping the puzzle piece I used to hold between my fingers.

Everything turns gray. The puzzle no longer has color to it. It's now gray and empty. Colin's blue eyes, the ones I've learned to love, they're gray and empty. His cheeks no longer having a slight touch of pink to them. No, he's pale. He's as dull as my world. Everything is painted gray. Like an old—*mute*—black and white movie.

"Lily?" I can see his mouth moving, but I don't hear a sound. He repeats it, again and again. But I don't hear him.

His hands take mine. His heat rolls over my hands, spreading through my body. He's warming me. His touch is comforting. But it's not repainting my world with colors.

It stays gray. Everything stays gray.

"What's happening?" His voice is muffled. He is so far away. So endlessly far gone. And yet I see him sitting in front of me. His face so pale, so lifeless, so worried. *He is worried.*

He speaks again but I can't hear it. He is taking my face in his hands again, forcing my eyes to look into his. *I am looking at you, Colin.*

I can feel his touch. I can feel every part of my body his hands come in contact with. It's stinging. Burning. Everything is burning.

My heart is hurting. It's hurting so much. Why does everything always have to be so painful?

"Lily." I still hear no sounds, only muffles. It's so quiet. But he speaks. I can *feel* my name roll over his lips. I can feel everything. Feel his worry, his angst. I feel his hands shake when they're touching me. I feel his eyes on me. I feel his breath on my skin when he moves his face closer to mine.

Chapter 27

***"she has the power to save you, the only one who's got enough of you to break you"**—She by Jake Scott*

Colin

HER BODY IS SHAKING. IT'S EVEN WORSE than it was when she was late for class. She doesn't listen to me. I think she is trying to, but it's like Lily isn't even inside of her own body right now.

"Lily," I repeat for the fifth time. Still no reaction. Her eyes are on mine, but she doesn't react.

Her breathing seems to be normal, maybe a bit faster than usual but not as bad as it was the other day.

Lily's hands are cold when I hold them—she is cold. It's like holding the hands of a corpse in mine. If she wasn't breathing, I would assume she just died on me.

"I'm taking you upstairs, okay?" I feel the need to tell her what I'm doing. I don't want her to panic just because I'm picking her up. If she's conscious, I think she will appreciate me talking to her. "You're okay, sweetheart."

I don't know if she truly is. I'm not sure if I told her this for her, or for my sake.

She has to be okay. I can't lose her. Not yet, not this Friday, and not ever.

Picking up Lily from the sofa, I carry her upstairs, calling out for Aaron in hopes he might know what the hell is going on. I mean, maybe this happened before, and he was around when it did.

"Aaron!" I repeat half-way up the stairs. It's only ten, he's still asleep but I don't care. I believe he won't care either once he sees his sister motionless in my arms.

Though, she's not too motionless. I can feel her fingers pressing into my nape. Additionally, her head isn't hanging low, so she does still have some kind of control over her body.

Aaron's room door wings open. The angry look on his face quickly vanishes when he sees Lily in my arms. "What…what is going on?"

He holds his bedroom door open, indicating for me to carry her inside. Would have preferred to take her to my bedroom, but his will do.

"I don't know what happened," I say, my voice filled with concern. "She just started trembling and stopped acknowledging her surroundings. I'm not even sure if she can hear us. She's not responding, not reacting. She's not doing anything." Gently easing Lily onto Aaron's bed, I allow myself a second to panic before snapping back into protection mode.

"Has this ever happened before?" I ask, coming off a little snappier than intended.

"I don't know."

"What do you mean you don't know!"

"I'm not exactly familiar with her condition. I never asked if she takes any medication. She's depressed, that much I know. So I assume she's taking antidepressants. But what the hell do I know if she's ever done…*this*?" He points over to his sister that's currently lying on his bed. Her eyes are still on me, which tells me that she is here with us.

Groaning, I rake my hands through my hair. *What do I do?*

"Does your father know?" I ask in a rush. Aaron shrugs. "Call him." It's not a question, it's a command.

"Maybe we should take her to a hospital?"

I look over to Lily. Her eyes are wider than before. She's scared. It breaks my fucking heart. I know she doesn't want to go to a hospital. They would figure out what this is about faster than anything, especially with Aaron there.

Aaron would tell the doctors that his sister is depressed and now "she's doing this." Maybe that would be the right thing to do. Perhaps even the only thing we should be doing. But I can't betray Lily like that. Can I?

But what if her condition has nothing to do with her mental health? What if this is some kind of other illness that has not yet been diagnosed?

"She doesn't like hospitals," I inform Aaron. Not sure if that's a lie or not. "She's afraid of them. You can't do that to her."

"Are you kidding me?" He laughs, once. "Fucking look at her!" I regret calling for his help.

I am looking at her.

I can't blame Aaron for freaking out on me. This is his sister. She looks pale. Emotionless. *Dead*. She's even as cold as a corpse. But I know she's alive. She is breathing, and she can hear us talking, I suppose.

"Carter, she can't die on me," Aaron says, his voice breaking. It's barely even a whisper anymore. I don't think I've ever heard him speak with so much pain in his voice.

He takes a seat on the bed, right next to Lily. Looking down at her pale face, he brushes a few stands of hair out of it, tugging them behind her ear.

I'm filled with guilt. Aaron should know about Lily's plans. He should know she's not doing alright at all.

"She can't die, Colin," he repeats. "I've never been the best brother, but she's all I have left from my mother. And even if that weren't a reason, she's the other half of me. If she dies, I don't think I could get through this."

For some reasons, I know exactly how he feels. I felt the same when Aiden died. Or when I had to learn that my sister is dying. I didn't want to accept it. I felt as though the whole world was crashing down on me.

I still feel like that sometimes. But Lily makes it better.

"She's not dying."

"She looks dead." Normally I would hit him for saying that, but she does look exhausted. I think dead fits it pretty well.

Though I'm not sure what the hell is happening to Lily, I feel like she just needs some rest. She did say she was exhausted. I didn't think it would ever get to this point of exhaustion, but what do I know?

"I'm calling an ambulance." Aaron is about to get up from the bed when Lily wraps her hand around his wrist. She shakes her head when he looks at her. It's so weak—she is so weak. "Lily..." before he gets to finish his sentence, Lily's eyes fall shut.

Another wave of panic comes over me. With her eyes no longer open, it's way harder to figure out if she's here with us. The only source Aaron and I have is her breathing, the way her chest lifts and falls with every single breath she takes.

"Colin," Aaron speaks, "it did happen before. She was fourteen then. It was the scariest day of my life." His eyes remain on Lily, and yet I can tell he's serious. "At least I think that's what it is."

"How did...*this* come to an end?"

"I'm not sure. Our father sent me to Ana. An hour later he came back from my room—where he kept Lily. He told me she'll be fine and that she's just in shock." *Shock*?

Suddenly I'm wondering if I'm the cause of her unconsciousness—or what I told her about Aiden.

"I'll call my father. Will you stay with her?"

"I wouldn't move one bit, Ron."

The second Aaron walks out of the room, I'm next to Lily again, holding her hand in mine. She's not opening her eyes, doesn't even react one bit to my touch.

For my own sanity I'm telling myself that she's asleep. I keep telling myself that she's alright. She's just exhausted, needs a good, refreshing and long sleep.

I'm not sure how much time passes until Aaron comes back. He's still on the phone, talking to his father. At least Aaron looks...relieved?

"I'll put you on speaker, dad. Lily's asleep, as far as I can tell." Removing the phone from his ear, Aaron presses the speaker button. "Colin is here as well."

"Colin?" Emerson's voice comes through the phone. "What did you do to my daughter?"

A bit startled, I answer, "Nothing. We were puzzling and then—"

"I'm kidding, son." A slight chuckle comes through. "Lily will be alright," he reassures...me, I think? "It's a temporary reaction caused by anxiety. Just, at least one of you, stay with her for a little while so she's not alone. Let her sleep it off. And don't let her attend classes tomorrow. I think she should take a day off to calm down."

"Dad, I don't think either of us is going to leave her," Aaron responses with no hesitation whatsoever.

"Good," Emerson says, sighing. "If either of you boys hurts my Lily..."

"Dad, have I ever intentionally hurt Lily?"

"You best believe you did."

With a dropped jaw, Aaron's eyes meet mine like he expects me to disagree.

"And Colin? I didn't get to threaten you yesterday, but I think you might have a second for me to do so, am I right?" I'm not even sure that's a real question at this point.

With Aaron's eyes still on me, I say, "Sure, go ahead."

Emerson snickers, kind of like he wasn't expecting me to let him.

I used to be so rude at all times, not to him but almost to everyone else. I never would have let anyone tell me anything.

But I guess ever since Lily came along, it all just doesn't matter anymore. Suddenly some father threatening me seems about right.

"WHAT ARE YOU doing here?" Grey asks when I storm into his bedroom only an hour after Emerson Marsh threatened to murder me if I let anything happen to his precious daughter. I would've gotten here earlier but I needed to get Sergeant Froggo from Lily's dorm room and give it to her.

Not going to lie, I was about to tell Emerson that I would protect Lily with all that I have. But I'm not going to risk this family hating me any more than they will—that is *if* Lily will die.

Once they figure out, I knew about it, and I didn't open my mouth…even Aaron will hate me.

"We need to talk," I tell Grey. Yes, I did come back here for advice. Grey is the safest person to speak to. "Like, in private. It's important."

It's not that I don't trust Aaron. I would give my life for my best friend. But Grey is easier to talk to. He has a clearer head. Doesn't judge. Come to think it's good that he's a psych major.

And Miles…well, he has plenty to deal with of his own. No need for me to add more to it.

"You do see Izan here, right?" Grey asks, chuckling.

I nod. "It's about Lily. I wouldn't come and interrupt if it weren't important, Grey. I guess it could wait another day, but then, I really don't have much time left."

Izan's attention is suddenly on me. I don't know him very well, but what I do know is that his mother is a shrink. Maybe letting him hear all this isn't too much of a good idea.

"Is it life-threatening?"

Is it? I chuckle to myself. "I'd say so, yes."

"I'll leave," Izan says and gets up from the bed.

"I'm really sorry, Izan. I promise I'll cook for you on, I don't know, Saturday?"

That earns me, not only one, but two snorts. "I'll hold you up for it once you've learned how to cook." He walks over to kiss Grey goodbye, and then I watch him leave, closing the door behind him.

Once the door is closed, I climb onto Grey's bed—like we're some teenage girls at a slumber party, about to reveal some deep dark secrets.

He laughs and lifts the blanket, offering me to slip underneath. And since it's already given, I do.

"You're so weird sometimes," Grey laughs, shaking his head.

"That's alright with me," I say. "I need momma Grey for a moment."

"Oh, that serious, huh?" All of his amusement gone.

As much as I hate that I left Lily back at home with Aaron, I really need some advice. And since she's asleep, I might as well go and get it now.

"It's about Lily." *Okay, this is harder than I thought it would be.*

"Look, you only know each other for a little while. Maybe you shouldn't propose yet. I know you've never been in love but—"

I cut him off before this gets silly. "She wants to die."

Grey inhales sharply, blinking a couple of times, waiting for me to say that I'm kidding. I wish I was. But unfortunately, it's the truth.

It does feel good to say it though. It feels good to finally tell someone about that one thing that has been killing me for nine days now.

"Colin, I will need more information than that."

I know he does, but it's really difficult to speak about her when I promised I wouldn't say a word to anyone.

"I've known for a while…" and then I tell him everything. I tell him what I've read in her notebook when I found it. I tell him the reason why I needed to give it back to her so desperately. Why I'm actually spending nine days showing her "the world"—that not being bet reasons. Why I can't let her live on her own right now. How I promised her I wouldn't say a word. As well as the reason why I *need* her to stay alive.

"Well, fuck." He's in shock, still processing all the information I've just given him. I wish I could say this feeling of shock will get lighter. But it won't. Not for me anyway.

I bob my head, agreeing to whatever he cussed at.

"You need to tell Aaron."

"I can't, Grey." Desperation rushes through my body. *That's why I came to talk to you.* "I promised I wouldn't."

"So you're going to see what happens?" Even though Grey doesn't know Lily very well—or at all really—he seems to be concerned for her. "You have what? three days left? You said she's in some kind of shock right now, what the hell do you think will change?"

And there is it. One question I have no answer to.

What *am* I expecting to change? I can't just magically erase suicidal thoughts from someone's mind. No matter how much time I spend with her. No matter what I'm showing her, how much fun she might have. I can't *heal* her.

Lily needs to want to be alive. If she doesn't want to be alive, there is no way I could ever keep her.

"You're not a therapist, Colin. You can't fix her. No one can fix her. You can't just take her on some fun dates and expect her to feel alive. Not to the point where she magically *wants* to be alive."

I guess he is right. *What was I thinking?*

"She's depressed. Lily is *suicidal*. Get her the goddamn help she needs. She might not want it, hell, she might hate you for betraying her. But what would you rather be the outcome? The girl you so clearly adore and obsess over being dead, or her getting better thanks to professional help?"

"I can't have her hate me, Grey."

He sighs and puts his hand on mine. I really do feel like some teenager talking to his mother about his first love and some broken hearts. It's ridiculous, really. I wish this was about some heartbreak and not Lily's death.

"She will hate you," he says, straight forward, no soothingly removing the band-aid. "But she will get the help she needs. She might even start to realize you've done it for her own good. And then, if you're lucky, maybe she won't hate you as much as you might think."

"Lily would cut me off completely," I say, feeling my throat clog up. I feel like I can't breathe, but I know air is getting into my lungs.

"She might. But at least she would be alive."

"It's not that easy, Grey." I know Grey is right. I know I should get her help. It doesn't matter that Lily will hate me for getting her help, she needs it. Getting help for Lily is more important than avoiding her hatred. *She would be alive...but she would hate me.*

I want her alive, but I also want her to like me.

Chapter 28

"there were fires burnin' and my hands learning to paint with passion"—Charing Stars by Alesso, Marshmello, James Bay

Colin

IT'S OFFICIALLY DAY SEVEN, which means I only have two more days left…and today. But that doesn't matter, not right now at least.

Lily is much stronger today. Not one hundred per cent back to her (more or less) joyful self, but she's doing better.

After my talk with Grey yesterday, I decided to do something really, *really* stupid. Maybe it's not that stupid. I don't think it is.

Okay, maybe it is. Doesn't mean I regret it though. Now I'm just hoping Lily won't see it earlier than necessary.

"How are you feeling?" I ask when I walk into my bedroom, carrying a tray with food and a glass of water.

Lily starts to laugh when she sees me, or the tray, or both combined. "That's sweet, but I'm not hungry."

I bet she just doesn't want to let go of her precious frog. She snuggled up to Sergeant Froggo all night, when instead she could have snuggled up to me. *Can't believe that frog is better than me.*

"That wasn't my question, Lilybug." I set the tray down on the nightstand, taking the glass of water and handing it to her. "Drink," I order.

She hasn't been getting much liquid into her system yesterday. She's been asleep all day and night, mostly. I woke her up a couple of times so she would take at least one sip of water…and eat a piece of bread for that matter. I couldn't let her eat and drink nothing at all, not all day long. So despite hating to wake her up for that, I've done it anyway.

She seemed glad about it. At least she didn't wake up with a major headache this morning. Though, she was starving.

"How was your day?" she asks, still ignoring my previous question.

"Without you? Lonely," I answer. "But now that we're united again, I'm feeling much better."

"You're so weird sometimes, Mr. Stinky." Chuckling, Lily takes the glass, taking a couple of sips before she hands it back to me. "Your hair is wet."

"It's still raining," I let her know. "Just hope it'll dry before I have to leave for practice. I'd rather not have frozen hair."

"I don't think your hair would freeze, but just in case, why don't you blow-dry it?"

Shrugging, I say, "I don't even know if I own a hair dryer. And if I do, I'm sure I have no idea how to work it."

Next thing I know, we're in my en suite bathroom and Lily is blow-drying my hair. Usually I'd find it weird if someone were to do anything to my hair, but it's different with Lily. Every single touch of hers is wanted—even if she's just blow-drying my hair.

But of course I can't let her dry my hair without messing with her. I mean, I have to sit on a closed toilet so that she can reach the top of my head properly, might as well mess with her a tiny bit.

Tracing my fingers up her smooth legs, I can feel her shiver. She tries to hide her goosebumps by moving around but she's always near me, right there for me to touch her.

I love that she's not wearing any pants, thinking the t-shirt she's wearing should be enough. It's more than enough for spending her day in my bed, I would prefer her naked with me buried deep inside of her, but I'll take half-naked, hair-drying Lily as well.

Actually, I'll take any Liliana Heaven Reyes.

Well, if it's my Lilybug. I only want—*need*—this one. The one that's currently laughing at my hands on her ass while she stands between my legs, drying the front of my hair.

"Lilybug?"

She hums, showing me that she's paying attention.

I know this is a bad idea and I know how displeased my father will be with me when he sees her, but I just can't hold myself back. "Come to practice with me."

It's not that anyone would really care about Lily being around during practice. My whole team keeps mocking me about her living here already, so might as well give them something else to mock me about. Though, I know they're all glad to see I have a heart, I guess.

My father, he's a difficult guy when it comes to hockey—especially when it comes to *his* team. It was a miracle that he gave me five minutes to go talk to Lily the other day. Having her around, distracting me, won't be on the good page of his likes and dislikes.

I know he likes Lily, he told me so himself when we left the house the morning of her birthday.

According to my father, bringing the girl you kind of have a thing for to hockey practice will complicate a lot. I don't see much of a difference to bringing her to a game or bringing her to watch the team practice.

Perhaps he just sees practice as something…private?

Hell, what do I know? I wouldn't even care if he saw it as such.

I can't leave Lily alone for much longer. She's been at the house by herself all day long already. I had a few classes to attend, and neither Aaron nor I allowed her to attend hers today.

Have some mercy on me.

This is a serious situation. I've already had to deal with Grey's disapproving looks when I told him I couldn't tell Aaron. And then when I told him Lily was all by herself back at the house. Surely I won't spend another two hours away from her, leaving her all alone.

"Can't," she says, "I've loads to do."

"That's a lie and we both know that."

Lily shrugs, smiling. "I didn't attend any of my classes today, I can't just show up at the arena to watch your team practice when I'm 'sick', Colin."

I suppose she has a point.

But my team won't rat her out, so she's fine. And it's not that any professor really cares anyway. As long as she hands in her assignments and knows her stuff for exams, she'll be good.

"I'm taking you to a pumpkin patch after practice," I inform her. "And when we're back home, we'll do some chocolate tasting." It's not like she asked for information about what we're doing today, but I figured telling her is better than continuing to pretend that she wouldn't be spending the next two hours at the arena.

"To how many weird tastings are you going to drag me to?" she asks, chuckling.

"I bought a bunch of different chocolate bars, even ordered some in from different countries. The guys are beyond excited for it."

Another laugh from her follows. "You invited them?"

"Excuse me?" Aaron's voice comes from the bathroom door. "He didn't need to invite the team, it's an open invitation. Always."

"Shut up, Ron."

"Is that true?" Lily goes to unplug the blow-dryer and sets it down onto the counter to let it cool.

We're in my en suit bathroom, not the one down the hall that's accessible for everyone, and yet Lily doesn't question Aaron's presence.

"Kind of," I answer. "We have this group chat. The guys always know exactly where the others are. Plans don't really go lost on each other. They know what we're doing today, so if they want to tag along, they most likely will."

Lily looks at me through the mirror, her mouth standing open in either surprise or shock. Maybe both. "That's like the ultimate stalking."

"Not really. It's voluntary, not a rule or anything. If plans are supposed to stay unsaid, they will," Aaron explains. "The guys always knew when I went off to see Winter."

"Gross."

"Not as much. It's weirder when *your* boyfriend sends a text saying he's about to get laid by you and I have to read that text." And that's my cue to get up and punch Aaron.

Before I can do that, Lily shoots me a warning look. I'm not sure if it's because she knows I'm about to murder her brother, or because she is asking me what the hell this is about. I'm not so good with reading minds.

"I have not once texted that."

And like Lily is waiting for more information, her eyebrows rise as her arms cross in front of her chest. It's cute whenever she does that. Like she believes she has some more power when her arms are crossed. It's like an armor.

She doesn't need that armor. This woman could ask me to rob a bank and I would do it for her.

Most likely my father's bank account, but same thing.

"Lily it's not that deep. We're just having the other's location at all times. You know, in case someone sends an *SOS* and doesn't have time to send their location. And the plans just kind of became a thing we do."

"And besides, most of the team knows when tagging along is okay and when it's an absolute dick-move to do," Aaron adds, crossing his arms in front of his chest just like Lily has it. "Chocolate sounds amazing though, and I bet at least 40% of the team is in."

I bet so, too.

"I know Grey and Miles are," I say. "Maybe even Brooke."

"Obviously," Aaron responds, chuckling. "It's free chocolate, and a good show because Lily will make you carve a pumpkin and put it on your head."

I eye Lily, waiting for her to laugh and tell me Aaron is kidding. But instead she shrugs pitifully.

He is not fucking joking.

But you know what? Fine. I'll do it. I survived a fairy costume on ice, I will survive turning into a pumpkin. I hope.

Chapter 29

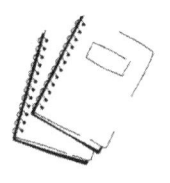

"lately I've been feeling not alive but you bring me back to life"—Cloud 9 by Beach Bunny

Lily

"I HAVE GOOD AND BAD NEWS," Colin says as he walks into the locker room where he left me to go and take a shower.

He could have easily left me waiting outside, but no, Colin refuses to let me do that. So instead, he forces me into the locker room, waiting for him, while his teammates are also present. At least he had them all march into the shower room with him.

The sight of naked Colin—completely naked except for that white towel wrapped around his waist—has me nervous. Though, not as nervous as knowing that when Colin just got out of the shower, twenty-one other hockey players are about to follow.

Colin lets his towel drop to the floor right in front of me, like I'm not even here. And the fact that a really hot and very naked hockey player is standing in front of me only has my blood rushing through me quicker, making it feel like it's a million degrees in here.

At least his back is toward me. I don't think I would have survived looking at his chest. More like, his tattoos. Who would have thought I'd ever be into tattoos? Certainly not me. But hell, they're sexy as fuck. Or maybe they're just sexy because they're on Colin's body and I happen to find him sexy? Either way, he's way too good-looking. And I hate it.

But I also love it.

Oh, the sight of his ass is quite the show as well. Not as intriguing as his bare chest covered in tattoos.

"We don't have to carry twenty-three pumpkins on our own," he tells me while drying his body. "However, we do need about twelve." That can only mean that more of his teammates decided to tag along for our plans today.

As much as I'd rather spend time with Colin alone, I begin to think that maybe today could be fun. I mean, as far as I know, the guys are fun to have around. Not once did I hear someone complain about spending time with one of the hockey players—well apart from sex rumors about Colin, which also aren't true at all. This man is a sex god, and can be, no *is* really sweet afterward.

"We'll be thirteen in total. Is that okay with you?" Colin turns his head to meet my eyes, yet his body stays in the same position, almost. It has a slight turn to it now, but not enough for me to view his abs. He isn't turning around completely, not sure why. I mean, I've seen him naked before, technically there is nothing more to hide from me. Unless he isn't trying to hide his body parts, but something that is on his body…like a tattoo. Or maybe he just thinks it's inappropriate right now—which it is.

"Thirteen of your teammates just decided to tag along to a pumpkin patch?" I ask. It's amusing, really. Never thought twelve super attractive, massive and...*tough* guys between the ages of eighteen to twenty-two would even consider going to a pumpkin patch. Voluntarily.

"Nine, plus Izan, you and I, which makes it up to twelve people in total. And Miles asked to bring Brooke, like I predicted. So thirteen. They're sharing a pumpkin though."

"So, who are the other six guys?" I'm assuming three of the tag-alongs are Aaron, Miles and Grey.

"Kaiden, Zac and a bunch of guys you probably never even heard of. They're all nice. Have fucked up brains though. Don't worry, you won't even notice they're with us."

I snort a laugh, watching as Colin finally finishes getting dressed and turns to face me. "That seems unlikely."

"They'll probably challenge you to do dumb stuff. But they know how to have a good time. If you want them to stop annoying you, just threatening them with me. Is that okay?"

"I don't mind. Sounds like a fun evening."

"Are you sure?" Colin sits down beside me, taking my hand in his as he caresses the back of it. "If you'd rather do something alone with me, I'm happy to ban them from joining."

"I think this is more about you wanting to be alone with me than the other way round."

"Obviously. I'd rather stick my dick inside you without people watching. But I can work with some viewers." I slap him about three times before he starts to laugh. I'm sure me hitting him hurts about...not at all. "Seriously, I'm talking about whether or not you have the strength to socialize today."

I want to roll my eyes and scream. Not because Colin cares about me, but because these few words have my heart skip a beat. Or two. Or a hundred. I don't know, I feel like this is a dream.

Maybe I'm already dead and Colin is my afterlife.

"YOUR HEAD DOESN'T even fit into it," Wees, so I've heard Colin call him, yells from across the pumpkin patch. Colin holds up his middle finger, flipping Wees off.

We've been here for good an hour and we're still looking for pumpkins to take with us. Of course Colin would pay. He voted for everyone paying for their own pumpkin, except for me, of course. Colin would never let me pay, even now that it's a new month and I have some extra money.

But because Colin is rather unlucky with Aaron around, he will have to pay for every single pumpkin as going to a pumpkin patch was his idea.

When Colin said he'd pay for mine, he earned a few slaps from his teammates, or friends…and Izan. Not sure why, but I suppose that's what guys do?

From what I've heard from Winter, guys aren't too good with that whole feelings stuff. And often times, if one guy develops feelings for someone, their friends will try to humiliate or make fun of them.

It's sad, truly sad. Love is supposed to be something good, something relieving to know there's this one person that loves you for who you are. That there's a person to call home and be yourself with.

So why would anyone make fun of it?

I don't see anyone making fun of Izan and Grey for being in love. Come to think it's a male-female-relationship thing only.

Well, or this team is just afraid of Grey or Izan. I know I am.

Grey hasn't stop eyeing me every now and then ever since he spotted me at the arena earlier. I know he's aware of Colin and my fake-relationship thing. But it's still odd, the way he watches me, I mean.

"Stop ogling at my best friend," Colin whispers as his arms wrap around me from behind. His chin rests on the top of my head, I could swear right before he'd rest his head on mine, he placed a kiss on top of my head. "You should be in love with me, not Grey."

I chuckle. "Grey has a boyfriend."

"So do you," Colin says. Before I would get the chance to protest, Colin twirls me around, cupping my face with his big hands and presses his lips to mine, sweet and soft.

This guy does want me dead after all.

"No face eating in public, captain," speaks Kaiden, tapping his hand to Colin's shoulder a couple of times.

Something seems odd the second Colin looks up and his eyes meet Kaiden's. It's like all of Kaiden's courage just leaves his body.

I've seen that happening a few times when someone spoke to Colin—with people that aren't his three idiotic best friends, that is.

"No one ever cared when you did that," Colin utters, his hands sliding down my body until they come to a stop by my waist.

"Yeah, but you should spare Aaron the show. He's about to cry and vomit at the same time."

Trying to hold in my chuckle is almost impossible. The thought of my brother crying because his best friend kisses me occasionally is pretty hilarious.

But then another thought crosses my mind. What if Aaron has other reasons to dislike Colin and me together? *Not that there is a "Colin and I."*

I excuse myself and walk across the pumpkin patch to get to my brother. He is comparing pumpkin sizes together with Grey, Izan and Miles. Though, Miles barely pays attention as his daughter clings onto him like a tiny monkey.

Brooklyn looks so much like Millie, it's almost scary. She even wears her blonde hair the same way Millie always used to. In two braids. Though, I suppose that's more an adult's doing than her own. And by the looks of it, most likely Miles's.

When I approach the guys, all of their heads turn to face me at the same time. And Brooklyn, she smiles up at me, yet keeps on hiding behind her father's leg.

"Can we talk for a second?" I ask Aaron. I am solely speaking to him, yet Grey is watching me with suspicion.

Something in Grey's aura has shifted since the last time he'd seen me. Yesterday morning, Grey was nice, calm and fun to have around. And today…he seems cold and as if he's judging me. It's weird.

"Sure." Aaron lays the pumpkin in his hands down before taking a few steps to get away from the other two guys. "What's up?"

Now, how do I phrase this? "Ron, I need to ask you something." *That's not the way to go, Lily.*

"Alright?" I can tell he is confused by the way his forehead wrinkles slightly. "Something happened?"

I shake my head. "Why do you hate the idea of Colin and me so much?"

He laughs, just once, one loud *Ha!* "Lily, I don't hate you together," is what I get in response.

"Then why are you so tense all the time? Kaiden said you're about to vomit and cry at the same time just looking at us."

Aaron puts his hand onto my shoulder, smiling at me softly.

"I'm happy for you," he says in the softest voice I've ever heard him speak in. "You deserve some happiness, Lily. And it's pretty obvious that this big guy over there is head over heels for you."

Lies, I want to say, luckily, I can stop myself before it slips out.

"How would you know?"

"Are you serious?" He laughs again. "Lily, I know Colin. He's an asshole to everyone that isn't Grey, Miles or me…and you, apparently. It worries me that he might start to cut you off like the dick he is. I don't want to see you hurting, not over some guy. And especially not over my best friend. If he hurts you, I will have to cut him off as well. That would be such a shame. However, I've also never seen him happier this whole time I've known him. I've never witnessed Colin seeing one girl for longer than one night, that is *if* it lasted a night. He moved you in with us in a heartbeat, only because you can't deal with Winter at the moment."

A smile tugs at the corner of my lips. *Stop smiling, Lily.* I hate that my body is betraying my head. And I hate it even more that my heart is doing little jumps.

"He didn't even ask if I was okay with it. He just informed me you'd be staying with us. Said if I had any complaints about it, I could move in with Grey and Miles."

Another jump. With those goddamn *dragonflies* in my stomach.

Didn't Colin tell me he *asked* all three of them? It doesn't matter.

"He cried, you know," Aaron says, lowering his tone. I raise my eyebrows, not understanding what he's talking about. "When he got Kermit—"

"His name is Sergeant Froggo now," I correct. I don't even know why I correct him, I just do.

Aaron's jaw drops slightly, but his open mouth quickly forms into a soft smile. I understand the jaw-drop. It was Aaron naming him after all. And for all those years I've had him, I've never changed the frog's name.

"I see." He presses his lips together, inhaling deeply. "When he got that frog and came back, seeing you half dead lying in his bed—after I figured that's where you'd rather be. I heard him sniffing and saw him wiping away some tears. Not that he'd ever admit it, so I never brought it up. But I know what I saw, and I heard what he said to you. Not a clue what it meant, but you know, probably something lovey-dovey."

Probably something like: "I should have let you go."

Wrapping an arm around my neck, Aaron asks, "What's the actual reason to came to ask me?"

I hate that he knows me well enough to know when I had other intentions. Luckily, he doesn't know me enough to see through my skull and read my mind.

"I thought that maybe…" I trail off, not knowing how to phrase it without making it awkward.

"Finish your sentence, Lily." Bemused, he looks at me with that nasty grin. He knows my assumption, I don't have to phrase it.

"I thought you might…you know…like him."

Aaron laughs, rubbing his knuckles over the top of my head like our dad used to do when we were younger. "I've seen enough of this guy to know I am not—in *any* possible way—attracted to your boyfriend."

"Too bad." I shrug. "Colin knows how to work…bodies."

Gagging, yet also laughing, Aaron pushes me away, holding his hand to his stomach. "I don't need reminders of what I've seen, Lily. I'm good with fake-sleeping while he fucks some chick next to me, if that chick isn't you."

"Wait, what?"

"Can I get my *girlfriend* back?" Colin's voice comes from behind me at the same time as arms wrap around my chest.

Why is he empathizing "girlfriend" like that? Just to make our fake-relationship seem more realistic to Aaron, right?

It starts to rain just when we're on our way back to the cars. It's not a light rainfall. No, it's pouring. All of us are soaking wet in seconds. Not a clue where that came from so suddenly, but I like rain.

Maybe I like it a little too much because I stop walking without even noticing. Just looking at the sky as I let the cold water run down my body.

Something about rain is freeing. Something about the cold water is washing away some stress and anxiety of mine. It truly is the most relaxing thing ever. It's easy to tip your head toward the sky and let the raindrops hit your face, shoulders, arms, chest and heart. And the feeling it comes with—the feeling of relief—it's unimaginably easy to accomplish with some rain.

But what's more of a benefit, tears are almost invisible in it.

I stand in the middle of the parking lot, head held up toward the sky that's crying on me.

Maybe that's why I find rain freeing? It looks like the sky is crying. If the sky can cry and let its frustration out, so can I.

The sky can look so dull, so sad for a moment and then the next thing you know, the sun is shining in all its glory. Everything is happy and sunny, and so bright. But even the sky has moments of sadness and anger.

Ignoring every single one of the guys as they walk past me, carrying some pretty heavy pumpkins to the cars we came here with.

I feel their looks, but I ignore them. Because what matters is that the sky is upset and cries. And although I don't have a particular reason to be upset right now, nor do I feel any kind of sadness for a moment, I still want to feel the cold drops on my skin, savor them.

Headlights from the cars turn on, but I ignore those as well. I just want to stand here for a minute, letting the rain drop against my chest, opening my heart.

"I haven't seen her do this in years," I hear Aaron say. He's watching me, probably with that same soft smile he used to give me back when we were kids and I stopped walking to look toward the rain.

"She's done this before?" I think Zac asks.

There's no response, so I'm guess Aaron nods as an answer. But a second later I feel a presence right next to me. At first I assume it's Colin because he's always right beside me, but it's not.

It's Grey.

"Is this any good?" he asks, his voice small and calm.

"The best feeling in the world." I don't look at him, but I know he's copying the way I stand. His arms open to the sky as he looks up.

When I feel another presence next to me, I'm certain it's Colin. So when I look up and find him standing there, doing the exact same thing Grey and I are doing, I can't help but smile.

Not sure if I should be happy or mad when Colin intertwines our hands and pulls me to him until my back hits his front.

"Lily," he whispers, sounding almost out of breath. It still feels weird when he says my name, though technically it's still a nickname.

He turns me to face him. My hands find his shoulders almost instantly.

"Tell me what you said to me when I was asleep," I demand, not caring that Grey is still beside us. Colin seems to care though. He eyes Grey who nods and makes his way over to the other guys. The ones that are waiting in the cars because it's pouring.

Colin knows what I'm talking about. And judging by the horror in his eyes, I'm assuming he thinks I've heard him talk. *I wish I did.*

"I didn't hear it, but Aaron did. He told me." He sighs in relief. "Tell me what you said."

He shakes his head, closing his eyes like he's dismissing his own thoughts, his own words.

"Lilybug, you won't understand it."

"Tell me anyway, I want to know."

"*Eres el amor de mi vida, mi sol.*"

And now I will forever wonder what he said. I bet he won't give me a translation when saying it to my face—in a language I don't even understand—is so difficult for him.

"*Siempre te amaré.*" Oh, okay, apparently there is more. I'm not quite sure if that should make me nervous.

"What does it mean?" I find myself asking, leaning my forehead to his as he tilts down enough for me to reach him.

"Can't tell you. At least not yet."

Chapter 30

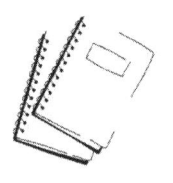

"wise men say only fools rush in, but I can't help falling in love with you"—Can't Help Falling In Love by Elvis Presley

Lily

"I HAVE NO IDEA WHAT FLAVORS THEY ARE," Colin says as he places a box down onto the coffee table.

The living room is a bit small for ten huge hockey players, and one massive soccer player…and me. Well, maybe the living room itself isn't, but the sofa most definitely is.

We're only five people (Wees, Aaron, Zac, Miles and I) sitting on the sofa while the others seated themselves on the floor, and it's getting a bit crowded. And well, Brooklyn is fast asleep behind her father.

Colin is still standing, as of now. I'm sure in less than a minute I'm going to be sitting on him instead of a comfortable sofa.

"Chocolate, obviously," Miles states the obvious with some great sarcasm.

"Duh," Kaiden adds to the conversation.

Colin rolls his eyes and takes a deep breath, trying hard not to make some comment about his friends' stupidity.

He takes my hands from my lap, pulling me up to my feet. When I'm about to protest, Colin sits down and as predicted, seats me onto his lap.

His arms wrap around my stomach, holding me close to him. "You okay?" he asks quietly so that only I can hear.

I nod, then voice a quick, "Yes."

"Are you tired?"

I am. I really am. It's only eleven, yet I'm exhausted. If I wasn't excited to see some hockey guys rate chocolate, I for sure would have gone upstairs already. I don't even know what's so exciting about jocks tasting chocolate, but it just is.

"I'm not," I lie, "but thank you for asking."

"Come on, does anyone not know what Hershey's tastes like?" Wees, I'm still not sure if that's his actual name, asks, chuckling. He pulls out a box filled with Hershey bars, setting it down on the coffee table.

"This is a chocolate tasting, Ezra"—I guess it's Ezra then—"we'll try *different* ones. Hershey's clearly should be on the list," one of the other guys says. I have absolutely no idea who's talking. Maybe I should have asked Colin for their names.

Miles rips open the box and then opens up one bar, handing one piece to each person. To our luck, we're exactly twelve people and this Hershey bar has twelve pieces to offer, so there's no waste at all. Except for the rest of the box, but we're not talking about that. They're closed and will be eaten eventually, I'm sure of it.

On the count of three, we're all eating this one piece. It's nothing new to either of us.

Some of those guys take the tasting part really seriously, savoring the flavor, opening another bar to get yet another try.

"I'll rate it two out of five Oompa Loompa's," I say, starting the rating. If only I had known my rating would have about nine heads from sports guys turn toward me like I've insulted someone.

"What the hell is an Oompa-Padoompa?" Zac looks at me with wide eyes, eyebrows raised and impatiently waiting for an explanation.

"Oompa Loompa," I correct. "From Charlie and the Chocolate Factory?"

"Do we have a chocolate bar from there, too?"

Miles laughs, bringing his hand to his mouth to cover it. "It's a movie."

"As if not one of you guys know it?" I look at Colin, praying he's seen the movie, but when he shrugs instead, I almost fall off him and onto the floor. "We'll change that once we're done here."

After the guys give their ranking, we move on to the next chocolate bar. It takes us good thirty minutes to get through the next three options, simply because Colin, Ezra and Zac take the rating a bit too seriously. They're analyzing each piece to the gods, comparing them to previous ones. If they were only comparing tastes, it would be understandable, but no, they're comparing price to volume and all that.

It's ridiculous, but fun…in some ways. I assume Colin does that mainly to make me laugh, and it does make me laugh. A lot.

Every time he reaches for another piece and makes those tasting sounds—which, by the way, annoy the hell out of me—I can't help but laugh.

Another half an hour passes, and we're finally down to the last bar. My stomach is hurting, protesting to try the last bar that's being handed around right now.

I feel like, if I were to eat one more piece, I'll explode. The guys seem less like it. In fact, I think they could go on for another hour. I'd love to see how that would play out.

Something about this last piece of chocolate seems off though. Well, not that it's expired or poisoned...but something tells me that trying this is a bad idea.

When Parker, apparently Wees's best friend, counts down from three, telling us to hurry up because he wants to try it oh so badly, my brain suddenly starts working, trying to figure out what is wrong with this piece of chocolate in my hands.

It isn't until Parker reaches the number three that I realize why this is a bad idea.

"Wait." I wrap my hand around Colin's wrist, stopping him from plopping his piece into his mouth.

His eyebrows draw together, eyes locked on mine as he waits. I'm sure there's even some concern for me drawn over his face, but I ignore that. He should be concerned for himself.

"Lily, this is just the same piece of chocolate we've tried before. Different taste, probably, different brand, but still just chocolate," Zac says, chuckling. I'm sure he's making fun of me in some ways, but I couldn't care less right now. Especially not when Colin glares at Zac with heat in his eyes, as if he's telling Zac to fuck off.

Taking the piece of chocolate from Colin, I turn to Miles. "Give me the wrapper," I demand, holding my hand out. He picks it up and hands it to me, his brows drawn together just like everyone else's.

I check the wrapper, reading every single word until I find what I'm looking for. It takes me a hot minute, but then on the back, written in the tiniest font size I could think of.

"It contains coconut," I mumble, mostly to myself. "Why didn't they write that information right on the front?"

Maybe it's unreasonable to get angry at this, but I do get angry. I know allergies, especially nut allergies can turn into a matter-of-seconds kind of situation.

How many people with allergies must have eaten this, thinking it's milk chocolate because that is what it says on the front of the wrapper?

And the worst bit, you can't even smell the coconut. Maybe that's also good? Considering that some people just have to smell the product they're allergic to and trigger it.

"You don't like that?"

Ignoring whoever just asked that, I look at Colin, seeing his dumbstruck expression. I want to touch his face, but I doubt that's such a great idea, so instead I stand up, take his hand and force him to the next bathroom with me.

He doesn't talk, which is unusual because Colin usually speaks a ton when he's around me.

"Are you okay?" I ask, starting to panic. What if it's already too late and his airways are about to clog up and he's going to die? "Can you breathe?"

He nods lightly, so lightly I barely see it.

"Colin, you need to speak to me, please." I don't think I've ever begged someone to speak to me. "Should I call an ambulance?" Fuck it, I might do it anyway, just to be sure he's completely okay.

"You—"

I grab my phone from my back pocket, struggling to unlock it with my Face-ID. Why is it that whenever you're in a rush your phone just doesn't want to corporate?

"Lily," I hear Colin say, at the same time as water starts to run. I think he's washing his hands. Typing in the emergency numbers, I'm about to dial when Colin takes the phone from me. "I'm fine," he says, lifting my chin up so that our eyes meet.

A light breeze of air hits my face as he sighs. When he places his other hand to my face, tracing his thumbs underneath my eyes, only then do I notice tears running down my face.

Why am I crying? *Lord*, what is happening?

"Sweetheart, I'm alright," he speaks softly, calmly. His voice is flat and low but reassuring. "I'm alright," he repeats. I'm not sure if he's trying to convince me or himself.

"You could have died," I mumble, once again, to myself, but of course he hears it.

Tears continue to slip past my eyes, running down my cheeks. The thought of Colin dying is too absurd, too much to think about, too *painful* to think about.

What would I have done if he ate it? What if he would have died?

The only source of light in my life can't die on me. Colin can't die on me. He can't die even if he wanted to. Not ever. Okay, maybe of old age, but even that is almost crossing the line.

I need to get a grip. I can't feel the way I do about Colin. It's not fair to him.

Sure, Colin didn't want me to die right from the start, but this is not about him dying that's bugging me so much. I mean, I don't want him to die, but the pain I feel just thinking about his death…that's what's bugging me.

The way my heart shrinks and my lungs tighten when I think about losing this guy. The way my head starts to hurt, and my eyes begin to water when I think about never seeing him ever again.

"Colin?" I sniff, still crying.

"Please stop the tears, *mi sol*, my heart can't take those." He wipes the couple of drops away as quickly as they came, just that they keep on coming. "You're breaking my heart, Lilybug. I can't stand to see you cry."

You're breaking my heart by saying these words, Colin.

A knock appears on the door, followed by someone asking, "Everything alright?" I don't recognize the voice, but I'm sure Colin does.

"Yup, all good." Colin talks a bit louder as to when he talked to me before.

"I'll call an ambulance," the guy informs Colin, I guess.

Colin shakes his head but of course his friend can't see through the door, so he speaks. "No, it's alright. I don't need one, Wees."

Oh, Wees, aka Ezra.

"You sure?"

Colin sighs, chuckling slightly. He seems annoyed by people caring about him. That's quite ironic given that this guy cared, and still cares more about me than my mother ever truly has, right from the start.

As he walks off to open the door and speak to Ezra face to face, I use that time to wash my hands, freeing myself from any kind of coconut remains.

"The guys have cleared the room from everything coconut, so you're safe to come out," I hear Wees say, followed by a quiet chuckle from Colin.

"I figured you'd call some more people in and ask them to bring coconuts."

"I was thinking about it," Wees laughs, "just to mess with you. But the risk wasn't worth it."

"I'm alright, Wees, I promise. I didn't smell it, and even if I did, I don't think it would have caused me to die. I don't react to smell, just the intake of it."

"That means, hottie saved your life." I bet Wees is smiling cockily.

"Her name is Lily."

"Everyone deserves a nickname."

Drying off my hands as a distraction, I try to stay calm before I'd punch Wees in his average-looking face. Okay, who am I kidding? This guy is handsome, and I thought he was nice…before those words left his mouth.

"Lily has one, in fact, I have a few for her. She doesn't need any more, especially none that are based off of her appearance."

In a matter of seconds, Colin reaches out for my hand and pulls me to his side, wrapping an arm around me like he's just offered himself to be my own personal shield. Which he is. I know he is. Colin wouldn't let anyone do me wrong, I just know he wouldn't.

"Could you tell everyone to go home. I think I need some time on my own. You know, dealing with the fact that I almost died." Colin's grip on my waist tightens, but not in an uncomfortable way, quite the opposite. It's comforting.

Ezra nods. "On your own, with your girl."

"Yeah, she doesn't bother me. Like you said, *my* girl."

Damned if that doesn't have my cheeks heat up, feeling as though fire is tingling on my skin. For some reasons my body loves that feeling of fire on my skin now. It happens a lot with Colin around.

As much as I keep telling myself that I can't let Colin get this close to me, that I can't keep hurting him any more than I already did, I can't seem to stop it.

It's like this man is giving me some kind of strength that I never knew was possible to receive. He's not only a light bulb, shining some brightness into the clouded space that is my life. No, he is the whole sun. Giving me light, warmth, helping flowers grow through rainy days.

I don't even notice when Ezra leaves and Colin leads me upstairs into his bedroom. Or I subconsciously crawl into his bed and throw the covers over my body. It's not that I'm tired, maybe I am, with Colin so close to me, I stay in my head and don't even notice what I'm doing until I am.

"*Mi sol*, you should probably change into something more comfortable before going to sleep." I hear him rummage through his closet.

Sending a silent prayer that Colin is about to hand me one of his shirts to sleep in, I allow myself to watch him looking through his clothes.

I love his scent. Colin smells like rosewood most of the time—every single day—and yet the scent that is *Colin* never passes me. He always smells nice, warm and comforting. I never even knew someone could smell *comforting* until I met Colin.

Maybe it's some broken piece in my brain that says he smells comforting, but then again, I don't mind it. Colin gives me comfort at all times, even when I don't want him to. Just knowing he is here—*with me*—not letting me go without a fight, feels right, peaceful.

And as if my prayer has been heard, Colin throws a shirt right into my direction, landing on my head. He laughs, filling my chest with some weird warmth. A warmth I grew so familiar with.

I pull it down, making sure to savor the smell of Colin. It brings an immediate smile to my face, to my broken and shaken soul.

Not caring that Colin's eyes are on me, my body, I lay the shirt down in front of me and start to strip off my own. The gasp that rolls over Colin's soft lips when I sit on his bed in just my bra and jeans quickly turns into a low toned groan when my hands reach behind my back, unclasping my bra.

To put up a show for Colin—as I pretend, I wouldn't know he is staring with hunger in his eyes—I stretch. My back arching, pressing my breasts a tad more into the air.

Avoiding Colin's eyes, which I'm sure are more focused on my breasts than my eyes, I pull his shirt over my head, slowly lowering it over my breasts, then pull it down over my stomach a bit quicker.

Couldn't have him think I did all this on purpose.

My eyes follow his body as he walks over to my side of the bed, coming to a halt next to me. Colin removes the blanket from my legs, then gently, yet firmly, tugs on them, causing me to lie on my back.

I don't question him. I wouldn't dare to do so. Colin could do whatever he wanted with me for all I care. Okay, maybe that's a bit exaggerated. But right now, I would let him do anything. Except for maybe bad stuff, like…drug me.

Feeling his warm hands on my body sends another wave of comfort through my veins, just like his laughter had before. To my displeasure, it also leaves me craving him.

My breathing quickens when Colin pushes my shirt up until my stomach is freed again. Anticipating his touch, I'm disappointed when he bends down and plants a kiss to my stomach, then undoes the button of my jeans, pulls down the zipper only to remove my pants from my body. The second my jeans are no longer on me, he tugs on the shirt, covering me up.

Grunting, I roll my eyes at him when I figure out, he only collects my clothes from the bed and isn't about to jump me.

Why do I even care? Colin and I aren't supposed to go at one another like rabbits. We're supposed to be friends, and nothing more than just that.

He is supposed to try and convince me that I want to stay alive—which we all know won't really work anyway.

We're not supposed to have some kind of friends with benefits arrangement. And yet I'm longing for his touch. Longing for the sweet relief I know he would give me.

"What's that movie called again?" I hear him say but my mind is still elsewhere.

My mind is still focusing on his hands on my body, skimming, gliding, caressing every inch. His lips on mine when our tongues meet. His hips pressing against mine, his erection pressing against my core right before he leaves me breathless, oblivious.

"Lilybug?" He sounds amused. *Oh God, have I said all those things out loud?* My eyes meet his and I'm sure my face is turning red when he grins at me knowingly. "The movie? With these chocolate figures."

I can't help my chuckle. "They're not chocolate figures. They're Oompa Loompa's."

"Oompa Loompa, Hoompa Poompa, Chocolate Shooter. It's all the same thing. What's the movie called?"

"Did you just say, 'Chocolate Shooter' to 'Oompa Loompa?'" I laugh, genuinely laugh.

He shrugs. "I might have. Name?"

"Charlie and the Chocolate Factory."

Less than a few minutes later, Colin is in bed with me, pulling me close to him when the movie starts to play on his TV.

Chapter 31

"we're on the right side of bad karma"—Rock Bottom by Hailee Steinfeld, DNCE

Colin

STEPPING INTO THE KITCHEN AT SIX in the morning is something I never learned to like.

Until I figured that it can be pleasing.

The second I walk down the stairs, the kitchen coming into view, my eyes land on Lily standing in front of the stove.

She is making breakfast. Again.

I don't remember one day this house smelled like fresh strawberries or bananas, or even just pancakes. But ever since Lily is forced to stay here, she's been making breakfast every morning.

And I'm quick to learn that she loves pancakes. Not the normal ones. No, Lily puts strawberries and bananas in the batter. I think these have become my new favorite kind of pancakes.

To be fair, I didn't even know this was a thing. Apparently it is, but I'm not mad about it.

"Good morning," says Lily in a soft and sleepy tone. I don't think she's been awake for too long yet, at least according to her sleepy voice.

She doesn't look at me, just continues to cook as I make my way over to her.

Standing right behind her, I slowly, and ever so gently wrap my arms around her, lowering my head until my mouth is at the same height as her ear. "Good morning, *mi sol*," I whisper, then plant a tender kiss to her temple.

She shivers, but I don't think it's because of my touch. Her skin is cold, she is freezing.

"You should have put on some more clothes before getting down here." Rubbing my hands up and down her arms to bring some warmth to her, she giggles.

"Maybe I wanted you to warm me."

Before I get the chance to answer, my phone vibrated. As much as I hate checking my phone with Lily around, I know I have to.

I pull away from the comfort of Lily and grab my phone from my pocket as I walk over to the kitchen island, taking a seat.

Eira: What are you up to?

Whatever Eira is planning (at six in the morning), it can't be anything good. She never asks what I'm up to.

Colin: About to eat breakfast. ¿Por qué?

Eira: You didn't come home yesterday. Can we do something fun today? I know you have classes and practice, Papá told me. But Colin, I really need you today.

How could I say no to her? Ever.

Eira: And bring Lily, if she wants. ¡Te quiero, Colin!

Sighing, I fight the urge to groan. Telling Eira that Lily is my girlfriend—which is a total lie, sort of—was the worst thing I've ever done.

Lily doesn't know it yet, but she totally is my girlfriend.

Instead of continuing to text my sister, I decide to call her. It's not only easier, but also, I need to hear her voice before it's too late.

She picks up right away. "*¡Ay, Colin! Es bueno que llames.*" Of course it's good that I'm calling. I know Eira prefers calls over texts as well.

"What do you want to do, *enana*?" I ask, having not only Eira's but also Lily's attention.

"Does Lily skate? We could go to an ice rink, *quizás*? Oh, we can teach her if she can't skate. That would be fun too!"

Eira is way too excited for someone who is supposed to be bed-bound and can barely even stand on her own anymore. Especially too excited about possibly going skating.

"Hate to burst your bubble, *enana*, she can. But I don't think she'd go. I'll ask her though."

I know for a fact that Lily will turn her head, then frown at me the second the question leaves my mouth. But for Eira's sake, I have to ask.

"Lilybug?" She hums, telling me she's listening. "Eira asked if we could go skating together. Now, I know you don't step foot on the ice, but—"

"I can't," she interrupts, turning toward me, frowning. A cute, little and irritated frown. "You know I can't. I know I'll love it, and I can't find back to something I used to love only to leave it behind again in a couple of days."

And those couple of days are less than I'd like. It's the fifth of October today, meaning there's only three days left. Two dedicated to me.

I hear Eira gasp through the phone. She must have heard Lily.

What Lily doesn't know yet, she will step on ice again. I wouldn't let her die without at least feeling the freedom of what she once loved one last time.

I'm sure if I told Lily why it's so important to me that we go with Eira—*hold on.*

"Can you even go? Eira, you're not that strong anymore," I ask in Spanish, not wanting Lily to ask questions afterward.

"I'm fine, Mr. Nurse. I know you'll hold me up. Mamá doesn't like the idea of me going, but she certainly isn't going to stop me. You know why."

I do know why. And I hate it.

"Lily, I really have to go with her. I have to give Eira that much. I haven't gone to visit her yesterday, it's the least I could do." *And maybe I should tell you the whole truth…but I can't.*

"You can go. I have classes anyway. I can also annoy Aaron for a while, tease him about liking some girl or something."

Nine Days

As intriguing at that sounds, I need Lily to come with me. I know she will ask questions—ones I can't give her answers to—but I need Lily around.

"She has to come, *gigante. Please*." Even my sister is whining for Lily to accompany us.

"I need you, Lily." Running my hands through my hair, I let out a soft sigh. "If anything happens, I need you to call 911 for me."

She shoots me a *what-the-fuck* kind of look, silently asking me what that is about. I wish I could tell her, but it would only guilt trip her.

"Eira is a bit clumsy, and she has thin skin, easily breakable bones," I explain, lying. But maybe it's not too much of a lie. She can get hurt so easily.

Eira snorts, knowing very well that I'm not being honest.

"You're such a liar," she blurts out in Spanish. "No cancer talk, got it. Bring her, *por favor*."

It required a lot of persuading and promises—*and a couple of milkshakes afterward*—but I got Lily to come with me.

Eira is sitting on the stairs to the entrance of the ice rink in New York. It looks like it's closed today, probably my father's doing. My mother is standing next to Eira, handing her probably six different gloves and a million scarfs.

We all know Eira is easy to break these days, but come on, seriously?

"*¡Ay, hijo!*" my mother shouts when she sees Lily and me exiting the car. "*¡Y sus novia, Lily!*" Suddenly I'm wondering how I was so confused when Lily found out I speak Spanish. My mother doesn't exactly try to hide her Spanish genes.

I suppose neither should I, but I've always found it difficult not to feel judged for it. It's like that one single incident—back in middle school when I used to have an accent and other kids would make fun of me—just completely ruined it for me.

Okay, and apparently, I switch between languages on the phone, even in front of her. Which, not going to lie, threw me off track when Lily told me.

I barely notice when I switch languages. But I do, however, know I don't go around showing off my Spanish genes.

"Take care of your sister, will you?" The concern in her voice doesn't stay unnoticed. I can't blame her, Eira shouldn't be outside anymore. I get that she loves it, that she wants to live but it's simply not too possible at this time around.

"I wouldn't let anything happen to her, Mamá."

"Good, good. Make sure Eira wears her gloves, and stockings, and a helmet, and scarves and—"

"Estaré bien, Mamá," my sister reassures. *"Estoy enferma, no muerta."*

My mother glances at her, so do I. It wasn't funny the first time Eira had said this, and it isn't now. It *especially* isn't now.

I hold my hand out for Eira, helping her up. "I can walk, Colin," she says, knowing I would very well carry her inside.

"That's good, otherwise I wouldn't know how you'd skate."

As we're standing in front of the ice, Eira can barely wait to get on it. She used to love skating, just like Lily. The difference is, Lily stopped skating because she didn't have the motivation to do it anymore, Eira was forced to by her doctors.

I got Eira one of those cute penguins, little kids use when they learn how to skate. I have no idea why, but this ice rink just loves being extra. So instead of those normal skate helpers, they have penguins. *Obviously they're not real.*

It doesn't even matter what they look like, it's only for some support. Eira isn't able to skate all she wants, she will need the help.

"You're a figure skater?" Eira asks, looking Lily up and down.

Despite Lily not wanting to come here in the firsts place, she refused to possibly go skating without wearing one of her costumes. She said something about if she is going to do this, she will do it the right way.

I don't really care if she's wearing shorts or jeans…or a figure skating costume. As long as Lily will step on the ice, I will throw a party…silently. I wouldn't want to scare her away.

The smile Lily offers doesn't quite reach her eyes. The sweetest green eyes are filled with pain as she nods just as softly. "Former figure skater. I haven't been skating in years."

"Like me," Eira cheers, grabbing onto Lily's hand. "I never skated professionally, my father wouldn't let me. But Colin and Aiden used to take me skating a lot."

"My brother used to sneak me into the rink when I wasn't allowed to be there because of hockey practice," Lily says, smiling at the memory.

Eira grins brightly. One of her many talents is brining smiles to people's faces. Genuine and shining smiles. Somehow Eira has always managed to grow flowers even when it's storming.

"So come on, Lily, let's skate." Eira pulls on her hand, but Lily isn't budging. Cocking an eyebrow, she let's go off of Lily's hand, taking a step back. "Maybe Colin can change your mind more easily than I can."

I place the penguin onto the ice for Eira, helping her step onto it. When I'm sure she's all good, I smile at her warmly and watch as she—slowly and carefully—begins to skate away.

I'd lie if I said I'm completely chill about it. I'm truly afraid something will happen to Eira in the next couple of *minutes*.

"I can't do this, Colin," I hear Lily whisper.

I turn to look at her, taking her face in my hands, looking deeply into her summer green eyes.

Chapter 32

***"he's gonna save my life like superman"*—Hide Away by Daya**

Lily

"Step on the ice, Lilybug," Colin says, never breaking his gaze from my eyes. His voice is strict. No, he is strict, demanding.

I don't think he will stop *demanding* me to start skating until I finally do.

As much as I want to, I just can't. So I tell him. Again. "I can't," I whisper through gritted teeth.

He is aware that skating has played a huge role in my life, he doesn't know how big, but I guess he has an idea. However, I put skating to ice when my motivation froze. There is no way I can get back out there without drawing a panic attack out of me for it.

It's not that skating scares me. It's merely the fact that I am afraid I won't like it anymore or that I might like it too much.

I'm afraid skating will come back into my life like I've never put it in the freezer to rot there until I die.

"I can't force you," he says softly. "Do it for yourself, Lilybug. For the little girl that used to love standing on the ice, feeling like she's floating, jumping from cloud to cloud. I know that's what skating used to feel like for you. Freeing. Like you're floating through the sky, above the clouds, reaching for the stars. Do it for the little girl that had big dreams, dreams she shared with her favorite person in the universe. *The* dream that had you on the ice between hockey halves to show the audience—with a huge smile—that skating doesn't require a puck and sticks, goals and massive guys that try their hardest not to send their opponent into a long-lasting sleep. Think about the little girl that couldn't wait to get back on the ice the second she stepped off of it. The same little girl that would hate herself right about now if she knew her older self put her dreams to rest, burying it under tons of layers of regret, blood and tears. Make her happy, just this one last time."

I hate him. I do. Why does he have to say smart things when I need him to be stupid?

I'm sure Colin knows this would somehow get to me.

I bet Aaron told him all about the dreams I used to have. There is no way he knew that much from the little information I provided for him. Then again, Colin is smarter than he shows to be, and he certainly knows the feeling of skating over ice.

Damn him. And he doesn't even stay for me to yell at him. No, Colin is running away, skating over the ice right to his sister.

The same girl that would hate herself right about now if she knew her older self put her dreams to rest.

He is not wrong.

I hate that he's not wrong. If I were ten and learned I would stop skating at the age of nineteen, never starting again either…I would have thrown a tantrum. Never would I have believed it for a second.

Skating was my life. It was what breathed air into my lungs. What would let me forget pain, let me forget that my family wasn't one anymore. It would make me happy, make me smile, laugh.

Apart from bringing out the competitive side in me, skating has taught me how to release frustration. Maybe my coach caused most of the frustration by pushing me, but that doesn't matter right now.

I'm standing right in front of the ice. It takes one tiny step, and I would be on it. I would feel my feet slip, the blades of my skates gliding over the ice in a smooth motion like I know they would.

Is it possible to forget how to do what you once loved to do?

What if I forgot how to skate?

That's unlikely, right? My muscles must remember how to do it. They have to. It's all I have left.

Eira is laughing, causing my head to jerk up, my eyes following Colin and Eira as he pulls her after him, skating over the ice so effortlessly.

She screams something in Spanish while laughing. And when a cough follows, Colin immediately halts and turns to her, putting his hands on her shoulders, analyzing her face.

I still don't understand what all this is about, but I no longer think this is just a flu. It has to be something more, otherwise neither Colin nor their mother would react the way they do. Parents and siblings don't usually get so worried about skating, unless there is a serious reason behind all of it.

As much as I want to know the real reason, I won't push Colin to tell me. If he wants me to know, he will enlighten me.

Then Colin's word come back into my head. *Make her happy, just this one last time.*

Something is seriously wrong with Eira, and I'm here whining about my passion possibly no longer being my passion.

Even if it's not, what do I have to lose? Nothing. And it sure would make child-me a whole lot happier, knowing I died and still did what I loved at least one last time before my death.

Taking a deep breath and clenching my hands into firsts, I carefully set one foot onto the slippery ice. My breath is shaky, my heart pounding like I've been running a whole marathon. I can feel the *thump-thump* through my entire body, being awfully aware of every inch of myself.

I know better than to step on the ice without doing a little push before coming to a stop, but I can't help it right now. I need to do this slowly, ignoring that I might fall right away.

Inhaling one more deep breath and exhaling it once it's been inside of my lungs long enough, my brain turns off, muscle memories activate themselves. And before I even realize it, my left foot—the one that's not on the ice—is pushing me away from solid, non-slippery ground, causing both of my feet to glide over the ice.

I don't trip, don't fall. I just glide over the ice. I don't move though, just letting this one push, the one my body did without me realizing, come to a natural stop.

And when I do stop, my eyes open slowly, my breathing still shaky, still weak.

I can't feel Colin's eyes on me, but he must have noticed me stepping on here. I'm glad he knows better than to approach me and make a comment. He always knows better for some unknown reasons.

When the feeling of me being back on the ice finally settles within me, it's like the sunrise I've watched with Colin on day one—or more like day two.

Something inside of me rises, shines and glows, bringing warmth to my heart in the way only Colin ever managed to. It's this kind of warmth that screams comfort, passion, *love*. It's as though my body knows this is what I was supposed to do, where I'm supposed to be: on the ice.

The feeling of something missing I felt in my heart just a few moments ago is completely vanished. I know I've missed skating. Ever since I gave up on it, I knew I would miss it more than anything. And now that I'm standing back on it, I realize just how much I actually missed it.

I'm wondering how I ever thought that giving up what I love would help getting through dark times?

How could my body, my own mind betray me like this?

How could my own thoughts tell me I didn't want this anymore? That I didn't want to skate anymore, didn't want to pursue my dreams when clearly it's still a part of me?

How could my own mind betray me, when all I ever did was listen and act in its favor? Not once have I done something my head told me not to do.

We were in for a long run with skating, until my brain wasn't anymore.

My heart kept yelling for me to go back, put those skates on and do what I love, but my brain tuned those cries down, left me thinking I didn't want it.

When did I stop listening to what my heart wanted? When did I allow awful thoughts, an *illness*, to come between me and my passion?

I know this is temporary thinking. I know by the time tomorrow arrives, hell, maybe even in an hour, my depression will get to me again. It will rip me to piece, *again*. Throw me under the bus like it always has.

But until then…I will—*have to*—make this time count.

With a smile on my face, I allow myself to skate, skate as though I've never once stopped. As though I haven't laid my dreams to ice and let it rot together with my will to live.

It gets even more magical when I remember that I used to be a figure skater, being able to ace jumps and spins. I'm not quite sure I could still pull them off, especially without any warm-ups, but I can try.

Of course I wouldn't be me if I'd choose the easiest jump I knew, or just normal jumping up and seeing if I could even still catch myself doing that. No, instead I decide to go for the Lutz. Skating backwards has always been my favorite— it's more exciting, at least to me.

Like the Lutz isn't one of the hardest jumps for a lot of skaters, and yet I choose to go with it for my first jump after years.

Best believe I will break some bones.

Taking off from the back outside edge, I do as I'm supposed to; performing a long glide in a long arc right into the corner of the rink, doing everything to get ready to shoot up into the air. I've never been one to take the easy way out—apart from my plan to end my life in a couple of days—so counterrotation it is. I mean, otherwise it would be more of a Flutz and not a Lutz, anyway.

The jump actually works out better than I expected. I thought I'd end up with broken bones, but I land pretty safely, a bit wobbly maybe, and definitely not as professional-looking as it used to, but hell does that feel good.

The sad thing to realize in life, you only ever start missing something when you no longer have it. Eventually that can turn into your new "normal." A life without that one thing, but it's never going to be the same again. You start to forget what it was like, what it felt like with your passion still being in your life. You learn to live without it, and it becomes natural. And then you get it back—if you're lucky enough, that is—and only then do you realize how much you've missed it.

I never want to let skating go ever again. Dammit.

That's what I was afraid of. Loving skating again. Having skating to hold on to. Having skating become a lifesavor, again.

Well, at least until my depression makes a reappearance.

It will return. Depression doesn't just leave because you actually do what you used to love for once.

If it was that easy…there's no use talking about it, it's not nor will ever be this easy.

Overcoming depression will never be easy, if overcoming is even a thing. Lord knows, it might stay forever.

Turning around, I find Colin and Eira watching me. Eira has a huge grin on her face. So does Colin.

I'm sure they're for two whole different reasons.

Eira's smile looks more like an amazed smile. Kind of as if she is fascinated by my jump. Colin on the contrary, he looks proud. He has this *I'm-oh-so-proud-of-you* dad-smile plastered on his face.

I'm proud of myself. Colin might have given me the push, but I did it. I stepped on the ice because I wanted to.

Hell does that feel good.

"*¡Dios mío!*" Eira shrieks as I skate over, approaching her and her brother. "I've never seen someone pull that off in person!"

"I didn't think I could still do it…" I reply in all honesty.

As much as I will hate myself for doing this afterward, I fall into Colin's arms, being in desperate need for a hug. Not because I sort of pulled off this jump, but because I am skating.

My eyes want to tear up, but I suppress the urge to cry.

His arms wrap around me immediately. "I'm so proud of you, *mi sol*." I can feel him plant an ever so soft kiss on top of my head. So soft and gentle, it tightens my chest.

"What did you call her?" Eira asks Colin.

I turn my head so I can look at her, seeing that her eyes are widened and something that I can't put a label on is sparkling in her eyes.

"*Mi sol*," answers Colin with a rather shy but happy smile, cheeks slightly flushed. Those reddened cheeks must come from the cold.

"I still have no idea what it means," I tell her. "Care to enlighten me?"

Eira shakes her head. As soon as Colin's words seem to settle in, her jaw drops and only a second later, the corners of her mouth tug into a wide and joyful smile. "Oh, Aiden would love that! He has to be so damn pleased with himself right now. And he'd be proud of you, obviously."

"I suppose."

"Colin, if Aiden were here and he would have heard you say that, he would be flashing a smile as bright as the Eiffel Tower when it's doing this sparkly shining thing."

Chapter 33

"I'll take your bad days with your good, walk through the storm, I would. I do it all because I love you"— Unconditionally by Katy Perry

Colin

"Colin always called dibs on the front seat, forgetting that both of our parents would be in the car. He would get so mad and then refuse to get a milkshake from McDonalds by the end of the day."

Eira is laughing. I don't think she ever stopped laughing even once since we've walked into The Retro Diner.

Neither has Lily.

And as it turns out, Lily loves listening to my sister telling her all about my embarrassing stories.

"When we'd be back home, he would throw a tantrum, crying and throwing pillows, breaking anything only because he didn't get a milkshake. You know, the very one *he* refused to get because he was mad for not sitting in the front seat."

Lily continues to laugh with such delight, I somehow wish Eira wasn't here. I want to keep Lily's laughter for myself, and I want to be the reason she's laughing. At least I get to hear it.

"You okay, *enana*?" I ask when Eira starts to cough from drinking her milkshake way too fast. I'm pretty sure she's not even supposed to drink it. But hell, how could anyone say no to her?

Eira nods. "I'm a bit tired."

"I'm sure you are. We'll take you home after this, or do you want to leave now?"

"No thank you. I'd rather spend more time with you and your *fake* girlfriend."

Lily gasps but doesn't speak. I feel her eyes on me, most definitely waiting for me to say something.

Before speaking, I take Lily's hand in mine, laying them both down on one of my thighs. "She's not my fake girlfriend. Lily and I are a real couple. She doesn't know it yet, doesn't want to accept it yet, but we are." My eyes find Lily's. Her cheeks are slightly darker, having a bit of a blush going on there. "Wouldn't you agree, *mi sol*?"

Lily rolls her eyes, but she can't hide that slim smile of hers. I know she wouldn't admit to it, but if she wasn't so keen on dying in three days, we would totally have put a label on *us* by now.

Eira winks, her whole face shining brighter than the sun. "You're certainly sure about it." She only says that because of the nickname. "So when you lied to me, you weren't lying?"

"Lily has been mine from the second we met. There were no lies in me telling you she's my girlfriend."

Eira shrieks excitedly. "Yeah, '*mi sol*' doesn't sound like something *not* serious."

I swear, Eira is planning my death as well. Lily has been doing so right from the start, and now Eira is giving her even more fuel.

"Can someone please tell me what that means?" Lily's forehead creases and a groan slips from her throat.

"My sun," Eira translates for me. To my luck, she doesn't tell her the *meaning*.

The meaning being connected to Aiden. To twenty years old Aiden, only one month before he died.

"If you ever find someone that makes you want to rip your heart out and hand it to that person on a silver platter. If you ever find someone that warms not only your bed but also your heart and soul…hold onto them forever. They're your sun. They're what's bringing light into your life. If they can ease your pain with just being there, lighten your mood, brighten up your days by simply being in your life. Colin, Eira, el o ella es tu sol."—he or she is your sun.

"*La amas, ¿verdad?*" Eira asks, clearly aiming her question at me since Lily doesn't speak one bit Spanish.

I exhale deeply, feeling terribly sorry for Lily because she probably feels completely left out since she doesn't understand a thing. I'm glad she doesn't though. If she did, this would get embarrassing for me.

"Mhm," I hum as a quick response. Eira's smile widens. "Now, could we quit the Spanish? I don't want Lily thinking we're talking about her." But we are…in some ways.

"You know, I can repeat it in English if you'd like?" Eira cocks a brow at me, grinning. Mischievous, that's what she is.

"Drink your milkshake or I'll do it."

Eira grabs her glass in a matter of seconds, shaking her head at me. "You refused to get one. Get yourself a brand new one and don't come for mine."

I could let her have it that way, order myself a milkshake—which I most definitely wouldn't finish because I just don't like them that much anymore—or I could steal my sister's.

Instead of stealing my sister's milkshake, I go with Lily's. Personally, I always preferred strawberry milkshake to chocolate milkshake anyway. It is only convenient for me to steal hers instead.

Unlike my sister, Lily doesn't complain, much to my displeasure. I kind of like it when she acts all feisty, probably because anything is better than seeing her sad. Not that she's sad right in this moment. Lily looks happy…but I know she is pretty good at faking it.

Eira yawns, which tells me that it is about time that we leave. She certainly needs the rest.

But Eira wouldn't be Eira if she didn't try to find anything to speak against her tiredness.

"I swear, Colin, it's not even that bad. Just thirty more minutes, then you can take me home."

I hate to say no to her, especially these days, but I'm also aware that she needs to get the rest her body clearly requests. "Fifteen," I offer.

"Bien. Quince minutos."

Eira doesn't fight for another fifteen minutes once the time is over. I don't think I could have said no.

So once those fifteen minutes pass, I go to pay for the drinks and fries my sister so desperately wanted, and we leave.

"Okay, you took me skating today, what are we doing tomorrow?" Lily asks just when I walk into my bedroom. She's lying on my bed, reading a book. She doesn't even look up when she speaks.

"Are you cold?" I voice instead of answering her question. Truth is, I have absolutely nothing planned for tomorrow. Tomorrow is day nine, the last day I get with her before I'll find out if she wants to live or if she's going to stick to her plan. Well, I doubt I'll find out tomorrow, probably Friday morning only, which would be in two days.

"No, why?"

"You're wearing a skirt and a baggy sweatshirt."

Her eyes meet mine as she lowers her book. "It's called fashion, look it up."

"You know what I'd rather do?" I walk over to the bed. Without waiting for an answer, I crawl onto the bed, making my way up until I reach Lily's legs.

In order to watch me, Lily spreads her legs, offering me a view I normally would enjoy if I didn't have other plans.

"What are you doing?" I can hear her ask when I spread her legs a little farther apart and lie down. A gasp that turns into a soft chuckle draws out of her throat when I lift her sweatshirt enough for my head to fit underneath. "Colin?"

Once my head is under her shirt, my head lies on her stomach, pressing my ear to it. "What does it look like I'm doing?" I wrap my arms around her hips, which must be a bit uncomfortable for her to lie on, but that's not my problem.

"You're so weird." She laughs, her hands tracing over my head that's covered with her sweatshirt. Then she shrieks, laughing just a tiny bit more. "Did you just lick my stomach?"

"Yeah. I had to make sure you still taste like mine."

I remove my arms from underneath her, realizing it's even uncomfortable for me. So instead I rest them right under her breasts, just above my head.

"Taste like yours?" She lays her book aside, at least that's what it sounds like she's doing. "How does that even make sense?"

I don't provide her with an answer, instead I hope to distract her with planting some kisses along her stomach and ribs.

"Colin," she speaks breathy. Her back arching the lower I kiss. The second I reach the hem of her skirt, I stop and lift her shirt up, crawling out from underneath it.

She giggles. "You're crazy."

"Crazy about you, *mi sol*."

She freezes as I crawl up her body until our eyes meet. I can feel her hot breath rolling over my skin. Our lips almost so close together, I can taste her on my tongue.

"Colin," she sighs. "You're not supposed to say things like that, let alone feel that way about me."

Chapter 34

"I fell for you all the way to rock bottom"—24 Hours by Alexander Stewart

Colin

"WE'RE GOING TO BE LATE FOR OUR CLASSES."

Today's classes aren't on my mind at all.

Lily is sitting on the kitchen counter right next to the stove, while I—for once—make breakfast. It's not as fancy as Lily's fruity pancakes, but I'd say it's edible. Don't think there's much to mess up by pouring cereal into a bowl.

"Seriously, Colin. You know what happened the last time I was late. I refuse to have another panic attack."

I sigh, setting the cereal box down onto the counter. I walk over to Lily, standing between her legs, laying my hands down onto her waist.

"We're not attending today." We're truly not. I figured since it's the last day I have with her, we'll stay here—well, not here at home. I have plans. The plan being *Build-A-Bear*.

Besides, it's not like Lily really needs those classes anymore. I truly doubt she will change her mind at this point, so it doesn't matter whether or not she's attending.

"I have to. What about my grades?"

I narrow my eyes at her, trying to make sense of her caring about her grades when they won't really matter.

Lily places her hands onto my shoulders, one of them sliding down over my chest. "Maybe it's good we're staying home. We can do…other stuff."

Smirking, I take her hand from my chest, kissing her knuckles before pressing her hand right against my crotch. "All in for 'other stuff.'"

I'm expecting Lily to make fun of me because she's definitely not good for a man's ego, but she surprises me when instead she traces her fingers along the outlines of my cock, palming me through my boxers.

"Are you cold, Colin?" she asks, smirking. "You're not wearing any pants, but you are wearing a shirt."

"It's fashion, look it up," I repeat her own answer from yesterday to her.

"You're hiding something, Carter." Lily reaches for the hem of my shirt, lifting it up. I stop her the second she's about to pass my abs. "So I'm right. What are you hiding?"

I choose to remain silent, but I should know better. Lily will find a way to get the truth out of me.

"I love your dress, where did you get it?" I ask, sliding my hands up her thighs, hooking my fingers into the elastic of her panties. With a bit of a strengthened pull, I manage to remove her panties, sliding them down her silky soft legs.

I keep her panties tugged in my fist, using my other hand to trace along the inside of her thigh.

She gasps softly, but she knows this is me trying to distract her. As an attempt to distract me just as much, her hand slips into my boxers, wrapping around the length of my dick. Her thumb glides over the tip of my cock, eliciting a groan out of my throat.

"Tell me, Carter, what are you hiding?" she says while her lips almost brush mine. "Or do you want me to suck an answer out of you." Her mouth is so close to mine, if I moved even just the tiniest bit I would feel her soft lips, getting a taste of the fuel to my addiction.

She strokes me in my boxers, making it harder to breathe. "What's wrong, *baby*? Not so mouthy anymore, are we?"

I want her mouth on mine, shut her up and fuck her until she forgets her own name. Right. Fucking. Now.

But I won't be the first one to cave.

"You want to kiss me, don't you?" A tease, that's what she is. She moves in closer, but her lips never touch mine. Lily kisses the corner of my mouth, then plants a couple more kisses along my jawline and down my neck.

Her hand pulls away from my cock. With a soft *thud* on the floor, Lily slides off the counter, kneeling down in front of me. She looks up at me, her gaze filled with lust and something dangerous for me—mischief.

"Where's Aaron?" she asks, hooking her fingers into the elastic of my underwear.

"Early practice," I breathe out.

Grinning, she pulls down my boxers until my erection springs free, her soft hand instantly wrapping itself back around my cock.

I inhale sharply when her tongue darts and crosses her lips, licking along my dick.

Hissing, my free hand finds into her soft blonde hair, gripping it firmly, yet not to the point where it would hurt her.

Lily's still looking up at me, and if I didn't know any better, I'd say she's asking me what to do next.

Then she plants a kiss to my tip before opening her mouth and wrapping her lips around the tip of my cock, sucking.

My head tilts back into my neck, breathing growing heavier the deeper Lily takes me.

"Fuck, Lily," I rasp, savoring the warmth of her mouth wrapped around my dick.

She moves so teasingly slow, it's torture. The part of my cock that doesn't fit into her mouth, Lily pumps with her hand, using slow and gentle strokes.

After a couple of torturously slow strokes, Lily moves quicker, her grip around my cock tightening just enough for her touch alone to send me off to see stars.

Pretty sure my groans and grunts grow a bit louder when Lily forces as much of my dick into her mouth as only possible, to the point where she would *almost* gag.

When I think she couldn't surprise me anymore, she does.

Knowing that she's not even wearing panties at the moment doesn't exactly help against my urge to come.

The last time I felt like coming after a couple of moments when receiving a blowjob, was back in high school. Lily has managed to have me completely lose my mind. For her.

"Lily, you have to stop," I grit out, pushing her away from my cock and pulling her up onto her feet.

My mouth immediately slams against hers, I'm no longer able to stay away from her lips. With no hesitation, I push my tongue into her mouth, waiting for that all too familiar tiny whispery moan to elicit from her.

And when it comes, that soft sound shoots right into my balls.

"I need you, Colin," she speaks against my lips, her voice hoarse. "I need you inside of me, right now," Lily corrects when I reach my hand down to her pussy, gliding a finger through her folds.

"So impatient, Lilybug." Giving Lily as she wishes, I lift her up and carry her to the kitchen island, sitting her down. She spreads her legs, letting me stand in between.

I grab my erection, stroking the tip of my cock through her folds, spreading her wetness around, covering my tip with it.

With her lips on mine, my hands on her ass, I gently ease inside of her, pushing in piece by piece, watching her face for signs that it hurts. When they don't come, I feel somewhat relived.

If there's one thing I refuse to do, it would be hurting Lily. In any possible way.

Once I'm completely inside of her, Lily holds my shirt in her hands, lifting it up. And although that's the last thing I want right now, I'm not fighting it. I help her take off my shirt, but to my luck, Lily doesn't pay much attention to my body when I start to thrust in and out of her.

She moans my name, leaning back on the island, holding herself up by her arms. "More," she demands, and so she gets what she wants.

Digging the tips of my fingers into the skin over her hips as I hold onto her tightly, I move faster, pushing into her deeper, rougher.

"Fuck, yeah," she cries out, lying down on the counter, her arms no longer holding her up.

"You like that?"

She moans out loud in response, bringing a grin to my lips.

One of her hands traces down her body, her fingers finding her clit, rubbing it. Her other hand rests on her covered breast, giving it a squeeze. She's doing all the things I want to do, to herself.

But God, it's hot watching her. Watching as her fingers get covered in her own wetness when she circles her clit just the way it is the most pleasurable for her.

Yet as much as I enjoy watching her, I take over, using my thumb and rubbing the pad of it over the swollen nub.

I can feel her walls tighten, clenching around my dick. "Let go, sweetheart," I order, looking into her eyes.

She's staring back at me, her mouth forming the perfect "O" as more moans roll over her lips.

"I want you to come with me."

She's panting heavily, so am I. Drops of sweat rolling down our bodies, making it appear as if neither of us took a shower just an hour ago. But hell, I'd take a shower every hour if that meant Lily would blow my mind like this in between.

I only manage to nod, pushing into Lily just that tiny bit deeper. And when she comes with my name leaving her mouth, I come inside her, marking her even more as mine than she already is.

Lily takes a lot longer to shower than I did, so by the time she's coming downstairs, freshly showered, I've already finished my breakfast.

After my shower I threw on some underwear and sweatpants, which means I'm still shirtless. But it's not like Lily didn't see my new tattoo before.

I know she has, just refused to ask me about it…until now.

"Why did you get a lily tattooed on your chest, right over your heart?" she asks, taking a seat on the barstool next to me.

"I like the meaning, Lilybug."

She chuckles, yet raises her brows at me. "What meaning? Purity?"

"Not purity."

Her arms cross in front of her chest. "What kind of other meaning is there?"

"Devotion."

I can hear the sharp intake of breath from Lily, but instead of losing her shit like I'm expecting her to, she says, "It doesn't even fit in with your other tattoos."

I shrug. She's right. All of my tattoos lack of color, simply because black ink seems to fit me better.

Except for my new one.

It has a couple of green strokes along the peddles. The same color of green that I see when I look into Lily's eyes.

All of my tattoos have important meanings though. Important to me, at least. Lily's isn't too unique on that part. And yet somehow it's still the one that means the most to me.

"It fits to the mark I have on my heart."

A bit startled, Lily hops off the barstool and stands in front of me, tracing her index finger along the outlines of the lily on my chest.

"We both know that you got this tattoo because of me."

"Not even trying to deny that."

"Devotion, huh?" She pauses, inhaling deeply before she continues, "You'll regret it, Colin. I mean, you've already committed to it, so there's not much you can do about it anymore. But why did you get it in the first place?"

I blow out some air in a rough sigh.

"I want the truth."

"Cause, *mi sol*, even if you're going to die, I'll always remember you. You'll always be a part of my life, of my heart. Even if *this* ends in pieces of glass, shattered. You've made my life better in a couple of days. You've shone through the layers of fog that clouded me. You *do* have my ultimate loyalty, even after you've died. I couldn't move on from you. I don't even want to. You're all that I am, Lily. I feel like I'm suffocating when you're not around. And when I do breathe, you're in every breath I take. You're everywhere I look, everywhere I go. You're everywhere. And that's how I want it to be."

I add, "I didn't want to get this tattoo after you've already passed. I wanted—needed—you to know that you've got me. You'll always have me."

A tear rolls down her face, one I want to wipe away, but Lily isn't letting me.

"This is crazy," she says, crying. "*You* are crazy."

"Perhaps it is. Perhaps I am. But that doesn't mean you mean any less to me."

"This wasn't supposed to happen!" She takes a couple of steps back. "You weren't supposed to…do this, *feel* this! You were supposed to show me beautiful places, get a couple of good, glowing memories into my head before it's all black for all of eternity."

"Life doesn't always play out the way you want it to. Guess you should know that."

Lily rolls her eyes at me, turning away. She starts to walk toward the stairs, probably to get her stuff and run away. Then she turns around again and starts to speak, "I can't do this, Colin. I can't do *this*—*us* anymore." She takes a deep, shaky breath. "You're hurting the both of us. Unnecessarily."

"It wouldn't hurt you if you didn't feel the same way about me."

My phone chimes just as Lily storms off, muttering something about life and the world being cruel.

I check my phone, just in case it's about Eira before I go to run after Lily.

As I read the message on my screen, my whole world stops for an entire second. I push whatever I feel in my heart aside. Taking a deep breath, I shove my phone into my pocket and run after the woman that owns my heart.

She's in my room, sitting on my bed as she holds her legs tightly to her chest.

"Lily," I say calmly. My eyes wander to my window, watching for a moment as it's pouring. My room is dark from the lack of sun, but it fits everything going on inside of me right now.

"Stop," she cries. "I can't deal with any more cruelty."

I'm two seconds away from losing my shit. And when Lily mutters something under her breath, I can't hold it back any longer.

"Yes, Lily, the world is fucking cruel. It's breaking you down, taking away every good thing you have. It's painful. It's dark. It's making you lose your goddamn mind."

I shake my head and press my lips together. "But it's also bright and filled with joy. It has good things to offer, if you fucking let them in." I let out a disbelieving chuckle. "You're living on a floating rock filled with water and you're expecting life to make sense. Well, breaking news: It doesn't make any kind of fucking sense to anyone. Your whole existence doesn't make sense. For all we know, we could be a part of someone's imagination and wouldn't even know of it because *this*, our current life, is all we're familiar with. Yet you're here. You're here for a reason, regardless of it maybe not making sense at all. Your reason to be here certainly isn't to die earlier than you're destined to. You have so much more to experience, so much more to see. And you're wanting to throw it away.

"I showed you the world. I threw the fucking world to your feet and you're still complaining about it not being a happy place. It's not a fucking happy place, but you *can* get life to suck a little less if you'd only tried to."

She's crying more than before, and it breaks my heart. Perhaps all I'm saying is all the wrong things, but at this point, it's all I have left to offer.

"I can't get through life on my own, Colin. I can't. I'm not that strong. I'm falling apart at every single *tiny* thing that fights back. I can't keep living, feeling like a broken piece that's never going to be whole again."

"For fuck's sake, Lily!" I say louder than intended, being seconds away from hitting something—*not Lily*—with my fists. "You are not alone!"

"I am."

"Say that again, I dare you."

"I am alo—"

Nine Days

"YOU HAVE ME!" I yell from the top of my lungs. "You have me. You'll always have me, Liliana Heaven Reyes. You've had me since the day I found you crying in the arena. I've done nothing but to love you all these days. I took you on silly dates. The happiness you've experienced all this time, it wasn't because the places were oh-so-magical. You felt alive. You felt *loved*."

"So what? You just played with my heart?" Her eyes are red from crying, her nose too. She sniffles, wiping away tears that I swore I'd never be the reason for.

I run my fingers through my hair in frustration, inhaling a deep breath while looking at the ceiling. For someone who's naturally smart, she comes off as pretty stupid right now. "To hell with that, Lily." My eyes meet hers.

I hate that she's crying. And I hate it even more that I will have to leave in a few seconds. My phone keeps vibrating in my pocket, so whoever tries to reach me…it won't be good news.

"I fell in love with you, Lily. I spent eight, or seven, however many days I've actually had with you, trying to make you fall in love with me too."

She opens her mouth to speak but I cut her off before she gets to do so.

"I know I'm fucking selfish. But yeah, there you have it. I love you. Now, go on, break my heart, Lily. I don't care what you do with it, you have it all. Throw it on the streets and let a car run it over, step on it, I really don't care, as long you're the one breaking me."

This time she's not even trying to say something anymore, probably because she's sobbing too much to do so—or because she just refuses to say anything.

"Look, I have a second car parked down the road. It's a black BMW, you can use it to get away if you want to. The keys are downstairs. I have to cancel today, not sure if you'd even want to go out anymore anyway. This is going to be so shitty of me, but I have to go."

Chapter 35

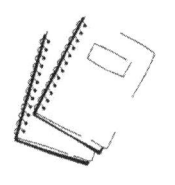

"and you don't know how you feel but you're getting real close"—I Need You to Hate Me by JC Stewart

Lily

IT'S BEEN HOURS SINCE COLIN LEFT ME HERE ALL BY myself.

He hasn't sent me even just one text, didn't even care to call me, not that he has to. Yet a quick notice that he's okay, that he reached his destination in one piece would have been nice.

But I can't blame him.

He loves me. That's what he said, straight into my face.

And what did I do? I cried.

No one's ever openly admitted to loving me. Never have I thought my first reaction to that kind of confession would be to cry.

And yet here I am. Hours later and still crying.

Although technically I still had enough time to get ready and attend at least my last few classes for the day, I decided against it. I didn't feel like listening to my professors talking about the film industry—I still don't.

Aaron hasn't come home yet either. It's past four and I know his classes—*at least today's classes*—end shortly after two. So now I'm wondering if they have hockey practice, even though they have had one this morning.

Also, why haven't I gone back to the dorms yet? Colin did say I'm free to go. So why do I stick around?

The texts I've allowed myself to send him have stayed unanswered, so I'm not even sure he truly wants me around still.

I go downstairs, Sergeant Froggo tugged in my arms, to get something to eat. My stomach has been growling for something to get inside of it for the past two and a half hours, I just never had the strength to get up.

Just when I reach the last step, the front door opens and Aaron marches inside. He's alone, no signs of Colin whatsoever.

"Are you okay?" he asks first thing he spots me. His brows draw together, his head tilting slightly to the side as his eyes follow my figure from head to toe and back up. "You look like you haven't slept in days."

Maybe I do. I certainly feel like I haven't.

After Colin left, I'm pretty sure I did nothing but roll over in his bed, crying, screaming, messing up my hair.

My eyes must still be puffy from all the crying, not that I ever truly stopped.

"Doing just great," I lie. It's a really bad lie. I don't even sound convincing, nor do I look like I am close to being alright.

"Lily, what the hell happened?" Aaron doesn't give me a chance to avoid him. He grabs my wrist, pulling me into the living room where we both take a seat on the couch.

Nine Days

I really don't feel like talking, especially not to Aaron, not about Colin. But maybe Aaron knows more about where Colin is at than I do.

It's truly a surprise to me. I've never been the one to care if someone doesn't respond to my texts. But Colin ignoring each and every single one of them is so…not like him.

I am worried. Worried that something happened to him.

Maybe he's gotten in an accident, being too much in his head to concentrate on the road.

"Did you have hockey practice?"

Aaron shakes his head no. "Was out with someone, getting some lunch. Practice had been called off a couple of hours ago."

"But you had it this morning?"

"Nah," he laughs. "I was home most of the morning. Didn't leave until nine, when you were in the shower."

Oh, so Colin lied to me about Aaron being at hockey practice. What else did he lie to me about?

"Coach sent a message early this morning, maybe at six, told us we're off for the day—and the rest of the week—because of something going on at home. The guys think it's a divorce, I highly doubt it. I think it's Eira," he tells me. The huge question mark on his forehead doesn't go lost on me. "Didn't Colin tell you any of this?"

It's my time to shake my head.

"I wasn't sure he would, to be honest. He's definitely at home now. I mean, when it's about Eira, he sure wouldn't stay away."

"I have no idea where he is, Ron." I sigh. At least I now know he should be home with his parents and siblings. Still doesn't help the fact that I'm not quite sure if he's okay or not.

"Fell out with the boyfriend, huh?" He nudges my side with his elbow. "How bad is it? Do you need me to call your mother?"

I chuckle ironically, almost like a really soft snort. "Aaron, this woman, the one you rarely refer to as *your* mother, she hates me just as much as she hates you."

He freezes. Aaron looks so lost, like he has no idea what I'm talking about. And he doesn't, because I've never told him any of this.

And so I spend the next thirty minutes telling Aaron every single thing about our birth mother, everything about when she started to dislike me to the last encounter I've had with her. He doesn't seem too surprised about it though.

"Dad kept in touch with her, you know."

He did what?

"No, he didn't." I don't believe a word.

"He did. Every Sunday, mom knew you were with us. Remember that day at court, when we were asked who we wanted to stay with? I chose dad, hoping you would too. You didn't even choose one, you said both. Dad won custody over me, because I said I never wanted to stay with our mother, but they had shared custody over you."

Does that even make sense? The judge could have chosen for me to stay with my father as well, or not?

"I could have chosen both as well, but I didn't. I used to hear our mother talk on the phone, and whenever it was about you, she only ever said cruel things, complaining about your obsession with figure skating when you should be into princesses and whatever she considered girly. I was so mad at her at all times. I've never been surprised that she didn't want to reach out to me."

Why am I just learning about all this now?

"I don't remember a lot from when we were four or five, or younger, but I do remember our mother saying those things in connection with your name. Every single skating lesson you've taken were paid by our father. Competition fees, mom didn't pay as much as one dollar. Your college tuition, it's all paid by dad, not one dollar is coming from her. Even the private high school we went to, she didn't pay for. Dad tried to get you out of there for so long, but you always said you liked having both parents in your life. If you had, even just once, said you'd rather stay with dad, you would have been out of there."

And like I haven't just stopped crying twenty minutes ago, the tears are back.

At least my skin stays hydrated. More or less.

"Lily, you've always been that kind of person to make her life more complicated. I'm not sure why that is, but you have that talent. You come up with the most complex plans instead of just letting life take you where you belong. You came up with a plan to hide the fact that we're twins, because God forbid our mother finding out you're in touch with your own brother. When, by the way, by the time you turned eighteen, she couldn't have told you to quit the contact to me even if she wanted to. You also tend to think you have to go through life on your own and refuse to get help." *Did Colin mention something?*

"I know you're allowed to skate," he tells me. "I didn't question it when you told me you'd quit skating with a lie. I did question why you'd want to stop though. I was certain it was about your mental health. I don't know what it's like to live with depression. I have no way of knowing what it does to you. I also didn't want to force you to speak about it, so I just let it be and accepted your excuse."

He takes my hand, giving it a light, comforting squeeze. "I know it's getting worse, you're getting worse. No idea how bad, but I know you're not okay. Colin knows too, otherwise he wouldn't have insisted on you staying here."

"Wait, did Colin mention something?" I ask, feeling a wave of panic rush through my veins.

"He didn't have to, Lily. I'm disappointed he didn't say anything, but I'm almost ninety-nine per cent sure he didn't because you forced him not to."

When I meet his eyes, his are filled with pain, something I've never truly witnessed before. Whenever I thought he was hurt…this tops it.

"I've read your notebook," he admits. Maybe my death will come earlier than expected. "You know, when you so desperately wanted it back."

I nod, knowing exactly what he's talking about. Which few pages he is talking about.

"At first, I thought it's some kind of writing for a short movie you're working on in class, a screenwriting practice perhaps. It didn't look like one of those scripts though, yet I still didn't think much of it. Until I've come to read the '*Dear Ana*' pages. After we met up, and I was back home, I would start throwing pillows around the house in anger, frustration. I tried to come up with anything that would save you. For the next couple of days I would still try to figure out how to keep you alive. My only thought was to send you off to a mental hospital and get you the help you need. But I knew that's something you'd hate me for, even if it would possibly save your life," he tells me.

"It wasn't until I noticed Colin getting closer to you, and you guys hanging out daily, Colin skipping practice, that I would finally shove the thought aside. He took you out to try and save your life, didn't he?"

I nod, not being able to speak through my tears.

God, Aaron knew this whole time?

"How many days do you have left?"

"One and a half." My voice is a whisper, weak and broken. I don't even recognize my own voice.

"There's nothing I can do, is there?" he asks with pain in his eyes, even in his voice.

I shake my head slowly, seeing as tears build up in his eyes.

For once I don't feel an ounce of pain.

I should be crying. I should be begging him to help me. I should be feeling bad for him.

But I don't.

All I can feel is…nothing. I feel absolutely nothing at all.

Chapter 36

"and I didn't think it'd go this way; can I please have one more minute"—Heaven's Not Too Far by We Three

Colin

My parents are both seated on Eira's bed as I walk into the room.

My mother holds her hand, her eyes barely open. She's trying her hardest not to cry.

It's what Eira wanted.

"I don't want to die watching you all cry, ¿vale?" Had Eira said so many times, it's carved right into my brain.

I lied. I lied to Lily when I said my sister is cancer free. She never was. She never had a chance to survive this.

My family knew it though. We had years to prepare for Eira's death. Years to make more memories with her and say goodbye.

But no matter how much time you have to prepare, losing someone you love to death is never not going to hurt.

Eira gives me a weak smile as she spots me by her door. She blinks so slowly, she might as well keep her eyes closed for ever any second.

She tries to reach a hand up but is too weak to do so.

I walk over to her, take a seat next to her on the bed as my father frees some space.

Taking Eira's hand in mine, I can feel how close she is to death. She's cold, colder than her hands were yesterday after skating for hours.

"*Gigante*," she says, her voice so weak, so quiet…I barely recognize her.

"*Enana*."

She giggles, though it's less of a giggle and more of a really heavy breath.

"I printed out a picture for you," she says weakly. "Of me."

I chuckle. "Of course you did."

"You're going to take care of Lily for me, won't you?" she asks, attempting to squeeze my hand.

I shake my head. "I think you're more likely going to have to do that for me."

Eira attempts to shake her head. "She'll live."

With a soft smile on her lips, Eira looks at our parents, her breathing getting weaker with every second.

I can feel my fucking heart break. I am so not ready to say goodbye to my sister. I don't think I'll ever be.

I knew this was going to happen. I knew Eira was going to die. But it's only now getting…real.

"*Sin lágrimas.*"

My mother rolls her eyes. "*Vale, lo prometimos, nada de lágrimas.*"

No tears.

The room quiets down just as Eira whispers, "I love you." She takes her last breath, eyes closing…and they never open up again.

It's been two days since I'm home, my childhood home. Two days since I've left Lily in my own house, all by herself.

But two days later also means…it's October 8th. Lily's day of death.

I'm certain after what went down on Wednesday, Lily will go through with her original plan, that being her death.

I haven't answered any of her texts or picked up her calls. To be fair, I also didn't see them until right now, when I finally pick up my phone and see I'm left with only one per cent battery.

Truthfully, I had my bets on it being completely dead at this point. How the hell did it last two whole days?

"You're leaving?" My father stands by my bedroom just when I finish getting dressed. He leans against one side of the doorframe, crossing his arms over his chest.

"What else am I supposed to do here? Watch Mamá cry? Listen to another round of you trying to explain to Reece why Eira isn't coming back home anymore?"

My father shakes his head slowly, sighing as he does.

"We knew Eira was going to die, and we all knew it would be pretty soon. Eira wouldn't want me putting my life on hold over her death, not when she was way too excited to go on a new adventure. So staying here for the next week until her funeral is no option," I say.

"The team's been asking why practice is off since Wednesday. I know you didn't tell them about Aiden, but you will have to say something about Eira. As far as I'm concerned, they all adored her."

I chuckle. "Dad, they loved her. You remember Eira's quinceañera? They went nuts planning it for her." Then I pause, sighing softly. "I'll tell them, just not over the phone."

"I'll keep coaching the team for the rest of the school year. You don't have to be alone when you tell them. That is, if you want me to be there with you."

I nod, appreciating his offer.

"Did something happen between you and Lily? The whole hour before you arrived Eira has been hoping you would bring her."

I take a seat on my bed, looking down at the floor. "Dad, Lily is suicidal. She didn't even know Eira was about to die. I felt bad about telling her, was worried that it would somehow guilt trip her."

"I understand," he says as he walks into my room and takes a seat next to me. "You've spent a suspicious amount of time with this girl. I figured something must have been up. Well, either that or you fell in love."

Without having to look up for a confirmation, I know my father has a slight smile on his lips. I also don't have to say the word, he knows option two is also quite the reason.

"I have no idea what to do. Aaron doesn't know about her condition. I couldn't bring myself to tell him, which is so stupid, I know. I've done the same mistake with Aiden. And now I'm not even sure Lily will be alive when I get back home."

"Colin, Aiden's death wasn't your fault. You were nineteen. Kids that age often joke about death, even when you shouldn't. Of course you didn't take it seriously, especially knowing that Aiden was the type to say, 'might just die instead of doing this assignment' whenever he was doing homework."

I don't answer. Dad has been trying to tell me this for two whole years.

Plugging my phone into my charger, only long enough for me to be able to call someone in case of an emergency on my way home, I skim over a few messages Lily sent me yesterday and the day before.

Lily: Are you okay? You haven't been answering me all day. Please just give me one sign that you're alive. I'm really worried.

Lily: Okay, it's the next morning. Aaron said you'd be with your parents. He mentioned something about Eira. Colin, I am so sorry…

Lily: I tried calling your house telephone, your dad picked up. He said you made it home in one piece. At least now I know you're alright, physically. My deepest condolences to you and your family. If you need anything…I'm here for you.

"You didn't tell me Lily called yesterday?"

"Well, your sister died, so forgive me for that." I don't think he meant to come across that harsh. "You also didn't tell her you were here, or even just let her know you didn't get in an accident on the road."

He's right. I had plenty of free moments to send her a quick text. But then again, I didn't really think Lily would have cared, not after the way I left her.

"Do you want me to take Reece with me? Give Mamá and you some space?" I ask.

Given that my mother hasn't stopped crying Wednesday, I figured maybe taking Reece home with me will give her at least something less to worry about.

Dad stands up from my bed, taking a few steps toward my door before saying, "No, I think it's good that at least one of your mother's kids is still at home."

He might have a point.

"Colin—" he pauses and turns around "—give Aaron a call and tell him everything there is to know about Lily. You won't be home for another hour. One hour can change everything. Even if you risk losing your best friend, and possibly the woman you love for opening your mouth. Saving her life is more important than risking some hatred."

My father disappears just as quick as he appeared.

Once he is no longer in sight, I make my way down the hall as well, right to my little brother's room. The only sibling I have left.

His room door is open, it always is. I mean, he is only three.

Reece smiles at me brightly when he spots me watching him from his door. He always smiles. I know eventually his smiles will get less the older he gets, that's how life goes. But for now, his smiles are still present and never seem to run out.

"Eira went to the beach," he tells me, giggling. "Mamá is sad because *enana* left, *gigante*."

Stepping into his room, I sit down beside him on the floor, offering a half-smile. "Very sad."

"Daddy said she visits Aiden now."

I nod, pulling Reece in for a much-needed hug. He doesn't understand any of what happened yet, nor does he know what happened to Aiden or why he never truly got to know him.

He has also only ever seen Aiden on pictures and heard stories.

Again, Reece is three years old, of course he doesn't have a clue what is going on.

"But Eira comes back like you do."

Sighing, I press a kiss to his head, holding him against me just a tiny bit tighter. "Yeah, bud, she will come back eventually."

Is it cruel to tell a three-year-old his sister died and will never ever come back again? I think so.

He will understand it eventually, once he's a bit older. But for now, Reece doesn't understand the whole concept of death, so why take his still present happiness from him earlier than necessary?

"Can we go to the park?" he asks, pushing himself out of my grip.

"Tomorrow, alright? I have to go, but I will be back tomorrow and then we'll spend all day at the park, okay?"

He nods, quick and hysterical. "And Lilybug?"

If Reece wasn't my so much younger brother, I would probably get pissed at him for using the same nickname as me, but I actually find it adorable.

"I'll ask her to come."

Chapter 37

"I'll remind you of the world and it's wonder"—Wait for you by Tom Walker

Colin

BECAUSE I'M SO GOOD WITH TAKING ADVICE, I didn't call Aaron.

Calling him seemed unfitting. Sure, I could have asked where Lily was at, if she's still staying at our house or if she went back to her dorm. But I feared that bringing up more questions.

At least I sent him a text saying I'd be home in approximately an hour…but that was seventy minutes ago.

I'm standing in front of our house, too anxious to walk inside.

As of now, I have no idea whether or not Lily is still alive. The second I walk in there, I'll receive an answer to a question I'm not sure I'm ready to get.

If I walk in there and Aaron is devasted, Lily has died. If he's unbothered, she might still be alive, or she hasn't been found yet.

Great, either I will know she's dead for sure or I'll still be in the dark about it.

After a short moment of hesitation, I take a deep breath, unlock the door and walk inside.

I can barely keep the air inside my lungs when I notice the wrecked-up state our house is in.

The barstools are lying on the floor in various positions, none of them standing by the kitchen island. Our sofa isn't in its usual position either. It's turned upside down and looks like someone took a hell lot of anger out on it. The TV is broken. The screen is now covered with what looks like two to three punch holes. Counter decorations, papers, pieces of broken glass are splattered all over the floor. It genuinely looks like this house has been met with a tornado.

"Aaron?" I yell out as I don't see him in the living room.

Silence.

Maybe he didn't hear me, so I call out for him again. This time I hear his bedroom door open, shortly before footsteps sound through the room as he makes his way downstairs.

The second I can get a glimpse of him, my heart shatters.

He looks awful. His shirt is ripped from what looks like being pulled on too strongly. His hair is messy and standing in various directions. His eyes are red and puffy, just like his nose and cheeks, his face tear stained.

I can see his hands ball into fists as he sees me, but he loosens them up soon enough and starts to sob.

His legs begin to tremble, a shaking hand finding to his mouth as he falls down to his knees. His shoulders hake as he lets out painful cries.

"She's gone, Colin." His voice is nothing but a whisper.

My heart breaks for the second time in a couple of days, and as shitty as it sounds, this time it hurts even more as to when I watched Eira take her last breath and close her eyes for all of eternity.

"I couldn't keep her," he cries.

I would make my way over to him, but I can't. I'm frozen on the spot. I can't seem to find the strength to move just one bit.

"I had this whole plan and she looked right through it," he hiccups. "She left a note for you…it's in your room."

Once the words leave his mouth, I sprint upstairs, leaving Aaron by himself. I'm such a shitty best friend, but I also don't really care at this moment.

My room is just as wretched as the rest of the house. Everything looks upside down. Aaron has been in here, throwing stuff around, breaking my own personal belongings. And the worst bit, I can't even blame him for it.

I find a piece of paper lying on my desk, the only part of my room that doesn't look like I've thrown ten parties in one day.

I pick it up, finding Lily's handwriting.

I am so sorry we didn't see each other again.
I'll be where it all started.
Make of it what you will.

Lily

Great. Not only did I lose Lily as well, but she also made a fucking riddle for me to find her dead body…because seeing her dead body is exactly what I need.

I know I've promised I'd take care of the letters, but never did I truly believe it would come this far. And never did I allow myself to think I would be the one to make the call to get her body transported out of the room she had died in.

I don't know what I imagined it would be like, but it wasn't that. Not at all.

I'll be where it all started.

What the hell does that even mean?

There are at least ten different places.

The hospital she was born in (I doubt it's that one); her childhood home, the place where she had to say goodbye to Aaron and her father to; the ice rink...

The. Ice. Rink.

The hockey arena is the only place near that would truly connect to anything to her life.

The ice. The place where her passion begun. The place where she will end her life to reconnect with it.

I run downstairs. Maybe she isn't dead yet. Maybe if I hurry up and by the time I get there, she is still breathing. I only have to call an ambulance, get her help, pray to God she will survive.

"What time did Lily leave?" Words rush out of me, faster than ever before. Aaron is still on his knees, crying.

He barely acknowledges me, but I can't blame him for that either.

"I couldn't make out that riddle, Colin," he speaks through sobs.

"I have my bets on the hockey arena. When did she leave?"

His eyes meet mine, breaking my heart all over again. I never thought seeing my best friend heartbroken would hurt me the way it does. I never thought it could punch me in the guts and force me to swallow my own vomit that's wanting to come out.

"During the night," he says quietly. "We talked and she promised we would get her help first thing this morning. I made her stay in my room with me…but when I woke up, she was gone."

"What the *fuck*, dude!" I have no right to yell, I'm fully aware of it. Yet I can't suppress my urge to do so anyway. "Why didn't you get her help right when you found out!"

I'm praying he doesn't know I knew about her condition. But of course he does. "Because you have room to talk." He scoffs, chuckling ironically. "Why didn't *you*?"

"I had no right to," I answer truthfully. It doesn't even matter if I had the right to or not, I still should have done it. "She was no one to me. I couldn't have cared less if she died or not. I didn't even know she was related to you."

"Well, you got to know her, and you still didn't get her the help she needed."

Fighting about this now won't bring her back either, so instead of saying anything, I walk out the door, sprinting to my car and probably driving like a maniac toward the arena.

I don't look back.

The parking lot is empty, completely empty. Except for one car. My BMW. *She's here*.

This is a big arena, she could be anywhere. By the time I find her, she's probably already dead…if she isn't already.

She's not on the ice itself, that much I can tell by just walking inside and having a great view of the ice. It's empty.

This whole arena seems empty, and so much colder than usual.

I go to check the locker room next, when it's empty, I check the shower room—also empty. So is the other locker room.

Before I go to check the upper half of the arena, I have one more *seat* to check.

I didn't see blonde hair anywhere before, but that doesn't mean she's not lying on the floor somewhere.

Running to the other side of the arena, to the seat I first found Lily two weeks ago, I'm more or less surprised to find a mint green notebook lying on the seat.

The notebook of horror.

The very same that is going to make my heart ache a million times more.

She planted it here. That means I'm too late. Lily just placed the notebook down to keep me occupied so her death is even more guaranteed.

I mean, God forbid me finding her still breathing.

This girl had her death planned out for weeks, there was never a chance for me to save her.

I drop myself down on the seat beside the notebook, sliding my hands down my face while letting out a long, pain-filled groan.

Grabbing the notebook, I take a deep breath, slowly opening it.

This book is all I have left from her.

Wouldn't even be surprised if she didn't leave a letter for me.

Oh God, the letters. I promised her I would make sure they'll get to everyone.

That's not what I should worry about right now. I have to read it. Everything.

I have to understand why her mind didn't change…and maybe I'll come across a glimpse of hope she had at least once.

I don't skim over the pages. I read every single one with care.

My heart breaks just a little more with every new page, finding out how much pain this woman truly carried within her.

By the time I come to the more recent ones, I notice a lack of something.

Letters.

The last one I've come across was dedicated to her mother. That one is good twenty (or even more) pages back now. Judging from her previous pattern, she had a new letter every ten to twelve pages.

So where the hell is Aaron's letter?

Dear Colin Baby,

That's new.

they say time heals all wounds…
they were wrong.
As you already know, this is my unalive journey 101.
The book that will break a couple of people's hearts.
At least that's what I told myself.
I told myself that there are at least three people out there that truly love me.
You want to know who these people are?
Yeah, I'm sure you do. But I'm not in a rush right now, so I'll keep you waiting and take my sweet time before telling you.

By the way, no, this is not your letter. You deserve a better one than this. I still wanted to address this to you.
You left me today.
I'm not sure why, and you're not answering any of my texts or calls.
I'm worried about you.
I'm worried you got into an accident and you're lying somewhere on the side of the road, dying.
I'm worried you will never come back to me.
I'm worried I'll never see you again.
I was mad when you left me. At least for a short while.
I was so mad because you dropped this huge "I'm in love with you"-bomb and then you ran away before I had the chance to respond.
I couldn't even say goodbye or tell you to drive safely.
Aaron told me something happened back at home, which only increased my worry-level.
You didn't tell me what was going on, where you had to go to or why you had to leave in the first place.
It's not that you have to tell me anything, but right at this moment, right after you dropped that bomb on me…I felt like I deserved at least that much of an insight in your head.
Anyway, I can't be mad at you.
A couple of hours after you left, Aaron got home. I was still crying, the very same as I did when you left me.
Of course I couldn't hide my tears from my brother, so we talked.
Or he talked.
You know Aaron, he loves to talk.
My talkative brother has of no importance right now.
Actually, he does.

NINE DAYS

He knows.
He knew from the day he gave me back this notebook. He read it, just like you did.
Aaron knows of my desire to die.
Now you may think "then why the hell wasn't he trying to get you some help?!"
The same question aims at you, Colin.
Why the hell didn't you get me some help?
I know I made you promise not to.
But you said you loved me, yet you still risked my death so you wouldn't break a promise.
You had the chance to give this book to the counselor, anonymously. He would have been forced to speak to me and get me some help. And all that before you offered me those nine days.
Before you devoted *nine days of your life to me.*
Maybe this is wishful thinking...
but I'd like to think you're a little bit selfish when it comes to me.
I'd like to think that you'd rather have me all to yourself or nobody is allowed to have me at all.
That means, if I don't fall in love with you, the way you fell in love with me...you don't want me to be alive, so I don't get the chance to fall in love with anyone else. Anyone that is not you.
But that would also mean you would have fallen in love with me way before we even truly knew one another.
Maybe it was love at first sight on your part, but we all know it really wasn't.
Anyway, that might also seem a bit...asshole-like.
You're not an asshole.
You did nothing wrong, Colin.

You did as I asked you to. You didn't get me the help I didn't want. And I am grateful for that.
Although you might have lost me in exchange for your silence.
Aaron also knew of my depression going deeper than…surface level.
Just like you, he had no idea how to deal with it.
Unlike you, he had no idea how to approach me and ask me what he could do to help me.
You helped me. Or tried to at least.
The past seven days were the most fun days I've had in a very long time.
I'm saying seven days because I'm not sure we can count day one as day one.
Day one: The day I had a panic attack in one of our school's hallways.
You took me home with you, let me meet your siblings, your mother.
I have to admit, that was weird for me.
A guy, the hockey team captain, taking me home when he didn't even know me. And I didn't know him either, not in the slightest.
Yet even that day was fun.
Day two: You took me to watch the sunrise. I never liked sunrises, never thought they'd be anything close to miraculously beautiful. Yet you proved me wrong.
Sunrises are amazing.
Day three: Coffee tasting. Hell, that was some fun. Especially the part when you dead-ass let your teammates, and friends, drink the cold coffees that you spit into.
Not only did we find a place, our place, we had tons of fun together. Driving around and tasting coffees.

Nine Days

I never would have thought tasting coffees would be enjoyable.
Day four: we stayed at your parents' house. Over night. I was scared shitless. It was weird, but I was still so excited. After the night before...I felt like our relationship had shifted.
And you only proved that when you told me to harm you if I feel like harming myself.
The words you said to me...Colin, they were the most pain-filled and most loving words I've ever heard.
"You can have a death wish all you want, but if you're going to hurt yourself, you'll hurt me too."
I hurt you. With every new day.
I didn't know friends wouldn't say things like that. Not a normal friend would offer their skin in exchange for your own.
And you also tried to understand me...You could never imagine how much that meant to me.
Day five: My birthday. You met my mother. You were there when she told me to die.
And what did you make out of it?
You took me to a plate smashing place.
You gave me the chance to let go of my anger, let go of words that hurt me.
When I wished for you to be happy, to find a girlfriend that loves you unconditionally. Someone to be alongside you when I can't be there anymore. The plate didn't break.
Colin, do you believe in miracles? In the universe sending signs?
What if the plate didn't break because the wish wasn't supposed to be granted?
What if you're not supposed to find a new *girlfriend.*

Now that sounds awful. I'm sorry.
What if the plate didn't break because the universe was trying to tell me, or us, that there won't be any unconditional love when it's not me?
Wishful thinking round two?
Also…you were right. I'm totally digging frogs.
Day six: We stayed home because of my panic attack that paralyzed me for a short while.
You know what you did?
You went to get Sergeant Froggo for me, because earlier that day I told you I couldn't sleep without him.
You drove a whole fifteen minutes to the dorms, broke into mine, only to get a stuffed animal for me to be able to sleep.
Day seven: The pumpkin patch. That was something. Not that it was very interesting, but watching a couple of tall as fuck hockey players walk through a pumpkin patch, trying not to step on the tinier ones…it was art. I wish I videotaped that.
Carving those pumpkins and rating each one…the laughs that came out of me were unbelievable. God, when Miles almost cried because I rated Ezra's mouth better than his. It was incredible.
We don't talk about the chocolate tasting. I refuse to think about almost losing you.
Day eight: Ice skating.
Is there any more to add to this?
I loved it. Every single part of it. The whole three hours the three of us spent playing some games on the ice. Even the part when Eira made me teach you how to do a "not awful-looking" jump.
I'll never forget it.

Nine Days

Thank you for giving this to me.
Day nine: You told me you loved me.
Do we finally get to the three people that I think truly love me?
One being my father. You can imagine why. He's my father, the man that paid for my dreams, my education. He took care of me even when my mother was supposed to do that most of the time.
Then there is Aaron. It's self-explanatory. He's my brother. The guy that stuck with me when I thought we weren't allowed to.
The very guy that held my hand when I was too afraid to go to the toilet late at night because it was dark, and we were eight years old.
Yup, I'd say he has some love for me after doing that.
And the third person being you, Colin.
Not only were you the first and only guy to ever say those words to me (apart from Aaron and my father, but you know, it's a different kind of love). You were also the first guy I felt something back for.
You didn't give me the chance to reply, but honestly, even if you had, I probably wouldn't have known what to say.
Colin, you said it yourself. You took me on dates. You loved me as an attempt to save me.
Not saying your love is platonic and solely based on whether or not you managed to keep me alive.
You showed me what love is.
You showed me that I don't have to be alone. That I'm not alone.
Now, I think love needs more time than nine days to properly develop...but our hearts were in a rush. Our days were numbered.

*Of course, the love part would try and sneak in way faster.
I'm glad it did.
At least now I've heard it before.
Also, I'm sorry. I'm sorry for leaving the way I did. You deserve better than that.
Colin, I'm not here. I'm not at the arena where you found this notebook (hopefully this is you reading).
Go back home. My body has been taken care of already.*

Lily

Fuck putting up the cold-hearted man.

How could I possibly not cry after the woman I love basically just told me all about how she loved me in form of a diary entry, without even directly saying it?

And all that while I know this is her goodbye.

Fighting against the urge to skip right to the end to hopefully find the letter that's truly meant for me only, I turn to the next page.

It's empty.

Maybe she just missed a page, it happens.

Not thinking much of it, I turn to the next page.

Empty.

So I turn another, and another, and probably another couple of pages. All of them empty.

I skip to the last page and my heart skips a beat…or two.

Dear Colin Baby,

*I told you to go home. There is nothing more to find here.
I never managed to continue writing after day six.*

NINE DAYS

Somewhere along the way you had me thinking I could actually do it. You had me thinking I could live, that maybe life doesn't need to be painless.
When you gave me time to truly think about everything...I concluded that life truly doesn't have to be perfect, that it doesn't have to be painless...
but I've been too burnt to continue to live anyway.

Lily

Chapter 38

"what you did boy, I'll never forget"—Wasting All These Tears by Cassadee Pope

Colin

JUST LIKE LILY HAS TOLD ME—two times by now—I drive back home.

My BMW is still parked outside of the arena, but I don't care enough to even try to find out why that is. I just go with believing Lily left it here as a sign she's been here.

But I can't help thinking about where she died. How she died. Was it painful? Did she jump off a bridge? A building? Did she overdose?

Not sure why I feel the need to know all that, but I do. And for some reasons my brain has a hard time believing she's truly gone.

With every person that died in my life, I've seen the evidence for it. I've seen their lifeless bodies, hell, I *watched* my sister die.

I watched as Eira's weak smile slowly faded and her last breath drew out of her lungs. I could feel her muscles loosen up. I witnessed the moment she left us.

I may not have seen Aiden die, but I saw his lifeless body. I had proof of his death.

It sort of makes sense that my brain refuses to believe the only woman I ever loved, the only woman to ever bring light into my life died.

When I get back home, I'm startled for a second.

The living room, the same that looked like a complete mess one and a half hours ago, is completely tidied up.

The couch is back in its usual place. The floor is cleaner as it has ever been. The barstools are by the kitchen island. Even the TV is no longer broken. It's as if the mess I've seen before never happened.

Was I hallucinating before? Is that a thing? Hallucinating from anxiety? Hallucinating from fear of having lost the most important person in one's life?

This time I don't call out for Aaron. I can't face him right now. I can't tell him his sister has died. My presence without her would be the confirmation.

Her body wasn't there. She's been taken care of already.

Did Aaron find her? No, that can't be. He would have told me she's dead already, right?

What do I know?

I don't care enough to think about this any longer. I'll just be waiting for an announcement from the school that states a student has passed away and we're all invited to a ceremony to say goodbye, a get-together to grief.

Can't wait.

I head upstairs, needing nothing more but to take a long shower and...cross that. Needing nothing but to crawl into my bed and cry to the smell of Lily that is hopefully still on my bedsheets.

My bedroom is completely tidied up…and some of the clothes Lily left on my floor when I left two days ago are in my laundry basket. This means, either Lily put them away before she passed away, or the mess I've seen before wasn't me hallucinating after all.

Either way, that's not of much importance right now.

To my surprise, when I inhale, I'm greeted with a *strong* scent that is Lily. It's not even faded. She sure has a strong perfume.

Or she was in here shortly before she left, and her scent just didn't escape this room yet.

But I could swear I didn't smell her this heavily when I entered this room earlier. To be fair, I also didn't pay much attention to the way my room smelled in the hurry I was in.

I look at my perfectly made bed, feeling the sting in my heart, even more so when I see that damn frog on my bed.

Staring at it for a moment, I sigh deeply and walk over to Sergeant Froggo. Although that frog creeps me out, I grab him and press him to my chest as I take a seat on my bed.

God, this frog smells so much like her. I miss her. I miss her so much, it's ridiculous.

When I cross my legs and go to stare at my door, I notice something on my bed. Something that I'm sure wasn't here before.

My eyebrows draw together as I look at the green envelope with a frog face on it.

In a matter of seconds, I have the envelope in my hands, opening it carefully so I wouldn't ruin it. I'll keep this stupid envelope forever.

Taking out a couple of papers, I stare at them for a short while before I find the courage to read.

Dear Colin Baby,

they say time heals all wounds…
they were wrong.
But you know what they don't tell you?
You don't need wounds to heal when there is tape.
You didn't heal me, Colin…but you sure as hell held—
hold—me together.
You're the medicine that's making pain disappear. You're the antidote to the poison in my life.
I get it, Colin. I finally understand.
Everyone fights demons.
Everyone struggles in their own ways.
When I hit rock bottom, on the verge of giving up…I've been sent someone to—not to show me the most beautiful places—but to show me that I don't have to fight my demons on my own.
You know how people tend to give advice but don't practice what they preach?
I figured out why that is.
We think we have to fight on our own. That we're a burden to anyone we ask for help.
And yet, we don't think of someone as a burden when we're asked for advice.
In fact, we always give the best advice, yet never find the courage to get some ourselves.
They got their advice, their help. And we're still struggling, thinking we're not worthy of help.
But we are.

Nine Days

My past will always be my past. But that's where it is...in the past.
I will always carry the scars, they'll never fade. But that doesn't mean I have to keep the wounds open.
I have the choice to put some tape over it.
Sure, tape eventually opens back up, but there's always more tape.
Maybe it's not the healthiest way to deal with pain, but it still seals the wound.
The kind of wounds I have...they won't disappear.
It's always going to be a part of me, but it's in my hands how much tape I use to cover those open wounds up with.
Maybe I'll get some stitches, they'll heal eventually.
I want *to heal.*
I want to tape my past away and move on, become the happiest version of myself as I can be.
I don't have to be happy at all times, I get that now.
I want to be alive, Colin.
Even if you won't stay in my life after this day...
you'll always be the person that saved me. The person that loved me back to life.
The person that showed me that there is happiness in cruelty, that there is light in the darkness.
No matter what will happen between the both of us, please know;
I will always think highly of you.
You're the only person that ever tried to understand me.
The only person that dug deeper and tried to make me happy.
You wanted to understand how I felt, and you tried your very best to accept my feelings rather than tell me they're not valid because I have no reason to feel the way I do.

So, thank you, Colin. For Trying. For being there. For understanding.
Thank. You.

Lily

I hastily turn each page to hopefully find more. But there's nothing more she's written.

"So, they say time heals all wounds, Colin..."—I look up, my breath getting caught in my lungs—"maybe they were right. You taught me that wounds can't heal when I keep stabbing them. Maybe it'll leave a scar, reopen at some point...but all that doesn't matter. It doesn't matter because life is too precious to give it up too early. Just when I thought I've been through with it, when I gave up on life...*you* happened. You threw my whole world upside down and for what? Apparently there's always at least one thing to hold onto...you happen to be mine."

"Lily," I breathe out shakily. I remain seated on the bed, frozen, not knowing whether she's truly here or not.

Lily has a fainted smile on her lips as she walks closer to me. With every step she takes, I stiffen more and more. If this is a dream, I will hate myself the second I wake up.

Then my mattress dips slightly as she takes a seat right next to me. *This is a very realistic dream.*

Her hands brush my skin, wiping away some of my tears. Her touch is so gentle, it's like this is only the ghost of her. *What if it is?*

Chapter 39

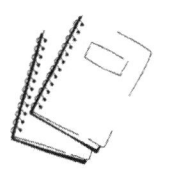

"if I was dying on my knees, you would be the one to rescue me"—Brother by Kodaline

Lily

COLIN IS BREATHING HEAVILY. His hands are shaking and I'm sure he can't figure out if I'm really here or not.

I can't even take it badly. I don't think I would react much differently if I found out the person I loved died and then suddenly they're standing right in front of me.

His eyes are locked with mine, and his muscles tense when I touch him, but he doesn't speak.

"Colin," I finally say. "You can believe this. It's really me."

I'm sure that in about five minutes, maybe ten, I will have to explain why I let him believe I died, but that's not what I should be focusing on right now.

"Lily," he whispers. His voice is filled with so much pain, I could actually start to cry from hearing it.

Then his forehead leans against mine and his eyes close. Colin's arms slowly sneak around my waist and he pulls me into him. I sit on his lap, straddling him.

His grip tightens, pressing me closer to him. We stay like this for a short while.

"I need to be able to breathe if you want me alive," I remind him. And the second those words leave my mouth, his arms loosen around my body, and he slowly inches his head away from mine.

"You're here," he says as if he's just realizing it.

Colin takes a deep breath, exhaling shakily but definitely steadier than before.

"You didn't leave, *mi sol*." I'm sure at this point he's more talking to himself than to me, but that's alright.

"I didn't."

Although he's heard me talk, felt me on his skin, his palms find my face again, cupping it as if to make sure I'm really present. He is holding my face so close to his, I can taste him.

"You're alive?" he asks, still looking at me as if he doesn't trust himself right now.

"I am, Colin. I am alive, and I don't plan on dying today, or tomorrow, or for the next years."

A tear slips from his eyes and I quickly wipe it away. He lets out another deep breath then lightly nods his head a couple of times as the realization finally settles in.

"I am so sorry about Eira, Colin," I say. "If I had known—"

He smiles at me softly, shaking his head. "I knew she would die. It's alright. Eira would kill me if I wasted more tears on her. She was excited to start a new adventure."

"This is a stupid question, but are you okay?"

He looks up at the ceiling for a second, then back into my eyes. "I will be." Then his hands leave my face, but he's not pushing me away. *That's a good sign.* "Why did you let me believe you've died?"

"I didn't know when you'd be back. As much as I love Aaron, we both know he couldn't have convinced me to stay if my mind changed again. When I woke up this morning and I was still going strong with wanting to stay alive, I needed to see my mother. I needed to tell her that she drove me this far. That because of her, because of her actions, I am way too close to make her wish come true. She didn't even flinch when I told her I wanted to die as much as she wanted me to. All she did was stare at me with this emptiness in her eyes, the same I'm sure I've shown you plenty of times," I tell him.

"Colin, I wasn't sure if I'd come back. I wasn't sure if I'd still be alive after I witnessed my mother still not giving a fuck about me. I could have called Aaron, probably even should have. I should have given him a sign that I'm still alive when he texted and called me a million times after he woke up. But I didn't want to give him some hopes that I'd still be alive five minutes later.

"When I left my mother's house, I was mad. I wasn't sad that she didn't care one bit about me. I was *angry*. I went to the arena and planted the notebook there, being sure to go through with dying. The next thing I know, I found myself in front of a mental hospital. I was sitting on the concrete in front of the building, crying, trying to find the courage to walk inside. And when it finally came…I wanted nothing more but for you to be there with me. For you to hold my hand while these people talked to me and admitted me. They asked me if I want to call someone, I said yes. I looked at my phone and saw Aaron was calling me, so I picked up. He was screaming at me, but I cut him off and told him where I was," I explain. Colin doesn't react much, all he does is look at me with the tiniest attempt of smile on his lips. A smile I believe to be pride *and* relief.

"I asked one of the women that work there if I could go home today and come back tomorrow. Of course she said no, granted, she kind of had to be worried given my state so I wasn't too surprised. But that's when I knew I needed more time. So I asked Aaron to mess up the house to the point where it would look like he was so desperate and frustrated when he didn't find me. I needed more time, Colin. I wanted to be home when you came back so I could proudly tell you I'm getting the help I now *want*. I needed to do this on my own."

Colin wraps his arm back around me, pulling me in for a much-needed hug. I wrap mine around his body as well, leaning the side of my head against his.

My heart aches for this man. A good kind of heartache.

"I needed to be *home* to tell you about the help I'm getting. I didn't want you finding out by me being at the mental hospital already. And I needed more time to convince them to let me go. I am so, so sorry I had to hurt you so much to tell you this personally."

I kind of expect Colin giving me a speech about how fucked up my way of thinking was, but he's not doing that. Instead he says, "I am so proud of you, my Lilybug," and holds me just that tiny bit closer.

"But I have to warn you, you're stuck with me now, *mi sol*. For as long as you'll have me," he whispers and pulls away from the hug.

Tilting my head enough for his lips to easily meet with mine, he eases us into a powerful kiss that's still gentle and loving. A kiss so good, it leaves me breathless.

When I pull back, in desperate need for some air, it's my turn to lay my hands on his jawline. Looking deeply into his eyes, I begin to speak again. "I love you, Colin Carter. Truth be told, if it weren't for you, I wouldn't be standing here anymore. You saved me, Colin."

"Sweetheart, I'll save you a million times more if that keeps you by my side." His lips brush mine again, softly. "I'd burn the whole world down if that saved your life." He takes on a slight pause, then speaks again. "But Lilybug, this wasn't my doing. This was all *you*."

"Okay, how about we try not to put our lives anywhere near the death-line? I don't think you would survive another heart attack."

He chuckles, pressing his lips to my forehead. "Lilybug, we both know I'll have to survive tons of those when I'm with you. Especially with your judgmental Sergeant Froggo in my bed. That frog creeps me out when I wake up at night. I swear he stares right into my soul and debates on murdering me right there."

I laugh, shaking my head in disbelief. "He's a stuffed animal, dumbass. He won't murder you."

"Did you look at that thing? He's so totally murderous. But if you promise to tell him to let me live, he can stay."

"Deal." When I press my head into the front of his shoulder, Colin rests his chin on the top of my head, caressing my back with his hands.

I'm not quite sure when my head started to tell me this is where I'm supposed to be, right in Colin's arms. But I'm glad I finally listened.

I'm glad I finally realized that I don't have to be alone. That there are people willingly holding their hands out to me for support, even if they can't help.

Knowing that I don't have to go through a dark period of time on my own is as much help as I could ever ask for.

Pain comes in all sorts of ways. Some might get hit worse, some less, but there is always pain in life.

The amount of pain doesn't matter, pain stays pain, and it sucks. It will never leave, will always be present.

But it's on us to decide whether or not we will let it consume us.

Epilogue

"I wouldn't have made it if I didn't have you holding my hand"—Control by Zoe Wees

Colin

Two weeks later

"FIVE MORE MINUTES!" MY FATHER YELLS as I skate past him. It's not like I don't have eyes and couldn't read the scoreboard myself. I guess he just has a great time reminding me of the pressure I'm supposed to be under.

St. Trewery University and Princeton University are playing for a win. As of now the board reads 3-3. However, five minutes can change a lot. In only five minutes, if it goes smoothly, we could possibly score at least one more goal, if extra smoothly, even two or three. *Maybe not three.*

Parker, our goalie, he does his best trying to keep the puck away from our net, but Princeton players are ruthless. They play with much more body than any of us.

Hockey is known for its brutality, but hell, these guys are cruel, not brutal.

Parker came in an as exchange for Kaiden five minutes ago. Only because Nico Cams, one player of the opponents, decided to almost break Kaiden's arm.

The puck is currently in possession of Grey, and he appears to be winging it.

My guys try to keep the Princeton guys away from Grey as good as only possible. However, their goalie is great. Getting past him turned out to be harder than we have practiced for. It appears Beck got quite the amount of practice in before facing us.

Grey is so close to the goal, almost ready to shoot when one of the Princeton players comes up from behind and presses Grey up against the wall, the puck gliding over the ice like it's dancing to a classical song.

Time seems to be frozen when a few players, me included, make their way over to the puck in no time.

Since we're so much closer to the enemy's goal and I made sure to stay close to Grey, it's an easy game for me to reach the puck first.

Not wasting any more time, I turn to the goal, pick up my pace and shoot for a win.

Thinking back to time freezing when players run up to the puck, it's nothing compared to what I feel now that the puck is so close to a win.

Ten seconds left.

Everything moves in slow-motion. And then finally, *finally*, the puck hits the net, the sound of sirens ringing as a point for St. Trewery adds to the scoreboard.

Another loud siren going off when the time runs out.

St. Trewery U wins.

I spend a quick moment saying a few words to the other team captain, and then my very cheery team skates off the ice and runs toward the locker room.

Everyone but me.

When I exit the ice, I'm greeted by two lovingly green eyes and blonde hair. The one person I grew so close to in a matter of no time at all.

She smiles at me so brightly, I can feel heat rushing to my heart.

"Congratulations, Mr. Stinky!" Lily screams all excitedly while jumping into my arms. Mind you, I'm still in skates, but I'd gladly fall to the floor for this woman. Even in front of a crowd.

I spin her around as much as I can before setting her down to the floor, then take off my helmet to kiss her breath away.

Lily's lips are still my obsession, my addiction. I'm addicted to her. Maybe that's not too healthy, but I don't give zero fucks. This woman owns my body, heart and soul.

"What are you doing here, *mi sol*?" I ask, completely dumbfounded by her presence when I thought she was at the mental hospital.

God, I missed her so much. I haven't seen Lily in three whole days. Haven't really touched and kissed her in two weeks.

It was torture. But at least I've got her back now.

"You weren't supposed to get out until later today. I thought I am picking you up," I say, stealing yet another kiss of hers.

"I wanted to watch your game, so my dad picked me up and drove me here. He should be around still."

I want to get out of my clothes, at least the hockey gear. I want to feel Lily against me, body to body. Hug her without any of my protective gear in between.

"Dad invited you for dinner in a couple of hours. Well, he asked if *we* would like to go out for dinner with him," she tells me, taking my hockey stick from me as we walk toward the locker room.

"Sure, just let me take a shower first, okay?"

She laughs, nodding. "Of course, Mr. Stinky."

"I do not stink."

"You're right. You just smell like sweat and old, stinky equipment on a daily." Lily smiles, getting onto her tippy-toes before planting a chaste kiss to my lips right when we stop in front of the locker room doors.

"Sweetheart, where do you think you're going? You belong in that locker room. Now, close your eyes and get your cute butt inside."

Laughing, she obeys, holding onto my arms—her eyes closed—as I lead her inside the locker room.

Lily

We lie in bed, my head resting against his shoulder as his arm is wrapped around me.

Colin's laptop is set down on his legs and he makes sure we both have a good view.

"Okay, Lilybug, our topic was life's beauty," he says as he presses the play button and our film directing project begins to play.

Videos of me crying start to show, only seconds of my body shaking, my hands covering my face, me screaming by the hill he took me to as we watched the sunset.

Pain. He is portraying pain.

"Life's beauty isn't about the magical and perfect side of life."

His hand reaches out to grab mine as we walk toward his car. I turn to look at him. My eyes are red and puffy from crying, but a smile appears when our hands touch.

"Truth is, there wouldn't be one beautiful thing if there wasn't anything bad to it."

We're at The Retro Diner. I'm laughing at Colin because only two seconds ago he was trying to push the whole burger into his mouth, but it didn't fit. Instead, the sauce dripped onto his shirt, ruining it forever.

"We wouldn't know how to cherish what we call 'beautiful moments' when there weren't any bad ones."

Another video of me crying, sitting on Colin's bed with my notebook in my hands.

The next clip shows me in the rain, spinning with my head held high, letting the cold raindrops hit my skin.

I didn't even know he filmed that.

"Life's beauty isn't about the happiness only. It's not sunshine and flowers. It's the pain, scars that tell a story. It's about darkness and the tiny source of light shining into the depth of the forest."

More clips of me struggling appear, but they're all fading into other clips of me smiling, laughing, portraying happiness through sadness.

One clip shows the moment when I step onto the ice, my face lighting up like fireworks, a big smile spreading across my face.

"Life might seem warm and bright for one moment, and the next it's all back to gray, back to darkness and freezing temperatures. It beats you down after rewarding you, then rewards you again only to get another hit from it. The true art in life is to see beyond the pain. See that there is a source of light in everything."

The video cuts to videos of Colin and me.

Colin running up to me in a fairy costume, making me laugh.

Colin smiling when I try to lift a way too heavy pumpkin.

Us, dancing in the middle of a bar with tons of eyes on us, ignoring every single one of them because what truly matters is Colin and I being there together.

"Love," he says. *"Life's beauty is connected to the one thing we all seek. The one thing that brings people together, splits them up. Pain wouldn't exist without love, and love wouldn't exist without pain. Whether it's family, friends, a pet, sports, a significant other, anything or anyone. Loss is the pain that comes with love. The true criminal, but without*

it, beautiful things wouldn't exist. If you don't fear losing it, if you don't fear it leaving you…it's not on the side of beauty it should be at."

More videos of Colin and me together, hugging, laughing, videos of the ways we look at one another when the other isn't looking.

"Love and loss are life's beauty. Both comes unexpectedly. It can destroy you, but it can also be a savior. Whatever it is, it comes together. One follows the other. They will keep on coming to remind us to cherish even the smallest number of times we get to have with Love. *But it's there, and if it's not yet, it will come when it's least expected."*

I sniffle, wiping away some tears.

Colin closes his laptop, a second later I'm completely cuddled up to him, wetting his t-shirt with my tears.

He chuckles, but he pulls me into his embrace and plants a kiss on the top of my head.

"That was beautiful," I tell him between sobs.

"I will deny making this. I will say you had me say a couple of words and mixed them all together."

Now it's my time to laugh. I look up, finding his eyes. Colin wears a smile on his face, one that says he's proud of himself for creating something so beautiful. And maybe also a bit of "I regret this more than anything."

"I'm not that talented, dumbass."

"Hm, they don't know that." He puts a chaste kiss to my lips. "Professor Meisner said he won't show it in class because he doesn't want to humiliate you and your 'crazily good acting' because it 'might seem too realistic.'"

At least that's something. I don't think having a couple of hundred other students see me cry is something I ever want to experience.

"NO, DAD, DO YOU know what your daughter is capable of? She's been home for a whole two hours and then…the whole goddamn *living room* looked like the decoration section of an IKEA." Aaron slides his hands down his face, letting out a desperate groan.

"I thought you guys needed a bit more color in there. Your whole house it made of white and gray's. It needed some color," I defend myself.

"Sweetheart, mint green is not a color that fits in our house." Colin clearly has a death-wish. How dare he be on Aaron's side instead of mine? "And your frog obsession still creeps me out."

"Thank you! These tiny frog statues are everywhere." Another groan comes from Aaron.

Honestly, if they didn't want me "girl up" their house, they shouldn't have offered me to stay. Well, it's not like I have any other choice. Colin insists on me staying so he can have an eye on me, and Aaron…he doesn't have much to say when it comes to me. Not when Colin already decided.

I mean, I sure do have a choice to stay at the dorms, but why would I when I get to annoy my brother with my presence at all times instead?

I didn't get to do that when we were younger, so I have some making up to do.

"Guys, you leave Lily alone, otherwise you will find killer frogs in your bed, and I doubt that's what you want," Ana says. At least someone is on my side.

"Thank you, Annie."

"Not another of those Sergeant Froggo's, *por favor*," Colin begs, making a face that looks like he's in pain. "It's bad enough that Lily loves that frog more than me. I don't need more of those in my life."

I roll my eyes, trying to appear annoyed but my lips betray me, keeping a smile on them.

"Ladies,"—my father motions his hand around the table then stops when it's in front of me—"and frog lover's." Everyone chuckles. "If mint green decoration and frogs make the woman happy, then you all will have to make some sacrifices."

"But dad, I can't," Aaron growls. "You don't live with us. You don't have to see those creepy creatures all day, every day. I, however, do."

"Sucks for you, Ron." Colin shrugs while winking at me.

Aaron grunts, disapproving. But just like it was for me, his mouth is betraying his annoyance.

And then the question I've been waiting for drops. Not that I was looking forward to answering it, but I knew it would come eventually.

"Will you have to go back?" Ana asks. "To the mental hospital, I mean."

There wasn't any need for clarification, but I'll give her an A for trying.

"Not for now. Before they released me, I've had a talk with a psychologist. She said I'm making great progress. Sure, I won't magically get better from one day to another, but she is positive that with some more work I can live almost to a 'normal' life," I say, probably explaining it worse than the psychologist did.

"It's going to be a hell lot of work to get near 'normality,' whatever that shall be. I honestly don't think there's a thing such as 'normal,' but whatever, that's not the point. I will still struggle sometimes, just like everyone else. Though, if I continue taking my meds and stick around the people I love, the same that love me too, even I am certain I can get through this without keeping up the desire to die. It's not gone yet, sometimes I still think it would be better if I did die, but you know, it's not like I think it's the only solution anymore. And of course, I will have to continue to go to therapy. But apart from that, if my condition doesn't get any worse again, I'm good to stay away."

Colin takes my hand in his, giving it a soft squeeze. His eyes are on mine and he smiles widely. It's not a pitying smile. He is proud of me.

No matter how small my victories might be, Colin makes sure to tell—or show—me how proud he is.

He couldn't visit me daily, the visiting hours wouldn't allow him to, neither would his schedule…but whenever he did visit me in the last two weeks, Colin listened to me telling him all about what I've learned. But most importantly, he always smiled at me like I was making him so proud.

It felt, and still does feel, good to know I'm not the kind of disappointment I thought I was for years.

Colin makes me feel better. And with the help of my family, I do feel as though I am doing better.

Of course I still have a long way to go, and I'm sure my depression will never go away (mainly because there's no cure whatsoever), I do feel like I can conquer so much more with love in my life than I could when I was all by myself.

HOURS LATER WE'RE finally back at home and I'm all cuddled up in Colin's bed. He's still in the bathroom, so in the meantime I figure it would be fun to hide something under his tiny part of the blanket.

Yup, about three-fourth of the blanket is mine. There is no discussion needed. Even if Colin wanted to argue with me, he will lose.

"What movie are we watching?" Colin asks just when the bathroom door opens.

He's only wearing some sweatpants, granting me the sight of his bare chest. Ever since I know of his not-so-new-anymore tattoo, his chest seems so much more interesting.

"Barbie, obviously."

He groans, causing me to laugh.

"Listen, *mi sol*, you can torture me with Barbie movies for the rest of our lives, but not tonight. It's your first day back home, let's watch something…good."

He walks over to his side of the bed, looking down at me with pleading eyes, he even adds the pouty lips.

"Are you saying Barbie movies are bad?" I'm totally not offended by that. Nope. All good.

"No, I'm saying I want to watch something like any Marvel movie, really. Or some horror movie, like paranormal activities."

I hum, pretending to think about it. "Alright. *The Notebook* then."

Colin narrows his eyes, slowly lifting the blanket. "That doesn't sound like anything *action*."

"Oh, it has quite the action in it. Like…love."

Thankfully, my words go lost on him when he flinches from the stuffed animal under his side of the blanket. The one that lost an eye from Colin's last fight with it.

I can't help the horribly loud laughter spilling out of me when Colin holds his hand to his heart, breathing heavily as he tries to come back to life.

"Oh, you're so done, Liliana," he speaks through gritted teeth.

Colin throws the frog across the room, getting onto the bed and hovering right over me. His face is so close to mine, I can feel his breath tingling on my skin. His chest presses against me, so close, I can feel his heart beating against mine.

He lowers his face, his nose gently touching mine before his lips come into touch with my lips in an ever so heart-exploding, mind-erasing kiss.

My tongue pushes past his lips, dipping into his mouth to deepen the kiss. And because I get way too touchy with this man, my hands automatically reach up to caress his back, scratching his skin with my fingernails.

"I love you, *mi sol*," Colin whispers, like he only wants me to hear it. "I finally have my sun back."

"I love you too, dumbass." I kiss him.

"What's the notebook about?" he asks, now lying next to me, keeping me in his arms.

"It's about the power of love and—"

"Mi sol, I mean the one on my nightstand, not the movie," he chuckles, picking up the mint green notebook to show it to me.

"Oh." I grin, scrunching up my nose. "I have a few letters to write. They'll be about how much I will miss you when Sergeant Froggo has murdered you."

Colin snatches the stuffed animal from me and throws it to the other side of the room. When I'm about to run after it, he holds me tighter, peppering my lips with kisses while hovering right over me.

"He can try, but I'm pretty much invulnerable, immortal even. For as long as you're with me, my Lilybug."

The End

Acknowledgements

This book would not have been possible without those people back in school that decided to make my life a living hell. So thank you so very much for the experience. You helped me grow, realize who I definitely don't want to be and see how not to raise my future children. I really hope that if *you* ever do have children, you will raise them better than whatever went through your heads back in the days.

I'd like to thank Joel Böhm for answering my very stupid questions about Ice Hockey. Also, if it weren't for you talking all about hockey most of the days on the bus on our way to school, I probably wouldn't have picked hockey for these books in the first place. So thank you for talking all about it.

A big thank you to Sofía Elizabeth Cortés for letting me bug you for Spanish translations, without context or anything. I couldn't have done it without you, honestly. I would not have been able to scratch up my little knowledge of Spanish to make it work myself. So, thank you, so, so much! I owe you.

I'm seriously indebted to the handful of my friends that I asked to read the first drafts to let me know whether I am writing complete nonsense or not. You've had to put up with so much, especially name changes, or me simply adding a couple more scenes in between, listening to minutes long voice notes of me explaining what changed et cetera.

So, Rana, Jane and Vanessa, thank you so much for reading this ahead of time with a million mistakes. And, of course, for your humbling but honest opinions!

Also, thank you to my parents and grandparents for believing in me, celebrating every other chapter with me, even though you had absolutely no clue what I was writing for the most part until I came up with translations.

To my mom, thank you so much for always believing in me, even when my plans seem absolutely ridiculous and completely unrealistic.

To my grandma Rike, thank you for spending your Sundays with me, discussing further steps for this book and plans as to how I can promote it. Without you and, my mom and my other grandma, I wouldn't have gotten as far as I did.

Thanks to my friend "What-is-a-Laur," aka my TikTok account manager (that didn't get to the managing part) for…well, doing nothing really. But you are emotional support, you know? Having you in my life stresses me out but it's also a blessing. Seriously, I couldn't go through life without you by my side. Thank you for all the unpaid therapy sessions in the middle of the night because we're both a little too stupid to function as humans.

I'd also like to thank the girl I called my best friend for so many years, I lost track of how many. I know we're no longer talking, but if there is a chance you're reading this…Paige, I want you to know that I love you and I am so thankful for everything. You were a huge part of my life, helped me through so much, I'll never forget that.

Because I know you two won't read this, which means I will not have a talk with you about this; thank you to my brothers, Tim and Noel, for…I'm not quite sure yet, but I felt like you should get a line or two as well. Let's be honest, my life would be a lot more boring without the two of you in it.

And thank you to everyone that has read this book. Writing wouldn't make much sense without you.

To everyone out there struggling, I promise better times are coming. I didn't believe so myself, but for whatever reasons, the universe decides to throw good and bad things around like money was free. They're both coming, always. But know, good things *are* coming your way.

At very last, thank you to my old English teacher that tried telling me I couldn't speak English. F you, look at me now.

Printed in Great Britain
by Amazon